# THE MAYOR OF
# OLONGAPO

# THE MAYOR OF
# OLONGAPO

## Hamlin Tallent

*Aura Libertatis Spirat*

# THE MAYOR OF OLONGAPO

Copyright © 2011, 2019 by Hamlin Tallent

**Braveship Books**

www.braveshipbooks.com

*Aura Libertatis Spirat*

**Cover Artwork & Design by Rossitsa Atanassova**

ISBN-13: 978-1-64062-068-1

Printed in the United States of America

# FOREWORD

Through his novel, *The Mayor of Olongapo*, Mr. Tallent has acknowledged the relevance of the Philippines and its people to the United States, and he has frankly and graphically explored the unique and unparalleled relationship between the two countries. I did not realize until after reading his manuscript how immense and deeply rooted was my desire for such an acknowledgment. Additionally, *The Mayor of Olongapo* brought me to the realization that, despite America's soul-searching and quest for historical honesty, she has conspicuously left the Philippines out of the discussion.

*The Mayor of Olongapo* contains characters and circumstances that touch the very issues my mind has anguished over for all of my life. It turns on the single greatest lament of all Filipinos: our lack of relevance with the rest of the world. It focuses on our invisibility.

*The Mayor of Olongapo* challenges us to know our contingent circumstances, our histories, and, ultimately, ourselves. It is the type of story rarely written these days, and from Mr. Tallent's labors arises a fascinating tale as intriguing as and certainly more exciting than many of the popular works of fiction I have read. It is a careful exploration of a complex subject matter and a link to our past. The Prologue speaks of Spanish and American brutality and of Filipino inability to unite for the most noble of purposes. Later chapters, particularly those including the bar and nightclub scenes, are graphic and difficult for a Filipino to swallow, but they contain ugly truths and they grip the reader. Mr. Tallent is able to dutifully report both the town's and the visiting sailors' transgressions and captures the essence of the place as a shield against life's temporal harshness, injustices, and disappointments.

In my never-ending search for my true identity and role in life, Hamlin Tallent's *The Mayor of Olongapo* has single-handedly helped me define myself. Sincere understanding and acknowledgment from this one American was all I needed to begin to find peace with my perceptions of apathy and disdain for the power corridors of America. It is an authentic spirit raiser and suggests that human friendship, in spite of political or government alliance, is a warm record of trials met and affections reciprocated and that Filipinos and Americans can be the best of friends as long as both are equally relevant to the other.

Every country and its people want to gain a sense of mission in the world. I feel the Philippines is in constant motion, trying to define this mission but hampered by years of colonization and interaction with aggressors. The current pulse of Filipinos around the world is to seek avenues to help in this process of national image building. For me, *The Mayor of Olongapo* has become a part of that building process.

Marilyn Picardo Rivera
Founder
Philippine American Literary Sports and Arts Foundation of Hampton Roads, Virginia

*Oh, sing to me, my lover, let my name be your song.*
*On your knees in front of me, how can this be wrong?*
*I want to let you love me, I want love to be our pact,*
*I fear to free my heart; I fear I will never get it back.*

*God plants an orchid in our forest of old*
*For every lie to a Filipina told.*
*Filipina hearts are young, and their love is flowing.*
*The orchid forest is overgrown.*
*God plants an orchid in our forest of old*
*For every lie to a Filipina told.*
*Filipina hearts are young, and their love is flowing.*
*The orchid forest is overgrown.*

*So love me, oh please love me like you said on nights so long.*
*I feel my heart beat faster, for sweet words on your tongue.*
*Now I have fallen, lord, I have fallen. Mama sew me a new white*
*dress.*
*Papa, don't fret and worry, he says he loves my brown island face.*

*God plants an orchid in our forest of old*
*For every lie to a Filipina told.*
*Filipina hearts are young, and their love is flowing.*
*The orchid forest is overgrown.*
*God plants an orchid in our forest of old*
*For every lie to a Filipina told.*
*Filipina hearts are young, and their love is flowing.*
*The orchid forest is overgrown.*

*On this day he caught me. I know our hearts are to the task*
*Because truth is a hard master. We'll have to face the past.*
*Our history twines us together but the pain's so deep and cold*
*You will rock my chair when I have grown old.*

*God plants an orchid in our forest of old*
*For every lie to a Filipina told.*
*Filipina hearts are young, and their love is flowing.*
*The orchid forest is overgrown.*
*God plants an orchid in our forest of old*
*For every lie to a Filipina told.*
*Filipina hearts are young, and their love is flowing.*
*The orchid forest is overgrown.*

*Today you are gone from me, your heart closed to the sun.*
*Perhaps our cultures can never join as one.*
*Time goes by and the sun goes dim.*
*Your heart strays and forgets its oath.*
*The loneliest word is love, when not shared by both.*

*God plants an orchid in our forest of old*
*For every lie to a Filipina told.*
*Filipina hearts are young, and their love is flowing.*
*The orchid forest is overgrown.*
*God plants an orchid in our forest of old*
*For every lie to a Filipina told.*
*Filipina hearts are young, and their love is flowing.*
*The orchid forest is overgrown.*

*Now I am alone in a faraway place, the jungle far away and gone*
*There is nothing here for me; I miss my island home.*
*I stand in line to get some food, people look at me and curse.*
*I look at your baby and wonder, did God plant an orchid for her?*

# PROLOGUE

## APRIL 1901

## NORTHERN LUZON, PHILIPPINES

Bayani's breathing was heavy and strained as he fought through the forest. He had been running, stumbling, and falling since dawn, and his legs, unused to such exertion, were heavy and sore. He had to stop often to rest and wipe the stinging sweat from his eyes. His face was covered with the welts from a never-ending supply of mosquitoes, and his once-white pantaloons and shirt were muddy and torn from the many encounters with bamboo. His soft hands were a mass of cuts and bruises and ached in protest to their treatment. Others may toil in the fields or behind the workers' bench, but he was a man of education and culture who had even studied in England.

As Bayani stumbled along in his misery, he tolerated his condition by concentrating on the last time he had traveled through the region. Of course, that trip had been along the main road and things had been very, very different. Then, he had traveled in a beautiful Spanish carriage pulled by two fine mares, and he had enjoyed sitting deeply in the plush, red leather seats. The beautiful Anita had been at his side, they had picnicked on eggs, bread, and wine, and afterward in a moment of passion, he had kissed her. She had kissed him back!

Anita's sweet kiss was now a distant memory, lost in the blood and despair and loss of war. There had been no time for picnics and kisses, no time for rides in the jungle behind fine mares—not since the Americans had come and helped defeat the Spanish and then, forgetting their promises, decided to stay. Bayani coughed and cursed a thorn that caught his arm, but then he quickly repented his words. This very forest was his future and the future of his country. This forest contained a treasure far beyond the beauty he and Anita had gazed upon or beyond the bounty of its resources, for deep in its wildness and high on its mountains hid their heroes and saviors. This magnificent forest hid the men who had freed them from the Spanish, and it hid the men who were now trying to free all Filipinos from the Americans. He knew that every bit of impenetrable bamboo, every stinging fly, every escarpment, and every river was a blessing to their future. He breathed a bit of resolve and rededicated himself to his task.

It was late afternoon when Bayani stopped for a brief rest. But as he watched the sun touch the tops of the trees and the forest grow dark, he suddenly felt afraid. He had heard of strange things that lived in the forest and tried to forget the childhood stories of huge snakes, ferocious boars, and giant bats. He glanced into the shadows of the towering trees, half-expecting to see the glow of little red eyes. Despite the heat, he shivered and quickened his step and recalled why he was there.

"Go up the mountain," Joaquin had said. "Go and find Santiago. Tell him the news."

"I am an accountant," Bayani had pleaded. "How will I know the way? I am from the city."

"Do not worry," Joaquin had assured him. "Go, climb, head upward always. You will find him."

He went even though he was afraid, because he knew there was no one else to send. The rest were dead, except for Joaquin and the boy. He also went because Joaquin was his compadre, a member of his extended family. To deny his request would be unthinkable and would be considered *walang hiya*. It would be most shameful.

While Bayani struggled through the jungle, the man he sought, Colonel Reynaldo Santiago, sat by his cooking fire, appraising the American visitor before him. The visitor was big and blond, and his tailored uniform fit him well. He sported the shoulder patch of the Nebraska National Guard and the insignia of a United States Army captain. Santiago had observed him intently since his men had led him into the camp. Despite the blindfold, the American had stepped off his horse with unexpected assuredness. He had been calm and had exhibited no hesitation as he was led to the fire. When the blindfold was lifted and the big man was able to survey the glares, wicked knives, and cocked rifles of the hundreds of men surrounding him, Santiago noticed he displayed no nervousness. Now, the eyes of the man seated before him were neither windows nor slits. They were not wide with expectation or narrowed with evasiveness. They were like the eyes of a shark, two spots on the head offering nothing. Santiago frowned as he looked into the American's calm face. It was a bit upsetting, given the situation the man was in, and Santiago felt a pang of intimidation as he looked at his well-fed, well-clothed enemy—an enemy that had systematically defeated every Filipino force sent to confront it and had chased him and all of the men left fighting into the mountains. He dropped his gaze for a second and looked around. He knew the torn shirts and pantaloons of their uniforms must appear ragtag and almost comical to the American. He knew the fact that they were hiding here so far from the cities—and the people—must make them seem irrelevant. He shifted his eyes back to the American and gently kneaded the old Spanish bullet fragment in his shoulder.

"A war wound, sir?" The American nodded toward Santiago's shoulder.

"Yes," replied Santiago.

"I'm sorry."

"It is not from you. It is from the Spanish. It is from the Spanish Army you and I agreed to defeat together ... so that we could have our freedom."

The American did not respond to Santiago's barb. His shark eyes held no understanding or acknowledgment.

"What is your name?"

"Lawrence," replied the American. "I am Captain Stanville Lawrence, Nebraska National Guard, United States Army."

"You are a long way from Omaha, Captain. You are a long way from your corn fields, from your family and friends."

"Yes, sir."

"Why are you here, Captain?" Santiago's voice was soft and even.

"I have a message for you from General Funstan."

"No, I didn't mean 'why are you here in my camp?' I mean, why are you here in the Philippines, fighting us?"

"I am a soldier, sir. I joined the army to fight the Spanish. You know what they did to the *Maine*."

"That's odd," said Santiago. "I read in your newspapers that the last of your National Guard units left the Philippines for home two years ago." He paused and looked at Lawrence.

"We are still here, sir." Lawrence shrugged and looked into Santiago's eyes.

"And so you are." Santiago nodded in agreement. "I also read that there were so many volunteers that you formed two battalions. Is that true, Captain? Despite the fact that your unit was sent home, did you stay here just to fight us?"

Santiago watched the shark eyes flicker in surprise. It made him feel good.

"I don't know about that," said Lawrence.

"You don't know if you are a volunteer?"

"My tour was up. I signed up to stay in the army."

Santiago detected frustration in Lawrence's voice. He looked intently at the man and then slowly smiled into his eyes. "So, you don't really know why you are here, do you, Captain?"

Lawrence sat quietly. Santiago saw a frown crease his otherwise smooth forehead. He leaned forward toward the captain. The night was rapidly creeping across the jungle and into his camp, and he did not want to miss anything. "Perhaps you wanted a chance to shoot some brown men," he whispered. "Perhaps you and your friends wanted a chance to go hunting for something other than doves and pheasant, something just a bit more cunning and threatening.

Maybe you wanted a chance to return to Nebraska at the head of a parade. After all, you Nebraskans haven't had a good parade since you murdered Crazy Horse in 1877."

Lawrence's shark eyes opened wide for the first time since he had entered the camp. Santiago saw uncertainty in them. He watched the big tunic rise and fall with heavy breath.

"Sir," said Lawrence, "I have a message from General Funstan."

"Ah, yes." Santiago nodded and sat up straight. He waited a moment for one of his men to throw fresh kindling on the fire. After the men stoked the fire and they were again alone, Santiago cleared his throat. "I have been reading what your general has been saying about us. I believe it was a paper from San Francisco. Yes, now I remember. General Funstan said Filipinos are a lazy lot. He said they are born tired, they live tired, and they die tired." Santiago looked intently at Lawrence. "What do you think, Captain? Is that what you see too?"

Lawrence said nothing. He swallowed and returned the colonel's gaze.

"He also bragged about executing us. Of course, it was for good reasons. He told the papers that some of his noble and brave soldiers had gotten themselves killed, and it was okay to execute civilians to even things. Is that the way you see it too?"

Lawrence dropped his gaze and stared at the ground.

"Well, never mind," whispered Santiago. He stood, stretched, and then sat again. "By the way, where is General Funstan?" He did not expect a reply, since such information would be a closely guarded secret.

"He is in Palanan."

Santiago jerked erect and stared at the American. His hand instinctively flew to the trigger of his rifle.

"Where—where did you say?"

"Palanan," Lawrence repeated. "You know, sir, the headquarters of President Aguinaldo."

Santiago was stunned. He did not know what to think.

"May I show you something, sir?" Lawrence motioned toward his pocket.

Santiago narrowed his eyes and picked the rifle off his lap. He nodded.

Lawrence carefully placed his hand into his pocket and drew out the letter. He slowly handed it to Santiago.

Santiago looked at the letter and noticed the seal. It had the insignia of the US Army stamped into the wax. He carefully broke it open and began to read.

*Dear Santo,*

Santiago felt his chest tighten. Santo was the name Aguinaldo used for him when they were alone. He had given it to him after the Battle of Imus. Santiago looked up at Lawrence, trying to find an explanation. Lawrence sat expressionless.

*Dear Santo,*

*I hope this finds you and your men in good health, and I apologize for the directness of it but there is no time for greetings. I am afraid we have suffered a great treachery. Funstan was able to lure Filipinos from Pampanga, the Macabebes, into his court. They infiltrated our lines, and I have been duped. I am a captive of the Americans.*

*I am so sorry, Santo. Perhaps, if I had listened to you, those who turned against us would have remained loyal. However, it is no matter now. I beg of you not to continue. Lay down your weapons and go back to your family. Go back to Marian, the girls, and your new baby boy. Let your men return to their homes. Santo, I am so tired. We have lost nearly 200,000 of our fellow citizens, and most of them were innocent civilians, women, and children. We cannot win this kind of war. Let us end it now.*

*Magdolo*

Santiago slowly crushed the letter and closed his eyes. Magdolo was Aguinaldo's nickname from the old days, from the romantic beginning when he first formed the *Katipunan* to rise up against the Spanish.

He sat that way for a long time and, although he was aware that the American was watching, he put his head in his hands and sighed deeply. *Was this the way it was to end?* He lifted his head and looked at Lawrence. The captain held a slight smirk in the corner of his mouth.

"When did this happen? How is Aguinaldo?"

"He was captured a week ago. As far as I know, he is being treated fairly."

"Fairly?"

"He has agreed to stop fighting and support our presence here. You read the letter." Lawrence smiled and nodded toward the crumpled ball in Santiago's hand. "He understands it is best that the United States rule the country for now. "

"Am I supposed to surrender my men to you?"

"No. Lay down your arms and let your men go. Only you and your officers must come with me to see General Funstan."

"And why is that?"

Lawrence pursed his lips and looked at Santiago. "Let us just say it is for insurance."

"What do you mean?"

"Your men may be content to go back home. However, you and your officers have been up here a long time. In addition, you fought together against the Spanish. General Funstan thinks it better if he were given a chance to discuss things with you."

"Oh," said Santiago. "Some of General Funstan's men discussed things a month ago with villagers not far from here. The discussion turned into a quick court, and four civilians were executed. Is that the type of discussion the general has in mind?"

"Look, Colonel, I don't know what happened in that village. All I know is that President Aguinaldo is a prisoner and almost all of your fellow citizens have accepted that fact. They have surrendered, and the fighting has all but stopped except for up here with you. If you and your officers come with me, the bloodshed will end."

"I see." Santiago took a deep breath and opened his fist, dropping the crumpled paper into the fire. He stood and gently rubbed the wooden stock of his rifle. "I will have my men lay down their arms. We have carts and horses. You can take the weapons to Funstan."

"Good." Lawrence smiled as he stood. "You have made the right choice, Colonel."

"But my officers and I will retain our arms, for self-defense. We will not be coming with you."

"But you don't understand."

"I do understand, Captain. However, I do not trust Funstan. I do not trust you either."

"But, Colonel Santiago, that is the deal General Funstan is making—all or nothing. You and your officers have to come."

"No." Santiago firmly shook his head. "No, we cannot … we will not do that."

Lawrence looked at Santiago and took a deep breath. He exhaled slowly and spoke very quietly. "If that is your answer, then I must show you something else. May I reach again into my pocket?"

Santiago leveled his rifle at Lawrence and frowned. "You have big pockets, Captain Lawrence. Be careful what you bring out of them."

"It is just this handkerchief," said Lawrence as he fished a small cloth from his pocket. "Your men saw it when they patted me down. However, they didn't see what was inside of it. It's for you." Lawrence stretched out his hand.

Santiago noticed that the captain's fingers were trembling. Santiago stared into Lawrence's eyes and saw a flicker of something new—fear?

Santiago leaned his rifle against the stool and took the small cloth bundle. He opened it carefully and gasped when he saw what was inside.

"Sir, you must understand," blurted Lawrence. "I did not want you to see this, but you gave me no choice. I am just operating on my orders from the general."

Santiago picked up the bloody piece of flesh and bone and held it up for Lawrence to see. His hand shook as he noticed a tiny nail still attached to the stump that was once a child's thumb. He swallowed, coughed, and fought the desire to take the captain's head with his bolo.

"My son?"

"Sir, please do not blame me. Funstan has your wife and children. He was afraid you would not come in like the others. He wanted you to be sure of his intentions. He will keep your family until you surrender."

"And if I do not come in, if I do not surrender?"

"You are to accompany me back to General Funstan. If you come back with me, your wife and children will be returned. Colonel Santiago, General Funstan admires your great military skill. He just wants to talk with you and to convince you to lay down your arms."

"You did not answer my question," replied Santiago. "What happens if I do not return with you?"

"Then." Lawrence looked at Santiago. "Then, your family will be killed."

Santiago slumped onto his stool and dropped his rifle to the ground. He would rather die than risk his family to the American desire for retaliation. His desire to kill Lawrence had passed. Lawrence was just the messenger.

"God," he whispered to himself, "what did we ever do to deserve this?"

"Colonel … Colonel Santiago!"

Santiago lifted his head and looked in the direction of the cries. He squinted in the darkness and saw his soldiers carrying a man toward him. The man was covered in sweat and dirt.

"Give him some water. Where did you find him?"

"At the southern perimeter," replied a soldier. "He says his name is Bayani. He says he is a messenger from Joaquin."

Santiago frowned. Joaquin was his great-uncle. His wife, Marian, and the children had been staying in his village.

"Here, sit." He led him to his stool. "Take some water."

Bayani quickly grasped the offered flask and gulped the water. He stopped to take a breath and gulped again.

"Enough, friend," said Santiago. He gently took the flask away. "You can have as much as you want later. Now, what have you come to tell me?"

"I have terrible news, sir." Bayani looked into Santiago's face. "The soldiers came to the village. They came and began shooting."

"What?" Santiago swung his gaze to Lawrence.

"Yes, Colonel. They killed many. They killed your wife and girls. Only the little boy escaped."

"Are you sure?" Santiago felt the lump in the handkerchief.

"Yes, sir. The soldiers had him for a day. They took his thumb." Bayani knotted his brows and frowned. "I do not know why." He looked at Santiago. "But they cut it off."

"But he escaped?" Santiago squeezed the man's shoulders and stared into his eyes. "My son escaped?"

"Yes." Bayani nodded. "Your aunt stole him from the jeep, and she has him now in hiding."

Santiago glared at Lawrence.

"Sir, I swear this is news to me." Lawrence took a step back and held out his hands. "Your family was fine when I left the village to find you."

"Liar!" Bayani stood from his stool and pointed to Lawrence. "He is a liar! He was with the soldiers. He had the long rifle. He shot the ones that had reached the top of the trail."

"Take him and hold him." Santiago pointed to Lawrence. "And take care of Bayani. Give him a place by the fire and food. Make arrangements to escort him to wherever he needs to go in the morning." He turned toward Bayani and held his hands in a tight clasp. "I cannot thank you enough, my friend. I cannot thank you enough for your courage to come up here."

"It was nothing, Colonel. I am glad to have been of some service."

"You will take a message to Joaquin for me. You will tell him to guard my son Pablo with his life."

"I will tell him, Colonel."

Santiago turned to go.

"Sir." Bayani touched his arm. "Will you continue to fight? Will you continue now that President Aguinaldo is a prisoner?"

"I will fight on," replied Santiago. "I hear General Malvar still has a solid force with him. I will go and join him with whatever men want to go with me. The rest can go home."

Santiago turned and walked into the shadows at the edge of camp. When he was sure he was alone, he sagged to his knees and placed his face into his hands. He bent over and held his sobs to his chest so the others couldn't hear.

*Oh, Marian, my darling Marian, how can I live without you? How can I live without you and the girls?*

He cried for a long time. He cried until the tears were gone and his eyes were dry and burned. He cried until his breath was a rasp against his throat. He forced himself to accept the fact that the core of his life, the essence of his life, was gone. It was gone forever and could never be reclaimed. He forced himself to whisper her name and the names of his daughters. He forced himself to remember his wedding day and the births of his dead babies. He thought about them long into the night, and the next morning he walked back into the camp.

Lawrence was tied to a tree and looked as if he had not slept. The once-calm shark eyes were now bloodshot and tinged with fear.

"Prepare the fire," Santiago said to his men.

Two days later, Sergeant Ernie Hoyle winced as he walked into the dimly lit tent. The smell inside the makeshift surgery room made him gag. He hated the smell of doctors' offices: alcohol, disinfectant, the cling of feces and urine and blood. Worse, this tent smelled of something else. It was cloying and sweet and burned.

"What do you have, Corporal?" He coughed softly into his hand.

The corporal looked up from his notes and nodded. "Good morning, Sarge."

"Who is he?" Hoyle walked to the edge of the bed and looked at the patient.

"Sir, he is Captain Lawrence, from the Nebraska unit."

Hoyle opened his mouth slightly so he wouldn't have to breathe through his nose. The smell of burned flesh was very strong. He noted the gauze bandages wrapped around the patient's legs and the bandage on the man's crotch. Tubes were needled into both arms.

"What happened to him?"

"According to the report from the patrol, they found him unconscious with his hands tied behind his back. He was lying in a pool of water and—get this, Sarge—there was a length of wire ten feet away with one end hammered to a tree stump and the other end still tied to his—"

"Tied to his what?"

"Well, you know, to his ..."

"Sarge, what are you talking about?"

"The wire was tied to his penis, sir. His penis and balls."

"What?"

"Yeah, looks like whoever did this must have sat him on the stump, wired his privates to it, and then set his legs on fire. There was a kerosene can next to the pool too."

"Holy Jesus!" Hoyle gasped and looked away from the man.

"I guess they wanted him to make the choice. You know, to burn up or rip his dick and nuts off. Doc said he probably had to lunge a bunch of times to rip himself free and get into the water."

"God, why would they have done this to him? Why not just shoot him?"

"I don't know, Sarge," replied the corporal. "A couple of guys from D troop said they heard of such things though. They said that in some Filipino families they have strange traditions to pay back people that hurt them. They say such traditions are handed down from generation to generation and never die."

# CHAPTER 1

## 1976

Blue Morrison sat at his desk in the stateroom he shared with three other junior officers—or JOs, as they were called in the navy. He was trying to write a letter to Cathy but just couldn't find a way to start. Every time he put his pen to paper one of the other guys would distract him. He sighed and began to write when Head McGinnis waved to him from his perch on the top bunk.

Head grinned at him and nodded down toward their roommate, Spot, and winked. Spot sat in his chair, head back and snoring. It was his usual position in the room except when he was lying in bed and snoring.

Head quietly slipped off the bunk and went to his locker. He took out a plastic bag and climbed back up on his bunk. He opened the bag and extracted a gray, stiff sweat sock. Blue chuckled when he saw the infamous sock. Head's socks were notorious throughout the ship, and supposedly he had not washed them once during the five months of cruise. The rumor was that he wore them for every flight. Blue knew his pal was a superstitious fellow and was totally convinced that his magic socks were the reason he was leading the air wing in landing grades. They were why he had been able to get his plane aboard the carrier without fail.

Head received his nickname because his enormous noggin was roughly the size and shape of a cement truck. In fact, he had to have his flight helmet made especially for him.

Blue looked at Spot and smiled. He remembered the day Spot got his call sign. It happened at an all-officers meeting, an AOM, and it was just before the showing of the evening movie in the ready room. Spot was called to the front of the room to be introduced by the skipper, but when he turned to face the crowd he unfortunately revealed a nice, clear, wet pee stain on his khaki trousers. Spot grinned and placed his hands on his hips, as if he owned the place. There was a moment's silence followed by a growing laughter. Then from the back of the ready room where the most junior of officers were banished came the chant, "Spot. Spot. Spot. Spot …"

Now, Spot snored away, unaware of the plot developing against him.

Blue could smell the faint odor of the rancid sock even from across the room. He covered his mouth to keep from laughing as Head dangled the sock above Spot's mouth.

Spot must have gotten a whiff because he gulped and closed his mouth with a snort. Still asleep, he frowned and wrinkled his nose. Blue held his breath to keep from laughing. The stench of the sock was clearly interrupting Spot's slumber but had not brought him to full consciousness.

Blue was fighting to keep from bursting out in laughter. Head lowered the sock, and it just touched Spot's nose. Spot snorted again and gulped. He frowned, coughed softly, and raised his right hand toward his nose but then fell back into slumber.

Head again lowered the sock and put it on Spot's nose. Spot half-opened his eyes and gulped. He opened his eyes and took a deep breath. Head dropped the sock into his mouth.

"Ahggg," coughed Spot as he lurched out of his chair. Still half-asleep, he fell against the dresser and then down to the floor. He coughed and spit as Blue and Head howled.

"Wake up," said Head, laughing. "It's time to go eat."

"I think I'm going to puke," coughed Spot.

"Save it for chow," said Head as he bounded down from his bunk. "You can hurl it on the meat loaf. You coming, Blue?"

"No, I'll go later. I have to write this letter to Cathy."

"Suit yourself. Come on, shit breath." Head punched Spot on the arm and pushed him out the door.

Blue stared at the wall and thought of Cathy. He had met her in a bar in Virginia Beach that summer. Blue, Head, and some of the other guys in the squadron were partying one Saturday afternoon when Cathy and a couple of her girlfriends walked in. Blue couldn't take his eyes off her, and he eventually mustered up the courage to ask her to buy him a drink and bear his children. She had laughed, and before Blue knew it the bar was closing. Blue soon met her family, including her father who was also in the navy. He wore the silver eagles of a United States Navy captain and was a fighter pilot with F-8 Crusader and F-4 Phantom time in Vietnam.

Cathy's parents quickly embraced Blue, and so did all of her friends. Of course, Cathy was a hit at all the squadron functions, and she fit in whether it was a party on the beach, a baseball game, or just hanging out. Because he and Cathy were "a couple," they were invited to couples' types of events, such as dinner parties, movies, weddings, and even games of charades. Blue enjoyed these events to some extent, but they also bored him. All of the talk was "married people talk," and he found himself detaching from the conversations. He laughed at the stories about babies who threw up on aunts, listened to discussions on the perfect wall paint, and commiserated with the trials of backyard maintenance, but he did not embrace them as revelations to his near future. He wasn't ready to make those conversations and the activities they portrayed part of his life yet. Blue enjoyed Cathy's company and thought maybe he would love her one day, but he was not ready to make any commitment. It was not that Cathy failed to be the woman of his dreams; it was that he had no such dreams.

The situation became more uncomfortable when Cathy began to change their relationship from dating to practically married. The first time she met Blue's parents she called them Mom and Dad, and the way she fawned over his baby pictures made Blue uncomfortable. His parents really took to her though, and that complicated things even more. And just before Blue sailed on the deployment, while walking downtown, Cathy stopped in front of a china store window and suggested they pick out a pattern.

When the ship finally sailed, Blue was ready to escape the lie he was living. He knew he should have discussed their relationship with Cathy before he left, but a part of him hoped that somehow he would change his mind. A part of him wanted to give in to the situation and to fall in love with Cathy as much as it appeared she had fallen in love with him. Blue was still staring at a blank piece of paper, trying to think of how to write his thoughts, when Chin Anderson stuck his head in the door.

"Hey, Blue, Skipper wants to see you."

"Okay, thanks, Chin." Blue was glad he had a reason to stop. "Where is he?"

"Ready room."

"Thanks. Any idea what he wants?"

"No." Chin shrugged. "Just said to get you."

Blue brushed his short brown hair and put on his khaki uniform. It had the silver bars of a US Navy lieutenant junior grade (LTJG) on the collars, and over his left shirt pocket were the gold wings of a naval flight officer. His yellow-and-black name tag was pinned over his right shirt pocket, and it carried the hooded skull insignia of the Death Angels of Fighter Squadron 57. At six feet two and 175 pounds, Blue was in good shape, and he kept himself that way through a daily regimen of jogging and weight lifting.

Blue's real name was Jack Morrison. He was from a small Midwest town on the outskirts of St Louis, Missouri, and was proud of his Middle America heritage. His mother and father had raised his brothers and sisters on a dairy farm and had scrimped and saved to send them through college. He considered himself a regular guy. While a lot of guys gave themselves call signs in the training command, it was actually their first fleet squadron that had the unwritten but clear right to provide the call sign. When an aviator reported to his first squadron, he could call himself whatever he wanted, but if the squadron decided to change it, then that was the way it would be. Of course it was the junior officers, or JOs, in the squadron that actually did the naming, and often call signs were conjured up at the spur of the moment to optimize a humiliating situation or exploit a shortcoming. The only real requirement of a call sign was that it must be appropriate to use over a radio and to be painted on the side of an airplane. Because of this, many naval aviators did not have the call sign they chose.

Blue got his call sign during a training flight in the F-4 Phantom. While students like Blue normally flew with instructors, there was one set of syllabus flights that crewed the students together. It was dive bombing. Blue and his pals wondered why dive bombing utilized a student-student crew and surmised it was either to give them an opportunity to develop crew skills … or it was because the instructors didn't want to be with students as they hurtled toward the ground. At any rate, for safety's sake, the syllabus was rigid and the flights static with hard altitude numbers for the target pattern roll in point, ordinance release point, and minimum pullout.

The F-4 Phantom relied upon a two-man crew: the pilot up front and the radar intercept officer, or RIO, in the back. The RIO's job was to handle navigation and communications chores as well as operate the radar and other weapons' computers. Blue was a RIO, and his pilot was a lieutenant named Bill Smith. Bill was about as dynamic as his name, and that huge dollop of personality earned him the call sign of "One Each," as in "there's a tray of pencils over there, take one each and fill out your forms."

Blue and One Each were on their last mission of the four-flight syllabus, flying on the Dare County, Virginia, bombing range when Blue's naming occurred.

Everything went smoothly until One Each misjudged his closure to the roll-in point and overshot. In his attempt to correct the situation, he yanked too hard on the stick, pulled up the nose, and stalled the Phantom. The big plane shuddered and then snapped to the left, exhibiting all of the flying characteristics of a Coke machine.

The nose of the Phantom whipped down, but as airspeed began to build, Blue thought they were out of trouble. Then, for some reason One Each panicked and jerked the nose up again, causing the right engine to compressor stall. The Phantom went into a spin, and as it descended five thousand feet, Blue pulled the ejection handle between his legs and they both rocketed out of the airplane.

They were both picked up quickly and taken to the hospital in Portsmouth, and both were okay. Somewhere in the ejection sequence Blue lost his helmet and received a blow from his parachute straps; the right side of his face had a large bruise. The day he came out of the hospital the guys in the squadron began calling him Blue Patch. Eventually the patch part was dropped, and Jack Morrison became Blue. The subsequent accident board cleared Blue, but old One Each was given his walking papers. Rumor had it he went on to fly for a major airline. Blue thought of that every time he booked a flight home to see his parents.

Blue left the bunk room and walked up onto the flight deck. He smiled as the warm sun and fresh breeze found his face. He slid his sunglasses from their perch on top of his head over his eyes and paused a moment to look around. The sight of the carrier's flight deck never ceased to impress him, despite the fact that he was now a cruise-seasoned veteran. Its four and one half acres of steel stretched over a thousand feet, and from where he stood it was six stories to the blue water below and another six stories to the top of the mast above.

The ship in which Blue and the rest of the crew cruised was the USS *Constellation* (CV-64). She was one of two ships in the Kitty Hawk class and was a grand lady indeed. She was a mammoth testimony to American maritime might, and she carried a crew of over five thousand men and a lethal air wing of eighty aircraft. She had her own bakery, barbershop, and chapel. She had her own medical and dental center, television studio, and library. She could distill her own water from the sea and could feed twenty thousand meals a day. When angered, she could launch hundreds of armed aircraft capable of engaging any of America's enemies. She was one of the most powerful things man ever made.

Blue stopped in mid-deck and allowed himself to drink in a bit of the scene in front of him. He saw knots of men all over the deck, gathered around the airplanes, and marked with grease and hydraulic fluid. The breeze carried the sounds of their shouts and tools, and it carried the smells of stack gas, jet fuel, saltwater, and lunch.

Despite all of the activity, Blue acknowledged the calm that surrounded one of the most dangerous places on earth. During flight operations, the tranquil scene in front of him would be transformed into a maelstrom of screaming engines, hot exhaust, whirling blades, and sharp edges. Aircraft would be launched from four steam catapults accelerating in seconds from zero to over 140 miles per hour. Other planes would land in what many thought of as "a controlled crash," slamming down at up to 140 miles per hour to be immediately brought to a halt as the hook on their tail snagged the steel cable across the deck. All the while, young men, most less than twenty years of age, would work feverishly. They aided the crew as they manned up. They armed the guns, bombs, and missiles. And they fueled the tanks and fixed the machines that broke.

But as Blue surveyed the deck that morning, the dangerous environment of flight was calmed by the sounds and actions of maintenance, because this was a much needed no-fly day. The ship and its air wing were standing down from flight operations to perform maintenance on the airplanes. They took off one day a week for such work as well as to catch up on neglected paperwork and conduct meetings. Blue's smile widened as he strolled. He sensed an extra air of good feeling and thought he could see added crispness in the sailors' actions and hear it in their voices. He attributed it to a few possibilities. Maybe it was the beautiful sunshine, maybe it was the fact that their cruise was ending, or maybe it was the upcoming port call in the fabled Philippine city of Olongapo.

Commander John "Heart" Valentine sat in his squadron's ready room with his feet propped up on his stool. He drank from a cup of steaming coffee adorned with the squadron patch design and the initials CO stenciled in gold. His stool also had CO stenciled on its side, a small benefit of aviation command. Pecking rights earned Heart the cup, the stool, and his seat in the front of the room. Sitting next to him was Commander Roy Saratoga, the executive officer and number-two man in the squadron. He had XO stenciled on his stool. Roy's call sign was Prince.

In a good navy fighter squadron, the skipper sets the tone. He is the commander and has the authority and the opportunity to press his personality into the group. That was true with the Death Angels. Heart was a solid professional, but he also loved to joke and give crap to the other officers, especially to the young JOs. Because of the friendly and boisterous atmosphere, the ready room was a lively place and there was always a crowd gathered around the duty desk or the coffeepot. Prince, on the other hand, was harder to read and harder to deal with. He had an aloof manner, and his gray eyes held no warmth. However, he was second-in-command, and since the executive officer would one day move up to replace the commanding officer, Prince was a force to be reckoned with.

Behind Heart and Prince were seats for the rest of the aviators in the squadron. Not surprisingly, there was also a pecking order for them. Immediately behind the two commanders sat the lieutenant commanders. There were four or five in each squadron, and they served as heads of the various departments in the command: maintenance, operations, safety, and administration.

The lieutenant commanders were in fierce competition, because in order to command a squadron one day they had to be assigned to either the maintenance or the operations officer billet and had to excel once there. While this competition was often graceful and balanced, some officers resorted to all manner of backstabbing and ass kissing. Of course, the JOs quickly discovered these traits and did their best to undermine the officers who bore them.

In reality, lieutenant commander was a difficult rank. It was not senior enough to garner much privilege, but it was too senior to avoid responsibility. When things went wrong, a lieutenant commander's ass would be chewed shortly thereafter. Lieutenant commander was also the rank of demarcation, whereby an officer could no longer claim the wild and innocent free play of a junior but had to admit to being a "company man." Since the lieutenant commanders directed the JOs and made them actually work for a living, the JOs actively sabotaged them. Individually, a JO was a decent human being and could be trusted to do all manner of things, including flying an airplane. However, as a group, they could hover on the edge of control. They possessed unbridled enthusiasm and imagination fueled by above-average intelligence, unhampered by the stains of maturity. The JO lot consisted of three ranks, the lowest being ensigns barely out of the training command. The single gold bar on their collars marked them as raw nuggets, and the best thing about them was that they were so naive and green that they couldn't get into that much trouble, even if they tried. This was not a problem for the lieutenant (junior-grade) officers. These men had been in the navy for a couple of years and, of course, had "seen it all." Their single silver bar gave them power over their ensign brethren and marked them as those who might—or might not—know something.

The kings of the JO world were the double silver bar–wearing lieutenants (or railroad track–wearing lieutenants). These officers had been in the navy from four to eight years, depending upon their time in that rank, and formed the core of naval aviation tactical war fighting. Lieutenants dropped more bombs and shot down more enemy airplanes than any other rank in the navy. They also led the various divisions in the squadrons that, when combined, formed the departments that the lieutenant commanders ran. If a squadron possessed a crop of solid lieutenants, the command would thrive if properly led. If not, the command was doomed to mediocrity regardless of the level of leadership.

Fortunately for the Death Angels, they were blessed with good officers and enlisted men and a great leader in Heart.

Heart guzzled coffee and smoked a cigarette as he glanced around the room. There were about a dozen officers standing around talking and laughing. The mood was the way he liked it, light and relaxed. He felt very comfortable around his young charges. Whether they were officers or enlisted men, he felt he belonged with them, and he was smart enough to cherish that feeling. He knew fellow commanders who avoided the ready room and contact with their young people. After all, it was a challenge to be both part of the group and the leader of the group.

"Hey, Spider." Blue stopped outside the ready room door and spoke to Spider Thomas. Spider was from Texas, and somehow the combination of that and the fact that he was only five feet six gave him a complex Spot described as "bubba Napoleon." The most obvious affliction of this complex was his filthy language.

"What's going on?"

"Bunch of fuckin' guys kissin' the skipper's ass and givin' each other shit." Spider grinned and continued down the passageway. "You know the usual slurp fest."

"Yeah, I know," said Blue as he pushed open the ready room door.

Giving each other a hard time was normal. In fact, the officers expected it and even enjoyed it for the most part. In a fighter squadron ready room, everyone gave everyone crap—that is, everyone but the skipper and the XO. They were the only ones who had the option of giving without necessarily receiving. Giving them crap required skill and tact and, like the old Indian act of counting coup, was highly admired by the JOs.

"Sit down, Blue." Heart motioned for Blue to sit on his stool, a coveted position for which a couple of the lieutenant commanders would have knifed their mothers.

"We have a little problem, but I think it will turn out to be a good deal for you." Heart's smile widened.

Immediately Blue felt nervous. The term "good deal" was notoriously misleading. When someone, especially someone senior, said he was giving you a "good deal," it usually meant that it was a "good deal" for him and a screw job for you.

"The admiral had his orders changed," continued Heart. "In order to get a job on the Joint Staff in the Pentagon, he is having his change of command early. In fact, he is having it at sea prior to our pulling into Olongapo."

Blue listened intently, still unsure how the "good deal" angle would play.

"In fact," Heart continued, "he is having his change of command in about ten days, and as you know that is before the ship pulls into port."

Blue nodded, still wondering how any of this affected him. The admiral didn't know Blue from a corn muffin.

"So that means we have to get him a gift in Olongapo, and that is where you come in."

Blue frowned. "Do you want me to take up a collection, Skipper?" This *was* going to be the crappy version of a "good deal."

"No," Heart said with a laugh. "It means I want you to fly to Olongapo early and have something made for him."

Blue immediately brightened. "Fly. Me? To Olongapo?"

Immediately the JOs surrounded Heart and Blue. Blue looked around as he felt the crowd shuffle close. He knew he was witnessing the shark feeding frenzy phenomenon of a navy ready room. He had seen it before. It was the time when the words "good deal" actually meant a good deal and not a screw job. When Heart said the word "fly," it caused the pack to perk up their ears. And when he said "to Olongapo early," it caused them to try to cash in.

"Yes, fly into Olongapo," answered Heart. "By the way, the reason you get to go is because you are finished with your enlisted evaluations unlike some other people I know." Heart panned the crowd, smiling slightly at the assembled officers. They either grinned lamely or looked at the floor.

"So, you are the lucky guy," continued Heart. "However, Blue, this is a big deal. The officers in the ship's company chipped in and bought the admiral a special-edition Winchester rifle as a going-away present. They ordered it months ago, and it has arrived. Now, the air wing is under the gun, so to speak, to get him something of equal value. The air wing commander thinks that a matching gun case would be ideal, and if the CAG thinks that then that is what we will do."

"Do they make that kind of thing in Olongapo?" Blue frowned and looked at the skipper. From what he had heard from the "old salts," all the town had to offer was prostitution and alcohol.

"Son, they make everything in Olongapo. So that gives you less than ten days to get the gun case done. You're leaving on the first launch tomorrow morning."

"Skipper, I would consider it an honor to fly Blue to Olongapo. I will have my evaluations completed by tonight." Just Ed Valentine shoved his way to the front of the crowd. He was called "Just Ed" because his last name was the same as Heart's. Since he was obviously not important enough to have the same name as the skipper of a fighter squadron, the JOs had stripped him of his last name.

Heart looked at the young pilot and smiled. "I appreciate the sacrifice but I really want someone with just a little more experience. I want someone who has been to Olongapo before. Besides, you're on the XO's shit list. He says you owe him a Combined Federal Campaign status report."

Heart winked at the crowd as Just Ed mumbled, looked away, and then slinked into the crowd. A few JOs clapped him on the back, and there was a chorus of "Nice try."

"So who is going to be my pilot?"

Heart smiled again at Blue and then looked around at the young, expectant faces. They were practically salivating. He looked at Blue and said, "I'm going to send you with Magic."

"Magic?"

"Yep, the legend himself."

"Wow, this is gonna be great." Blue grinned broadly.

"I think so," said Heart. Then his eyes became serious. "But don't make it too great. Remember that I am expecting you to do some business for me. I am tasking you, not Magic, you understand?"

"Yes, sir," stammered Blue.

"Magic is one of the best pilots in the navy, maybe the world," said Heart. "But he is no good at doing this kind of thing. He would play around with the whores in Olongapo or go over and hang out in Hong Kong until the last minute and then bring back a piece of shit."

Blue smiled and nodded his head in agreement.

"Or he would get in a fight with some marine or air force puke and wind up in jail."

Blue nodded again.

"So get the job done and try to keep some of the magic out of Magic."

# CHAPTER 2

**B**lue whistled as he walked down the passageway toward Magic's stateroom. He was ecstatic about the adventure in front of him. To fly off early was a tremendously good deal, but to be crewed with a guy like Magic was beyond a good deal. Blue considered him the best fighter pilot in the navy. Magic had shot down two MIGs in Vietnam, and he regularly out flew even the Top Gun pilots at their famed school in San Diego.

Blue thought it was cool that Magic didn't look like the movie-star version of a fighter pilot. He didn't have the perfect physique and he wasn't all white teeth and sparkling eyes. In fact, he looked pretty average, with the beginnings of a paunch starting to push out the front of his flight suit, and his hair was already thinning on top. Blue thought Magic mocked everybody's ideal of what a fighter pilot should look and act like. Besides being a good pilot, Magic knew many important things. He knew what stereo systems were the best buys and how to overhaul a V-8 engine. He knew what night blue crabs would molt and transform into a soft-shell delicacy. He knew how to install a hot tub and that Jimmy's Kitchen in Hong Kong made the world's best French onion soup. He knew how to plan an air strike against a target defended by the best Soviet–style air defenses.

Blue also knew the story about Magic being an orphan, and that added to his mystique. His mom and dad died in a car wreck, and his uncle had raised him.

Blue didn't know how, when, or why Magic got his call sign. Nobody else seemed to know either. But it didn't make any difference. Magic just seemed to fit.

Blue was still one hundred feet away from Magic's room when he began to hear his stereo. By the time he got outside the door, the strains of "The Duke of Earl" were deafening. Blue knocked and walked in; he smiled at what he saw.

Magic stood in the middle of the room, eyes shut and singing along with the song. He held a beer bottle in his hand as a mic. He swayed in a circle, and when he opened his eyes and saw Blue, he waved him in but continued to sing.

Blue stood next to the bed and watched as Magic moved around the room. Magic was wearing a maroon smoking jacket, the kind Blue had seen in old movies. It had the left elbow patched with a piece of an old flight suit. Underneath the jacket he wore jungle fatigues, and on his feet were a pair of scuffed cowboy boots. Blue grinned and shook his head as he looked around the room. He had heard about the place but had never been inside.

Magic's room was a typical two-man stateroom that people with the rank of lieutenant commander shared. However, Magic lived by himself and had for two months since his roommate, Swede Anderson, had developed mononucleosis. Swede had gotten so sick that he was flown to a military hospital in Germany and eventually back to the States.

The room was twenty feet by twenty feet and painted haze gray like everything else on the ship. Magic had removed the top bunk so the room looked larger than normal. Along one wall were two closets and a chest of drawers. There were no photos or pictures on the walls, save one large poster of Raquel Welch. It was the one of her in an animal skin for the movie, *One Million Years B.C.* Blue laughed when he read the handwriting on the poster. In a flowing feminine hand it read, *Magic, you are the beast with the big one. I will always love you, Raquel.* Magic's stereo and album set lined one whole wall of his room. He had purchased the components during previous cruises and was quite the music aficionado. A television stood next to his speakers.

As the last sound of the song died to a whisper, Magic walked to the stereo and flipped it off. He spun around and flashed Blue a huge grin.

"Have a seat, son." He gestured to a stool that looked exactly like the one Heart had, except it was red. It had CO stenciled on the side in black.

"Where did you get the stool?" Blue asked as he sat down.

"Oh, I took it from our pals in the other Phantom squadron."

"You did?"

"Yeah, went in there one night and took it." Magic laughed. "Their skipper is a pussy, a lousy pilot, and a piece of shit. I crawled up his ass, put my gun sight on the back of his airplane, and gunned his brains out, and he refused to admit it. So I took his stool."

Blue laughed and looked over Magic's shoulder at the wall.

"Is it true about the desk?"

"The what?"

"The desk, your desk. The rumor is you had one of the guys in metal frames come up here and weld it shut." Blue laughed and pointed toward Magic's cabinet.

"Yeah, it's true." He walked over and tugged at the cabinet. It did not budge.

"Why did you do that?"

"I was afraid it might fall open one day and I would accidently do some paperwork." Magic laughed and winked at Blue. "That would ruin my karma as the greatest living fighter pilot."

"You hate paperwork that much?" Blue settled onto his stool.

"I don't hate it. I just don't do it." Magic chuckled. "I tell you what, son, if you ever catch me doing any paperwork you have permission to cut my balls off and have personnel assign me to the nearest air force base."

"I'll do that." Blue laughed.

"So how about a cocktail while we talk about our trip?"

Blue smiled back. "Sure, diet Coke if you have it."

"Nah, Cokes are for the chaplain." Magic walked over to one of his closets and pulled open the door. Inside was a full-sized refrigerator.

"You have your own fridge? How did you ever get it in here?" "I stole it out of the admiral's galley during the yard period." Magic had his back to Blue and was rummaging around inside the fridge. "So how about a martini?"

"I don't think I have ever had one."

Magic whirled around and looked at Blue in disbelief. "You've got to be kidding me."

"No." Blue shrugged. "I don't think I have ever had one."

"Christ, you *did* go to college in this country, didn't you?"

"Sure, but we drank mostly beer."

That's the trouble with you guys these days." Magic shook his head as he fished a bottle of gin out of the freezer section. "You don't have any sense of tradition. How old are you, twenty?"

Blue laughed and straightened the stool beneath him. "I'm twenty-five."

"Christ, I'm thirty-five. It only took a decade to turn us from hard-charging gin drinkers to light beer pussies. What a shame."

"I guess it is a pity." Blue laughed.

Magic put gin, a dash of vermouth, and some olive brine in each glass. He stirred and handed one to Blue. "There you have it."

"God, but that is strong." Blue grimaced as he took his first sip and shivered as the liquid went down his throat. He took his drink, walked back to the chair, and sat down. "So what is it like in Olongapo?"

"Kid, it is a fucking blast!" Magic took a seat on his bunk bed.

"Really." Blue grinned. "How so? I mean, there are so many stories going around the ship. Most of us are East Coast sailors and haven't been there. And we never know if what we hear is a bunch of crap. But, from what I hear, the place is pretty wild."

"Yeah, I guess 'wild' is a good word," said Magic as he took a sip. "But the martial law that President Marcos imposed keeps it pretty safe for us. Marcos's goons know to leave us alone, and they keep us from being screwed with too much. The US brings a lot of money into the Philippines, and that among other things keeps Marcos in power. So it's a strange situation where the outsiders, like US sailors, are treated better than the locals, the Filipinos themselves."

"That's weird." Blue took another sip.

"Yeah, as long as you're off the streets by midnight or back on base, and as long as you don't go messing around in the jungle, you'll be all right."

"What about disease? I mean, the place is kind of a dump, isn't it?"

"Gee, kid, you're not going to raise a family there. You're just visiting." Magic laughed and took a sip. "It's like Mexico. Don't drink the water, and wear a rubber. Simple."

"I guess there is a lot of clap and stuff, right?"

"Yeah, but that's the deal with any port city, kid."

"I guess so." Blue nodded. "But every guy who says he's been there brags about one thing, and that is sex! Sounds like there is a hooker on every street corner."

"Well, they are right about that. But remember, kid, a guy that has been to Olongapo is expected to brag about that kind of stuff. What do you expect them to do, talk about how much fun they had in the base library?"

"I guess you're right."

"Besides," continued Magic, "a lot of these guys are still kind of kids. They haven't ever been with many women, if any. In fact, the only titties a lot of them have seen were their mamas when they were wearing diapers."

"Yeah, I guess." Blue chuckled.

"So they walk into a bar in Olongapo and some little girl jumps their bones. It gets their attention, and it makes them feel good."

"Yeah, but they're hookers." Blue frowned. "What's to brag about? It's business, not charisma, that gets the girl."

"Kid, it amazes me what you don't know about your own species. Every guy that ever bought a woman secretly thinks that at least a little of the transaction is personal. If the hooker is good-looking— and a lot of them are—a guy thinks that she has been looking around all night to find him. After all, she could have turned down his money and gone with someone else."

"Umm," grunted Blue. He had never been with a hooker.

Magic refilled their glasses, and they drank in silence for a moment. Then Blue cleared his throat.

"You act like you have spent a lot of time with them. I mean *with* them, not just watching from a bar stool."

Magic munched on a cracker and slowly nodded his head. "I guess you are right about that, kid."

"What are they like? I mean, really?"

"Filipinos? They're real nice people. Smaller than we are, somewhat skinny for the most part, and of course, brown. They're pretty laid-back."

"Umm," grunted Blue as he took a swallow. The second drink was beginning to mellow him out. "These martinis are pretty good after all."

"They're real big on family."

"How can a city of prostitutes be big on family?" Blue squinted his eyes and looked at Magic.

"Don't be stupid, kid. Most of them are shop owners. They sell stuff. Hell, they make everything you can think of over there. Look at this." Magic opened his jacket and displayed a worn T-shirt with the words *Duke of Eral* written in bold letters. "See."

"Yeah, but it's misspelled. Earl is misspelled." Blue laughed.

"Yeah." Magic shrugged as he winked at Blue. "Quality control does need some work, I guess." Magic settled into his perch on the bunk and slurped his martini.

"Times are tough in the Philippines. They always have been tough. The government is run by a bunch of corrupt fuckers who take most everything off the top. So a lot of people are left with making do any way they can."

"Sounds like an excuse to me."

"Might be." Magic nodded. "Might be at that. But you wait until you've been there, and then we can chat about all this some more."

Blue nodded and sipped the last of his drink. He smiled and handed his glass to Magic. "Thanks for the martini. It was great."

"My pleasure, kid. Get some rest. We got a big day tomorrow."

"Yeah, we are on the 0730 launch."

"I saw that on the schedule," said Magic. "I figure we are around three hundred miles away. It should take us around an hour to get there."

"Then what?" Blue stopped at the door and turned. He was very excited about what was going to happen the next day.

"Well, then we land and the advanced detachment maintenance crew will bed down the jet and we will get a ride up to the Cubi Point Officers' Club."

"Cool."

"Cool is right," said Magic. "We will rest up, have some chow, and then head into town tomorrow night. We can start on your education, kid."

"Cool." Blue opened the door and walked down the passageway toward his bunk room. He grinned in the semidarkness and then laughed aloud. Yep, this was going to be a good deal, all right. It was going to be a *great* deal.

# CHAPTER 3

A s Blue walked back to his bunk room, the enlisted men in the Death Angel power plants shop, the men who maintained the mighty J-79 engines and fuel systems, were relaxing in their berthing area. They sat around a battered table, smoking cigarettes and drinking Cokes. The room they shared was the lounge area in one of the Death Angel berthing compartments. Actually, "lounge" was a generous term. It was really only a cleared part of the sleeping area, reserved for the men to watch television and talk or play cards. The compartment stretched across the center of the ship and contained bunks for eighty-seven men. The bunks were stacked three high with barely enough room to turn around without touching shoulders on the bunk above. Each man also had a small locker to store his sea bag of uniforms, with a little room for personal items.

The compartment was kept dark most of the time, except when it was being cleaned. Since the squadron was divided into two shifts of twelve hours each, someone was always trying to sleep at any given time of the day or night. There was a close, damp smell of sour towels, dirty laundry, and stale tobacco smoke. Accompanying this bouquet was the sharper odor of aerosol deodorant and foot powder.

Next to the compartment was the bathroom or head. It was a "four-holer" with a line of urinals to match and no doors or curtains for privacy. A man using this accommodation was destined to sit with his pants around his ankles and the world in his face. Two of the commodes were not working and were taped over. An evil smell issued from them, and a yellow-brown liquid pooled on the floor. It was not a good place to sit and read.

Benny Benitez stood at one of the sinks, shaving in the mirror. He had finished showering, and his thick black hair was combed straight back. Beads of sweat popped out on his forehead. Benny was a Filipino American, the first in his family to be born in the United States. Most of his Filipino shipmates served as cooks and clerks, since they did not have security clearances. But Benny was an American citizen and did have a clearance. He was the only Filipino maintenance technician in the entire air wing.

"Hey, Benny, come on. He's just about to start." Jimmy Rogers stuck his head in the door. "Hurry up, man."

"Coming," said Benny. He wiped the shaving cream from his face and tightened his towel around his waist as he walked into the lounge area. He didn't want to miss the captain's nightly announcement.

Benny eagerly looked forward to such talks. It was a time when the captain could tell them about upcoming events, dispel rumors, and publicly praise sailors. In fact, the day before, he had praised Benny and his crew for the job they had done fixing one of their F-4 Phantoms. One of their engines had had a compressor stall during flight, and the plane had to come back to the ship with only one engine working. Benny had diagnosed the problem, and the plane was back on the schedule that night.

Benny had no sooner taken a seat than the captain appeared on the carrier's closed-circuit television station. As usual, he began by acknowledging the crew for the work they were doing, particularly those who had participated in the previous night's refueling evolution. After passing out a round of "atta boys," he abruptly turned the microphone over to the ship's training officer, Commander Johns.

Commander Johns had the task of ensuring all hands were briefed concerning the customs, opportunities, and pitfalls of each coming port visit. He was a tedious man with a love for details, and he attacked his task with all the charisma of a librarian. He began

his delivery with positive words about the friendship between the
United States and the Philippines, and he briefly described some
of the topographical features of the islands. But soon Commander
Johns's message became more negative and pointed.

"There are thousands of whores in Olongapo," he said. "And
every one of them has gonorrhea or syphilis or both. I know what
some of you men are thinking, and I know what some of you have
been told. But I am here to tell you to be careful about what you
poke into."

Benny winced at the laughter that burst from the men.

"And be careful of the bars," Johns continued. "If you get drunk
in there, they will spike your drink and steal everything you own.
In fact, the *Ranger* was in Olongapo last month, and there were so
many incidents of robbery that the town was placed off-limits for a
week." Johns paused to let it sink in. "That cost them an awful lot of
money, and it really pissed President Marcos off. You all know that
the Philippines is under martial law and the cops can do anything
they want. They don't want to shoot Americans. They will shoot
their own for nothing, but they won't shoot you unless you get in the
middle of something." Johns stopped and looked into the camera.
He seemed to be satisfied because he smiled and said, "Nuff said."

When the commander finished and the television went blank,
the men began talking in excited tones about what they had heard.
Benny sat quietly and looked at the floor. He could tell out of his
periphery that his shipmates kept glancing his way. He figured they
wanted to talk about the whores and the booze and the wildness of
the place they were about to visit. He also figured that they didn't
want to offend him.

"So, Benny." Gary Olds looked across the lounge at his friend.
"What's the real deal with Olongapo?"

"Yeah," chirped a chorus of voices.

"What's it like?"

"You ever been there?"

Benny looked around the room and shook his head. "Hey, guys." He smiled. "I've never been there. Besides, my folks were from Manila. Nothing but virgins and good Catholics there."

"But Commander Johns made it sound like all of the Philippines was the same."

"Commander Johns doesn't know the Philippines." Benny stopped smiling. "He doesn't know anything about us, and neither do most of the guys who are spouting stuff about the place. Olongapo is Olongapo. It is a port city. Much of what it is ... is what the people who visit have made it."

Benny looked around the room and noticed Petty Officer Franks sitting by himself in the corner. Franks was a new arrival and the work center supervisor, but he had rejected Benny's friendship.

He was a petty officer first class, but he didn't seem to know much about the Phantom.

Franks's ugly grin widened when he saw Benny look his way. "I've been there," he said. "I've been to Olongapo."

The noise in the compartment suddenly died down. Everybody turned to look at Franks.

"I've been to Olongapo," Franks repeated. "I was there on my last cruise." Franks looked around the room and slowly exhaled the smoke from his cigarette. He smiled and looked at Benny.

"So what's the deal?" A voice came from the back of the crowd.

"What's Olongapo really like?"

"Is it like the commander says?"

Franks smiled wider as he stubbed out his smoke and looked at Benny.

"Well, it's not *great* pussy ... but all things considered ... it's not bad either." Franks grinned broadly as the sailors whooped and clapped. "All you need is a handful of pesos and those girls will give you all you want of whatever you want all night if you want."

The sailors cheered again and pushed forward toward Franks, leaving Benny alone in his chair. Any sensitivity toward him appeared to be forgotten.

"You young boys from back in the sticks will love these girls. They'll suck your cock like a calf sucks its mama's teat."

The sailors cheered again, and every eye was fixed on Franks, following his every word.

Benny was shocked by the abruptness of Franks's words and his language, but as he heard the sailors cheer and clap he frowned and looked down at the deck. It seemed that everybody was more than willing to believe the worst about the Philippines. In fact, Benny knew that he had been pretending all along that the ship's visit to Olongapo would be just like the visits in France, Spain, and Italy. Although he had never been to Olongapo, he knew about it. It was a place that was famous for catering to American sailors with all of their money and all of their desires. In Olongapo you could pay a man a peso and he would feed a baby duck to an alligator. In Olongapo you could pay a woman a peso and she would have sex with a donkey. In Olongapo you could give a child a peso to watch him dive into a sewer. And it seemed that there were plenty of people who wanted to see such things, and plenty of people who were willing to do them—and, of course, there were plenty of pesos.

Benny knew that once the crew hit the city and saw all of this, they would link the Philippines and all Filipinos with what they saw there. He shifted his eyes toward Franks and found him staring coldly back.

"Yep." Franks grinned. "Olongapo is like the rest of the Philippines. A bunch of whores and pimps and not much else."

The crowd started to cheer again but then fell into a nervous silence. Benny felt the blood rush to his head as he stood up. He had never wanted to hit someone so much in his life. He wanted to walk over to Franks and tear out that stinking, filthy tongue of his. He felt the eyes of the others on him, and he felt their silent urge for him to punch the man. But he also felt his father's presence, and his mind flashed to a small man with the ever-smiling face and the white apron. He thought of the man who made a living cutting up ducks, chickens, and pigs all day for the market where he worked, the wonderful man who had come to America from the Philippines and who was so proud his son was in the United States Navy.

Benny felt his father's ring on his finger. He slowly rotated it with his thumb. He knew that no matter how much he wanted to hit Franks, to do so would ruin his career. The navy took a very dim view of sailors fighting sailors for any reason, and when it involved a junior hitting a senior it was a career ender. Benny took a deep breath and dropped his hands to his sides. He looked around at the men in the room. When his eyes returned to Franks he saw the smirk on his face that told him Franks realized that he was in no danger. Franks's smirk grew to an open smile, and his arms akimbo exuded a growing confidence.

Benny turned and walked out of the lounge into the quiet darkness of the sleeping compartment. He went to his bunk, sat on the wool blanket, and stared into the dark. His father had told him that the navy was a magnificent place to begin his life. But he had also warned him that it was not an easy place. His father too had been in the US Navy. He had served for four years as a compartment cleaner. He made beds and took out trash and later was given the opportunity to cook for the crew.

"I wonder," he whispered, "if this is the way it will always be."

# CHAPTER 4

"Hey, take a look at vulture's row." Blue spoke into his oxygen mask and pointed up at the carrier's superstructure. A handful of the Death Angel JOs stood there. They were watching the launch from the perch above the flight deck. Of course, Head was mooning them.

"Nice." Magic laughed. "I can't tell. Is that Head's ass or Prince's face?"

Both men laughed and then concentrated as they pulled out of their parking spot toward the catapult. Blue looked from one side to the next to ensure their wings were clear, and Magic followed the signals from the yellow shirts. Blue shirts pulled off the chocks, brown shirts picked up the chains, and red shirts stood ready in case of fire. Green shirts readied the catapult, and black-and-white checked shirts gave a final thumbs up.

Blue and Magic taxied over the shuttle into position, and green-shirted crew attached the launching bridle to hard points on the wings. Seconds later, Magic jammed the throttles into full afterburner, and the Phantom shuddered under the power of nearly 36,000 pounds of thrust. Orange-yellow flames shot out of the back of the burner cans and crawled up the steel blast reflectors behind them. The noise made teeth rattle, the heat backed men away, and the pronounced nose and squatted rear made the Phantom look as if it was ready to leap out of its bridle. It looked like it was alive!

"You ready, kid?"

"Ready to go," said Blue. He put his helmet against the ejection seat and waited for the shot. Out of the corner of his eye, he saw Magic salute the catapult officer.

Blue gasped as they blasted forward, grateful for the acceleration. He hoped he would never get used to how great a catapult shot felt.

"Gear's up, flaps coming," sung Magic as he jerked the aircraft sharply to the right to clear any other aircraft. Blue could see vapor coming off the wing tips as he grunted under the g-forces. They turned back toward the ship's heading and accelerated to 400 knots per hour. Then Magic brought the nose up and pointed it toward Olongapo.

Two hours later they were lying in the sun beside the Cubi Point Officers' Club pool.

"So what do you think?" Magic lifted his sunglasses and looked at Blue. He smiled and leaned back against his plastic beach chair.

"Man, this place is paradise," said Blue. He settled into his wooden chaise lounge, put down his hot dog, and lifted his head slightly to survey the area where they lay. The pool was of medium size with a diving board at one end and a hoop for water basketball at the other. The Bachelor Officers' Quarters (BOQ) management had placed a mix of standard pool furniture around the area, and young men like Blue and Magic filled chairs and chaise lounges. Most were assigned to the local aviation squadrons that performed fleet services, such as towing target banners and flying logistics flights. The pool was attached to the BOQ, and its hotel amenities provided towels as well as a pool drink service.

"You can go in there and get oiled up." Magic had pointed to the massage room as they walked to the pool.

"Is it a massage as in getting your muscles worked on, or a massage as in getting your other muscle worked on?" Blue grinned at Magic as he looked at the colorful sign on the door.

"Oh, she will be wrestling with Jimmy if you let her." Magic laughed. "About the only time you won't have the opportunity to get the other muscle worked on around here is when you order a hamburger."

Blue finished the last of his hot dog and frowned at Magic's napping face. "This place is paradise, but the world-famous Cubi dog is kind of disappointing." He looked at Magic.

"How so?" Magic grunted but did not move.

"Well, all of you Vietnam guys talk about the Cubi dog like it is something out of this world. It's just a hot dog."

"No," said Magic, "it's a Cubi dog, a world-famous Cubi dog."

"But why is it world famous? It's just a hot dog."

Magic turned his head toward Blue. "It's a world-famous Cubi dog because we are eating it at the world-famous Cubi Officers' Club pool, where the world-famous Cubi dog was born."

"Oh." Blue laughed. "That explains everything."

"Besides, where else can you get a hot dog and a cold beer for fifteen cents?"

"Well, you have me there." Blue laughed. "But speaking of beer, I can't decide if I like this beer or hate it." He looked at the brown San Miguel bottle and scratched at its painted label.

"Then choose to like it." Magic laughed. "It's all they have outside the base. Besides, it's a classic."

"Yeah, like the world-famous Cubi dog is a classic."

"Exactly. I'm glad you are starting to catch on, Blue boy." Magic laughed and slumped back into his chair.

Blue took a deep breath and wiped sweat from his cheek. The pool water was perfect, and he had already been in to cool off a couple of times. Magic had convinced him that, since it was Sunday, it would do no good to go into town to start the hunt for a gun case maker. He had assured Blue that he knew of the perfect place to have the case made and that they would be open early in the morning. That left the afternoon and evening for an appropriate introduction to the pleasures of Olongapo.

"Have you called Cathy yet?" Magic grinned at Blue and sipped from his drink.

"Jesus, Magic, why did you have to ask? I had forgotten about that." Blue groaned, and the euphoria he had been feeling vanished.

"I thought you were in love with the pride and joy of Virginia. That is what your buddy Captain Joplin thinks."

Blue groaned louder. Captain Joplin wasn't his friend. He was Cathy's father. Worse, just before they had left for the deployment, he had been assigned as the chief of staff for the *Constellation* battle group's embarked admiral. Blue had spent the entire cruise feeling that he was being watched.

"I don't know what I think about ..." Blue trailed off lamely. "Christ, I don't know." He took a sip from his drink.

The whole thing about Cathy confused him. The strange part was that he thought Cathy was a perfect companion for a naval officer. She was beautiful, she was funny, she knew the service traditions, she was prepared to accept the rigors of deployment and separation, and she was deferential without kissing up. The problem was that Blue wasn't ready for a full-time companion, no matter how perfect she was. The issue had not surfaced while they first dated, but now Cathy was putting pressure on him. It was subtle—she didn't stamp her foot and demand to get married—but it was there. Blue felt selfish about the whole thing. He had accepted a middling status quo relationship, but Cathy wanted more. She wanted much more. She had joined him during the ship's import period in Cannes, France, and instead of relishing every moment with her he found the whole thing stifling. He had tried to tell her, but there never seemed to be the right moment for that kind of discussion. He was relieved when Magic interrupted his thoughts.

"Why did you get into this business, kid?" Magic got up from his chair and perched on the edge of the pool. He splashed some water over his shoulders.

Blue paused a moment and wiped some suntan lotion from his face.

"I don't know. I guess it was ordained from birth. My grandpa flew in the navy, and Dad flew Hellcats in World War II. I guess I started thinking about it from childhood."

Magic nodded and looked at the pool. He flicked some more water on his shoulders and grinned.

"Yeah, you have the look of a lifer."

"Hey, nobody said anything about doing this forever." Blue laughed.

"No." Magic nodded. "Only as long as it's fun."

"What about you?" asked Blue. "Why did you join?"

Magic took his feet out of the water and hopped back into his chair. He signaled the pool boy for another round. "I got into this business because of vacuum cleaners."

"Vacuum cleaners?"

"Yep, vacuum cleaners. You see, kid, I know this is going to be hard to believe, but I screwed off during much of my undergraduate career."

"No." Blue laughed. "You? I can't believe it."

"Yes." Magic nodded his head. "I know it comes as a shock, but I wasn't always this paragon of perfection that you have come to worship." When Magic's drink came, he took a long pull on the glass and leaned back into his chair.

"I had a real good time in college." He looked at Blue and grinned. "My uncle died and left me with a wad of cash that I used to enhance my social awareness. I made many good friends. I chased many women, caught some of them too. I had little time for the dean's list."

"Well, I must say, I am totally shocked." Blue laughed.

"Anyway," continued Magic, "I screwed off for four and a half years, and all of a sudden one day I graduated."

"What did you study?"

"Well, I didn't actually study anything." Magic laughed. "But I majored in history."

"Bullshit," said Blue.

"No, really, I am not kidding. I even have a teaching certificate."

"You are a teacher?"

"Well, no, not really. I mean I could be, but I never did actually get hired to teach anyone."

"Jesus Christ," groaned Blue. "Someone even considered putting you in a room with impressionable children?"

"Hey, buddy," Magic reached over and swiped at Blue's arm, "I'm not that bad."

"Why history? And why teaching?"

"Well." Magic took off his sunglasses and squinted at the lenses. He began to polish them with his towel. "Some guys take a long time figuring out what it is they want to be when they grow up, and I guess I am one of those guys. I had no idea what I wanted to do the entire time I was in college. I just drifted. History was just reading, and I have always been a good reader, so it was the path of least resistance. My goal was to get a degree and see what happened. I guess I was waiting for someone or something to make up my mind for me."

"So a vacuum cleaner made up your mind for you?" Blue laughed and took a final sip from his drink.

"Yeah," said Magic, joining in with Blue's laughter. "You see, I went to St. Louis to stay with a friend while I considered my options. I saw this ad for playboys in the *Post Dispatch*. Naturally, that caught my interest, so I read it. The ad said if you liked to stay out at night and wanted to work afternoons and make big bucks then to give them a call."

"And you fell for that?"

"Well, kid, sometimes we hear and see things we want to believe. Anyway, I answered the ad, and it turned out to be a job announcement to sell vacuum cleaners."

"Hmm, let's see," said Blue, rubbing his chin. "And I guess the punch line has something to do with sucking?"

"Hey, kid, there is no punch line. I am giving you the straight skinny."

"Well, I can't imagine you with a vacuum cleaner in your hand, that's all." Blue shook his head and laughed.

"Man, but that was a goofy job, I have to say." Magic chuckled. "We would gather in the late morning at the office and get our assignments. The company said the assignments were requests from people who wanted to see one of our vacuum cleaners. However, the real story is that the company put ads in the paper that announced a free vacuuming of any three rooms in a house. So when we got there we had to turn the free cleaning into a sale."

"Ohhh that sounds like fun." Blue laughed.

"Yeah, you can count on that. You can imagine the folks that replied to those ads. Man, what a mess some people live in. They needed a backhoe, not a vacuum cleaner!"

Blue was laughing so much his eyes watered. He just couldn't imagine Magic, famed MIG killer and fighter ace, standing in someone's living room pushing a vacuum cleaner.

"So how does that lead to the navy?" Blue wiped his eyes with his towel.

"Oh, yeah, that. I had forgotten why I was telling this dumb shit story anyway." Magic laughed. He took another sip of his drink. "So I answered this call, and when the guy opened the door I started my pitch. But as I started to talk, this tooth," Magic pointed to his right front tooth, "fell out and dropped into my hand."

"What?" blurted Blue. "What?"

"Yeah, I had the tooth knocked out playing football, and it never was fixed right. It kept falling out all the time. I have to say it made for a pretty funny Halloween deal though." Magic laughed and winked at Blue. "So, anyway, luckily my hand was open so the tooth plunked right into it."

"What did the guy do?"

"He looked at me like I was a toothless idiot. What do you think he did?" Magic and Blue both threw back their heads and roared.

"Can you imagine how stupid I felt?"

"No, I don't think I can." Blue laughed and fell back on the lounge.

"Man, I never felt more like a piece of whale shit than then," said Magic. "I mean, I think I heard myself hit bottom, you know?"

Blue looked at him and nodded his head.

"I knew right then that I had to do something to make it all right. I had to do something to make up for screwing off and just for my general scumbag behavior."

"So you decided to be a fighter pilot?"

"No, not really," answered Magic. "I drove around for a while, thinking about how a guy in high school that had been all-conference football and who had graduated near the top of his class and who had so much potential wound up trying to sell vacuum cleaners to guys in trailer parks. I wound up going downtown, and all of a sudden I saw this complex of recruiting offices."

"You got to be kidding me." Blue shook his head and grinned.

"No, really." Magic laughed. "I pulled the car over and went inside."

"You're not kidding?"

"Hell, no. This is the way it happened. So I go inside and the army guy tells me to get lost since he already has his quota filled."

"So they were all together?" asked Blue.

"Yeah, pretty much right in the same spot," replied Magic. "The marine was out doing push-ups or something and the air force guy didn't impress me."

"Looks like some things don't change." Blue laughed.

"Yeah," said Magic through his grin. "I didn't much like that shade of blue on their uniforms either."

"You passed up the air force because you didn't like the color of their uniforms?"

"Yeah, how is that for some fucking reasoning? Like I was some chick picking out a prom dress. The only reason I joined the navy was because it was the only thing left, and the reason I got into aviation was because it was the only thing the navy had left."

"That and the fact you were a scumbag looking for redemption."

"Yeah, I guess that's about right." Magic chuckled and settled back into his chair. The two friends sat, drank beer, chatted and dozed all afternoon. After several hours, Blue looked over at Magic and gently kicked his chair.

"So how did you really get your first MIG?"

Magic grunted, and a slow grin crept across his mouth. "Gook flew out in front of me."

"Yeah, that's all you ever say, but how did you really shoot him? What happened?"

Magic shrugged. "It's a long story."

"I got time."

Magic paused and looked at his drink. "Well, hell, I have already told you half my fucking life's story. I might as well continue. I tell you what, I'll tell you about the first one today and the other one later."

"Great." Blue grinned and settled into his chair. He had always wanted to hear the real story about Magic's MIGs.

Magic took off his sunglasses and polished a bit of dust off one lens. He put them back on and began.

"We were bombing down south of Hanoi day after day. I was a LTJG back then, like you are now. I was crewed with a lieutenant commander named Buddy Missions. Buddy was a great guy. He's dead now."

"Did he die in a plane crash?" Blue asked.

"Hell, no. He was too good for that. He died in a motorcycle accident. He was tying one on at the Miramar Officers' Club and decided to ride his scooter home. They say he left Pomerado Road doing ninety miles an hour. Old Buddy didn't get up from that one."

"That's too bad," grunted Blue.

"Yeah, too bad indeed." Magic nodded his head and continued. "So we were bombing every day and kind of getting used to it. I was carrying a basic load of bombs and missiles, plus I had a Zuni rocket pod. We would either fly a preplanned mission or go hang around the tanker waiting for the forward air controller to call us in on something. If we didn't get the call, we would jettison the bombs and head for the ship."

"What was the reason for all the bombing?"

"We were trying to break up Ho Chi's logistics lines, so we were going after anything that looked like it carried anything. Lots of trucks, stuff like that. Most of the time the FAC would just call up and give us some coordinates to bomb. So we would plot it out and go and drop. We couldn't really see anything through the trees so we would just roll in and dump the stuff. Shit, if God likes monkeys, I'm going to hell for sure."

Blue laughed, and they both took a drink.

"So one day, just as I was pulling out of my dive, Buddy screams, 'Break port! Break port!'! So I instantly pulled her left and tried to get sight of what was exciting Buddy so much. He didn't do a lot of talking back there, but when he said something, I listened. And just as soon as I started the turn I saw tracers heading right at us."

"Wow!" Blue sat up in his chair.

"Wow is right." Magic laughed. "Buddy saved our asses that day because we had a MIG-21 closing at nine o'clock, guns a blazing!"

"Holy shit."

"The MIG goes whizzing across our tail, but just as he goes by me, I noticed that he had started his nose up, so I started a slight nose-up climb, hit afterburner, and kept pulling port."

"What was your plan?"

"Plan?" Magic looked confused. "Hell, kid, I planned to kick the shit out of him."

"No." Blue laughed. "What was your game plan? Your tactic?"

"Oh, that." Magic laughed. "You know, kid, a lot of that classroom stuff kind of runs down your leg when the tracers start popping."

"I'm sure of that." Blue chuckled. He was fascinated with the story. "But what were you thinking?"

"Well, kid, I wasn't sure where he came from or how fast he was going. When he pulled his nose up, that told me he had overshot, but I also knew he would slow down pretty quick too. I didn't want to get too slow with him, but I had to pull hard enough to keep him from getting behind me, so I tried to keep the jet at around 375 to 400 knots. So I kept my turn in because I didn't want to give the gomer too much separation. Buddy read off my airspeed. I was holding the jet at the speed I wanted, but the gomer began turning inside of me even more. He apparently decided to go for the kill, because all of a sudden he snatched on all kinds of stick and crawled right up our ass." Magic's eyes were bright with animation, and he was describing the aircraft positions with his hands. The "MIG hand" snapped to align behind the "Magic hand."

"But just as he pulled behind me, he stalled. I noticed his airplane shudder and the nose drop off so I leveled my wings, said a prayer, and pulled my nose straight up."

"Geez!" exclaimed Blue.

"I zoomed up a thousand feet and saw him try to pull his nose up and shoot me, but it shuddered again so I knew he was out of airspeed. I pushed the stick to the left and buried it in my lap while I stomped the right rudder. My Phantom stalled and flipped nose down, pointed right at the MIG. I couldn't believe how she came around." Magic smiled and clapped his hands. "Cross-controlling is a beautiful thing when it works. So I selected rockets on the armament control panel, and as my nose swung through him I emptied my pod right in that gook's face."

"You have got to be shitting me!"

"I am sure that's what the gook was thinking." Magic laughed. "Because he tried to tear the wings off, getting away from all those rockets."

"Did you hit him?"

"No, the rockets went all over the place, but none of them hit him. Zunis aren't guided or anything, and my nose was moving around a lot when I hit the trigger. I didn't think I could hit him, but I knew I could get his attention."

"What did the MIG do?"

"He dumped his nose and made a run for it. But all he did was open enough distance to get into Sidewinder range, and when he did I put one up his tailpipe. The MIG exploded, and Buddy and I went back to the ship. The whole thing took about thirty seconds."

"Wow," gasped Blue. "Wow."

The two men continued to talk about airplanes, and Magic answered Blue's many questions about what it was like to fly over Vietnam back in "the good old days." The two had an easy conversation with their drinks and watched the sun begin to set. But one thing about Magic's story bothered Blue, so he looked at his friend and spoke.

"Magic, I don't want to sound like a wimp, but isn't it supposed to be real dumb to slow down and wrestle with a MIG when you are over Indian country? I mean, there could have been more of them, plus anti-air guns and stuff. Sure, if you get the MIG it turns out okay, but if you lose, then what? Two good guys dead or at least out of the war and a multimillion-dollar aircraft gone. It's a hell of a risk."

"You're not a wimp, kid, and you're right. Like my old skipper once said, 'nothing good happens after two in the morning and under 200 knots.' But then again this is a risk taker's business to some extent. It was a war. He was my enemy. I knew I could take him. The whole time, from the second Buddy had yelled to the second his plane exploded, I knew I could take him. Shit, kid, when you know you are going to win, there ain't any risk."

And for the hundredth time that day, Blue grinned, nodded his head, and wondered if what he was hearing was absolute truth or something else. He did know that his time with Magic would be a time for lessons. What kind of lessons, he wasn't sure.

# CHAPTER 5

lue and Magic lay by the pool, talking and napping and drinking San Miguel beers until late afternoon. Finally, sunburned and hungry, they went to their rooms to get ready for dinner. Blue met Magic at the front desk, and they walked to the Officers' Club bar.

"Are the burgers still as good as they used to be, Tony?"

"Mister *Majeek!* It so good to see you. You been gone long time." Blue smiled as he saw the diminutive waiter, dressed in a bright yellow "flight suit," hug Magic. His name was embroidered on the right side of his suit, and two crossed martini glasses were stitched to the left in the place of aviator wings.

Tony dropped his hands and frowned at Magic. "How you here? No ship in port. Connie not due for more than a week."

"It always amazes me just how good your intelligence is." Magic laughed.

"You guys know more about our carrier movement schedules than the Russians."

"But how you here?"

"We flew in early, to do some business in town."

"Ahh." Tony smiled. "It good to be back in Philippines. Yes?"

"Very good, Tony." Magic smiled. "Very good."

"Come, sit at bar. I get burger. You want fries?" Tony pointed to the long wooden bar.

"Sure, and two San Miguels."

"Coming, boss." Tony smiled. "It's really good to see you, *Majeek.*"

"Thanks, Tony, it's great to see you again."

The two men took seats on the red leather bar stools, and within seconds a cold beer was in front of each. They toasted with a clink of brown bottles.

"Wow!" exclaimed Blue as he slowly looked around the room. "Wow!" Every inch of all the walls was covered with squadron plaques and memorabilia. Blue had heard about the Cubi bar, but its testament to naval aviation, at least in the Western Pacific, was remarkable.

"Pretty neat, huh, kid?" Magic grinned at Blue's wide-open stare. "Every squadron that comes through here gets a plaque made out in town and puts it up on the wall in this place. They have a bunch of the old ones from years back in storage too."

"Where are you?" Blue swiveled on his bar stool and looked around the room.

"Look up there," said Magic. He motioned toward a large rectangular plaque set high on the wall behind the bar. The black-and-yellow death's head of Fighter Squadron 142 was carved into the wood with a banner over the top that read, *Westpac Combat Cruise 1969*. The silhouette of an F-4 Phantom adorned the center, and on each side of the Phantom was a list of the squadron pilots and RIOs.

"See on the pilot side, near the bottom." Magic smiled and pointed.

"Oh, yeah," said Blue. "LTJG Magic Sharentino. Was that your first cruise?"

"Yep." Magic nodded and set his bottle on the bar. "I was your age back then. I was a dumb fuck like you too."

"Good to hear." Blue laughed. "I am following in big shoes."

"I'm over there too," said Magic. He swiveled and pointed to the back wall.

"How did you know where to look?" asked Blue as he swiveled on his stool to follow Magic's finger.

"First thing you do when you walk in here, kid, is see where you are. They move the plaques around to make room for new ones."

"So you scoped the walls out as we walked to the bar?"

"Yep," said Magic. "You always need to know where you are, kid."

Blue found the plaque to which Magic pointed. It was even larger than the first, and it had the black panther of Fighter Squadron 21 carved into the mahogany. Its banner read, *Westpac Combat Cruise 1971.* Blue saw Magic's name midway up the pilots' list. He was listed as LT Magic Sharentino.

"Did you get your second MIG on that cruise?"

"Yep, shot it down coming off a bombing run."

"How did it go?"

"The kill itself was a piece of cake," said Magic, "but getting to the kill was pretty dicey."

"How so?" asked Blue. He had a second beer in front of him and took a sip.

"I was on a bombing mission near Haiphong going after a railroad switching yard." Magic burped and took a swig. "It was heavily defended, and the Vietnamese were pumping a lot of triple-A into the air. SAMs were launching from all over the place, and I remember my gear was screaming when their heads locked onto the plane."

"Wow!"

"Wow is no shit, kid. It was the hairiest flight I have ever been on. Anyway, it seemed like we jinked and jived for hours before we got to the target. I saw an A-7 get smacked by a SAM about a mile off my right wing. Just disappeared in a fireball."

"Geez," said Blue.

"So we jumped through our ass for a while. Then we got to the target and I rolled in and dropped my load. I pulled out and saw the bombs go high order right on top of a train."

"Man!" exclaimed Blue. "That must have been a sight."

"It was, kid. It was really cool. But the coolest thing is that I had practiced this a hundred times in training, and I had rehearsed it a million times in my head, and so as soon as I got rid of the bombs, I automatically selected heat on the stick grip."

"So you were ready to shoot a Sidewinder instantly," said Blue.

"That's right." Magic nodded his head vigorously. "Lots of guys missed kills, Blue, because they didn't have their switches set."

"So you come off target and noticed you hit the train. Then what?"

"I looked at the fireball and turned my head back to the front, and just then a MIG-21 flew in front of me. My Sidewinder howled when it sensed the exhaust, and I pulled the trigger. Wham! It flew right up his tailpipe and exploded."

"Just like that?"

"Just like that."

"That is a great story," said Blue. He felt even a deeper respect for Magic than he had before. Both of his MIG kills were due to discipline and coolness under pressure. They were not just good luck.

"Kid, I suggest we eat these burgers, then head across the river into town. You need a good introduction to the culture of this place, and I am just the guy to give it to you."

"Sounds great to me. I have always wondered what the fabled city of Olongapo was really like."

"Some people come away a little disappointed with it, kid." Magic smiled slightly and took a sip of his beer. "Places like Olongapo aren't for everybody."

"Why would I be disappointed? You said it was a blast."

Magic leaned back in his chair and looked intently at Blue. "It is a blast, kid, but in its own way. It isn't Las Vegas, and it isn't Disneyland. It is a lot more raw and rough than that. It's kind of like that movie that came out a couple of years ago. The one where Yul Brynner was a robot."

"You mean *Westworld*?"

"Yeah, that movie. You remember how it went. These two guys—I think Richard Benjamin and James Brolin played the parts—paid a bunch of money to go back to the Old West, where they could act like cowboys and realize their fantasies. You know, like having their way with women or beating up bad guys. But everybody but those two were robots, so nothing bad could really ever happen. It was programmed fun."

"I remember." Blue nodded. "But then the bad guy, Yul Brynner, really went bad."

"That's right," said Magic. "The guts of the movie turned on those two realizing that the fantasy was over and the real world was back and what to do about it. So, what I am saying is that sometimes sailors that visit Olongapo have a tough time realizing when the fantasy is over and there is a real world that has to be lived in."

Blue looked at Magic and shrugged. He wasn't sure what Magic meant.

"Have you ever been to Mardi Gras, kid?"

"Sure," replied Blue. "When I was going to flight school in Pensacola. I took a long weekend and went to New Orleans."

"Did you see the French Quarter?"

"Sure."

"Did you see it in the daytime?"

Blue frowned and shook his head.

"It's a run-down mess, kid: peeling paint, puke on the sidewalk, cigarette butts everywhere, red-eyed drunks in every doorway. Nothing like it is at night. It's ironic that the thing that man has feared the most for the longest, the dark, can often be the very thing that protects him the most." Magic took another sip and ordered a refill from a passing waitress.

"Blue, there is a poorness that you can see here if you care to look. I mean poor as in abject poverty kind of poor. I mean the kind of poor that people never, ever, get out of. And you and I can stand here on the base and we can see that there is only a chain-link fence about an eighth of an inch thick separating us from the Philippine people. And the thing that can get to you, if you care to look, is that the difference between having everything and having nothing depends upon which side of the eighth inch you were born on."

"I see," said Blue.

"This is a different kind of place," continued Magic. "At first blush, it is lively and exciting and wonderful, like the French Quarter is at night. But if you allow yourself to look just a little closer and linger just a little longer, you will see that underneath all of the lights and the glitter there are things that are not so good. There are people in real bad shape."

"Yeah, I can see what you mean, I guess." The conversation was sobering to Blue. But it was also fascinating.

"So I think a lot of sailors do take the time to see all of this, and some of it does bother them. You know, kids, sailors are pretty big hearted most of the time. I think this place makes some of them feel a little guilty. Understand?"

Blue nodded. "By the way, did you ever feel guilty about all of this?"

"Me? No." Magic laughed. "Well, maybe a little." He took another swallow of San Miguel and nodded. "Maybe a little."

"But you know this isn't our fault. We didn't make this place the way it is." Blue took a sip and looked sideways at his friend.

"You're right, it's not our fault. But I think that we do owe our stewardship to the place. I mean, we do need to consider what it is we are doing and asking for. Sometimes the guy with the money needs to consider what he allows people to do for it. Especially when that guy is in a place where people are so bad off they will do almost anything to get it."

"I see." Blue nodded. He started to continue the conversation when Magic clapped his hands and laughed.

"Enough!" Magic smiled broadly. "Enough of this heavy stuff for one night. I hope I didn't get you bummed out, kid, but to really enjoy this place you got to understand it."

The two continued to talk until the food came, and then they settled down to their dinners like most naval aviators—they attacked their food with little fanfare and even less talk. They wolfed down their burgers and fries, quaffed their beer, and almost simultaneously straightened up on their stools, ready for the next event.

"Come on, kid, let's hit the town." Magic leaped up and threw a wad of money on the bar. "If we sit here any longer someone is going to think we are a pair of shoes and ask us to check our balls in the coatroom."

Blue stood, laughing as he also threw money on the bar. Magic's comment about shoes referred to the name aviators gave to surface warfare officers in the navy. Aviators selected brown boots to wear with the khaki uniform because black showed too much of the dust that covered early airstrips. The surface navy officers clung to the traditional black color. So aviators began to refer to surface officers as "shoes."

"Shall I get you a cab?" Tony smiled as they walked out.

"No," said Magic as he put a ten-dollar bill in Tony's hand. "I have my own car."

Blue looked at him with surprise. "What car?"

"Don't worry, kid. I spotted Gladys in the parking lot when we walked in. The P-3 dudes or some air force pukes probably have her now."

"What are you talking about?"

"Here we are," said Magic as they approached a dilapidated old Ford.

"What's that?" Blue looked at the old car as Magic opened the driver's side door.

"Why, son, this here is Gladys. A '56 Ford Fairlane with a 223 cubic inch, 137 horsepower, single-barrel carb engine. Ain't she beautiful?" Magic gazed fondly at the old car as if it were a long-lost friend.

"But whose is it?"

"Well, I say it's ours." Magic settled into the driver's seat and motioned to Blue. "Get in."

Blue opened the passenger door. He slid into the seat and looked at his friend with confusion. "I don't get it."

"Look in the glove compartment, kid. Tell me what you see scratched way in the back."

Blue opened the compartment and was greeted with two empty San Miguel bottles, a bunch of dirty rags, and what appeared to be the remains of a sandwich.

Magic grabbed one of the bottles and sniffed it. "Yep." He smiled. "Been driven recently."

Blue lit a match and held it in the glove compartment. He could barely make out some rusted scratching.

"It says, *Smoke 67, Frankie 68, Magic 69, and Groper 72*," he said.

"That's right, kid. That means this car is mine."

"What do you mean?"

"Tradition, son, tradition. You see there are a bunch of these old cars on base. They were brought here over the years by sailors who eventually left and didn't want to ship them back to the States. Some of them, like old Gladys here, are kept in running condition and are used by visiting squadrons. And so it goes on and on."

"I still don't see how the car is yours."

"Because you are a new guy and new guys don't know shit." Magic smiled and shook his head.

Blue shrugged, and Magic continued.

"You see, the rules of Cubi Point are if you can prove you have the earliest claim on the car, it's yours while you visit the base and until you leave. In 1969 I scratched my name in the glove box during my first cruise. I know Smoke and Frankie, and both those guys are out of the navy, so that means it has to be mine for the time I am here."

"What a lovely tradition." Blue smiled as he settled into the old seat. "This sure beats walking or taking a cab."

"Sure does." Magic grinned. "Push."

"Push?"

"Yep, you need to get out and give us a shove until it rolls a bit down the hill and I can pop the clutch."

Blue got out and pushed the car a few feet before it started rolling on its own down the gentle grade of the parking lot. Magic popped the clutch and the old engine immediately fired. Blue hopped in, and Magic eased Gladys onto the street and down the mountain toward the main gate and the city of Olongapo.

As they rode down the mountain, Blue felt himself getting more and more excited. He was really glad the skipper had chosen him to fly off the ship. The great food and drink, the fact that he was in a strange and mysterious place, and the added thrill of riding in a car that was "borrowed" all added to his feeling of euphoria.

After parking Gladys in a lot next to the main gate, Magic and Blue joined the other sailors who were streaming toward a checkpoint. There was an electricity of gaiety and carnival in the air, and the loud talking and laughter of the crowd intensified as the two aviators neared the gate. The lance corporal on duty gave them a cursory check and a snappy salute and waved them through to a line of money-changing booths. Moments later, Magic and Blue were strolling across the short Magsaysay River bridge with their pockets full of pesos.

"Jesus, but that stinks. God almighty!" Blue blew out his breath as he frowned and coughed. The two men were about midway over the bridge, where the narrow river's aroma was at its peak.

"That is why everybody calls it the shit river, my boy." Magic chuckled.

"Look, look at that." Blue grabbed Magic's arm and pointed at the river. "What is she up to?" Blue was pointing to a young girl of about nine or ten years old. She was dressed all in white and stood in a small wooden canoe in the middle of the river. She held a wire cone in one hand and a garland of flowers in the other.

The image both fascinated and depressed Blue. The juxtaposition of the virginal girl and the cesspool was stark.

"Kind of puts a different spin on the notion of damsel in distress, doesn't it, kid?" Magic grunted and slapped Blue on the shoulder. "Of course, we have turds to slay here instead of dragons."

The girl smiled sweetly up at the two men. "Peso, Joe?" Her voice was soft, innocent, and shy. "Throw me a peso, Joe." She held the cone basket toward them.

"This is another thing you will only see in Olongapo," said Magic as he dug into his jeans for a coin. "There are usually three or four of them here every night, at least on Friday and Saturday night or when a carrier is in town."

"Hey, Joe." Another voice came from the canoe, and a small boy's head peeked out from behind the girl. He grinned broadly at the two men and waved. He was sitting in the back of the canoe, a paddle in his hand. He appeared to be six or seven years old and was wearing an old white sailor's Dixie cup hat. At least the cap used to be white. The name Henry was written in bold letters across the front of the hat. The *R* was backward.

Magic grinned at the young girl and flipped a couple of pesos into her cone. She smiled and curtsied, steadying herself in the canoe as she did.

"Thank you, sir," she said.

Magic nodded to her and then frowned at the boy. "Henry? Are you the same Henry that is Eve Mariposa's brother?"

"Yep." Henry smiled and showed a missing front tooth. "She is my big sister." He was about to say more when a sailor came stumbling up to them from the Olongapo side of the bridge. He had obviously been in town long enough to get a snootful, because he was wobbling back and forth. He had the look of a guy who had spent some time in a gutter. His jeans were filthy and wet, and his torn T-shirt was emblazoned with the words, *Eat Shit or Die*. The sailor leaned over the bridge railing and focused on the girl below. "Shh ... show me your tits," he belched. He looked at Magic and Blue and grinned stupidly.

"Hey, you." He raised his voice and pointed in the direction of the young girl. "Shh ... show me your tits."

"Hey, pal, why don't you go on back to the base and leave these kids alone?" Magic smiled amiably at the sailor and held out his hand.

"Bullshit," spat the sailor. "Hey, cutie, show me your tits and I'll give you a peso." The sailor thrust his hand into his pockets in search of a coin. "Show me your tits," he mumbled.

Magic grabbed the sailor firmly by the arm. "Hey, sport, why don't you just go on back to the base?"

The sailor jerked back, and Magic dropped his hand. Just at that moment Henry called from the boat.

"Hey, squid. I'll show you my ass for a peso." Henry grinned at the sailor and pointed to his behind.

"I don't want to see your ass, you little queer." The sailor was clearly agitated, and he glared at Henry. "I want to see the little whore's tits."

Magic grabbed the sailor by the arm and twisted it behind his back. The sailor yelped in pain as Magic quickly began walking him in the direction of the marine guard. Blue followed, wondering what was going to happen next. Magic half-carried and half-pushed the sailor all the way to the checkpoint. The sailor stumbled and cursed, but he was gasping for breath too and appeared to be just about out of gas.

"Lance Corporal, I am Lieutenant Commander Sharentino. My shipmate here has had a little too much to drink. He needs to get on the base before he causes any trouble."

"Yes, sir," the lance corporal replied.

The sailor drew back his right fist, and for a moment Blue thought he was going to swing at Magic or the lance corporal. The sailor swayed back and forth, and his fist trembled as he tried to focus. Luckily, the intellect that had survived the alcohol engaged and he dropped his hand and stumbled through the gate.

"Sorry about that." Magic looked at the lance corporal and shook his head.

"No problem, sir. At least he wasn't a marine."

Magic and Blue turned and walked back toward the bridge. As they once again reached the center of the span, they looked at the river and saw the young girl and Henry stepping out of the canoe onto the shore.

"Hey, Henry," Magic yelled down to the boy. Henry looked up and frowned.

"Come up here, will you?" Magic held a wad of peso notes in his hand.

Blue wondered what Magic could want with the boy, but he kept his silence. Henry quickly scrambled up the bank onto the bridge and ran to them.

"You want me to dive into the shit river?" He smiled.

"No, Christ no," said Magic. "You should *never* dive into that thing … *never.*"

"It makes me money, Joe." Henry looked up at Magic and shrugged.

"Maybe so, but that river will kill you."

"It makes me money, Joe."

"Okay, well, look. I liked the way you stood up to the drunk." Magic smiled at the boy and handed him a wad of pesos.

Blue smiled at the boy as he took the money. He was glad Magic warned him about the river.

The boy's face brightened, and he immediately stuffed the money into his pockets. He turned and started to scamper back off the bridge but turned and frowned at Magic.

"Why don't you want me to jump into the river? Everybody else does."

Magic looked at the boy for several moments and then shook his head. "Just don't, okay?"

"Sure, Joe." And with a smile he turned and vanished into the dark.

"Do you know that kid?'

"Not really. Eve wrote about her little brother a couple of times and described the cap. I figured it was him."

"He looks like he is part European or something."

"Hey, kid, everybody in Olongapo is part European or something." Magic laughed and clapped Blue on the shoulder. "Come on, kid, let's get to the party."

Magic had warned Blue that Olongapo was a raw town without much nuance or subtlety, and Blue found the warning to be true. His first indicator of this truth was when the strong smell of the Magsaysay River hit his nostrils. The river separated Olongapo City from the US naval base, and it was an open sewer, pouring the town's waste into the sea.

"Whew, does that stink." Blue shook his head and blew air out of his lips.

"Think of it as a welcome mat to the city." Magic laughed.

The two men crossed the short span over the river, and Blue found that the smell of sewage was gradually being overcome with the smells of gardenias, popcorn, beer, perfume and cologne, and auto exhaust. Overlaying all of that was the smoky smell of charcoal braziers. Blue saw them on every corner, their owners grilling hot dogs and skewers of what Magic had assured him was chicken and pork. Blue's eyes were filled with bright neon lights, and he marveled at how every store was garishly lit. People were everywhere, and they all moved with a glow of excitement and anticipation. Sailors and marines walked hand in hand with young Filipinas, and an unending array of vendors hawked everything from belt buckles to monkeys. The energy was infectious, and Blue could feel it grip him as he and Magic walked along the strip. On each side of the highly lit main street scores of stores and bars competed for the Americans' attention. The latest hits back in the States blared from loudspeakers, and in one block alone Blue heard "I Write the Songs" by Barry Manilow, "You Sexy Thing" by Hot Chocolate, and the Bee Gees'

"You Should Be Dancing." And his biggest surprise was when he looked inside and saw that the music wasn't coming from juke boxes. It was coming from local Filipino bands.

Magic and Blue walked for a few more blocks. Then Magic steered him into a place called The Rusty Spur. As they entered the dimly lit bar, they were mobbed by a half dozen girls. The manager welcomed them and, navigating by flashlight, led them to a table next to the stage. As soon as they sat down, the girls joined them.

Magic and Blue both ordered San Miguel beers by screaming over the noise of the band. The girls settled in, with Mimi on Blue's lap and Kitty straddling Magic. On Blue's left and right were Doris and Sally; Maureen and Dolly sat on either side of Magic. Each man had three eager girls rubbing their arms, caressing their legs, and cooing at them to buy drinks. Although Magic had warned Blue earlier that such drinks were really expensive shots of colored water, he ordered them anyway. At first, Blue was a little bewildered. He had never been in a bar where girls actually jumped in his lap and competed for his attention. He found that he liked it though, at least for a while. It was like a blind date with three girls, only unlike other blind dates Blue had been on; this one had a very predictable ending as long as he was willing to shell out the cash.

Blue also enjoyed listening to Magic talk to his three girls. He seemed to swell to larger than life, and his loud laugh was rich and expansive. He seemed totally sincere with the girls and talked with them about where they were from, what kind of music they liked, where they bought such nice clothes, and if they were married.

They sat there for an hour, and Blue drank two more San Miguels. Those in addition to what he had drank earlier put him in a festive mood. Mimi's thin cotton dress did little to hide her body, and as she squirmed and "danced" it rose higher and higher. Blue found himself holding her bare thighs, and she was soon hugging him and kissing his neck. He tried to play cool, but the girl was getting him aroused. She was practically naked, and he was now positive that she was not wearing any panties. And that was not all.

Despite Mimi's advantage on his lap, Doris and Sally kept sneaking in kisses and crotch grabs. "Blue, do you think I'm pretty?" Mimi whispered in his ear as she planted a wet kiss.

"Yes, you are very pretty." Blue winced as Doris pinched his arm.

"Do you want to go upstairs?" Mimi stuck her tongue about three inches down his ear.

"No." Blue squinted as Mimi's saliva ran down his neck. "Not now. Thank you very much though."

"Do you want to go upstairs after band plays?" Mimi nibbled his neck. "Thirty pesos for all my love."

"Well, not this time," said Blue. "I think we have plans to go to another bar. But thanks anyway." Blue looked across the table at Magic, who winked and grinned. His three girls had unbuttoned his shirt and were busy cooing over him and kissing his chest.

"I give you French love," whispered Mimi as she drove her tongue down his ear again.

"Well, thanks, but not tonight."

Mimi pushed away and frowned at Blue. "You don't think I am pretty."

"Oh, yes," exclaimed Blue. "It's just that—"

"If you think I am pretty then why not go upstairs with me?"

Blue looked at her and shrugged.

Mimi frowned and stood up. She gave Blue a suspicious look. "You queer? You like boys?"

"No," stammered Blue. "Absolutely not."

"I think you like boys." Mimi put her hands on her hips and glared at Blue.

"I like girls, I swear." Blue looked at Magic for support. Magic was grinning at him over the top of Kitty's head.

"Then go upstair with me." Mimi stamped her foot.

"No," said Blue. He smiled at Mimi in the darkness, hoping she would just go away.

"You queer," spat Mimi. She turned and walked away.

Blue looked across the table at Magic and grinned. "What was that all about?"

"You're a nice, clean-cut guy. She thought she could make a quick peso or two."

"Geez," said Blue. He took a drink of beer and looked at Magic. "Christ, man, how long are you gonna let them lick you like that?"

Magic rolled his head back and laughed. "I am getting a little sticky." He kissed each of the three girls on the forehead and stood up. Although the girls held onto him and whined in protest, he buttoned his shirt and threw some bills on the table. He glanced at his watch and strode toward the door.

"Let's go, faggot," he said over his shoulder. "I want to take you to my favorite place in Olongapo."

"Knock it off, Magic," said Blue as he followed him out the door.

Blue walked out after him and quickly caught up. The two men worked their way down the packed and brightly lit street, passing knots of celebrating sailors, street vendors, and of course, girls. As they passed each bar, music blared at them from outdoor speakers, and door barkers tried to lure them inside. The enticements ranged from the comfort of air-conditioning to ice-cold beer and the cleanest girls in town.

"What kind of place are we going to?" Blue grunted as he jumped a muddy ditch where the sidewalk ended.

"Oh, it's a place for grown-ups." Magic smiled.

"How did you find it?"

"Someone took me there a long time ago."

They walked on for a block and then, suddenly, Magic darted down an unmarked set of stairs. Blue followed him, and at the bottom they came to a door with a sign that read, *The Black Rose*.

Magic knocked, and seconds later a young man opened the door. He was wearing a *barong*, the traditional shirt of Filipino men. The barong was unique to the Philippines and, like the people, it was very flexible and practical.

The doorman frowned and slowly shook his head. "No seats left. Sold out last week. What you want?"

"I have traveled thousands of miles just to see Eve Mariposa's show," said Magic. "I hear she is the hottest thing west of San Francisco."

"Don't know about San Francisco. No seats!" The doorman began to shut the door when a deep voice boomed from behind him.

"It's okay, Manuel. Magic is an old friend."

"Richard!" Magic stepped inside the door. "I hoped you would be here." He leaned forward and hugged a large, silver-haired man.

"Welcome back, Magic." Richard leaned back and surveyed his old friend. "You have not changed one bit."

"Nor have you!" Magic laughed and grabbed his friend by the arm. "Richard, meet my running mate, Blue Morrison. Blue, this is Richard Rodriguez, owner of the best club in the Philippines."

"The best club in the world!" Richard corrected Magic and grinned broadly. He shook Blue's hand heartily. "Welcome to my club, Blue."

The three men walked through a dimly lit alcove and then out onto the main floor. Magic stopped and looked at the stage. It was empty except for a lone microphone. "She's still the main attraction, I see."

"Eve? Why, of course. Her shows sell out for months in advance."

"It's great to see you both doing so well."

"Come." Richard led them to an area near the stage. Some men were moving tables and chairs closer together, but the patrons didn't seem to mind. In a moment a new table and two chairs appeared.

"Sit." Richard beamed as he gestured toward the table.

Two ice-cold San Miguels quickly appeared, and Blue took a sip and looked around. "Where are the bar girls?"

"Not all bars in Olongapo cater to the sailor looking for female companionship." Magic grinned. "This is one of those places."

Blue nodded and sipped his beer as he looked around the place. It was dimly lit, as expected, with candles on small wooden tables that faced a raised stage. The air was thick with tobacco smoke and the noise of the growing crowd.

"What's so great about this place?"

"You'll see," said Magic, and he took a long pull of his beer. He burped and wiped his mouth with the back of his hand. "You will see."

After more small talk and beer, the din of the crowd dropped as music from a piano began to play. The stage lights brightened, and a singer emerged from the shadows. She was tall and very thin, and Blue guessed her to be in her late twenties. Her dress was a soft ivory that clung to her body, and luxurious black hair tumbled down her back and shoulders. Her smooth olive skin was blemish-free, and her dark eyes held an expression of soul and sorrow.

Blue thought she was a very beautiful woman, but when she began to sing, he knew why Magic had said this was his favorite place.

Blue had never heard anything like her. She was mesmerizing with a voice that was haunting and lonely. One moment she was strong, and the next, unbearably fragile. Blue found she didn't make him feel sad as much as she made him feel appreciative—appreciative that he had the opportunity to hear such a voice. Her words seemed too soft to hear at first, but as they lilted by Blue's ear and spun into his mind, he heard clearly. Her breathing and passion came through the microphone with a force that made him think she was singing just for him. Blue and Magic didn't talk the entire time she sang. She moved from song to song, never giving the audience any time to escape her trance. Finally, she paused and smiled at the crowd and nodded at the piano player. Instantly, the crowd grew even quieter.

"What's going on?"

"Shhh," said Magic. "Watch this. This is what they all came for."

"This is for all of us," whispered the singer. Her voice was low and smoky. "This is for all of us who live in the orchid forest."

It was only after a few notes that Blue realized he was holding his breath. He was holding his breath because he didn't want to miss a single word. But despite his concentration, he found himself looking around the room to see if other people were hearing what he was hearing. They too were mesmerized, all staring at the stage, drinking in every word. Their eyes were wide and soft as they reflected on her voice. Blue also realized for the first time since he and Magic had walked in that everyone there was a local except the two of them. Strangely, that made him want to understand the words even more. Blue leaned forward and closed his eyes to concentrate. The sound of the piano grew quieter and quieter, and when he opened his eyes she was standing alone in the spotlight, singing:

> *God plants an orchid in our forest of old,*
> *For every lie to a Filipina told,*
> *But Filipina hearts are young and their love is flowing,*
> *So the orchid forest is overgrown …*

Her crystal voice was soft and haunting, and Blue wondered what the words actually meant. What did she mean about lies to Filipinas? Whose lies? He told himself to ask Magic later. As she finished, Blue found himself on his feet, standing beside Magic. The rest of the crowd stood too. There was no clapping, not a word, not a sound. They just stood and held their breath until she finished.

Then they went nuts!

The cheering and applause intensified to a deafening roar as she shyly smiled and bowed her acknowledgment. It continued until she once again disappeared into the shadows.

"Whew," breathed Blue. "Who was that?"

When Magic didn't answer, Blue turned to his friend and started to speak. But when he noticed Magic staring into the candle, he sat down and nursed his beer. Finally, Magic looked up and smiled.

"So, kid, what do you think?"

"I have never heard anyone like her," replied Blue. "Never."

"Yeah, I thought you would like her."

"What's she doing here? She should be in Hollywood or someplace."

Magic arched his eyebrows and shrugged. "She likes it here."

"Yeah, but she could make so much money. They absolutely love her, especially when she sings 'The Orchid Forest.' What is the deal with that song anyway? What does she mean about lies to Filipinas? Whose lies?"

"I guess you have to be here a little longer to really understand it."

Blue looked at Magic in the dim light and waited for him to continue, to tell him about what the song meant. But when he realized that Magic wasn't going to say any more, he just nodded into his bottle. "I guess you're right. I still can't believe someone like that is here."

"Money doesn't mean everything to all people, I guess," said Magic. "Besides, she might feel like she can take better care of Henry here. There's an orphanage up the road a bit, and the father there looks after him pretty well, as I remember."

"The Orchid Forest" was the last song of the night, but despite the fact that the lights were being lowered and the customers were all filing out, Blue and Magic were in no hurry to break the warm mood and continued to talk about the songs they had just heard. Blue was trying to describe the effect the singer had on him when, suddenly, there she was, standing next to Magic. Both men slid their chairs back awkwardly and stood.

"Hello, Magic," she said as she put her hand on his arm.

Magic smiled broadly. "Hello, Evie." He hugged her for a long time and then sighed and dropped his arms.

"Miss Eve Mariposa, I would like to introduce you to LTJG Jack Morrison. We call him Blue."

"You were just fantastic," blurted Blue as he grinned and shook her hand. It was slim and firm and warm.

"Thank you, Blue." Eve smiled, and her dark eyes held Blue for an instant, enough for him to sense a power in her.

"Can you join us?" Magic motioned for her to sit in the chair next to his.

"Not this time, Magic. I only do one set an evening. Then I go and look after Henry. But, perhaps, if you are staying long enough, we can get together?"

"Great." Magic grinned. "We're gonna be here for a while."

"Good." Eve smiled. "We would love to see you." She kissed Magic on the cheek, smiled her good-bye to Blue, and then turned and was gone.

"Wow, she is nice," said Blue.

"She looks tired." Magic frowned.

"How do you know her so well? Did you have something going on with her?"

Magic stared at the candle and rolled his empty beer bottle in his hands. He looked at Blue and chewed his lip.

"No, kid," he said as he shook his head. "I had something going with her sister."

"Her sister? Wow! Where is she now?"

"Hey!" exclaimed Magic as he leaped out of his chair. "Let's get out into this town. I've got stuff to show you." He clapped Blue on the back and headed for the door.

"Sure," said Blue. *I wonder why he doesn't want to talk about this,* he thought. *For a guy that can talk about how to make a martini forever, he sure is close-lipped about other stuff.* When Blue walked up the stairs to the street, Magic was waiting for him. A big smile plastered his face, the previous reflective mood apparently gone.

"Come on, kid," he said, grabbing Blue's arm and steering him toward the street. "It's time for your education."

Blue smiled and allowed himself to be tugged along.

"Hey, how about it, pal?" Magic shouted to a passing jeepney driver who immediately darted his vehicle to their side and slammed on the brakes in a cloud of exhaust fumes and gravel. "How about a trip to Evelyn's?"

The driver grinned and nodded his head.

"Get in, kid," said Magic, pointing toward the back.

Blue walked around and had no sooner hopped in when the jeepney immediately took off. Three passengers—sailors, by the looks of them—were already on board, and Blue looked around them to see if Magic had gotten in. To his surprise, Magic was sitting in the driver's seat.

"What are you doing?"

"I'm driving this vehicle on a mission to the promised land, kid." Magic turned his head sideways and grinned. His after-dinner cigar was firmly clinched in his teeth. Blue looked at the driver, who just smiled and held up a twenty-peso bill.

"Yieeeee!" screamed Magic as he stomped on the accelerator. The three sailors in the back started screaming too.

"Yieeeee!" screamed Blue. He didn't know what he was screaming about, but it sure seemed like the thing to do. And what was this place called Evelyn's?

As they lurched along, Blue glanced about at their ride. He changed places with the sailor closest to Magic and yelled over the sound of the wind and the engine. "What is this contraption anyway?"

"This?" Magic turned his head to Blue, keeping one eye on the road ahead. "This, kid, this is a world-famous jeepney."

*Christ,* thought Blue. *Is everything in the Philippines world-famous?* "It looks a little like a jeep, all right."

"Yeah, the original jeepneys were converted jeeps, left over from World War II US forces. The industrious Filipinos painted them, put tops and more comfortable seats in them, and converted them into taxis." Magic grinned sideways at Blue and gestured with his free hand. "Look at this thing. It is perfect for the poor roads and rain. Later, a factory opened near Manila and those people began to produce them from scratch. These newer models are larger and more durable, and their owners personalized them with fringe on the tops, chrome, various animal figures for radiator mounts, lights, and horns."

"Hey, have you guys ever been to Evelyn's?"

Blue looked at his companions, who nervously glanced at each other and smiled.

"Yes, sir," said the one closest to Blue.

"What's there? I mean, why do people go there?"

The three sailors looked at each other again. They were deciding which one would answer. Finally, the one in the middle shrugged his shoulders. "Pussy." He smiled.

"Oh," said Blue, and he looked back up front.

They had gone about a half a mile and were nearing the end of the strip when another jeepney appeared on their left side. The driver had a full load of sailors who were screaming and cheering. The driver pulled even with Magic and grinned. Magic grinned back, screamed, and stomped the accelerator even harder. The race was on!

Blue looked ahead through the beams of the jeepney. "Uh-oh," he said as he noticed the traffic circle arcing to the left. There was only room for one car at a time, and both jeepneys were racing for the turn at breakneck speed. Plus, they were on the wrong side. Blue heard everyone in the jeepney take a breath at the same time. They realized the jeepney that led out of the turn would have a huge advantage on the hairpin road up the mountain. It would be virtually impossible to pass.

Blue was staring at the turn when all of a sudden the passengers in both vehicles suddenly notched up their screaming. He wasn't sure why. He just screamed too.

"Come on, Magic. Come on," screamed Blue. He looked over at the other jeepney; it was barely a foot from his face. He could see the passengers urging their little driver on. Blue glanced at the driver and grinned and screamed.

The little driver grinned and screamed back.

The turn raced toward them.

Suddenly, Magic slammed on the brakes and the other car shot out in front of him. He turned the wheel hard to the left, and the jeepney skidded around the corner. They shot into an alley that had no more than six inches of clearance on each side. The screaming stopped abruptly. Then Magic screamed and everyone else did too. The car hopped over a hump in the road, and everyone flew into the air. Blue felt his head hit the ceiling and held on tighter to the side railing. As they rounded a corner, two cats barely darted out of the way in time. One chicken didn't.

*More meat for the braziers*, thought Blue.

Suddenly, they squirted out of the alley and off to the right. Blue could see the lights of the other vehicle. He glanced at Magic, who screamed and gave the jeepney all the gas it had.

"Aieeee," Magic screamed again.

"Aieee," screamed Blue.

"Aieee," screamed the other sailors in the jeepneys. The two jeepneys were coming together again.

Blue flew up and hit his head against the roof. He grabbed the seat harder. They went down into a little valley and lost sight of the other jeepney for a second, and when they popped back up, Magic made a hard left turn and they bounced out onto the main road. The other jeepney jammed on its brakes to avoid hitting them, missing by inches. Magic let loose a victory yell, and Blue and the rest joined in.

The rest of the trip up the hill took about ten minutes and was uneventful. Soon, both jeepneys screeched to a stop in the gravel parking lot of Evelyn's Lounge. Magic hopped out of the car and shook hands with the owner. He clapped the back of his rival driver, also shaking his hand. Everyone was laughing and screaming and carrying on as they burst through the front door.

# CHAPTER 6

Viela Mayquez closed her book and sighed as she rolled over onto her back. The bed creaked beneath her, and the thin mattress squeaked against the dusty springs. She looked at the ceiling and thought of Clarise Hooper. Clarise was the heroine in her book, and she had read it ten times over. She frowned as she thought of the work she had to do, and she put the book on her nightstand. She would not be able to rejoin Clarise until the next morning.

Viela's pretty face turned into a frown again as her eyes followed the cracks and chunks of uneven plaster on the ceiling. It seemed she had always dreamed of being someone like Clarise Hooper. She did not have to be quite as successful as Clarise, but she did dream of being someone who used her brains to beat the best and worst the world could throw at her. She dreamed of being someone who was not afraid and who could be relied upon to take care of her family's future. Viela dreamed of being someone to be dreamed about.

"Christ," she muttered to herself, "quit wasting your time with such nonsense." She swallowed bitterly and began to feel tears form in the corners of her eyes. She hated herself for them.

Viela, like most girls who worked at Evelyn's, had wound up there on a trip to someplace else. They were not who they wanted to be, they were not where they wanted to be, and each had a story of how her life had been sidetracked.

Viela was the eldest of six siblings. The daughter of a banana farmer and his wife, she had grown up in a small town in northern Luzon, where the rest of her family still lived and where she had enjoyed a loving and happy childhood devoid of wants and problems.

She was an exceptional student and the most beautiful girl in the region.

As she grew older, Viela's parents began to earmark her for a destiny beyond the fields, and soon they took for granted that she would one day go to Manila and become rich and successful. Viela's grandparents, uncles, aunts, and other assorted relatives all regarded her as someone very special, and many bananas, eggs, and chickens were sold to bolster her departure war chest.

Viela arrived in Manila with an energetic determination to succeed and immediately made friends with a man who agreed to help her enter a prestigious business school. The school boasted accelerated courses and guaranteed success to its alumni.

It cost Viela nearly every cent of her money to enroll, and it was only too late that she found the school was little more than a diploma mill, producing undereducated students, armed with worthless credentials. Unfortunately, when she attempted to get her money back, she was presented with the small print that declared her contract binding and efforts futile.

Viela's bad fortune could not have come at a worse time, because her father fell ill and died, leaving the family destitute. Viela's relatives did as much as they could to help out, but times were very hard and there was no money to spare. So, when Viela heard that large amounts of money could be earned for acting and dancing to entertain American sailors in Olongapo, she decided to try it. Viela was certain this was the way out of her predicament and a source of needed income for her desperate family. However, she soon found the real money involved a bit more than acting and dancing. Eventually, she joined the other girls at Evelyn's. They were girls who all had similar stories of equal desperation and frustration. They were girls who all sent money home to hide their shame. They were girls who no one would dream of becoming. And they were girls who many could never understand, especially if those critics did not understand living in a country with no social safety net and where your life and the life of those you loved totally depended upon what you were prepared to endure.

Viela sat up and dabbed at her eyes with the corner of her bed sheet, leaving faint smudges of mascara to mark her sorrow. Then she stood and walked across the room to her dressing table to finish getting ready for her night's work.

*I wish I could be more like Tina,* she thought as she reapplied her makeup. Tina enjoyed the men, the way they pawed her and looked at her. Viela shuddered slightly as she heard a pair of jeepneys screech to a halt below her bedroom window, and then heard the loud, raucous laughter and screaming.

"I wish I was more like Tina," she whispered.

Viela looked out of her window and down at the parking lot. The dust from the two jeepneys roiled in the air, and the smell of exhaust filled her windowsill. She coughed and waved her hand in front of her.

Blue stepped out of the jeepney, laughing with the rest of the men. He clapped the other driver on the shoulder and looked up at the building in front of him just in time to see a girl wave. He looked around to see whom she was waving to and then shrugged and waved back. *Friendly people,* he thought.

Magic led the way inside with veteran's assurance, and Blue and the other sailors eagerly followed. Blue stepped inside, and immediately a girl grabbed each arm and led him to the bar. It was L-shaped with room for eight stools, and every one of them had a sailor atop with a girl on each side vying for attention. Magic nudged into a slight opening between Blue and the stool next to him and ordered San Miguels.

"My name Rose, you want blow job?"

Blue looked at the pretty face peering up at him. "Not yet. But thanks, Rose."

"Here's your beer." Magic grinned and handed him a frosty bottle. Both men took a long drink. The hair-raising adventure of coming up the hill had made them thirsty.

"You want blow job now?"

"Not now, Rose, but thanks." Blue took another swig and looked around. The place was mobbed with sailors and young Filipinas dressed in various types of lingerie. He guessed their ages to be from about eighteen to forty. Girls who hadn't found a sailor to latch onto sat by themselves, watching and waiting. He saw even more standing on the stairway leading to a second floor. Blue took another sip and noticed the high ceiling with its rotating fans, the walls decorated with banners of welcome to every ship in the fleet, and the dance floor next to the bar. It was very small, and Blue laughed into his beer as he thought about that. He guessed there wasn't much time for dancing in a place like Evelyn's. He also noted tables positioned here and there, and music came from a jukebox in the corner. A pool table was next to the jukebox.

Suddenly, three laughing girls grabbed him by the arms and began to drag him away from the bar.

"Hey, he mine. He mine," protested Rose. She frowned and tried to fend off the other girls.

"You too slow. He ours now," said one of the girls, and they led Blue toward one of the tables. Blue looked over his shoulder and saw two more with Magic.

Magic laughed and held up his hand. "Girls, girls, hold on now. First, I want to see Evelyn. Is she here?"

The girls giggled and nodded, and one detached herself and ran upstairs. Blue and Magic sat at a table, and in a second each had a thinly clad girl squirming in his lap and one waiting on "alert five," as Magic told them.

"What 'alert five'?" The girl next to Magic looked up at him and grinned.

"It means that you have to be ready to launch into me in five minutes or less."

"I ready launch now. You want blow job?"

"Well, not quite yet." Magic laughed. "But I like your attitude."

"Masheek." A female's voice boomed from the stairway. Blue and Magic looked up, and there stood a portly woman of about sixty. She held out her arms, and the sleeves of her kimono flowed. "Masheek."

Magic hopped up and ran around the table for the stairs. Evelyn met him at the bottom, and Magic picked her up and whirled her around in a huge bear hug. He kissed her on the cheek, hugged her again, and then sat her back down.

Blue stood as the two approached, and an instant after he was introduced to Evelyn he found himself inexplicably giving her a bear hug too. Like so many things so far that evening, it just seemed to be the thing to do. Evelyn sat down, and the girls positioned themselves behind the men's chairs.

"So, Masheek. You have come back to me?" Evelyn smiled and touched Magic's hand.

"Yes, my sweet." Magic grinned. "You know I couldn't stay away."

"And is this one new? I don't recognize him." Evelyn smiled at Blue.

"This is his first time in Olongapo."

"So you just got into town today?"

"If I would have gotten into town yesterday, we would have been here yesterday."

"That horny, are you?" Evelyn sat back and laughed.

"No, Evelyn, just to make sure I saw you again."

"You have always been my favorite." Evelyn squeezed Magic's hand. "So have you seen Evie?"

"Yes, we saw her. She looked tired." He took a long drink.

"I am glad you saw her." Evelyn patted Magic on the arm. "She works hard and I think Henry is something of a chore. Now, regardless of what you say, you didn't risk your life driving up here to see me." Evelyn winked at Blue. "You came to see my girls. So shall it be steam and cream?"

"Exactly what the doctor ordered." Magic smiled.

"Good," announced Evelyn, and she clapped her hands. "Girls, come over here."

The girls waiting behind the chairs walked out in front of the table, and a half dozen others joined them. Overall, there were ten from which to pick.

"Masheek," said Evelyn, "shall we begin?" She smiled and pointed to the girls.

"Why, yes, we shall," said Magic. He hopped up and began to walk up and down the row of girls.

"You know, girls, this may be the hardest decision I ever made. Of course, the decision to turn down Harvard Law School to join the navy was almost as tough." He winked at Blue and took a puff of his cigar.

"To put it in perspective," he said as he spread his arms, "if the whole world were an ice cream parlor, there wouldn't be a plain scoop of vanilla among you." He smiled, and the girls smiled too. Blue could see in their eyes that they didn't have a clue what he was talking about.

"So," Magic continued, "I will be forced to use a scientific technique that I have perfected over the years when faced with such a crisis." He walked to the end of the line and, starting with the first girl, moved down the line with each word. "Eenie, meenie, minie, moe, catch, an, island, queen, by, the, toe. If, she, hollers, make, her, pay, fifty, pesos, every, day."

The girl he stopped in front of looked at her companions and giggled. She wasn't sure what was going on. Magic took the cigar out of his mouth and leaned over.

"Looks like you and me, baby."

The girl squealed and clapped her hands. Magic grabbed her by the hand and led her back to the table. Blue thought she was very cute. She wore tangerine briefs under a filmy white blouse, and when Magic sat down, she sat on his lap like she owned it.

Magic picked up his beer, took a gulp, and looked at Blue. "Now it's your turn, kid."

Blue grinned and looked at the girls. He had been scoping them out during Magic's parade and had first chosen a lithe girl wearing a green teddy, but then the girl who had waved at him out of the window walked down the stairs. She wore a lacy outfit that barely covered her perfect body, and Blue found her aloof expression exotic. Although the cross around her neck momentarily unnerved him, he chose her.

"Excellent choices," beamed Evelyn. The other girls groaned and turned around, looking for other opportunities.

"Masheek, this is Tina, if you haven't already found out." She pointed at the girl on Magic's lap.

"Way ahead of you, Evelyn. We are getting married in the morning as soon as the chapel opens."

"Really," squeaked Tina.

"Well, maybe after lunch." Magic smiled, and as he squeezed Tina, she giggled and squirmed on his lap.

"Blue, this is Viela."

"Hello, Viela." Blue smiled uneasily at the girl. He was surprised at his discomfort. Truth be told, he had never had a prostitute before. He hoped when the lights went out things would go smoother.

"Hello, Blue." The girl smiled slightly and touched his hand. Her shyness made Blue feel a lot better. Maybe his uneasiness wasn't that strange after all.

"Okay, girls, you know what to do." Evelyn clapped her hands, and Tina and Viela hopped up and ran up the stairs.

"Masheek, do you remember the way?"

"Like it was my own house, mama."

"Get on then." Evelyn shooed the men toward the stairs.

"Come on, Blue, it's time to see the doctor."

"Doctor? What doctor?"

"Evelyn employs a doctor to check out clients like us," said Magic. "Of course, he probably never set foot in a medical school, but what the hell, it's part of the show."

The two men tromped up the stairs and turned left along a dimly lit corridor. There were rooms on each side, some empty with the doors open and others shut. Blue noticed soft music coming from somewhere, and the whole place smelled like lemon. He sniffed the air and coughed.

"Lemon-scented body oil, kid," said Magic.

Blue nodded, and the two continued to the end of the corridor. Magic pushed open the door and they walked in. The room was fairly small, with a wooden floor and bamboo-covered walls. At the far end was a bubbling hot tub.

In an adjacent room, Viela and Tina prepared for the bath. Viela sighed deeply as she thought about her situation. Although Blue seemed like a nice man, she still hated doing what she did every night. *Only one more year,* she thought. *Only one more year and I will have enough saved to go back to Manila and start again.*

"What's wrong, girl?" Tina frowned at Viela's lack of spunk.

"Oh, nothing," murmured Viela. "I'm just not in the mood tonight."

"Sister, you aren't ever in the mood. You're like the rest of these whiners. You waste too much energy hating yourselves and not enough on making money."

"What's it to you?"

"Look, if you drag yourself in there and ruin the mood, the boys aren't going to throw out the extra cash. If you don't like it here, leave. But don't screw things up for me."

"Okay, okay," said Viela. "I'll be ready in a second."

"So, how we looking, kid?" Magic and Blue were sitting on the edge of the hot tub, waiting for the "doctor" to come in.

"I'm having a great time." Blue smiled and looked at Magic. "Not used to this kind of thing though." He smiled again and looked at the floor. "When did you pay for your first woman?"

"I guess it was in 1963, in Tijuana." Magic squinted his eyes, remembering. "Yeah, that's it, 1963. A pal and I went down there one Saturday to a bullfight. You ever been to a bullfight, kid?"

"No, can't say I have."

"Well, don't ever go, 'cause in a bullfight, the good guy always loses. About a million jerks on horses beat the shit out of the bull with their spears. Then some fag in a nut-hugger suit dances in there and sticks him in the heart. What horseshit! Of course, there's always the crap about giving the meat to the fucking poor, like that makes the whole thing okay."

"You've convinced me," chuckled Blue. "I will never, ever go to a bullfight."

"Good. Magic laughed. "Anyway, my pal and I started driving around TJ, and all of a sudden we decided to get us some real Mexican whores. Quintessential, you know? Is that the right word? Like when you think of Corinthian leather, German engineering, French food—well, then ... Mexican whores. You see the connection? Anyway, we asked this cab driver where to get them. Of course, we had to each pay him ten bucks. Then he went off and dragged back the two raunchiest-looking women you ever laid eyes on. Hooey, they were some rough stuff." Magic shook his head, and the two men laughed.

"So, we took the girls to a motel, and each of us took one into a room. What a stinking pit that was! Cockroaches bigger than cats. Meaner too!" Magic grinned and took a swig of beer.

"So my chick pulls down her panties on only one leg. Can you believe it? Maybe she thought she was going to have to chase me or something."

"Maybe she thought you looked like the kind of guy that'd steal 'em." Blue laughed.

"Maybe." Magic laughed. "She sat down on the bed, leaned back, and spread her legs. Man, but it was ghastly. I almost became a homosexual on the spot."

"What'd you do, leave?"

"Hell, no, kid. I shut my eyes and pretended she was Bobby Franklin's sister. I always did want to poke her. Anyway, in about twenty seconds it was all over."

Blue took a sip of beer. "I don't know if I could have done that." He shook his head slowly and took another drink.

"If you knew Bobby Franklin's sister you could."

"No, seriously, I don't think I could." Blue looked at his beer bottle, rolling it in his hands.

"Nobody says you have to, kid. Look, a man has to have his own feelings and understandings about whores, or any woman for that matter. I mean, wars have been fought over a little pussy. Same's true for all animals. Bear pussy, frog pussy, tuna pussy. It's all the same. It makes the world go around."

"Yeah." Blue shrugged. "I guess."

"You're not having trouble with them being Filipino, are you?"

"Of course not." Blue frowned.

"Okay." Magic smiled.

"I mean, I don't think so."

"Okay, so, something for you to figure out." Magic lit a new cigar and puffed on it for a few seconds before looking back at Blue. "One thing is true though. Just because you make love to them doesn't mean you ever love them."

"Yeah, that's true," Blue agreed.

"Hello!" Both men looked up to see the door fling open. A small man in a white smock strode in and smiled broadly. He bowed slightly and placed the small stool he was carrying on the floor.

"Well, hello yourself," said Magic. "You the doctor?"

"Yes I am, and how you tonight?" The man smiled.

"Well, I guess that's what you're here to tell us." Magic laughed.

The man closed the door and sat down on the stool. He looked at Magic and Blue and smiled, squinting into the light.

"Okey-dokey, who first?"

"I guess I am," said Magic.

"Okay, take off skivvies, show dick."

"I like a man that gets down to business," said Magic as he laughed and stepped out of his underwear. He moved up to the stool, and the doctor gingerly put a gloved hand on his penis and inspected the end. He looked at Magic and smiled.

"You got claps?"

Magic laughed. "No, I don't got claps, Doc."

"Good, then you okay." He turned to Blue.

"Next."

Blue took Magic's place by the stool, and the doctor performed the same inspection. Blue also answered no to the question about claps.

"Have good time." The doctor smiled, picked up his stool, and walked out.

Magic and Blue hopped into the hot, bubbling water and had no sooner sat down when Tina and Viela walked in the door. Both girls were wearing fluffy white towels that reached from the tops of their breasts to their knees. As they entered the room, Tina turned to the wall and lowered the lights.

Magic and Blue smiled at the girls as they walked across the floor toward the tub.

"Come on in, the water's fine," said Magic.

Tina grinned broadly as she threw off her towel and stepped into the water while Viela looked at the floor.

Blue smiled as he observed the girls. He found himself growing more relaxed and figured it was a combination of the beer and the way Evelyn ran the business. The "doctor" thing was goofy, but the girls seemed pretty classy compared with what he had envisioned hookers to be. They actually acted discreet instead of just traipsing around in the buff.

The four soon engaged in a comfortable conversation about what they had done that day. Magic pretty much dominated the conversation, but Blue enjoyed it because he made everything fun.

"Hey, how about another beer?" Magic smiled at Tina and Viela and nodded toward the cooler across the room. The girls looked at each other, shrugged, and then stood and stepped out of the tub. Their hair hung in wet ropes down their thin backs, and soapy water glistened off their firm, round buttocks. Blue began to feel aroused as he watched Viela reach for the cooler. Her breasts were small but perfect, and her nipples were dark and inviting against her olive skin. Her narrow waist was accented by delicately curved hips that tapered to beautiful legs.

The girls looked up as they started back to the tub, and Blue averted his eyes. He didn't want to be caught staring. He glanced at Magic and chuckled. Magic was ogling them openly. Neither eye so much as blinked, and his mouth was half-open. Blue could almost see the drool and chuckled again. Magic was the essence of the basic man!

The girls stepped back into the water, and each handed her partner a beer. Magic took the bottle from Tina, but instead of sitting down beside him, she gently straddled his waist and sat down on his lap, facing him. She held his head with both her hands and gave him a long, passionate kiss. Tina leaned back from her kiss and smiled at Magic. "Let's go," she said.

"We're outta here," said Magic as he looked over Tina's shoulder at Blue.

"Yeah, so are we." Blue stood up, and he and Magic stepped out of the tub. Both men were in a state of semi-erection, and their towels stood out like they were stealing bananas. Pretty comical, actually, but no one was laughing.

The girls each took a partner by the hand and led him down the hall and into her room.

"Lie on your stomach." Viela pointed to a cushioned table that stood in the center of the small, dark room. The table was just large enough for Blue to fit, and it was covered with a clean cotton sheet.

Blue removed his towel and hopped onto the table, lying on his stomach, as instructed. Viela started on his neck and shoulders, and Blue couldn't believe how good the massage felt. The lemon-scented lotion made his skin soft and slippery.

Viela moved down Blue's back, rubbing deep into the muscles. He was amazed how much strength she had in hands so small. As she moved over his buttocks and down his legs to his toes, he felt himself starting to doze.

"Turn on your back," Viela whispered in his ear.

Blue rolled over and lay on his back. For a second he felt a little self-conscious, but the feeling quickly slipped away into the darkness of the room and wonder of Viela's hands.

Viela's hands never left him, as she continued the massage. She spent a lot of time on his face and neck before moving down to his chest. It was here Viela's hands became softer. Instead of a deep muscle massage, she lightly rubbed his lower chest and the muscles of his stomach.

They rolled toward each other and began to make love, but too quickly Blue was finished. And as the lust left him he felt himself falling asleep.

# CHAPTER 7

**B**lue awoke early the next day. In fact, he had never gone back to sleep since he and Magic had rolled out of Evelyn's in the wee hours and had hired a jeepney for the return trip to base. He lay in his bed in the BOQ for a long time, thinking about the events of the previous evening.

His head throbbed from all the beer he had consumed. He wasn't sure what he thought about his night with Viela. There was something about it that made him feel a little rotten—like he had taken advantage of something that he shouldn't have. Blue lay pondering the situation, but as the sky became lighter he rolled over on his back and looked around the room. Filtered yellow light fell through the cracks where the curtains had shrunk, and a ray cut a dusty swath to the wall where it struck the cheap print of some ducks. Blue studied the print as he stretched awake. The ducks were nondescript brownish creatures, and surprising enough, there wasn't even the archetypical green-headed mallard among them. They were just a bunch of girl ducks hanging out in some green-brown water surrounded by reeds. Blue laughed to himself when he saw the print was bolted to the wall. Just who did the management think would steal such a treasure? He yawned widely and looked around some more. The room had the traditional navy institutional intimacy that can only be truly captured by "the lowest bidder." Except for the ducks, it was similar to every other BOQ room in which Blue had stayed. Concrete cinder block was covered with off-white paint, and the floor was linoleum over the slab. Besides the bed, complete with gray sheets that used to be white, the furniture included two chairs, a dresser with drawers, and a secretary that doubled as a work desk and underwear drawer. A small refrigerator stood by the waste can. There was a private bathroom attached, and it was small but serviceable. The room smelled of mildew, the Right Guard spray deodorant of the previous occupant, and the main battery of US Navy cleanliness, bleach. Blue smiled as he surveyed his domain. It was familiar and made him feel at home. The smile worked wonders, and in a few moments his puzzlement over Viela left him. He began to feel better. In fact, he began to feel pretty darn good. He felt extra good when he remembered he was not on the ship anymore. He was on dry land, and any day on land was a good day.

Blue stretched once more, got up, and shaved and showered. Since he was going to town, he put on a pair of tan shorts and a bright-yellow golf shirt. On the left breast was an embroidered figure of a caped skull, holding a scimitar. The words Death Angels were stitched below the figure. After surveying himself in the mirror, Blue opened the door and walked out into the morning sunshine.

As he walked across the parking lot and down the hill to the Officers' Club, he noticed Gladys still parked where he and Magic had left her. He smiled and shook his head.

"God," he whispered to himself, "ownership of a car based upon the fact your name is scratched in the glove box. What a tradition."

He had a huge breakfast of eggs, sausage, and pancakes while he caught up with the rest of the world, reading the *Stars and Stripes* newspaper. After he washed down the last bit of toast with the dregs of his third cup of coffee, he walked outside into the growing heat and hailed a taxi for the ride around the bay to the gate.

His cabbie was the silent type and left Blue alone with his thoughts and the crackle of the dispatcher's radio to accompany the scenic drive along the coast. The fact that he was riding next to a jungle pleased Blue. It wasn't the zoo or some man-made adventure; it was real, and it was a world apart from the small Midwest town where he had been raised.

Blue smiled as the beauty flashed by windows.

The foliage grew right down to the edge of the road, and at times the car appeared to be in a long green tunnel. Blue marveled at the startling flashes of brilliant birds as they flitted about their duties, weaving the wind with their songs of good morning. He was surprised by how many groups of monkeys he saw, sitting together in treetop communes. They were doubtless holding meetings of great importance.

"What kind of monkeys are those?" Blue nodded toward the trees.

The cabbie glanced at the bands of animals for a second and then looked at Blue in the rearview mirror. "Black." He shrugged.

Blue smiled and nodded his thanks and returned to the scenery. The jungle occasionally broke into an expansive view of the beautiful Subic Bay. Everything looked so perfect. The mighty, gray navy ships were decked in ceremonial dress with bunting and bright signal flags flapping in the morning breeze. An occasional sailboat dotted the aquamarine water, and various motor craft carved back and forth, leaving foamy crescents. Even the hovels clustered on the far reaches of the bay looked more quaint than squalid, and one could imagine their occupants more peaceful than destitute. Blue leaned back in the car seat and relaxed. The wind ruffled his hair and brought with it the smells of the jungle: damp earth, musty leaves, a hint of sweet gardenia. There was something about the jungle that made him feel right, that made him feel like he wanted to be part of it and protect it. He wished he could somehow take a picture out his window and step into it. Blue shut his eyes and smiled. He was glad to be off the ship. He was glad he had been selected to come on the trip.

After arriving at the base and paying his fare, Blue walked to the nearby telephone exchange. It was a small building, run as a service to fleet sailors, and it housed telephone booths with a central connection to an overseas operator. The sight of the building reminded Blue that he hadn't even thought about calling Cathy since Magic had mentioned it the day before. He sighed as he walked in the door, dreading the conversation to come. The fact was that his relationship with Cathy was over and it had been for some time. At least it was for Blue. The previous night's antics proved that.

Blue had a personal rule that he stood by, and that was when he dated a girl steadily, he didn't mess around with any others. And as long as he and Cathy had been going together, that was the way he had conducted himself. So he knew there was no going back to Cathy, even if she never knew of his liaison with Viela. But he also knew he couldn't just walk out on her. They had spent too much time together and, besides, it was just not the thing to do. He didn't want to hurt her, although he knew he would.

And then there was the rest of Cathy's family. Although they had not discussed marriage directly, Blue knew that such a prospect had gathered an aspect of inevitability as time had gone on. He assumed it was now an anticipated event in the Joplin household. Cathy's mom had begun to treat him like he was already her son-in-law.

"Please call me Mom, Blue."

Cathy's dad, Captain Joplin, was a bit more reserved and, while he treated Blue wonderfully, probably didn't think the marriage deal was an automatic outcome. In fact, Blue felt "Dad" had been watching him and checking up on him during the cruise. He also suspected that somehow Captain Joplin would let Cathy know Blue had flown off the carrier early.

Blue filled out a form to place the overseas call and started to place it on the stack in front of him. But then he realized that it would not be good for the business he had to do in town if he began his day with the emotional drain a phone call to Cathy would surely bring. He looked out the window, and his thoughts were endorsed by the gently blowing palm trees. They appeared to be waving toward the gate. He smiled to himself, wadded the paper into a ball, and headed for the gate into town.

Anyone who has ever taken a sober Sunday morning walk in New Orleans's French Quarter knows the illusion of the reveling night as it meets the reality of the day. And so it is true for the town of Olongapo. The facade of neon lights and frenzied mirth of partygoers gives way to the starkness of dilapidation and the atmosphere of "just barely hanging on." As Blue walked over the bridge into town he could see that what had been a twinkling string of lights in the darkness was actually the outline of a nest of hovels. In the morning light he could make out the tin-roofed shacks, and he could see children playing in the dirt among the pigs and chickens. Dogs lay curled under the bamboo porches, and the smoke from outdoor cooking fires spiraled into the green canopy of trees.

Unlike the night before, there were no children in canoes and Blue guessed they would come out when the sun went down and the sailors with their pesos began their journey into town. As he walked down the strip, Blue noted that the city wasn't completely ready to give up the night, because he could still hear the blare of loudspeakers coming from the occasional bar that catered to day drinkers.

Blue ducked down an alley Magic had pointed out to him the night before and soon found himself standing in front of a small shop. The sign on the front glass read, *Olongapo City Wood Crafters.*

That morning while Blue had been studying the duck print in his BOQ room, Lori Santiago was awaking from sleep in her grandmother's house in Olongapo. She had gotten up as the first rays of light peeked over the jungle tops and had made a pot of coffee to take out to the front porch. She was on her second cup when her grandmother joined her, soon followed by her uncle, Raul.

"Good morning. Did you sleep well?" Lori's grandma gave her a warm smile and put a weathered hand on her arm.

"Fine, thank you." Lori smiled. Grandma nodded and took the cup offered her.

"And you, *Tio* Raul, how did you sleep?" Lori smiled at the tousled head of her uncle.

Uncle Raul had scurried out to the porch with Grandma, and he was now bent over a bowl of Cheerios, carefully lining the Os in a row on his spoon. He looked up, smiled, and went back to his labors.

A surge of compassion always coursed through Lori when she realized her uncle's fragile innocence. She had long since stopped wondering what he would have been like if he would have been born normal—if the umbilical cord had not been twisted. Lori loved him and accepted him like he was, and she was grateful for this time in Olongapo that she had to spend with him and her *lola,* grandmother. That was why she liked to start her days off at first light, to make them last longer.

Lori was finishing her coffee when the telephone rang and she automatically frowned. It would be Father, wanting to know when she was coming back to Manila.

Raul immediately hopped out of his chair, spilling his milk and cereal, and pointed toward the sound of the telephone.

"Mama, it's the phone." He nervously pointed again and looked at his mother. "It's the phone. Mama, it's the phone."

"Okay, Raul, go ahead and see who it is."

Raul dashed into the house, and Lori laughed as she watched him go. He was on strict orders not to touch the telephone without specific permission. The problem was that Raul was infatuated with it and had once been caught talking to someone in Alice Springs, Australia, about a kangaroo he had seen on television. Grandma had not been happy.

"Lori, it's your father." Uncle Raul stuck his head out the door and smiled. "It's your father from Manila."

Lori frowned again as she stood up and walked into the house.

"It's your father from Manila," repeated Uncle Raul.

"Thank you, *Tio,*" said Lori, and she gave him a quick smile as she took the instrument from his hand.

"Hello, Papa."

"Good morning, Lori." Her father's voice boomed over the receiver. It was the voice of wealth and confidence. It was also a voice that belonged to a man used to getting his way.

"Good morning, Papa, everything all right? How is Mama?"

"Your mother is fine. She is feeling very good this morning."

"That's because she knows I am looking after *lola* and *Tio* Raul." Lori decided to go on the offensive.

"She's feeling good because I told her I was going to insist you come home this weekend," countered her father.

"Oh, Papa."

"Lori, you have spent almost two weeks down there. I would think you would miss the city by now. All of your friends have been calling. Jose called yesterday."

"Jose works for you. Sometimes I think he calls because of you."

"That's not true. You dated Jose."

"Yes, I know, but—"

"Lori, I'm just looking after you. Jose is doing extremely well. I have given him his own accounts to manage. I usually don't do something like that for a man so young."

"But, Papa, I am having a good time down here with Grandma and Raul. I have been making some very good pieces. Grandma is very impressed."

"Lori, Lori."

Lori heard her father take in a deep breath, and she imagined him swiveling and fidgeting in his favorite oak chair, the chair that served as a throne in his Makati district office. She was proud of her father and appreciated his accomplishments. She knew that Pablo Santiago was a powerful man, and she knew that he loved her. But he could be so controlling.

"Honey, I remind you that I absolutely loathe the idea of you being in that filthy place. It's a national embarrassment! Hookers throwing themselves at anyone who walks by, beggars, thieves, and all to service the American sailors."

"Papa! *Lola* and *Tio* Raul live here. It's their home. Remember, it is also where my mother was born."

"Look, Lori, it's just that we miss you."

"I know," softened Lori, "I miss you too."

"So how about coming back home this weekend?"

"Oh, Papa, that is so soon. Let me call you back in a couple of days."

"You haven't met anyone there, have you?"

Lori heard her father's voice harden. "No, Dad, I haven't been carried off."

"It's not funny, Lori. Americans can be very persuasive and very charming."

"I know, Papa, I haven't even talked to one."

"Good." Lori could hear her father's voice begin to lighten. "Good. Well, call us in a couple of days. I expect you to say yes."

"I'll call."

Pablo Santiago hung up the phone and leaned back into his leather chair. He looked at the far wall and let his eyes rest on the painting of his father. It had been rendered from a photograph, and it featured Colonel Reynaldo Santiago sitting on a jagged rock, holding his rifle. The painting never failed to elicit complex feelings from Pablo, and maybe that was why he liked it so much.

The painting framed not only a likeness of his father, but it also framed a beginning for Pablo. It reminded him of the beginning of his life with his father.

He was living with his aunt, he was six years old, and she told him to go and wait by the forest path. She told him his father was coming home to see him. He was so excited! His aunt had told him many stories about his father and how he had fought the Americans after they had killed his mother and sisters. She had told him how he had refused to give up and had continued to fight these last five years as a fugitive, living in the mountains. Patrol after patrol had been sent against him, and all had failed. And now, finally, he was to be given amnesty if he would just surrender. Pablo remembered running down to the path, and he remembered his heart beating as he squinted his eyes and looked deep into the forest, hoping to catch sight of this legendary figure. He waited for what seemed like hours and then, far away, against the backdrop of a great mahogany tree, he saw a figure coming out of the shadows. His heart stopped in his chest, and he swallowed and held his breath, hoping absolute stillness would help him see better. The figure advanced toward him, and he remembered the wide smile flashing against the dark mustache, and he remembered crying and running toward it. He remembered burying his face into his father's chest and smelling the sweet smell of sweat, the sweet smell of the forest and soil, the sweet smell of reunion.

Later his father would tell him of what he had done during the war with the Americans and why he had done it. Much later, his father would tell him of what he had done to the American captain and that, despite the hate that had raged within him, the man's screams had not salved his loss. The screams had not diminished the ache that had left him all but lifeless, and they had not avenged the loss of his sweet wife and daughters, Pablo's mother and sisters.

Pablo and his father had been inseparable since the day of that reunion, and he remembered his gentleness and patience. He remembered his rough hands and his big, sad eyes, but he also remembered no bitterness or frustration. It was almost as if when his father had come down from the mountain he had left all bad things up there.

His father was a brilliant man and had a strong sense of business, and he turned all of his energies to positive pursuits. His reputation as a freedom fighter made him very popular as well, and this accelerated his success even more. Soon he built a successful importing business, and it was this business that Pablo had inherited. But despite the closeness of their bond, Pablo always felt a sense of mystery about his father. He always felt there was something just beyond his eyes, just beyond his words, that remained unseen and unsaid. Pablo thought about this on occasion especially when he caught his father staring out into the jungle, and sometimes he wondered if in fact all things had been left up on the mountain.

"Papa, do you ever have regrets?"

"Regrets about what, son?"

"About things that you have done?"

"What kind of things, Pablo?"

"Are you ever sorry about what you did to the captain?"

"No."

His father had answered immediately and without reservation and had continued to read his journal. And over the years and after his father's death, Pablo had recalled over and over how his father had casually said no. Pablo had come to believe that sometimes things needed to be done. They needed to be done, not for punishment, not for revenge, not to inflict pain, but just to bring an ending. And such things must then be accepted regardless of how they make you feel.

Now, Pablo smiled at the painting as he always did and nodded a salute. He thought of Lori and smiled again.

"Your granddaughter is a lot like you," he said. "She is brilliant, proud, brave, and stubborn." He turned his gaze to his desk and picked the family photo off his desktop. As he looked at his daughter, his smile faded to a frown and he set the frame down. Lori meant everything to him, and he knew he angered her by hovering over her. But he also knew his heart was in the right place, and if that caused some momentary friction, then so be it. He could always make it up to her later.

Pablo Santiago felt blessed to have a beautiful, young wife who had given him a child so late in his life. His first, dear wife had died in 1934 and had never been able to bear children. He had given up on the idea of having a family until he met Mary. She was so vivacious and energetic, and he had been so lucky the day he had dropped by the portfolio division and asked her out. He had been even luckier when she had said yes.

He was fifty when Lori was born, and that was twenty-six years ago. He realized the age difference between him and his wife and daughter might make it harder for them to see eye to eye. However, he also knew he was more determined than ever to ensure she had a good life.

Pablo sighed again and picked up his fountain pen. Why did Grandma Martinez insist on living in Olongapo in the first place? He could never figure that out, especially since Grandpa Martinez had died four years ago. Pablo had been sensitive to the fact that the Martinez family had been in the wood-crafting business for years and had offered to buy the shop for ten times its value. He even had an addition built onto their Manila home for her. Hell, he would buy her a house if she wanted!

But, no! She insisted on staying in that place in that dreadful port city. And Mary's insistence that Lori be allowed to spend the summers there was simply unrealistic. He had made his mind up about that. This was going to be the last summer of this nonsense! Pablo gripped his pen with his index and middle fingers and began to read and sign documents.

It was the only way he could write, since the Americans had taken his thumb all those years ago.

Lori shook her head as she hung up the phone. Her father's ability to hold a grudge against the Americans was remarkable. It was especially remarkable when one considered how much time had passed. She had heard the stories about Grandpa Santiago and the war time and time again, and she knew how the Americans had killed Grandma Santiago and the girls. She knew how her father had lost his thumb. But that was all so long ago, and what did it have to do with her meeting some sailor from America? It wasn't like she was going to run off and marry one. Besides, her father dealt with American businessmen all the time and had entertained them in their home. She shrugged and walked outside. Her father could be so old sometimes.

Lori's trip to Olongapo this summer was different than times before because she had graduated from the university with a degree in business. That meant she would soon be a part of the workforce and would not be able to spend long summers with Grandma and Raul. However, Grandma was beginning to show some signs of her age and was beginning to talk more and more about selling the shop and moving to Manila. Although the prospect of not seeing her friends in Olongapo saddened her, Lori was excited about having the family finally reunited in the capital.

"Do you want to walk down to the store with me this morning?" Lori sat her cup down and looked at her grandmother.

"I don't think so. Raul and I are going to go for a walk and feed the monkeys. Isn't that right, Raul?"

Raul drained the last of his milk and looked up. "Your father called, Lori." He smiled broadly. "From Manila."

"I know, *Tio*. Lori smiled. "Thank you."

Lori kissed her uncle and grandmother good-bye and walked into the house to get ready for work.

Since it would again be hot and steamy, Lori chose a loose-fitting white blouse and dark-blue shorts to wear to the shop. After showering and putting on makeup, she looked at her reflection as she gathered her silky, black hair in a loose knot. She had often been told she was attractive, and the constant attention from young men reaffirmed the comments. Whether in Manila at school or in the shop in Olongapo, she entertained a steady line of would-be suitors. Like most Filipino girls, she was proud but not haughty and genuinely appreciated being pursued.

"Being sought is as important as being caught," her mother had told her. "Relish the chase, and never show disrespect for a young man's heart."

At five feet five, Lori was tall by Filipino standards, and she had inherited her mother's striking cheekbones and large, expressive eyes. From her father, she had gained a strong chin and perfect white teeth that she often shared in her warm, friendly smile. Although she was thin, her body was muscular and firm due to the hour-long exercise session she religiously followed every day. Lori Santiago was indeed a catch, and any man would be overjoyed to snare her.

Lori quickly walked the five-block distance to the shop, and she was pouring over columns of inventory figures when she heard the jingle of the front doorbell. She stood and walked around her desk and out into the showroom.

A young man was looking at one of the display cabinets, and she approached him from behind.

"May I help you?"

He did not turn around, as she expected. Instead, he continued to look at the cabinet.

"This is really, really good," he finally said.

Lori could tell by his voice that he was an American, but she was surprised at her mix of emotions. She was a bit angry that he did not turn immediately and address her, but she was also proud that he was that captivated by the handicraft of Martinez workers. But he had used the word "good" instead of, say, "beautiful." Was that a judgment instead of praise? Or was it just her father's phone call getting to her?

"The tone in your voice indicates surprise. You did not expect this?"

The American turned around to face her, and his eyes crinkled into a smile. "I'm afraid I didn't know what to expect," he said. "I've never shopped for anything like this before."

"Anything like what?"

"Anything like wood."

"You've never been in a furniture store?"

"Heck, no." The American grinned. "The only thing I own is an old car and this shirt."

Lori laughed and nodded her head. "Just like most guys I know."

"It's the same the world over," agreed Blue. He reached out his hand. "My name is Jack Morrison. My friends call me Blue."

"Hi, Blue." Lori took his hand and smiled at him. "My name is Lori Santiago. This is my family's shop."

"Great to meet you, Lori." Blue felt the warmth of her hand and then let it go.

"So, what can I help you with? There are no cars or shirts in here." Lori smiled again and looked into Blue's eyes. He seemed okay ... for an American sailor.

"Well, I have a big problem."

"My, that sounds serious. Has one of the sailors tipped over the ship's liquor cabinet?"

"What makes you think I'm in the navy?"

"Well, let me see," said Lori. She paused and put a finger to her chin. "It could be your shirt with the skull on it. I don't see that every day around here. Or it could be that haircut. I had forgotten men even had ears with the fashions these days."

"You mean it's not my tan that gave me away?"

"What tan?" Lori laughed.

Blue joined her laughter and pointed to his white legs. "Exactly."

Lori laughed again. "Seriously, what can I help you with?" Lori looked up at him.

"Well, it's kind of hard to describe."

"Good thing you don't need a doctor."

Blue laughed again.

Lori also felt herself enjoying the exchange. The handsome young man with his quick wit, yet self-deprecating manner, was different than most of the young men who tried too hard to impress her.

"I need a gun case."

"A gun case? Why is that so hard to explain?"

"I don't have the gun that fits in it, and I've never even seen it."

"My, that was a full liquor cabinet, wasn't it?"

"Hey." Blue grinned. "Come on. I need help."

"You sure do." Lori smiled.

"It's a Winchester bicentennial-edition rifle."

"Well, we have never made a gun case, but if you have any idea what you want and the dimensions, we can give it a try."

"I have a picture of the rifle, and it is to scale. Can you create a fitted case with that?"

"I think so. If the drawing is to scale, I can shadow-trace it into a life-size replica. It should be no problem getting an exact fit."

"Really? That's great! My skipper, my boss, told me just to do the best I could so the gun doesn't rattle around too much. This is fantastic."

"What kind of wood?"

"Huh?"

"The wood." Lori smiled. "What kind of wood do you want?"

"Gosh, I don't know. What do you suggest?"

"Tell me again why they selected you to do this job?"

Lori burst into laughter, and so did Blue. She noticed that every time he looked at her he smiled. "Don't worry," said Lori. "I'll pick out something that'll work."

"How long do you think the job will take?"

"Oh, we should have it done in about a week. Is that soon enough?"

"Yeah, that's perfect."

"So you will be in our fair city for that long?" Lori was surprised she asked the question. It was a little forward.

"Looks like it." Blue smiled.

"Good." Lori grinned. "However, you need to come back and pick out the color of the felt inlay and choose a stain."

"How about tomorrow?"

Lori heard him stop short as he blurted out the question. She smiled at his eagerness. "Is tomorrow too soon?"

"I think I can have some samples for you to look at in the afternoon."

"That's just great," said Blue. "Just great. By the way, what will all of this cost?"

"I think I can do it for $250. Is that fair?"

"That's more than fair. Where do I sign the contract?"

"Here, we shake," said Lori as she held out her hand.

"Sounds good to me." Blue grinned.

Lori stood there looking up at him and smiled inwardly as he grinned at her, looked at the floor, and then looked up and grinned again. It was a little awkward and odd, but it made her feel good.

"So I will see you tomorrow then." Blue held out his hand.

"Tomorrow." Lori shook his hand and turned toward the door.

As they got to the door, Blue turned to Lori and started to speak but stopped. He looked at her as if he wanted to say more and smiled.

"So, until tomorrow afternoon, then?"

Lori looked up at him, smiling at his confusion. "Until tomorrow."

After Blue left, Lori closed the door, went into her office, and sat behind the desk. She returned to the papers she had been working on, but she realized that she was still smiling. It was a smile that would keep coming back to her the rest of the day.

Blue exited the shop and walked down the alley toward the main drag. He shook his head as he felt what must have been a goofy-as-shit grin split his face. *Wow! What was that all about? Why do I feel so weird?* He felt funny, but it wasn't a bad funny. He turned the corner at the main street and began walking toward the center of town. He felt his face growing red as his mind flashed to Lori. *I must have been at sea longer than I realized.* He forced his mind to concentrate on the job he had been sent to do. The weirdness evaporated, and he smiled at the great fortune he had to find someone who had the capability to do what he needed. If Lori could produce what she said, he was going to accomplish his mission on time, under budget, and with a product vastly superior to what anyone back on the ship expected. The feeling of weirdness came over him again as he thought of Lori, and he couldn't keep from laughing as he recalled bits of their conversation, but his awkwardness at the door was perplexing. He hadn't felt that goofy since the seventh grade. He was also surprised he was so eager about seeing her tomorrow.

As Blue strolled down the strip, he noticed several people in front of him turn down a side street. Curious, he slowed his pace and turned down the street to see what the attraction was. There, about two blocks away, was a large, open square with a bustling marketplace. Blue recalled his previous evening's conversation with Tina and Viela and realized that he was eager to see what sort of things were on sale. He quickened his pace and headed down the street.

As Blue neared the square, he saw the crowd busily picking through the produce. Most of the shoppers were women who carried small children on their backs. Their bright dresses and gay chatter filled the square with color and excitement. The square was jammed with stalls, shops, and carts all filled with produce from the surrounding area. One side of the square contained stalls of seafood. Mounds of anchovies, sardines, mackerel, squid, and prawns lay on beds of ice. The sharp tang of the fresh fish, seaweed, and saltwater was strong but pleasing. Next to the fish were shops with a wide assortment of fruits and vegetables. Shoppers eagerly picked from piles of coconuts, mangoes, papayas, pineapples, bananas, and breadfruit. Sacks of corn, sugar, and rice were stacked in front of wooden tables, their scoops full for sale. Mobile carts held cooked dishes of spiced pork, chicken, and fish. Shoppers could purchase paper cups of *pancit*—thin noodles mixed with vegetables, meat, and spices—and Blue saw many people eating as they shopped. Blue also noticed that some were eating what appeared to be a dark, discolored egg.

"What is that?" Blue asked a man who was carefully peeling away the shell of his egg.

"*Balut.*" The man smiled.

Blue winced as the odor of the egg and the man's breath hit his nostrils. "What?"

"Balut, it is fermented duck egg. It is very good." The man held the partially eaten greenish-yellow egg to Blue. The juices dripped from his hand and down his arm. "You want try?"

"No," said Blue. He gave the man his best smile and turned around.

Blue's mind flashed to his BOQ room print.

*Whew, what did he do to that duck?*

Blue was also impressed with the assortment of crafts. Wooden glasses, bowls, trays, and ornamental statues filled some of the stalls, while others held fabrics and dry goods. He was trying on a straw hat when he heard someone call his name. He turned and was surprised to see Eve Mariposa, the singer. A crowd of well-wishers and autograph seekers accompanied her.

"Well, hello," said Blue as he walked to where she stood. The group around Eve moved apart as he approached.

"I thought it was you, but since I didn't see Magic, I wasn't sure. It was a little dark in the club last night." Eve smiled and extended her hand.

"I think Magic is still in bed. We were out a little late."

"Did you have a good time?"

"Well, yes," stammered Blue. He felt his face flush. "Yes, we did."

"Good." Eve smiled.

The two of them fell into a slow walk and began to move among the stalls.

"Hey, Miss Mariposa!" a street vendor called over his smoking fire.

"Eve, you were great last night!" a little man selling T-shirts sang out.

"Miss, can I have your autograph?" Blue and Eve stopped for a moment as she bent to sign the fan's copy of "Orchid Forest."

Blue noticed that Eve took all of the compliments graciously, and she took the time to acknowledge her greeters with kind words, handshakes, and, of course, her smile. However, he also noticed that in the light of the morning, Eve had a gauntness that had been hidden in the candlelight of the club. In fact, it was when he watched her beautiful, brilliant smile fade into her face that he saw the thinness of her cheekbones and the light shadow under her eyes.

"So tell me," said Eve as she inspected a pineapple, "what are you doing out so early this morning?"

"I was tasked to fly in early and get a wooden gun case made, a gift for our admiral. Magic told me about a shop, and I visited it this morning. Wonderful girl manages it—maybe you know her, Lori Santiago?"

"Oh, yes!" Eve looked at Blue and smiled. "She comes here every summer to help her grandmother and uncle."

"So you are good friends?"

"Yes, but we do not see each other as often now. In fact, I haven't seen her since she came back.

Eve smiled at Blue again. "She has a lot of the young men in town interested in her."

"I can certainly believe that," said Blue. *Why does that bother me?* "She sure seemed nice. I mean, real easy to talk to, you know?"

Eve arched a curious eye in Blue's direction. "Yes, I know."

"Do you have time for a cup of coffee?" Blue asked.

Eve smiled and nodded. "Sure, there is a little patio around the corner. We can sit there."

The two of them maneuvered out of the square and walked down the street until they came to a small plaza. It was little more than a cleared space in the market and was ringed with the raggedy, wooden facades of stores that were obviously aimed at American sailors. T-shirts with any message imaginable—and many that were not acceptable—could be had for five pesos. A grinning man standing by a hot fire made metal belt buckles, and shops sold knockoffs of Gucci bags, Adidas running shoes, and Levi's jeans. All labels of pirated music were proudly displayed in storefronts and stalls. The aroma of American-style pizza mixed with the smells of exhaust, brazier fires, sewage, and the ever-present beckoning of gardenia blossoms. Blue and Eve sat down at one of the tables, and in a moment a server appeared. Although obviously starstruck with Eve, the young girl managed to take their order and soon had two steaming cups of coffee on the table. Blue spooned some sugar into his cup, took a sip, and looked at Eve.

"I am dying to ask you something." Blue smiled and sipped again.

"Well, what is it?" Eve's voice was rich and warm.

"I hope you don't mind me saying this, but I can't believe anyone with a voice like yours would be living here. Please don't be offended, but, hey, I think you belong on Broadway!"

Eve smiled at Blue's hearty laugh. "Thank you, Blue," she said. "I appreciate your praise. And I appreciate your sensitivity."

"Not at all." Blue smiled back. He took another sip of his coffee. "It's just that if I had your gifts I would not be here. And according to Magic, you have been here for over six years."

Eve blew softly across the top of her cup, cooling the brown liquid. She took a tiny sip and put the cup down.

"You want buy? Cheap, one hundred pesos."

Blue turned toward the sound of a man's voice and looked into the eyes of a small, gray monkey. The monkey was perched on its owner's arm, chewing a string of red licorice.

"No, no thanks." Blue smiled at the man and shook his head. "He is cute though."

"Eighty pesos." The man pushed his arm closer to Blue. The monkey didn't seem to mind; it kept chewing on the candy.

"Nah, not today." Blue shook his head again.

"Sixty."

"Sir, I don't want to buy your monkey."

The little man shrugged, put his partner on his shoulder, and left.

Blue and Eve both laughed as they watched him go, and then they returned to their coffee.

"You asked why I stay?" Eve looked at Blue.

"Yes."

"It is difficult to explain … completely."

"Oh, how so?"

Eve cradled her cup and looked Blue directly in the eyes.

"These people need me," she said. "And I need them. They give me something."

Blue nodded his head slowly.

"These people are my family."

Blue wasn't sure what to say. He had not expected this conversation. But he did appreciate what Eve was saying. He looked at her and nodded over his shoulder. "Is it hard living like this? I mean, you know, with so many in need, especially the ones down by the river."

"Sometimes it is. That is why sometimes I hate it when you Americans are here."

Blue frowned and straightened in his chair. "What do you mean?"

"Don't be offended, Blue." Eve reached across the table and touched his hand. "I mean no insult. It is just that you have so much and we have so little. Sometimes it hurts my heart to see what we are prepared to do for your money—what we do to each other and to you."

Blue swallowed and nodded.

"Last month, when the *Ranger* was in port, there evidently was a lot of petty theft, and so Olongapo was declared off-limits by your navy. Much money was lost because of it. Store owners complained, and the police caught a man who had supposedly stolen a sailor's wallet. They shot him. There was no trial or legal proceeding. They shot him dead as a message. That is the kind of thing we do to each other in the name of your money."

"Jesus," whispered Blue.

"So, you see, I can't leave these people. They are my family."

"I understand."

"Besides." Eve smiled and patted Blue's hand. "I need these people to help me with Henry."

"Oh, yes." Blue grinned. Eve's smile immediately brightened the mood. "I can definitely see your point. We met him at the river last night."

"What?" Eve's eyes turned hard.

"He was in a boat. We saw him when we came across the bridge."

"I am going to have to talk to that boy. He must have sneaked out of the dormitory house again." Eve took a deep breath and sighed.

"He seems like a great kid." Blue smiled and hoisted his cup.

"You're just trying to protect him."

"How is it he lives with you? Oh, I'm sorry." Blue realized he might be crossing a line. "It's not really any of my business."

Eve hesitated for a moment and then cleared her throat. "My family is from the north, and there are not many of them left. Both Papa and Mama died shortly after Henry was born. So he came to live here with me."

"How old?"

"A baby."

"Did he have that sailor's cap on his head?"

"No." Eve laughed. "He got that later."

"Well, he sure is lucky to have you as his big sister."

"Thank you, Blue." Eve smiled and nodded her head.

"Say, how did you meet Magic?"

Eve looked at Blue and laughed. "I met him on his first cruise here. I had just started singing at one of the local bars. This was before the Black Rose. No one knew me, and to be honest I wasn't sure if I was going to make it. And one day this guy shows up, and the next day he brings some of his friends, and by week's end the bar is standing room only."

"Really!"

"Really. The ship was in port for two weeks, and every night was standing room only. I was able to build a following, and even after the ship left the local population, tourists, others from as far away as Manila came to hear me. I have to say a lot of it was due to Magic."

"Is that when he met your sister?"

Eve looked at Blue and took another sip of coffee. She slowly nodded. "Yes, Magic met her, but Solang was just a kid then. It was when he came through on the second cruise that the two of them fell in love. At least they seemed like they were in love."

"Really? I can't imagine Magic being in love. That must have been something to see."

"He was something to see, all right." Eve grinned. "He hung around the Black Rose every night, just hoping to catch a glimpse of her."

"What did your parents think?"

Eve looked startled for a moment and then quickly cleared her throat. "Oh, Solang had come down here to live with me by that time. So it wasn't a problem."

"Oh." Blue nodded. "How long did this affair last?"

"Magic's ship was in need of repairs, so they were in here for over a month."

"I guess that's enough time to fall in love."

"I guess." Eve smiled. "Have you ever been in love, Blue?"

"I don't know." He laughed. He was a little surprised at her forwardness. He was surprised but not displeased. He thought about Cathy and remembered he needed to call her. "No," he corrected. "No, I haven't."

Eve looked at him for a moment and then continued. "Magic began showing up at the club more and more frequently until he was almost living there. I remember twice his squadron called because he was missing a flight brief."

"That's amazing, Magic missing a flight brief because of a woman. I can't believe it!" Blue was truly shocked.

"His friends really let him have it too." Eve smiled. "They started calling him the mayor of Olongapo."

"The mayor of Olongapo? Why?"

"Because he was in town so much." Eve laughed.

"So where is Solang now? Does she sing too?"

"No, Solang died shortly after Magic left for sea again."

"Oh, I'm sorry."

"Thank you. She has been dead for a long time now."

Blue sat quietly and looked out over the neighboring houses and shops. He felt terrible for bringing up the subject. He had assumed Magic and Solang had just broken off their relationship. He was about ready to stand and excuse himself when Eve spoke.

"I don't know what plans she and Magic had made, but I do know she was very happy while he was here. After the ship pulled out and went off the coast of Vietnam, Magic would write her letters and send her things. You know, little things from the ship's store. Cards, little gifts, things like that."

Eve paused to ask for more coffee from a circling waiter, and after he refilled both cups, she continued.

"Everything changed after Magic shot down his second MIG. I guess things were not going very good as far as the Vietnam War was concerned, so the navy sent Magic back to the States. They put him and some other pilots on a tour, to talk up the war. Anyway, when his ship came back for another rest period, Magic was not on it."

"Didn't he write her?" Blue frowned and sipped his coffee.

"In the beginning."

"Did they ever see each other again?"

"No," said Eve. "Shortly after Magic returned to the United States she died."

Blue nodded but remained silent.

"Well," said Eve, "I must get going. Henry will be home for lunch and I want to be there. We have some talking to do."

"Thank you for the conversation," said Blue. He stood and looked into her dark eyes, her smile again illuminating her gauntness. He shook her hand and watched her turn and walk toward the market. She was truly a beautiful woman, and for some reason Blue felt happy for her. He felt happy to see people call her name and to see her acknowledge them. He felt good that someone like her lived in a place like Olongapo. He watched her until she disappeared into the crowd, and then he turned and headed back to the ship.

# CHAPTER 8

That morning, Magic lay in bed for a long time after the sun came up. He had not thought about Olongapo, Eve, Solang, or any of that part of his life in a long, long time. It had been six years since he was last here, but as soon as they flew in and he saw the jungle, the Cubi landing strip, the Officers' Club, and Olongapo, it was as if he never left.

*But why am I thinking so much about Solang?*

He had suppressed thoughts of her for so long he wasn't sure what the truth was. Had he really been in love with her, or was it just some kind of island fever that had beset him? But even if he had not loved her, even if it had just been a cruise fling, that still did not explain how he had just dropped her. And then for her to die so young! He felt that in some way he was responsible. He remembered the letter from Eve, telling him how Solang had loved him and that she had drowned. He remembered going into his stateroom and sitting in the dark with tears rolling down his cheeks. He remembered it like it was yesterday. He and Eve continued to exchange letters over the years, and he had always read them closely and had always dreaded that one day she would blame him for her sister's death. But she never did. She told him about the town, about Evelyn, the Black Rose. She told him about her little brother, Henry, coming to live with her and the normal things in her life. Each time he opened her letter, he tensed with anxiety. Each time he finished reading it, he breathed a sigh of relief. He didn't know what he would do if she ever did blame him.

Magic sighed, rolled over, and sat up on the edge of the bed. He ran his fingers through his hair and rubbed his hands across his face, wiping away the last remnants of sleep. Then he stood and walked into the bathroom.

As he stood under the blast of hot water, Magic forced himself to drive the memories from his mind. He smiled as he began to remember the events of the previous evening and chuckled aloud when he remembered Blue's shyness and his confusion over the girls at Evelyn's. *What a kid,* he thought and wondered if he had been that naive when he was Blue's age.

"Ha!" He laughed. "I was never that fucking naive."

Magic smiled again when he thought about Tina and their moments together in the little dark room. He had even surprised himself with his lust.

After he finished showering and shaving, he put on a pair of shorts and a knit shirt and headed down the hill to the Officers' Club for breakfast. On the way across the parking lot, he noticed two men in flight suits next to Gladys. Curious, he walked to where they were standing.

"What's going on, gents?" Magic grinned broadly as he approached the men.

When they turned, he noticed they had US Air Force markings on their flight suits. They both were wearing the rank of major.

"We were just seeing about our car," drawled the taller man. He stood with his hands on his hips, an angry glare on his face.

"Yeah," said the other man. "Some son of a bitch took it last night from in front of the club. Now, it won't even start. The distributor cap is missing." The taller man looked sideways at Magic. He squinted in suspicion.

"Why are you interested anyway, sport?"

Magic smiled into the man's eyes.

"I'm the son of a bitch that took the car."

The two majors exchanged glances and then looked at Magic. "What?"

"I took the car. It's mine."

"Bullshit," spat the taller man. "Our squadron's been using this car for two months. We've been down here from Japan, fighting the A-4s at Cubi." He was referring to the navy squadron of A-4 Skyhawks, stationed at Cubi Point. The squadron provided services to the fleet, such as towing aerial targets and simulating enemy aircraft in mock dogfights.

"Well, I'm glad someone was able to put it to good use while I was gone. But, boys, I'm back now and I'll need my wheels."

"What?" sputtered the taller man.

"What makes you think it's yours?" the shorter major whined and frowned.

"Tradition, boys, tradition." Magic laughed. "Here at Cubi, the rules are the guy with the oldest claim to the car gets it. If you look in the glove box, you'll see my claim goes back to 1969."

"What kind of tradition is that?" the shorter man whined again.

"Like I said before … bullshit," growled the taller man.

"Well, boys." Magic smiled. "I'd sure love to stay out here in the sun and jerk off with you two some more, but I've got a slight hangover and need some breakfast. I'll catch you later." He turned and walked toward the club.

Magic walked into the club and proceeded to the dining room. He picked up a plate and started to walk to the buffet line when he felt someone grab him by the arm. He looked around into the eyes of the tall major.

"This ain't over, Bub," the big man hissed. "I want that fucking distributor cap, and I want it now."

Magic looked around the room. It was almost full, and he felt the eyes of the crowd fall on them as the hum of conversation stopped.

"Look, rocket boy," Magic whispered, "let's not cause an uproar. Everybody in here is looking at us, and that embarrasses me. Wait until I eat and we can go outside and talk it over."

"Eat shit, squid. I'm late for the golf course. I want the car, now."

"Take your hands off, pal."

"I said I'm late—"

Magic backhanded his ceramic plate into the man's face, hitting the bridge of his nose with a loud whack. The man yelled with pain and let go of Magic's arm. He grabbed his nose and doubled over. Magic gripped him by his flight suit and dragged him through the door. Once outside, he released his grip and the man staggered back against a tree.

"What's wrong with you two?" The shorter major had rushed over at the sound of his friend's yell and had followed them outside. He was now standing between them, his face a shock of disbelief.

Magic looked to see who was watching, but the door to the club was closed and no one was in the parking lot. That made him feel better.

"You rotten bastard. You could have put my eye out." The tall man gently held his nose, his eyes closed in pain. A trickle of blood ran between his fingers.

"Your fucking eyes are so close together you would never know the difference." Magic smiled.

"Okay, that's enough," said the shorter officer. He took his companion by the arm and started to lead him up the hill toward the BOQ. Then he turned around.

"The bottom line is you stole our squadron car and we want it back. We'll have to see what the commanding officer of the base says about your damn tradition."

"What do you fly?"

"What?"

"What kind of plane do you two pussies fly?"

"Phantoms. And fuck you."

"I'll tell you what. Being a sporting man, I bet I can beat both of you in a dogfight."

"What are you talking about?"

"Two versus one. Your two phantoms against mine. Winner gets the car, loser walks." Magic smiled and winked. "In fact," he added, "if you beat me and my RIO in our Phantom, we'll give each of you a hundred-dollar bill."

The two men looked at each other, and their frowns turned into smiles. Even the man with the cut nose managed a grin.

"You're on, prick," he said.

"Good." Magic smiled. "Be ready for a 0900 takeoff tomorrow morning. Don't be late."

"Fine," said the short major. "What weapons do you want to simulate?"

"Heat seekers," said Magic. "But you," he turned his gaze to the taller man with the cut nose, "I'm gonna gun you."

"Bullshit," spat the man. He turned on his heel and stomped up the hill.

Magic and the shorter officer watched him go, and as he got to the top, the short man looked at Magic and shook his head.

"Man, what's your problem?" he asked. "Why did you hit him?"

Magic gave the man a glare of pure ice. He curled his lips and almost snarled his answer. "Nobody ever embarrasses me, pal. Nobody."

The man looked at Magic for a moment and slowly shook his head again. "Well, I hope walking doesn't embarrass you or you better plan on taking a lot of taxi rides. I'm pretty good, but Rusty is the best pilot in the wing."

Magic smiled, turned around, and walked back into the club.

# CHAPTER 9

Head looked up from the *Division Officer's Guide* as Spot sauntered into the gloomy stateroom. He was glad for an excuse to put the dreaded thing away.

"The XO is such a dickhead!" Spot threw himself onto his bunk. "I can't believe he will actually be the CO in a couple of weeks."

"Well, believe it, little buddy." Head chuckled. "Heart's out of here."

"Ohhh," groaned Spot. He bunched his pillow and stuffed it under his head.

"What makes you say he's a dickhead? I mean, I agree that he is. But what makes you say it now?"

"Well, first of all, do you know how much flying we're going to do on our way home from the Philippines?"

"Zip."

"Exactly," replied Spot. "We aren't flying hardly any. So I planned to take leave the day the ship pulled into Olongapo and fly home on the DC-9."

"The one that makes the weekly run from Cubi?"

"Yeah. We have a family reunion and I would just make it in time."

"You mean, miss the port period in Olongapo?"

"Look, guy, I've seen monkeys and whores before. I don't mind missing Olongapo."

"You're just trying to get back to Margie."

"Well, that too." Spot smiled and twirled his pillow up in the air.

"Family reunion, my ass." Head grinned. "Do you even have families in Texas? I thought you all just humped cows down there."

"Eat shit, pud whacker." Spot laughed.

"But just think," said Head, "you'll miss the whole boat trip back to the States."

"Yeah, and since we won't be flying much, there isn't much to miss. I could fly home from Cubi, take some leave, and then check in with the advanced detachment in San Diego."

"And screw off while the rest of us are steaming back at fourteen lousy knots."

"Well." Spot grinned. "I prefer to think of it as redeploying forward to help the ship."

"Yeah, right," said Head. "And the XO told you to screw yourself, right?"

"Basically." Spot sighed. "Actually, he told me I could take leave the last day the ship was in port. That will make me late for the reunion."

"So are you going to do it?" Head bent and picked up Spot's pillow. He looked at it and made a face. "Do you drool at night, or did this get mixed up in your dirty underwear drawer?" He threw it back at Spot.

"Eat shit." Spot laughed. He picked up the pillow, inspected it briefly, and put it back under his head.

"You know, Spot, with all of the shit you have done to the XO, you should feel ashamed for even asking him a favor."

"Yeah, I know. Imagine what he would do if he found I was behind Weenie Kleegan?"

"Yes, I can imagine," said Head. "He would cut off your smaller-than-average penis and shove it into your larger-than-average mouth."

Head liked giving crap to Spot. He also acknowledged Spot as the ringleader of the squadron JOs. Generally, if something weird was going on, Spot was behind it. He had a great imagination sparked by an irreverent nature and spared no effort in antagonizing people he thought deserved it. He also liked to play with fire. That's why he liked to screw with the XO.

"So how did the Weenie Kleegan caper really start?" Head put his feet up on his desk and looked at Spot. "I never knew the real story."

"Well," said Spot as he bounced upright, "I will tell you the real story because I am the real story."

"How so, sir Spot?"

"Well, last December when we were at home in Virginia Beach, I was over at Just Ed's apartment. It was a rainy Saturday and we were drinking beer and watching TV, and this Frankenstein movie came on."

"The original? The one with Boris Karloff?" Head opened a can of Coke. It was room temperature, and he grimaced as he took a sip.

"Yep, the one with old Boris. Anyway, after a couple of hundred beers I came up with this great idea about how I could get some money from Just Ed and screw over Prince at the same time."

"You mean, a twofer?"

"Yeah, or a win-win, put another way." Spot and Head laughed, and Head took another hot sip.

"So I bet Just Ed ten bucks that I could create life, just like Dr. Frankenstein did."

"What did he say?"

"What do you think he said?" Spot laughed. "He said, 'huh?'"

"Yeah." Head laughed. "He is kind of a dumb shit. But did he take the bet?"

"Absolutely." Spot laughed. "So on Monday I went down to my buddy at base communications, and he helped me write a fake message from the Bureau of Personnel in Washington DC, to the squadron. It stated the squadron would soon receive a new air intelligence officer named Ensign William N. Kleegan."

"No shit!" Head laughed and gulped some more hot Coke.

"No shit. It really looked official, so I slipped it into the morning-message traffic."

"And that is how it showed up on the message board in the ready room?"

"Exactly." Spot laughed.

"I remember reading it." Head laughed and nodded.

"So I was the duty officer in the ready room. I had planned it that way because I knew I had to work the birthing a bit."

"Yeah," said Head. "Creating a message is one thing; getting it to be believed is another."

"Right, so I sat there waiting for Prince to come in. He would be my first test."

"Let me guess," said Head. "He came in, shit on you for a while about the coffee, and then asked for the message board, which was already on his seat."

"Bingo," declared Spot. "I see you have had the duty when the mighty Prince of dog shit enters. He did as you said, but he also asked if he had had any calls. I almost threw up my coffee. I mean, who in the fuck is going to call him at 0700 on a Monday morning?"

"What did you say?"

"I almost said, 'Sir, the president *just* called before you came in. He said he needs help with North Korea and the Russians.'"

Head threw back his head and laughed. He loved Spot.

"But I said, 'No, sir, no calls.'"

"Then what happened?"

"Well, he made the big deal out of taking his green pen out of his shoulder pocket like he always does, like he is preparing to sign the Magna Carta or something, slurped his coffee for a while, and then found the message."

Head was laughing so hard he dropped his Coke on the floor. Luckily it was nearly empty.

"So, he says, 'Looks like the bureau is sending us a new ensign. Name of Kleegan, new intelligence officer.'"

"How did you keep from laughing?"

"I tell you, I peed in my pants just a little," said Spot. He held his right thumb and forefinger up for Head to see. "Just a little."

Head was laughing uncontrollably.

"He reads some more and says, 'Looks like he'll arrive today. Duty officer, make sure Ensign Kleegan reports to me as soon as he checks in.'"

"I love the way he always talks to the duty officer in third person," said Head. "Why can't he just use your name?"

"Beats me," said Spot. "Just part of his gnarly nature, I guess."

"So then what happened?"

"Well, he was on the flight schedule that morning, which I had planned, and as soon as he left I got some of the guys and briefed them on my plan. But what really worried me was Heart. The skipper is way too sharp to fall for something like a fake message."

"Yeah, no kidding," said Head. "Not much gets by that guy."

"So, Heart comes in, grabs a cup of coffee, gives me a load of crap just because he likes me, and sits down. He picks up the message board, and I sat there peeking at him, hoping that somehow he doesn't figure it all out."

"Taking a big chance there, bud."

"Yeah, I know," said Spot. "I can see by his eyes and his smile when he gets to the message. He reads it and immediately looks at me. I pretend not to see him, but he just stares at me. I can't take it anymore, so I look at him and he just smiles and says, 'Gee, Spot, looks like we are getting a new ensign. Make sure he reports to the XO.'"

"You have got to be kidding."

"No, I almost pissed in my pants. I mean he knew that I knew, that he knew, and that Prince didn't know. It was a truly magic moment."

"Wow," said Head. "Wow."

"So the rest was easy. We used the fake orders and got him checked into medical, dental, the BOQ. We ordered him some flight gear and had a ready room seat made with his name on it. The hard part was finding ways to keep him from never meeting Prince. I sent him on leave, manufactured orders for him to go to school, heck, I even sent him to school out in California."

"And you put his name on the backseat of CAG's bird."

"Yep, that we did," crowed Spot.

"Tell me how you got the letter writing going with Face's sister. I remember you reading all of them to us at your house, but how did you get it going?" Head leaned back some more in his chair to enjoy the story.

"Oh, that is the best part," chortled Spot. "I talked to Face and he got his sister to copy a letter I wrote and to send it to Prince from her hometown in Potosi, Missouri.

"Where's that?"

"Fuck, who knows," said Spot. "Somewhere in the middle, I guess."

"Do you have the letter?"

"Sure." Spot leaped up from his bunk and reached for his drawer. He rummaged around for a second and then produced a letter.

"Read it to me."

"Sure."

*Dear sir,*

*I hope I am not inconveniencing you by writing, but William has been so impressed with the squadron I felt I must thank you for Mother and me. We were a little worried about him joining a real, honest fighter squadron, but his reports are so positive we both feel much better. William says he hasn't met you, but he is convinced the positive attitude of the squadron is all your doing. He says he is able to assume this from the remarks of his fellow officers. Well, once again, thanks so much from William's family.*

*Love,*
*Cookie*

*P.S. William asked for a photo of me to include with Dad and Mom's. We don't have his address, so I hope you don't mind holding onto it until he returns from California.*

"Can you imagine what Prince did when he saw her photo?" Head chuckled and shook his head.

"You mean after he went to the shower and slapped old chubby?"

"Yeah." Head laughed. "After that."

"Well, we know that he wrote a letter back to Face's sister, and I have that here too." Spot produced another letter and began to read.

*My Dearest Cookie,*
*I am writing to acknowledge receipt of your most thoughtful letter and to pledge I will safeguard your photo until William gets back. Although I have yet to meet William, I feel very close to him, as if I have known him for a long time. Perhaps it is the warmth of so thoughtful and caring a family as yours that I feel. At any rate, please be assured I will look out for your brother. I would like to close by saying I can only hope when I assume the ultimate mantle of responsibility as the commanding officer of this fine fighter squadron that I will continue to elicit the loyalty and support of young patriots such as William and of families such as yours. You do your country proud.*
*Very sincerely,*
*Roy Saratoga*

"You replied to that one too, didn't you?"

"Yeah, here it is," said Spot.

*Dear Roy,*

*Thank you for your very nice letter. Mother and Father were most impressed. In fact, Daddy is going to write his congressman today about the caliber of navy leadership, particularly in Fighter Squadron 57! I feel so sure William is safe now. Thanks to you, sir knight! I wish I could somehow repay you for your kindness. I hope someday soon we can meet person to person so I can know a man who seems so strong but also can be so sensitive and caring.*

*Love,*

*Cookie*


"So, anyway, this letter thing really took off, as you know. All the JOs came over, and we had the reading of Prince's love story. The best part was when Prince arranged for the secret meeting in Kansas City. It was at that point when Just Ed agreed that I had indeed created life and gave me the ten bucks."

"Yeah, I was there for that." Head laughed.

"Of course you remember we had to somehow end all of this?"

"Yeah, I think it was when CAG was in the ready room, right?"

"Yeah, he was in the ready room and someone mentioned something about Weenie, and CAG said that he had not met him yet and so we knew we had to eventually break the story. I was really nervous about what the XO was going to do when he found out."

"I don't blame you," said Head.

"Heart took me off the hook by telling CAG that it was all just a big joke that the JOs had come up with to see how long they could fool everybody."

"I remember CAG thought it was funny as shit."

"Fortunately he did. He was a pretty wild JO back in his time and so he thought it was really funny. He congratulated Heart on having such an energetic ready room."

"I remember watching Prince," said Head. "He looked shocked. Then he looked embarrassed."

"Yeah, I saw him too," said Spot. "His face got redder and redder, and he sunk lower and lower in his seat."

"What a great story. Thanks for telling me how you dreamed it up."

"No problem," said Spot.

"So, want to go eat?"

"Sure, let's go."

# CHAPTER 10

**P**olice Station 1 in Olongapo was east of city hall and was the main center of enforcement activity in the city. It was a modest building and, like most everything else, it was composed of cinder blocks and concrete covered with white wash.

The chief of police in Olongapo was Lieutenant Ocotillo Sanchez, and on the morning Blue and Eve were having coffee, he was reading crime reports and reflecting upon his extremely poor luck. He had requested the posting to Olongapo five years earlier because it was a sleepy town with a reputation for good kickbacks from US Navy contracts. The visiting sailors were somewhat of a challenge but nothing that couldn't be handled. His first year was wonderful and had been everything he had wanted. A secure retirement with a lot of cash was clearly in his future. But the next year, in 1972, President Marcos had to change it all by declaring martial law. While this martial law had been directed toward Maoist-inspired members of the New People's Army, the downstream effects meant every substantial report went to overseers in Manila, and they seemed to have nothing better to do than criticize his ability to control things. To make it worse, President Marcos felt that he was a personal friend to the United States president, and so all crimes against Americans were presented to him in a special daily briefing. Much of that crime was directed toward American sailors, and after reading his third report of a stolen radio, he screamed at the sergeant to report to his office.

"Have you seen these reports?" Lieutenant Sanchez slapped the sheaf of papers on his desk and looked at Sergeant Ortega, who quivered at attention before him.

"No, sir." Perspiration rolled down the sergeant's fat face and stained the collar of his khaki shirt.

"Well, they are *atrocious!*" Lieutenant Sanchez screamed and attempted to stand. Unfortunately, his chair was pushed too far under his desk, so he only half-rose and then flopped back. It made him feel idiotic, which inflamed him even further.

Sergeant Ortega continued to stare at the wall behind the lieutenant's head.

"How long have you been on the police force?"

"Thirteen years, sir."

"Thirteen years!" Lieutenant Sanchez stood and walked around his desk, drawing next to the sweating Ortega. "You got this disgusting in only thirteen years? Or did you join looking like this? Look at you! You look like a fat old pig. Your uniform doesn't fit. It has stains all over it. What is that?"

Sanchez stopped and leaned forward until his face was next to Ortega's shirt. "Jesus! It's fried egg! God, you are a disgusting mess, and look at your boots! You look like you fed the goats in them!" He looked into Ortega's eyes. "You don't have goats, do you?"

"No, sir."

Lieutenant Sanchez flung his hands in the air and returned to his chair, sitting heavily.

Ortega shuddered under his cold, cruel glare and continued to sweat.

"I got this job because of my connections, and I want to keep it a long, long time." He leaned forward and pointed a finger at Ortega. "But I won't keep it if my chief assistant is a worthless old hog who spends all of his time eating fried egg sandwiches and lusting after peasant girl radio operators."

Sergeant Ortega's eyes widened at the mention of Felicia, and he dropped them to look at the lieutenant.

"Oh, yes." Lieutenant Sanchez nodded and smiled. He picked up a pencil and twirled it between his fingers. "I see the way you look at her and follow her around like some dog. I am sure you dream of one day coupling with her, yes?"

Ortega swallowed and stared at the wall.

"It's pathetic!" Sanchez looked at Sergeant Ortega and waited for him to establish eye contact. When the sergeant looked at him, he smiled evilly.

"What would you think if I told you I slept with the lovely radio operator?" Sanchez smiled again and watched with satisfaction as the despair fell across the sergeant's face. "Yes, right here in this office while you were out getting something to eat, no doubt."

Sergeant Ortega stared at the wall. "Look, Sergeant, quit dreaming and get yourself together. I am going to clean up this town and I am going to be the chief of police here for a long, long time." Sanchez's eyes brightened, and he smiled. "I'm going to be the best chief this town ever had."

Sergeant Ortega let his eyes fall to the lieutenant. He smiled warily and grunted, "Yes, sir."

Sanchez stood and straightened his uniform. He picked up the report from his desk and held it up to Ortega's face. "This makes me look like I can't control a small town in the middle of the jungle. This looks like I'm in over my head!" Sanchez paced across the floor, slapping the papers against his leg. He whirled upon Ortega.

"I know you think these crimes are petty. You think it is just kids' play when one of these street urchins steals a camera or picks an American sailor's pocket. But I'll tell you, Sergeant, screwing around with the Americans is a big no-no. President Marcos is furious about this! He considers it an insult to him and his hospitality!"

Sanchez leaned his head forward and to the side to stretch his neck and closed his eyes. He grunted and then looked at Ortega. "We need the Americans, Ortega. We need them, and we need their money. I am giving you one warning to get yourself and your men out on the street and stop this street crime. If you can't, I'll send your fat ass back to the jungle where it belongs! Now, get out!"

# CHAPTER 11

"**I** challenged some air force guys this morning."

"You did what?" Blue looked at Magic and frowned. The two men were sitting in the Cubi Officers' Club bar, drinking beer and catching up on their first full day of activities in Olongapo.

"I challenged a couple of air force majors to an air-combat training flight."

"You mean a dogfight?"

"You bet," said Magic. He winked and smiled. "Might as well kick some air force ass while we're here."

Blue straightened up on his stool. "What do you mean a couple of air force majors?"

"Well, there were two of 'em."

"Were they a crew, like us? A pilot and a RIO?"

"No. Actually, they were both pilots. I challenged them both." Magic laughed again and took a sip of beer. "Piece of cake."

"So it's two of their airplanes against us in one?"

"Yeah, I guess that's about right, two versus one. Like I said, piece of cake."

"I don't know," said Blue. "Air force guys are pretty good."

"Yeah, I suppose they are." Magic burped.

"So what's the bet?" Blue leaned forward.

"Gladys." Magic shrugged. Then he looked at Blue and grinned. "Gladys and two hundred dollars."

"Are you nuts?" Blue set his beer on the bar and looked at his friend in amazement.

"Hey," said Magic, "two of us against some blue bellies. What could go wrong?"

"Well," said Blue, "if we can kill one of them right off with a long-range sparrow shot, maybe we can work it down to a one versus one. Of course, we're going to have to convince them the sparrow was within parameters."

"I wouldn't worry too much about that," said Magic as he took a sip of beer.

"Why not? It might work."

"Actually, I said we would only use Sidewinders on them."

"That means we have to get right behind them! What do you think the chances of that are?" Blue sat his beer on the bar and frowned at Magic. "Gee, Magic! Do you really think we can get that close to two US Air Force Phantoms and shoot them both from behind without one of them shooting us first?"

"Well, actually, we can't shoot them both with Sidewinders either."

"What?"

"I told the flight lead we'd gun him."

"Holy shit!" exclaimed Blue as he slapped his head. "That means we have to get within a thousand feet of the guy."

Magic grinned. "Actually, I like to get at around seven hundred. You know, fill the windscreen. Can't miss that way."

"Man, you are crazy. What do you think his wingman's going to be doing all that time, reading the *Air Force Gazette*?"

"Look, kid, take it easy." Magic smiled and put his hand on Blue's shoulder. "These are a bunch of fucking air force dickheads. The wingman will probably have his nose so far up his lead's ass we can kill them both with one shot."

"Do you remember when we went to that exercise at Eglin before cruise?" Blue swiveled on his bar stool so he could look straight at Magic.

"Yeah, sure. So what?"

"Those air force dickheads, as you call them, had the best radars I've ever seen, that's what. They could see us from fifty miles away. Sneaking up on these guys is going to be a real bitch."

Magic smiled and took a sip of beer.

"What the fuck are you smiling about? The radar in 207 is dog shit! On our flight in here, I couldn't pick up any traffic more than twenty miles away."

"Kid, you worry too much and you have no faith. You're a great RIO. You can make that radar sing! We'll work something out. Besides, it's really quite simple. All you have to do is figure a way to get our airplane next to their two airplanes without them seeing us. I'll do the rest. Now come on and let's eat."

After dinner, Magic stirred about half a cup of sugar into his coffee. He liked it sweet. "So, what did you do today?"

"Well, I told you I went looking for the woodworking place to get the gun case?"

"Yeah, how did that go?"

"Great! I can have the case done in a week. It'll cost less than Heart thought. I'm going by tomorrow afternoon to pick out the stain and the felt liner. Want to come?"

"No, thanks, kid. I was just about to ask you to go with me to Hong Kong for a while. I got a line on a flight that won't cost us a dime. We could leave right after the fight tomorrow morning. Pick up the gun case later."

Blue shook his head. "No, I want to be sure this is taken care of. Besides, I told her I would come by."

"Her." Magic smiled. "Who's her?"

"She's the manager of the shop." Blue smiled. "And, man, is she something!"

"Oh, in what way?"

"I don't know." Blue shrugged. "She's just, you know, something."

"Well, is she a good-looking kind of something?"

"Oh, yeah." Blue grinned. "She is a knockout by any standards. But she's not just good-looking. She's, you know, something."

"Well, how much time did you spend with her?"

"Oh, about fifteen, twenty minutes."

"That's quite an impression, kid. Not bad for someone you met for only fifteen or twenty minutes." Magic knitted his brows slightly.

"Yeah, I guess you're right. She did make an impact. Hey, I also saw Eve!"

"Oh, really. Where?"

"At the market. They have a really neat one just off the main drag about halfway up the street."

"Oh, yeah, I remember. So what did Eve have to say?"

"We mostly talked about you."

"Me? You two must have been pretty bored."

"She told me how you met. She said you started bringing guys to the bar where she sang and practically filled the place. She said you got her started."

"That's a stretch." Magic laughed. "But, I tell you, I did fall in love with her voice, and after a couple of the guys heard her and spread the word, it took off."

"She told me about Solang too. I'm sorry."

"Nothing to be sorry about, kid. It happened a long time ago."

"I guess she must have been crazy about you."

"Yeah, I guess so."

"Did you meet her in the same bar?"

"Not exactly. I mean, I started hanging out at the bar and she was there, but the first place I actually saw her was in church."

"Oh, bullshit!"

"No, really. Father Pat, the Catholic priest on the ship, rounded a bunch of us up and convinced us to go and paint a church. You'll probably see the same thing happen this time when the ship gets here."

"I'm amazed anyone would volunteer their liberty time for something like that."

"You don't know American sailors very well."

Blue shrugged and looked at Magic.

"Anyway, about half of the squadron showed up at this little church. Eve was there, and she entertained us at lunch with some songs."

"You had already heard her, right?"

"Yeah, drunk and in a bar. Man, for her to have an even greater impact on me while I was totally sober truly blew my mind."

"Where does Solang fit in?"

"I was sitting there, listening to Eve, and this girl sat down next to me. I looked at her and said, 'Have you ever heard anyone sing like her before?' The girl looked at me and said, 'Sure, but she can't cook, her room's a mess, and she snores in her sleep.'"

Blue and Magic both laughed.

"I thought I would die. She wasn't giving her big sister any slack at all."

"So what happened?"

"Nothing much. She was just a kid, but I admit I was attracted to her. I found myself hanging around the Black Rose more and more. Then one day we pulled out and went home."

"Did you write?"

"Nah, but I did think about her. When I came back on the next cruise two years later, she was still hanging out with Eve. I started coming over to the Black Rose, because I knew she would be there. I'd just hang around, that sort of stuff. She was mad over me, of course." Magic grinned and lit a cigar.

"Eve said guys started calling you the mayor of Olongapo, since you were in town so much."

"Yeah." Magic laughed. "That's right."

"So, what was the deal? Did you want to get into her pants, or did you really give a shit about her?"

"Strange question from one guy to another, don't you think?" Magic looked at Blue quizzically.

Blue nodded and picked up a soda straw. "Yeah, I guess you're right."

"Where does your interest in Solang and me come from?"

Blue rolled the soda straw with his fingers and shrugged. "To be honest, I am not sure. I guess a part of it is I just can't picture you in the situation."

"What situation?"

"A situation where you are … you know … vulnerable. Just doesn't track for me."

"And the other part?"

"I don't know." Blue looked at Magic and shook his head. "I don't know, something about all of this. Eve, the song, the girl at the store—I don't know."

Magic looked down at the table and picked up a toothpick. He snapped it and looked back at Blue. "This place isn't real, Blue. Just remember that. It doesn't exist outside of the city limits." He took a puff of his cigar and stood up.

"Better get to bed early. We got to kick some air force ass tomorrow morning. I'll come by your room at 0700." Magic dropped some bills on the table and walked out.

# CHAPTER 12

The next morning when Magic stopped by Blue's room there was a note taped to the door, saying Blue would meet him at the flight line. Magic thought it a little strange but shrugged his shoulders and walked down to the Officers' Club for breakfast. He hated fighting on an empty stomach.

After a hearty breakfast of coffee, eggs, and bacon, he climbed into Gladys and rolled her down the hill. He popped the clutch, fired the engine, and drove to the flight line. "How we looking, Mac?" Magic walked into the maintenance shack and shook hands with Chief Petty Officer Ronald Mackenzie. Mac was leading the detachment of maintenance sailors who had flown into the Cubi Point airfield earlier.

"Fine, Mr. Sharentino." Mac took his cigarette from his mouth and smiled. "Mr. Morrison and I were just now talking about 207."

"How's the bird?"

"I think she'll fly." Mac grinned again.

"So, Blue boy, I missed you at breakfast."

"I couldn't sleep. I kept trying to think of some way to sneak up on those guys. I bet both of them have better radars than old 207 out there."

"I'm afraid he's right, Mr. Sharentino." Mac frowned and puffed on his cigarette. "You slam them radars down on a flight deck day after day and the darn things give out. I'm afraid 207's radar has about had it. It might be good for twenty miles, max."

"We're going to have to trick 'em," said Blue. "We'll never beat them head-to-head."

"Now you're talking, kid. What's your plan?"

"First of all, we come at them from around forty or fifty miles away. Let them have a chance to get a look at us on their radars." Blue took out a piece of paper and drew two triangles at one end of the paper and one triangle at the other.

"Then, after we look good and juicy, I'm gonna pop out some chaff." He paused and grinned at Magic.

Chaff is a bundle of metallic fibers cut at certain lengths to correspond to airborne radar operating frequencies. The fibers blossom upon release and appear as a large, inviting target on radar scopes.

"Chaff? Where did you get that?" Magic looked at Blue and then Mac.

"I told Mac our problem and, presto, he came up with it."

Mac smiled proudly and took a huge drag from his cigarette. "Stole it from the A-4 squadron next door."

"That's great!" Magic clapped him on the back. "Now, kid, what's the rest of the plan?"

"I don't know." Blue smiled. "That's as far as I got."

Before Blue finished his sentence, Magic pulled out a pencil and began figuring. After scribbling for a few seconds, he looked at Blue and Mac. A big smile covered his face.

"Okay, kid, you've got your work cut out for you. Success or failure is on your thin shoulders."

"How so?"

"We start out like you said but keep in mind the speeds at which we will be closing. We'll have less than three minutes from start to the merge with the blue bellies."

Blue continued to look at the paper and waited for Magic to continue.

"When we start, punch the clock and wait for twenty seconds. That'll give them time to find us with their good radars. Then, you pop the chaff and I'll dive for the deck. Hopefully, the air force weenies will hang on to the chaff and won't pick us up going low."

"What if they do?" asked Mac. This was navy against air force. He had a stake in it too.

"Why, then they'll swoop down and kick the living shit outta us." Magic grinned.

"Aren't you taking a big risk?" Mac frowned.

"Well, we could take a more conservative approach, I guess." Magic shrugged. "Something less risky."

"No," said Blue. "No, I think we're going to have to hang it out to beat two of 'em. I like the plan."

"Good." Magic smiled. "Remember, as we head down we'll be closing fast. At the ninety-second mark, we'll be about twenty miles away. I'll start the nose slightly back up and start flying to meet them. You have got to find them on radar by then."

Blue nodded. "They'll be high and drifting away from the side we went down. I'll really have to crank the thumb wheel to find them."

"Exactly, kid. You'll have to look up there and find them fast. If you don't, we'll be going into them blind. Hell, we could pop up right in front of them if we time it wrong."

"Hell, Lieutenant," growled Mac. "That'll be no problem for you."

Blue looked at Mac and back to the piece of paper. "Thanks, Mac. I hope you're right."

An hour later, Blue and Magic were sitting at the end of the runway, waiting for the air force Phantoms to roll out of their line. They had already done their engine run-ups and were ready to call for takeoff as soon as the "enemy" showed. No need to take off early and run out of gas.

"Navy, this is Sierra One." Magic and Blue were listening to a frequency reserved for the air force squadron. A lieutenant had called the maintenance shack and provided it before they had walked to their jet.

"Go, Sierra," replied Blue.

"Do all navy Phantoms leak like that, or did you plant that piece of shit into the back of the ship the last time you landed?"

Magic recognized Rusty's voice and keyed the mic. "Interesting comment for some pussy that needs ten thousand feet of runway to land on."

"I'm going to gun your fucking brains out," hissed Rusty.

"Temper, temper, temper." Magic laughed. There was no answer as the planes came rolling into view from around the edge of the hangar. Seconds later, Rusty's caustic voice again crackled over the air.

"I'm going to enjoy this, prick."

Magic laughed into the intercom. "Call for takeoff, kid."

Blue made the call, and seconds later they were cleared to go. Blue expected Magic to nurse the plane off the runway to save fuel. However, Magic stroked the afterburners and let the stick fall back into his lap as the nose broke the runway. As soon as the main wheels cleared, he raised the gear and pushed the nose down until the plane was only twenty feet above the concrete. Magic raised the flaps, and the Phantom accelerated to the end of the runway. As he crossed the numbers, Magic smoothly pulled the stick back and 207 shot into the sky.

"I thought you would have saved the gas," grunted Blue.

"Nah," said Magic. "This will either work right away or it won't work at all. Better to look good when you can. You never know if you'll get a second chance."

Blue busied himself, getting ready for the mock dogfight. He adjusted the background and gain settings to optimize the radar and set the switches so that both he and Magic could release precise amounts of the chaff bundles. He lowered his seat so he could turn easily to check their rear from surprise attack. He also navigated them to a point about seventy miles from Cubi.

While Blue was getting himself ready, Magic did the same. He tightened his straps to ensure he would not come out of his seat during negative "G" maneuvers and demanded that Blue read him the combat checklist. At each step, he told Blue where each switch was set, and Blue did the same. Once their checklists were complete, they entered an orbit and waited for the air force planes to call. They didn't have to wait long.

"Sierra One is on-station, ready to play." Rusty's voice leaped into their headsets.

"How we looking, kid?"

"Radar's ready, chaff's armed, I'm ready to go."

Magic keyed the mic. "Navy is inbound."

"Fight's on" was Rusty's answer.

Blue punched the clock as Magic added power and swung the big jet toward the intercept point. Magic selected the hot microphone position on his communications panel. This allowed Blue and him to talk without keying the mic for each transmission.

"How we looking, kid?"

"That's twenty seconds," replied Blue. "Popping chaff." He hit his toggle switch and popped two bundles.

"Starting down." Magic banked the Phantom to the right and pulled the nose below the horizon. He shoved the throttles forward, and the airspeed increased to five hundred knots. They quickly descended through fifteen, ten, five thousand feet before they leveled at five hundred feet above the water and almost six hundred knots.

"Come left ten degrees," said Blue. He was conducting a mental plot of where the air force planes should be while he concentrated on finding them on radar. "How we doing, kid?"

"Eighty-five seconds," said Blue. "Let's start up." Blue now forced himself to use disciplined radar scan techniques. He took a deep breath to help him find his patience. He knew the impulse would be to move the thumb wheel too fast if he saw no targets on the screen. But he also knew that if he did so, the antenna could not settle on a target. He knew it was a common mistake, and often targets within the capabilities of radar went undetected.

Magic lifted the nose and started up.

"Looking for smoke," he said.

"Roger," replied Blue. A Phantom's GE 79 engines smoked badly unless they were in afterburner. If the pilot left his engines in basic settings too long, he could give away his position. As they started up, Blue also noticed the sun was near what he anticipated the "enemy" position to be. He cursed himself for not foreseeing that. Getting sight would be hard.

As they climbed through ten thousand feet with no sign of the air force planes, Blue began to get a little worried. Although he wouldn't allow himself to think the unthinkable, he dreaded the prospect of winding up in the middle of the air force formation. He guessed they were around fifteen miles away.

"I've got 'em," barked Blue as he saw the twin blips pop onto his radar screen. "Come left fifteen degrees."

Magic immediately swung the nose to the left and started looking for the planes.

"Ten degrees left of the nose at twelve miles, slightly high," said Blue.

"Paint me a picture, kid."

"They're flying side by side in combat spread about one mile apart. Come left ten degrees and put 'em on the nose."

Magic banked the airplane hard to the left.

"On the nose," said Blue. "Eight miles, slightly high. They will be passing from right to left. We'll hit them from underneath the left side."

"Tallyho!" shouted Magic. "I got one right where you painted 'em, kid. Six miles on the nose."

"Look through him, Magic. The other guy's one mile farther away."

"Tally two!" Magic's voice sung over the intercom. "Got 'em both."

Magic and Blue were approaching the air force formation from their left beam and below their altitude. This made it very difficult for them to be seen visually. Plus, they were outside the scan volume of the radars.

"Ha-ha, you fuckers." Magic chuckled over the intercom. "Don't see us, do you? I tell you, kid, there's nothing better than kicking the shit out of a couple of blue bellies."

Blue watched as Magic let the two air force Phantoms drift a little to the left as they climbed up to their altitude. They slowly swung in an arc until their Phantom was behind both of the air force planes, less than a quarter of a mile away.

"I seeee youuuu," Magic's singsong voice boomed over the radio. "I know where you are."

"Heater." Magic selected the Sidewinder missile position on his stick. The seeker head on the dummy missile under the left wing immediately growled in the intercom, indicating the missile was sensing the heat from the air force exhaust.

"Oh, Rusty. I see you."

Magic and Blue laughed over the intercom as they watched the two jets in front of them rocking their wings in an obvious attempt to gain sight.

"Fox two, dead six on the right-hand jet. You're dead, get out." Magic's radio transmission meant he had fired a simulated missile from directly behind, right in the heart of its performance envelope. Rusty, in the lead plane, saw the navy Phantom and immediately broke hard to the left in an attempt to cause an overshoot. Magic had already reduced power and thumbed out his speed brakes. As Rusty banked harder to the left, Magic rendezvoused on the inside of his turn. He closed until the green camouflaged Phantom filled the windscreen. There was no doubt he was in gun range. However, instead of calling Rusty dead, Magic abruptly leveled his wings and called, "Knock it off," over the radio. "Hang on a second, Rusty," said Magic. "I have an emergency light in the cockpit."

"What's the problem?" asked Blue. "What's going on up there?" Blue checked all of his circuit breakers and lights. Everything appeared normal. "What's wrong?"

"Hang on, kid." Magic's voice was calm.

"What is the problem?"

"I've taken care of it, kid." Magic started turning the plane back toward Rusty. "Okay, Rusty, I've taken care of my problem. Let's say we start again? Just you and me, two miles abeam."

"I'd love to, pal." Rusty's voice hadn't lost any of its caustic tone, despite the fact he had already lost a wingman and would have been finished himself, if Magic hadn't knocked off the fight.

"There never was a problem, was there?" Blue asked.

"Nope."

"Then why didn't you kill him and finish it? We won fair and square against two of them. Now we stand the chance to lose."

"Hey, kid, you did a fantastic job, and I'll sport the two hundred if we lose. But that prick over there is probably blaming everyone else for what happened. I bet right now he's blaming his back seater for letting them get bushwhacked. I need to let him know, once and for all, he ain't as good as me. I'm going to give him an even start, and then I'm going to gun his fucking brains out."

"I'm ready." Rusty's voice interrupted their conversation. Blue and Magic looked out the left side of their jet and saw the green Phantom level with them, slightly over two miles away. "How we looking, kid?"

"Ready to go. But, Magic, this time let's finish it."

Magic keyed the radio. "Fight's on." He lit the afterburners and banked the plane hard to the left. Rusty was in a hard right turn, and in seconds, both jets passed head-on at over five hundred knots each. They passed left side to left side, each pilot turning hard to get behind the other. Blue felt the force of over six Gs as Magic pulled toward Rusty. Within seconds, each plane had turned 180 percent, and they were now heading for each other again. However, this time Rusty's plane seemed to have gained some leverage. As they passed, it wasn't quite head-on. Rusty's plane had a slight advantage.

"Four twenty-five, 8.2," Blue grunted over the intercom. His body weighed six times more than normal, and he strained to keep sight of the air force plane and monitor the fuel and altitude. His transmission told Magic their airspeed and there were 8,200 pounds of gas left. This allowed Magic to keep his eyes on Rusty.

"Super, we're on the corner." Blue knew that Magic was telling him they were flying at the optimum airspeed to get the best sustained turn rate out of their Phantom. But as they passed again, it was obvious that the air force jet was gaining the advantage.

"Holy shit, Magic, he's out-turning us. Crank it on. Crank it on." As Blue pleaded for Magic to harden their turn, he heard Magic's characteristic chuckle.

"Relax, kid. He's right where I want him."

Blue couldn't understand how that could be true, but he concentrated on keeping sight and passing airspeed and fuel information to Magic.

The fourth time the planes met, Rusty had a decisive advantage. In fact, instead of meeting anywhere near head-on, he was digging into their side.

"He's kicking our ass, man," screamed Blue. "Turn it on!"

Just as Rusty's Phantom passed behind them, Magic leveled his wings and smoothly pointed the nose to the sky.

Blue took a deep breath as the g-forces came off their jet and watched Rusty spit out to the right. "Oh, shit," he said as he watched Rusty start his nose up.

"He's bringing his nose around," said Blue. "He's coming up with us."

"Relax, kid," said Magic. "We got a 150-knot advantage over him. He's right where we want him."

They watched Rusty's Phantom slowly creep toward them.

"You're right, looks like he's slowin' down pretty quick." Blue could easily see the green Phantom below and off to their right.

"Keep watching him, kid. He's about had it."

"Looks like he is stalling." Blue watched the air force Phantom shudder and then flip nose low in a stall.

"Watch this, kid," said Magic. "I stomp a little left rudder, plant the stick in my right side, and presto."

Blue lost sight as their Phantom suddenly pitched to the left and tumbled nose down. But he immediately acquired the air force plane just below and to their left. He smiled, as he now understood Magic's story of how he had fought the MIG back in the sky over Vietnam. He was doing the same thing now!

Within seconds, they were less than one thousand feet behind the air force Phantom and closing.

As he gained airspeed, Rusty made a last-ditch effort to turn hard back into Magic to negate the threat and cause an overshoot, but Magic saddled up on the inside of the turn, put his gun sight on Rusty, and pulled the trigger.

"Tracking," he said over the radio.

Blue smiled. "Tracking" was a special word in the fighter business. It was a word that, to a non-aviator, might not sound especially deadly, overpowering, or dominant. But deadly, overpowering, and dominant was exactly what the word meant. In this instance, it meant that through superior aerial skills, Magic had flown his aircraft to a position whereby he could kill Rusty any time he wanted and there wasn't a thing Rusty could do about it. It was a very personal word.

"Tracking," Magic repeated.

"Tracking."

Magic and Blue tracked Rusty for a few moments longer. Then they pitched off and headed back toward Cubi.

Magic keyed his mic. "The car is mine."

# CHAPTER 13

"I don't care what Daddy said. You should have called, Jose."

"Lori, your father said you were lonely and bored here in Olongapo. He said he talked to you on the phone and that I should drive up and pay you a visit."

"He talked to me, Jose, but I didn't say I was lonely and bored."

Lori sat down in the chair behind her desk and motioned for Jose to take a seat. She had been working on store inventory when he had suddenly popped into the office. She knew exactly what was at the bottom of the visit as soon as she saw him. It bothered her that her father would be so sneaky as to send Jose all the way to Olongapo just to spy on her. He could be so childish sometimes.

However, it was typical of him and, despite his methods, Lori knew his heart was in the right place. Besides, she couldn't be angry with Jose, and he did look very handsome in his light business suit. She sighed and smiled at the young man who fidgeted with his tie in front of her.

"You sure don't seem happy to see me." Jose Manteo looked across the desk at Lori and frowned.

"Of course I'm happy to see you. You should call first, that's all."

"Your father implied that you were in favor of my visit."

"My father implies a lot if it is to his advantage." Lori felt a pang of sorrow for Jose, getting caught in one of her father's tricks. He was a favorite of her father's and was destined for a management position, but that also made him vulnerable to her father's scheming.

"So, how is work? Is Father keeping you busy?" She wanted to ease the mood.

"Very busy, thank you. Your father just placed me in control of a new portfolio division, and I am very excited about it. I think I will be able to make a lot of money for the company."

"Great, Jose, that is great news." Lori smiled and reached her hand across the table. Jose shook it and smiled back. Lori liked Jose and they had gone out a few times, but their dates had just been casual affairs. She regarded him as more of a friend than anything else, but she also knew he thought differently. When she had told him of her plan to spend another summer with her grandmother in Olongapo, she had seen the disappointment in his eyes.

"I'm sure Father has the highest confidence in you."

"Thank you." Jose smiled. He glanced around the room and looked out the window behind Lori's chair. "How have you been doing, Lori? Haven't you missed Manila? It's been a lot of fun this summer."

"Yes, I have missed all of you." Lori smiled. "But I have been busy."

"You don't have a boyfriend down here, do you?" Jose grinned nonchalantly.

"No. Rafael has visited once or twice."

"Rafael?" Rafael was another young banker in Mr. Santiago's employ. He was Jose's chief rival in the next generation of company leaders.

"Yes, Rafael. He visited with Grandmother and me."

"Oh," said Jose.

Lori could hear the disappointment in his voice but stifled her grin. Rafael had been another of her father's tricks.

"How are Grandmother and Raul? I hope they are doing well this summer."

"They are doing fine," said Lori. "I will tell them you were asking about them. Grandmother will be very pleased."

While Lori entertained Jose, Blue walked through the gate past the marine guards and toward the river. It was early afternoon, and he whistled as he strolled and recalled their morning victory over Rusty and his air force buddies. After he and Magic landed, they celebrated with Mac for a few moments and then jumped into Gladys and raced to the base exchange. There, Magic purchased a dozen white roses and sent them to Rusty's ready room. He addressed the card with a poem.

*Ode to Rusty*

*Gather around boys and hear the story*
*Of an air force pilot who sought some glory.*
*He figured to have his way with a navy man*
*But he sucks and got his ass kicked.*

Blue burst into laughter as he read the card. "Magic, this is terrible. Your ode sucks. It doesn't even rhyme."

"Maybe." Magic laughed. "Hey, it gets the point across."

"Well, it certainly does that."

Blue sniffed the river as he crossed the bridge. For some reason the smell wasn't as strong as he remembered. He squinted at the bright sunlight and shielded his eyes. There were no river princesses standing in their canoes. He guessed they were resting for the main show later. Henry was not in sight either, and Blue grinned as he thought of the little boy.

The town was quiet; Magic had told him to expect that. He said that Olongapo was a nightlife town and most folks saved their energy for when the sun went down. Blue did see knots of people gathered at storefronts, and he spotted an occasional sailor, peering into the windows of the small shops that lined the main street.

"Want T-shirt, Levi's jeans?" A small man spoke as Blue walked down the sidewalk. He didn't bother to answer.

Blue turned into the alley that led to the furniture shop and slowed his pace in order to check his reflection in a store window. Satisfied with what he saw, he peeled the wrapper from a piece of gum, threw it into his mouth, and continued down the alley.

"Hello?" The doorbell tinkled over Blue's head, and he glanced at it as he walked through the door.

"Oh, hello, Blue. I hoped you would stop by." Lori walked into the front room from her office, a smile lighting her beautiful face. Blue smiled too and then noticed she was not alone.

"Blue, this is my old friend, Jose. Jose popped down from Manila this afternoon. Jose, this is Jack Morrison. His friends call him Blue."

Both men nodded stiffly and shook hands.

"Should I come back?"

"Oh, no. Jose, would you excuse us? We have some business to do. We are making Blue a gun case."

"Of course," said Jose. He smiled at Lori and took her hand. "Call you later?"

"Yes," said Lori. "I'll be home tonight."

Jose nodded at Blue and walked out the door.

"It's no problem for me to leave and come back later. You can call your friend to come back in." Blue nodded toward the door, glad that Jose was leaving.

"Nonsense." Lori smiled as she held out her hand.

Blue smiled and took it, but much to his surprise he felt himself blush. The touch of her hand reminded him of how he felt the day before, when he had first touched it. He had not realized how good it made him feel, or he had suppressed the feeling. And now, a new feeling coursed through him, a feeling he could not describe. He felt a sense of great happiness, but also a tingle of alarm. He dropped her hand, coughed nervously, and swallowed his gum.

"Come." Lori didn't seem to notice his discomfort as she turned and led him to a workbench. "Here are some examples of stain." She pointed to a series of stained wooden blocks. Each was beautifully finished in a different hue that ranged from light blond to deep cherry-red to ebony.

Blue stood beside her and looked at the expert workmanship. He smelled her next to him, soap and gardenia, faint and wonderful. He handled each piece of wood and carefully examined it before laying it down on the bench. He wasn't really sure what he was looking for, but he did know he enjoyed standing next to her looking for whatever it was.

A wave of nervousness touched him, and it surprised him. He wiped his hands on his shorts and cleared his throat. He remembered standing next to Julie Wilson during the junior high school graduation party. He had a huge crush on Julie, but he had been so nervous he ran to the bathroom without even asking her to dance.

"So, what do you think?" Lori looked at Blue and smiled.

"I guess this one ought to do." Blue shook off his memories and picked up a blond block.

"Yes, that is a pretty shade." Lori took the block and turned it over in her hands. "But, I'm not sure if it would be the best."

"Oh, why do you say that?" Blue was a little surprised she had not just accepted his choice. Once again, he didn't see much reason to make a fuss over the color of a gun case.

"You probably want to put some type of plaque on the case, don't you?" Lori held the piece in her hands and looked at Blue. "I imagine you want some brass that has the admiral's name or something?"

"Yeah, I guess so."

"Good." Lori smiled and reached into a drawer, pulling out a small rectangle of brass. "See how the brass seems to disappear into the light wood?" Lori held the brass plate against the blond block. "It looks nice but not quite bold enough. Now look at this." She took two of the darker blocks from the collection and laid them next to the blond block. The new blocks were stained a medium walnut, one slightly darker than the other. "Notice how the brass stands out? The overall effect is much more dramatic, don't you think?"

"Yeah, I see what you mean. The darker shades do look much better." Blue had to admit the effect of the combination was much richer. "Let me change my mind to that one." He pointed to the darker block.

"Excellent choice." Lori grinned.

Blue smiled, surprised at how much he enjoyed her praise.

"Now for the interior color." Lori took Blue's hand and led him to a table covered with colored pieces of velvet.

Blue looked at the swaths of cloth and started to pick one up when he realized he was still holding her hand. "Oops." He grinned. "Sorry." He slowly released his grip. She looked up at him, and he smiled. They both looked back down at the table, and Blue cleared his throat again.

*What is wrong with me?*

"I think the red would really look good against the walnut stain." Blue picked up a piece of red velvet.

"I agree. It would look very rich against the walnut." Lori held the walnut-stained wood against the rectangle of bright red velvet. "However, have you noticed anything special about the gun? Do you know what it looks like?"

"No. It's just a gun, I guess." Blue frowned slightly and looked at the red velvet again.

"Well, I found a color photo of your centennial Winchester in a magazine, and I have it right here." She walked into her office and seconds later returned with an opened magazine.

"See the finish of the stock?" Lori pointed to the picture of the gun. It was a beautiful piece of workmanship with intricate metal inlays. The wooden stock was a beautiful shade of purplish-red.

Blue looked at the magazine and nodded.

"Don't you think blue would enhance the color of the stock better than the red?" Lori held a piece of blue velvet against the magazine. Although it was only a photo and not the real thing, it was obvious the blue was the best choice. Blue looked at the magazine and smiled.

"Looks like you did it again. I'm sure glad I didn't have to do this myself."

Lori looked at Blue, and a smile slowly crossed her upturned face. "I'm glad you didn't have to do it by yourself too." They held each other's gaze for a second, and then Lori turned and headed into her office.

"How about a Coke?"

"Sure, thanks." He watched her walk through the door and open up a small refrigerator.

*What ... is ... wrong ... with ... me?*

"Here you go."

"Thanks." Blue accepted the cold bottle and took a sip. The carbonation felt good as it burned and tickled his throat.

*Why am I feeling like such a—*

"Come and have a seat." Lori motioned toward a rattan couch next to her office door.

"Sure, thanks." Blue followed her and took a seat on a cloth-covered cushion. A voice inside him urged him to get up off the couch and go back to the base. After all, there was no future in sitting there, chatting with a young Filipino girl, no matter how beautiful she was.

*Like Magic said, this place doesn't exist. She doesn't exist.*

But another voice whispered, urging him to stay.

Lori sat down beside him, smiled, and took a drink. They both took another sip and then another. Blue finally cleared his throat and glanced at her.

"Lori, when I was growing up, my parents had a couch like this."

"Oh, really?" Lori smiled quickly.

"Yeah, I liked it because I could play with the cat through the spaces." He grinned at her and stuck his fingers through the latticework on the side of the couch.

"Ouch!" he screamed.

Lori jumped to her feet, her eyes wide in shock.

"Damn cat." Blue laughed as he sucked on his finger. He smiled at Lori. "Got you."

"Oh, you." Lori gave him a swat on the shoulder.

"So how many of us do you know?"

"Americans?"

"Uh-huh." Blue sat his bottle down on the floor. He leaned back and looked at Lori.

"Well, let's see." She knotted her brows in thought and then looked at Blue. "I knew a couple of Americans that went to college in Manila with me. That's about it though. I don't know them well, just to say hi."

"So what do you think about us?"

"Oh, you're okay, I guess." She giggled and gave his shoulder a playful shove.

"Gee, thanks." Blue laughed and rolled his eyes. "I am glad we had such an impact."

"Americans are generally regarded positively." Lori nodded her head slowly. "Unless, of course, they do something to prove otherwise."

"Fair enough." Blue nodded in agreement.

"Why do you ask?"

"Oh, I don't know," said Blue. "I guess we just want to know what people think of us. In every port we visited I got around to asking the locals how they liked us."

"And what is the verdict?" Lori smiled and tilted her head to the side.

"Oh, we're okay, I guess." Blue laughed and gave Lori a playful shove on the shoulder.

Lori leaned her head back and laughed. "Good," she said.

"How about your parents, your grandmother? What do they think? This place has a lot of our sailors coming through. We don't always act the best."

"Oh, the sailors are not really a problem. They are young, they have money. Most of them seem to respect us."

"That's good." Blue reached down and picked up his drink. He took a sip. *Where am I going with this?*

"My father, on the other hand, has fairly strong feelings."

"Oh, how so?"

"Have you studied much of our history? The history between our two countries?"

"No, not really. I mean, we got a little bit on the ship."

"Well, it wasn't always friendly. Some bad things happened and, anyway, my father has memories and thoughts about that."

"I see. What would he say if he saw me sitting here with you now?"

Lori looked at him, her smile fading into the Coke she sipped. She frowned and gave her head a little shake. "I don't know."

Blue looked at her, nodded, tipped his Coke to his lips, and finished it. He sat the bottle back on the floor and stood up. "Well, I guess I better let you go home." Lori stood with him. "Jose will be calling."

"Yes," she said. "He will call." She took his hand and gripped it tight. "Come, let me walk you out."

He let her lead him across the floor to the front door, and for the second time that day he glanced at the bell as it jingled over his head.

"So." Blue looked at Lori and swallowed. He was surprised at how much he wanted to read her thoughts, to know what she thought about him.

"I ..." He cleared his throat.

"Yes?"

"I wonder, would you like to go somewhere tomorrow? It's Wednesday and the window says you will be closed." Blue nodded to the store hours placard, painted on the glass.

"I'm sorry but I have plans." Lori smiled.

"Oh," said Blue. His smile felt tight and false. He hoped he didn't appear as disappointed as he felt. "Plans with Jose?"

"No." Lori smiled and looked up at him. "I volunteer every Wednesday at the orphanage."

"Oh." Blue felt much better. Jose had looked pretty sharp in his suit. "Well, I guess I'll be going. I'll check by in a couple of days to see how the case is doing." Blue paused a moment, again wishing he knew what she was thinking. He smiled at her and then turned and walked out the door. He walked a few steps, turned, and reentered the shop. "What if I come and help you?"

"Help me? You mean work at the orphanage?"

Blue smiled at the surprise in her eyes. "Sure, why not?" He moved across the floor until he was next to her. "What's the deal on this orphanage anyway?"

"Well, it is called Blackjack, and it was built by a wealthy Manila financier for his wife. Here, have a seat again." Lori motioned to the couch, and they both sat down.

"Blackjack is a strange name for an orphanage, isn't it?"

"It didn't start out to be an orphanage. It was a mansion and a place for all the wealthy people from Manila to come to and gamble. The owner named it Blackjack after his favorite game of chance."

"Oh, sort of like Las Vegas in the States."

"Yes." Lori laughed and touched his arm. "Except with a jungle instead of a desert."

Blue laughed too. He was enjoying the story; he was enjoying her telling it.

"So, rumor has it that in the 1950s there was a house fire that didn't do much damage, but it did lead to the death of the owner and his wife."

"How so?" Blue settled against the rattan couch.

"The story goes that visiting houseguests and the couple all ran out of the house and stood on the front lawn waiting for the fire engine. Then they heard the sounds of a child screaming and so the financier's wife ran back inside. Her husband ran after her, and both were killed."

"Was it their child?"

"No, that's the strange part. They didn't have any children, no children were visiting the house at the time, and no child's body was ever recovered."

"Wow, that is weird."

"Now, I am not sure how much of this is true and how much has been made up." Lori shrugged and smiled at Blue. "A child's death that leads to the creation of an orphanage is a bit … contrived."

"Yeah, it sounds like something out of Hollywood." Blue laughed and reached for her hand. Lori laughed and held it out to him. He intertwined his fingers in hers and smiled. "So how did it actually become an orphanage?"

"Well, the strangeness continues," said Lori. "It seems that the couple had willed the estate to the town of Olongapo for the express purpose of using it as an orphanage. They both had been born poor, so they wanted to pay it back."

"Well, that's convenient."

"Sure is," said Lori. "But I am not sure how much of all of this is true. What is true is that a local church group took over the estate and turned it into an orphanage for children of this region. There is enough death here from disease and typhoons to generate a fairly large population of needy children."

"I see," said Blue. "Sounds like a success story for sure."

"It was for about fifteen years, until the group ran out of the dead couple's money."

Blue felt Lori squeeze his hand. He felt wonderful, sitting in the shop, listening to her talk.

"They didn't have a clue about what to do. And then help came from the strangest place."

"Another rich couple from Manila?"

"Hardly." Lori tossed her dark hair, grinned, and looked at Blue. "There is a lady in town who is very rich. In fact, she is very rich because of the services she provides to American sailors."

Blue felt the smile drain from his face. He squeezed Lori's hand.

"Her name is Evelyn and she runs a house of prostitution up the hill overlooking the city."

Blue felt his throat tighten. "Really?"

"Really," said Lori. She smiled and squeezed his hand again. "So, you see, your friends do good things without even knowing it."

Lori laughed, and so did Blue—at least he attempted to. *Jesus, I hope she never finds out about the other night.*

"Evelyn put her management staff on the job and within a year had the place out of real trouble."

Blue was relieved that Lori had not noticed his discomfort. His smile crept back onto his face as she continued.

"She took the land around the mansion and turned it into vegetable gardens and brought in chickens and pigs and so forth. Two years later, Blackjack was able to produce enough pork, poultry, and vegetables to sustain itself."

"That amazes me," said Blue. "I mean, a woman who owns a whore ... a house of prostitution would have a hard time getting public support for anything back in the States."

Lori smiled and nodded. "It is much the same here. But sometimes you accept what you must."

Blue nodded his head. He understood what she was saying. He was grateful for his conversations with Magic.

"So the people of Olongapo are proud of what Blackjack has become, and we demonstrate that pride in many ways."

"And one of those ways is to work there occasionally." Blue stood and pulled Lori up with him.

"Yes." Lori smiled as she stood, and they slowly unclasped their hands.

"What kind of work do you do?" Blue began to walk toward the door.

"The work is seasonal," said Lori. "Everything from tending vegetables to butchering chickens and pigs. You'll see."

"Sounds like ... fun." Blue laughed and found himself reaching for her hand again. He was glad when she held hers out to him.

"Are you sure? It'll probably be dirty work."

"I have stuff to wear."

"Great." Lori grinned up at him. "Meet me at the orphanage at nine. Do you know where it is?"

"Sure," said Blue. "Magic pointed it out."

"Okay, I'll see you then." He once again released her hand and smiled at her. He couldn't believe how she made him feel. However, behind the smile he offered her, there was a tiny sliver of … something. Was it doubt? *What am I doing?* flashed through his mind, but he quickly shoved it away.

Blue turned and walked out the door and up the alley toward the main street that led to the river.

As he walked, he worried. What kept nagging at him was the question of his motives. Just what was he looking for, and what were these odd feelings? In the past, when a girl had smote him as quickly as this, it had always been purely physical, and it was quickly over. This seemed so different. She wasn't like any other girl he had met. He hadn't ever felt like this.

Blue was deep in thought as he negotiated the crowds of merry revelers, and he didn't hear the blare of the loudspeakers or notice the lures of the barkers. He didn't even notice Henry's wave as he crossed the river.

When Blue walked into his BOQ room, he noticed a note on the floor. Someone had evidently slid it under the door. Ripping it open, he saw it was from Magic.

*Hey, kid,*

*Came by one more time to see if you wanted to go with me to Hong Kong, but I guess you're with the girl you met at the wood place. Too bad you'll miss the experience 'cause the ship ain't stopping there on the way home. Chance of a lifetime, buddy. I also wanted to congratulate you for a great job today with the air force pukes. Nothing is better than winning. Nothing. In fact, I just drove by Rusty on the way over here. He was*

*walking. Did I detect a limp? Ha-ha. Must be from all the lead
we drilled into his ass. Well, see you in a couple of days.
Magic*

*P.S. Be careful, kid. The jungle is a dangerous place.*

Blue frowned and wondered what Magic meant by the dangerous
jungle bit. However, then he yawned and shrugged. Magic was
always spouting some kind of philosophical gem. He tossed the note
into the trash can and changed for dinner.

# CHAPTER 14

"Doc, I'm fucked up, man." Just Ed forced himself to look at his instruments. His instincts told him he was in a nose low, right-hand turn, but his gyro and airspeed indicator said he was flying straight and level at 1,200 feet. Panic started to nip at him, and his chest tightened.

"You got vertigo, man. You're straight and level. You're okay, got it?" Doc Rogers leaned forward in his ejection seat and tried to see Just Ed in the front cockpit. It was dark as pitch outside, and all he could see was Just Ed's helmet and oxygen mask in the glow of the instrument lights.

"Okay, Doc, that's what I'm reading too." Just Ed breathed a bit easier. "Man, I still feel like I'm in a descending turn."

"Nope, don't believe it. Your instruments are telling you the truth."

Just Ed shut his eyes for a second. He hoped it would help him re-cage his brain. He blinked them back open but still felt disoriented. The vertigo really spooked him, and he didn't trust what his instincts were telling him.

"Ten miles, Ed. Let's drop the gear and flaps." Doc's voice was strong and confident.

"Roger," replied Just Ed. He reached over with his right hand, slapped the gear handle, and lowered the flaps to the landing position. He nudged his trim button as the landing gear and flaps lowered into the airstream. "Everything's in the green, looking good."

"Roger," replied Doc. "How you doin'?"

"Still goosy, Doc." Just Ed adjusted his trim a little to take out the pressure of the flaps being down.

"You're a straight and level goose."

"War Chief, 205, say your needles."

"On and on," replied Just Ed.

War Chief was the *Constellation's* radio call sign, and the final air controller was asking if he was receiving guidance commands from the carrier's Automatic Carrier Landing Control System, or ACLS. "On and on" meant that Just Ed was flying on centerline and on glide slope.

"See," crowed Doc. "You're lookin' good."

Just Ed didn't answer. He concentrated all of his energy on flying the needles and keeping them centered. Out of his periphery he saw the green speed chevrons that indicated he was on speed. He continued to fly his instruments as he closed with the carrier. The jet felt solid, and he started to feel better. Then, as suddenly as the vertigo had come, it vanished.

"I'm good, Doc," said Just Ed. He concentrated on the needles and the airspeed.

"All right," replied the RIO. "You're lookin' good."

"Three-quarters of a mile, 205, call the ball."

"Phantom ball 5.2, 205," replied Doc. At three-quarters of a mile, the aircraft transitioned from an instrument approach to a visual one using the Fresnel optical lens. Just Ed's task was to keep the orange-colored "meatball" centered against green lights to maintain glide slope.

"Roger, ball," replied Rocky Phillips. Rocky was the landing signals officer standing by the lens. He was a highly trained aviator, and his keen eye could see aircraft deviations quicker than a pilot in the plane could. Rocky could also feel the deck movement, something the pilot couldn't.

Just Ed concentrated even harder to keep the ball centered.

"You're going low," said Rocky.

Just Ed was breathing hard, focusing as hard as he could. He pushed the throttle a bit forward.

"On speed," cooed Doc from the back.

"Little low," said Rocky.

*Shit.* Just Ed pushed the throttle up some more.

"Little right for line up," said Rocky. He detected Just Ed drifting to the left.

*Shit. I am a little off.* Just Ed moved the stick to the right and added more throttle.

"Easy with the power," said Rocky.

"On speed," said Doc.

"You're going high," said Rocky

Just Ed eased the throttle a touch and focused on the meatball. Just as the jet touched the deck, the meatball flicked off the top of the lens. He added full power, and when he did not feel the familiar tug of the tail hook against the arresting wire, he knew he had missed all four of them and boltered.

"Bolter, bolter, bolter," said Rocky as he watched Just Ed and Doc touch down beyond the wires and take back off into the darkness.

"Dammit," shouted Just Ed. "Dammit."

"No big deal, Ed," said Doc.

They continued straight ahead and flew to 1,200 feet and then, at the direction of the controller, turned left to give it another try.

"How do you read, 205?"

"Two-oh-five has you loud and clear." Just Ed took a deep breath and made himself settle down. His last attempt to land was rough.

"Okay, Just Ed, this is Rocky." "Your last pass was solid, Ed, until right at the ramp. You looked like you got behind the airplane a little. Then you added too much power, and that put you over the wires, causing the bolter."

"Got it," said Just Ed.

"I want you to settle down," said Rocky. "You are getting a good start out there, but you got to keep that scan going. Now, fly a good airplane. On speed, on glide slope, on centerline all the way to touchdown. Okay?"

"Okay."

"Four point eight, 205 is four point eight." Doc made the radio call so everyone could hear. Since the Phantom used one thousand pounds of gas per landing attempt, they had enough to try again.

Just Ed was glad he had Doc with him in the backseat. Although he knew it was up to him to fly the jet, it helped to have an old hand looking over his shoulder. Doc had made two combat cruises to Vietnam, and this was his third deployment.

"How you doing up there, pal?" Doc spoke over the intercom. "How's the vertigo? You caged okay?"

"Yeah, I got my head upright."

They flew the pattern and soon intercepted the final bearing line. Once again, Just Ed flew centered needles until three-quarters of a mile.

"You're on glide slope, 205, on centerline, call the ball."

"Phantom ball, 205, 3.9."

"Roger, ball," replied Rocky.

Just Ed was sweating as he concentrated upon his instruments, the meatball, and the centerline lights.

*Looks good. Slightly high, just where I want it. Good. Airspeed looks good. Back to lineup. Looks good.*

"Little power," said Rocky

*Oops, he's right, the ball is starting to sag a little. Squeak on a little power. Good. Lineup looks good.*

"On speed," said Doc.

*Lookin' good, we got this one nailed. Little right, little power.*

Suddenly the red lights on either side of the meatball started to flash.

"Wave off, wave off," shouted Rocky.

*God dammit, I had that one in the bag.* Just Ed immediately pushed the throttles forward. He maintained his nose attitude, passed low over the landing area, and climbed up into the pattern again.

"Something blew out into the landing area, Ed," said Rocky. "Too bad, you had a real nice pass going there."

"Roger," replied Doc. "Fuel's 3.5."

"Three point five, damn," said Heart. He and CAG were sitting in the Carrier Air Traffic Control Center, watching and listening to the evolution unfold. All the squadrons had representatives there, and they could see the aircraft approach on cameras that viewed the stern and the landing area. They could also hear the radio transmissions. Squadron reps provided specific aircraft information when required.

"He's been pretty solid, hasn't he, Skipper?" asked CAG.

"Yes, sir," said Heart. "Just Ed's been one of my best first-cruise pilots."

"What kind of fuel is he gonna have on the ball next time?"

"Somewhere around 2.5, CAG."

"How far is it to Singapore?"

"It's over two hundred miles," replied Heart. "His fuel is too low to get him there."

"Okay," said CAG. "Let's tank him before we bring him back around."

Moments later, the ship's controllers directed 205 out of the traffic pattern and toward a specially designed A-6 aircraft. The A-6 had a steel basket and flexible hose fixture that the pilot reeled out from a fuel tank. Aircraft needing fuel could extend their own in-flight refueling probe, place it into the basket, and suck in the precious liquid.

"A little right, Ed. That's it ... little more ... little more."

Just Ed and Doc were snuggled up behind the A-6 tanker over the carrier. Doc's job was to look out the front right quarter panel and fine-tune Just Ed's attempts to tank. This allowed Just Ed to concentrate on flying in good formation as Doc talked him into the basket.

"Little up now. Good, keep it coming, keep it coming, keep it coming ... you're in!"

Just Ed took a quick breath and concentrated on keeping his jet from falling out of the basket.

"We're not receiving." Doc keyed the radio. Although Just Ed had a solid connection in the basket, for some reason, no fuel was flowing.

"Okay, 205," responded the tanker pilot. "Back out and I'll recycle the package."

Just Ed reduced power slightly, backed out of the basket, and maneuvered to the left side of the tanker. He and Doc observed the pilot reel in the hose and then deployed it once again. After receiving an okay from the pilot, Just Ed once again positioned his Phantom behind the A-6.

"How are you doing up there, 205?" Heart gripped the phone and frowned in the semi-dark room.

"Well, Skipper, we're down to 2.6, but we got a little problem with the tanker. We're going in for a second shot now." Doc's voice was surprisingly calm.

"Okay, give it one more shot. If you can't get the fuel to transfer right away, give us a call down here."

"Roger that, Skipper."

"It's not coming, Doc. I can't get it to flow." Just Ed gritted his teeth in frustration.

"Okay, Ed, go ahead and back out," said Doc. "Skipper, we're backing out. It's not working."

"Shit!" exclaimed Heart. He gripped the phone harder. "Okay, boys, what's your fuel?"

"Two point four."

"Okay, stand by for a second." Heart nodded to CAG. I recommend we put 'em in the barricade."

CAG sighed and shook his head. "God dammit! That's a hell of a risk."

"I know, sir, but by the time he gets here he'll only have around 1.8. That's only enough gas, for sure, to make one more pass. I would rather try to take him into a controlled barricade instead of having him suddenly flame out close to the water."

CAG looked at Heart and slowly nodded. "Okay, give me the captain and the admiral." Moments later, apprised of the situation and Heart's reasoning, the admiral and captain of the ship agreed.

"You up, 205?"

"Yes, Skipper, we read."

"Okay, boys, we're going to put you into the barricade. I want you to switch to final control on button seventeen."

"Yes, sir," replied Doc. "Switching to seventeen."

"Son of a bitch," growled CAG. "I was hoping we could get him to Singapore."

"I've never seen a night barricade," said Heart. "I've heard of guys doing it." CAG nodded. "But I've never seen it done."

"Control, 205, come to a heading of 030 and take angels two." The controller's voice boomed into the room, but both Heart and CAG were already running toward the tower.

"Rig the barricade! Rig the barricade! This is no drill. We have a low-state Phantom overhead. Get to it, men!" The air boss's order squawked over the flight deck loudspeakers, propelling the crew into action. The crew raced to a hatch on the side of the landing area and grabbed a large nylon cord that was splayed for easy retrieval. Petty officers lined the men up and directed their movements as they began dragging a heavy nylon net across the deck. The crew had practiced this event repeatedly during their training and all during the cruise. They knew that every second was critical and an aircraft out there was in a desperate situation. Within two minutes, twenty-foot-tall steel stanchions on either side of the landing area were slowly raised, spreading the nylon webbing across the deck.

They were ready.

"Okay, Just Ed, how you feeling?" Rocky's cheerful voice hid the seriousness of the developing situation. A day barricade landing was a true emergency; a night attempt was frightening!

"I'm okay, what's the plan?"

"Just fly a good pass, Just Ed. Give it all you got," said Doc. "If we make it, we make it. If we can't, we jump out. There's nowhere else to go."

"Roger." Just Ed breathed deeply to calm his nerves. He had always dreaded that this kind of night would happen—when everything went wrong. They called it "your night in the barrel," and it was turning out to be a barrel of crap.

"How do you hear, 205?" Rocky's familiar voice filled the cockpit.

"Loud and clear," replied Just Ed.

"Okay, Just Ed, fly a pass like the last one and we'll end this thing easy, okay?"

"You bet," said Just Ed. *Easy for you to say!*

"Good, you have to really keep that scan going and get her down here on centerline and on glide slope."

"Roger," said Just Ed. He knew he had to stay disciplined. Since he had virtually no depth perception at night, he knew he'd have a tendency to stare at the meatball and neglect his lineup and airspeed.

"Once we get you in close, you can't wave off. If you do, your hook will probably snag the top of the barricade and you'll come down like a safe."

"Yes, sir." Just Ed took another deep breath and fought off the rising panic. He had never felt like this before in an airplane. He had never been afraid before.

"Once you're at the ramp, the ball is gonna disappear on you. It's normal because of the barricade stanchion. When you lose the ball, just call CLARA, okay?"

"Yes, sir." CLARA was a term navy pilots used to indicate they couldn't see the meatball.

"When it happens, don't worry about it. Just get the jet into position, listen to me, and fly her all the way to touchdown. Okay?"

"Okay."

"Okay, Ed. Piece of cake."

"Roger, Rocky, piece of cake," replied Just Ed. He swallowed hard and took in another lungful of air. He had to stay calm and focused.

The ship steadied on course, and the captain ensured that the wind was coming directly down the angled flight deck. He didn't want Just Ed to have to fight any unnecessary drift. The air boss lowered the lights to reduce glare, and the crash crew stood ready. Medical personnel were waiting inside the flight deck locker, and all unnecessary personnel had been chased off the deck. Impending emergencies had a way of bringing out a crowd, all toting cameras, and the boss didn't want anybody taking a blinding flash as Just Ed and Doc were coming aboard. Those who remained could see the lights of the approaching Phantom and could hear the fluttering of the nylon as the wind sung through the net.

"Three-quarters of a mile, 205. Call the ball."

"Phantom ball, 205, 1.7." Doc's voice exuded calm and confidence.

"Got you, Ed, looking good." Rocky sounded cool as a cucumber.

Of course, Just Ed was shitting bricks. His mind was working overtime as he concentrated on his scan.

*Meatball, looks good, got a little crown, good. Lineup, good. Airspeed, good. Meatball, good. How's lineup? Looks good. Airspeed's still okay. Meatball, oops. Starting to sag. Little power to stop it. Lineup.*

"A little left for lineup," demanded Rocky.

*He's right. Shit.* Just Ed moved the stick ever so slightly.

"Little power," demanded Rocky.

"Shit, shit," said Just Ed as he squeezed a touch of throttle.

*Meatball? Looks okay now. Lineup, good. Airspeed's okay, meatball's okay.*

"Easy with it." Rocky didn't want Just Ed to go high. Although the jet was approaching the ramp, there was still a lot of flying to do.

*Meatball, looks good. Lineup, good. Airspeed, good. Meatball, good. Lineup, good. Meatball's going high. Shit! Take off a little power. Lineup, shit! Drifting left, come back a little right. Shit, lost the ball!*

"CLARA!" yelled Just Ed.

"Just a little power," replied Rocky. His voice was level and confident. He heard the Phantom's engines scream as Just Ed added power, and the instant he saw the airplane rise, he keyed the mic again.

"Hold what you got. Don't go high!"

As the Phantom neared the deck, Just Ed fought the urge to wave off. He was hurtling into a pitch-black tunnel with no idea what his position on glide slope was. He held the stick steady and gritted his teeth.

The Phantom screamed into the deck, and an instant later the huge main gear touched down, spewing puffs of burned rubber in their wake. The arresting gear glowed in a shower of sparks as it etched across the deck. The nose fell over, and Just Ed saw the nylon webbing whip into the canopy.

Doc grabbed the ejection handle and waited. If they slipped the net, he was getting them out. However, as the airplane met the nylon barrier and the hook engaged the arresting gear cable, the jet stopped. It had worked like a charm.

"Just a second, Master Chief." Heart held the phone away from his mouth and glanced at the door.

"Come in." He turned back to the phone, but not before he saw Just Ed enter the room.

"Go ahead, Master Chief."

"We checked her out pretty good, Skipper. The leading edges of the flaps are torn up, and the right gear door needs replacement, but, other than that, she's a flyer. We were real lucky."

"That's no lie." Heart smiled. "How are the engines?"

"The boys inspected the engine ducts, and both motors are okay. No damage. Hell, I think we can fly her in a couple of days!"

"Super, Master Chief. Thanks."

"See you tomorrow, sir."

Heart replaced the phone on its receiver and turned to Just Ed. He smiled and motioned for him to sit.

"Enough excitement for one night?"

"Yes, sir." Just Ed attempted to smile but didn't make it. "Sorry I screwed up, Skipper."

"You didn't screw up. You just had your night in the barrel."

"Yeah, but I boltered and almost lost the airplane."

"Ed, there were fifteen planes on the same recovery. Four of you boltered, including the skipper of an A-7 squadron, and he's one of the best drivers in the wing. It happens."

Just Ed took a deep breath and sighed. He looked down at his boots.

"Look, Ed, everyone knows the idea is to get aboard the first time. No one wants to keep the ship into the wind any longer than necessary. But this is a tough business and you boltered. But the important thing is you didn't fall apart on us. You didn't wimp out after you got the foul deck wave-off. You didn't wimp out when the tanker went sour. You sucked it up and did what you had to do."

"Skipper, there were a few minutes when I wasn't sure I could do it, when I couldn't get gas." Just Ed squirmed in his chair and avoided looking at Heart.

"It scared me," whispered Just Ed. His voice shook slightly. "I mean, I've never, ever doubted myself about anything. I never thought I ever would." He looked at Heart, his face a mask of anguish and confusion.

"And you don't ever want that to happen again?"

Just Ed nodded his head and once again looked at his boots.

"Look at me, son." Just Ed raised his head and looked at his skipper.

"I can't guarantee you'll never be in a position like this again, or something even worse. In fact, if you stay in this business long enough, chances are it might happen. But, Ed, that's the difference between a warrior and some guy who flies around in a warplane. A warrior knows the demons that await him. He knows what they look like and he flies anyway. A warrior doesn't defy fear, Ed. He doesn't deny it either. A warrior manages it."

Just Ed nodded and swallowed. He was beginning to feel a little better.

"The important thing is what happens next." Heart smiled and looked into Just Ed's eyes. "Because now you know you can be scared. Now you know you aren't superman. Now you know you aren't invincible."

Just Ed nodded.

"So do you man up on a bad night, when the chances are you just might have to go through something like this again, or do you quit?"

Just Ed looked at Heart and took a deep breath. He let it out in a slow stream. "I'll man up."

"Good." Heart smiled.

"Thanks, Skipper." Just Ed stood and grinned. He was starting to feel good again.

"No problem." Heart smiled as he shook hands with the young pilot and then watched him walk to the door.

"Oh, Ed."

"Yes, sir." Just Ed turned in the open doorway as Heart approached him.

"I almost forgot to tell you. CAG says thanks. No one in this air wing has ever done a night barricade. Frankly, we weren't sure if it could be done. Thanks to you, now we know." Heart smiled and closed the door. Just Ed stood in the darkened corridor for a few seconds and then slowly turned and walked down the passageway. He was whistling by the time he got to his stateroom.

# CHAPTER 15

"Hello. Hello, Mrs. Joplin? This is Blue. I'm calling from Olongapo in the Philippines. Is Cathy there?"

Blue was standing in the lobby of the Cubi Officers' Club, speaking into an overseas phone. He had been lucky and had gotten through on his first attempt. In fact, Mrs. Joplin had answered on the second ring.

"Yes, Blue, she's here." Her voice was cold and formal. "She's been waiting for you to call."

"Oh?" Blue frowned. "How did she know I was here?"

"Her father sent us a telegram from the ship three days ago. Said you had flown into the Philippines. We expected your call sooner."

"I had a project to do and I've been pretty busy."

"Really? Cathy was worried maybe something had happened to you."

Blue closed his eyes and imagined Mrs. Joplin, standing in the kitchen. She would be holding the wall phone, twirling the line while she narrowed her eyes to see into his brain. He had seen her do it often. Blue felt that Mrs. Joplin was the kind of woman who was never quite happy unless someone was apologizing to her. He also guessed that she knew he had not written to Cathy for over a month. Blue gritted his teeth as he held the phone.

"Is she there, ma'am?"

"Just a minute, I will get her."

Blue heard the sound of the phone being placed down and readied himself for the ensuing conversation.

"Hi, sweetie."

Blue swallowed and put his mouth closer to the receiver. "Hi, Cathy. I'm glad I caught you at home."

"I've just been waiting here, hoping you might find the time to call. You know, if it wasn't too much trouble."

Blue frowned at the sound of the martyr and prepared for trouble. "I had a job to do for the skipper."

"All you had to do was get an old gun case."

"How did you know that?" Blue was shocked.

"Daddy said so. In his telegram."

Blue felt like a noose was tightening around his neck. He was half-tempted to turn around and check if Captain Joplin was watching him!

"It was pretty involved." Blue winced at the limp sound of his voice. He couldn't think of anything else to say, so he just held the receiver and listened to the thousands of miles of static buzz between them. Finally, he cleared his throat and spoke.

"I had to find someone who could make the case so it wouldn't look cheap and cheesy."

"And did you?"

"I think so. I think I did."

"So why haven't you written?"

Blue sighed and rubbed his forehead. *Here it comes,* he thought.

"Listen, Cathy. I, uh, it just doesn't seem to be working for us right now. It hasn't for a long time."

"It worked before you left."

"Did it really? We argued about everything for months."

"But we had so many good times."

"We did, Cathy." Blue felt helpless. "But it isn't good for us anymore."

"What do you mean, it isn't good for us? It's good for me!"

"We fought the whole time you were in Cannes."

"That's because you were so picky about everything I said."

"Cathy, you can't treat people like that. It's embarrassing."

"Like what? What are you talking about?"

"You treated every waiter, every cab driver, every doorman like a dog. That is what I mean."

"Waiters are professionals in Europe, Blue. They aren't college kids making beer money. If they don't act correctly, they need to be trained."

"Nobody likes to be disrespected, Cathy. I don't care if you are from Europe or Idaho."

"You just don't know how it's done on the Continent," sniffed Cathy. "You've never been anywhere."

"Maybe you're right," agreed Blue. "But I don't like it."

"It was your damn buddies that caused it." Cathy's voice began to break. "You always wanted to be with them."

"Cathy."

"It's true," she cried. "Every chance you got, you made sure we were with a group of your friends. You didn't want to be alone with me. We didn't even have sex after the first night. And we were in Cannes! Everyone has sex in Cannes!"

Blue didn't answer. The truth was that she was right. He had wanted to hang out with his pals. He had a better time with them than with her. But it had been that way for a long time. Besides, he was just tired of their relationship. It was so tied up with her parents he always thought they were on a double date whenever he went to their house. Everything was so forced. He felt that he was already married.

"Cathy, I don't want to hurt you. I wish we could have talked this out when you were in Cannes, but I didn't have the guts to bring it up. Besides, I hoped my feelings would change. I'm sorry." He felt like a total jerk.

"You're so weak!" Blue grimaced at her cold voice. "You don't like the way I tell some slob of a waiter how I like my coffee, so you decide to leave me."

"Cathy, it's more than that."

"Is it? You think you're such a nice guy."

"Cathy."

"You tell me that you have had these thoughts for a long time, yet you don't tell me anything while we are together. You are aloof and distant, and now it's my fault somehow." Cathy was crying, sobbing into the phone.

"Cathy." Blue gripped the phone and took a deep breath. She was right. He had had the chance to bring this entire thing out in the open in Cannes and didn't do it.

"Good-bye, Blue." She hung up before Blue could respond.

There was no point in calling back, so Blue walked out of the club and up the hill to the BOQ. It troubled him when he had heard her call him weak. Was he? Was he the kind of guy who just walked away from the people and things that didn't suit him? Was he that selfish?

# CHAPTER 16

ori always awakened early on Wednesday morning, and this morning was no exception. She did it to allow herself time to do some work at the store but also give enough time to do some shopping at the market for the trip to the orphanage. She was browsing through a selection of fresh fruits when she heard her name.

"Lori, is that you?"

Lori turned at the sound of her name and smiled when she saw Eve.

"Eve!" Lori quickly covered the distance between them, and they embraced as they met.

"I heard you were back this summer. I hoped to see you in the Black Rose."

"I am ashamed of myself for not dropping by."

"Then promise me you'll come, as my guest, of course!"

"I promise." Lori laughed. She noticed the too-thin face and tired eyes. "It's so good to see you."

"It's great to see you too." Eve laughed. "How are your parents? I see Grandma and Raul occasionally. They seem fine."

"Everyone is just fine." Lori grinned.

"Let's sit for a while. Do you have time?" Eve pointed toward a small coffee shop at the edge of the market.

"Certainly, lead the way."

The two friends walked to the shop and took a table outside. Soon they were laughing and remembering over their steaming cups.

"When did you get in town?" Eve smiled at Lori and spooned sugar into her coffee.

"Ten days ago."

"Did you take the bus?"

"Yes," said Lori. "Just like we used to when we went to Manila together."

"But it's air-conditioned now."

"Yes, and no one was sitting in the aisle with a sack of chickens."

"Oh, I remember." Eve laughed. "Solang called the bus the 'chicken express,' remember?"

"I sure do." Lori reached across the table and took Eve's hand. "I know it has been six years since she died, but I just want you to know I think about her every day."

"Thank you, Lori. I miss her too."

They sat quietly for a moment, sipping from their cups.

"Do you still manage the shop during your summer visits?"

"Yes, but 'manage' isn't the right word," said Lori. "It takes me most of the summer just to get the books back in order from the previous summer. Grandma doesn't do financials anymore, and Mr. DeCastro does them just enough to create maximum confusion."

"Well, that explains why you haven't dropped by."

"I really intend to. I hear 'Orchid Forest' on the radio once in a while, but it's not the same as hearing you sing it." Lori looked at Eve and shook her head. "It's not the same at all."

"Why thank you. By the way, is your father still worried about you running off with some sailor?"

"Oh, yes." Lori laughed. "In fact, yesterday, a friend from Manila dropped by for a surprise visit. I felt so sorry for him. I think Father tricked him into coming down here after me."

"Surely your father didn't have to trick him very much."

"I suppose not." Lori smiled. "Jose has been fairly persistent, and last night he came over for coffee. He is a very nice man, and he is doing very well for Father."

"But today you are not seeing him?"

"No." Lori smiled. "I made other plans for today."

"I am sure Jose was very disappointed."

"And you? How are things with you? How is Henry?"

"Henry is a handful," sighed Eve, "for Father Joseph and for me. He is so wild."

"I don't suppose you have found someone to help you with him?"

"No, not yet," said Eve.

Lori did not pursue the subject. Eve's first husband had been her school sweetheart. He had died in a logging accident, shortly after they were married. "I am always surprised to hear you are still here," said Lori. "I expect each summer to have Grandma tell me you have gone to Manila or New York or somewhere."

"Olongapo needs me."

Lori was surprised at Eve's tone. There was a touch of defiance in her voice, as if she was defending herself.

"Yes, I suppose that is true." Lori nodded. As the memories flooded through her, a pang of sadness wrenched her heart. She reached across the table and took her friend's hand again. "I have missed you."

Eve squeezed her hand and returned the smile. "I missed you, Lori. It is good to have you here for a while. So tell me what you are doing in the market this morning. That is a big basket for you, Grandma, and Raul. Going to Blackjack this afternoon?"

"Yes," said Lori. "I'm going to carry this to the orphanage as soon as I drop off enough for breakfast." Suddenly, she grabbed Eve's arm, her eyes wide with excitement. "Oh, please say you are going too, to sing!"

Eve held open the bag she was carrying. It was filled with sweets. "Of course. I have been singing for the little ones almost every week since I can remember."

"Yes, I remember!"

"Well, I certainly plan on singing today." Eve laughed and stood. "Let's go."

"I must confess something to you." Lori glanced at Eve and then back at the crowd in front of them. Many people were heading to Blackjack, and the sidewalk was packed. The men were carrying axes, shovels, and other implements while women carried baskets of produce.

"What is that?"

"I am inviting someone to meet me at the orphanage today, a man."

"Jose? I thought he went back to Manila."

"It's not Jose." Lori smiled.

Eve grinned and squeezed Lori's arm, directing her off the sidewalk into an alley. "Who is he? Is he from Olongapo?"

"No, he's not from around here. He's just a friend."

"You aren't acting like he's just a friend," said Eve. "You're blushing!"

"He's an American. He's in the navy."

Eve's smile froze as she scanned Lori's face for an indication of humor. "You're kidding. Aren't you?"

"No." Lori smiled.

"When did you meet him?"

"The other day. He came by the shop to have me make a gun case for him. He was so nice, and when I told him about the orphanage, he volunteered to help!"

"Is his name Blue?" Eve stopped and caught Lori's arm.

"Why, yes, do you know him?"

"No, not really. Magic introduced him to me the other night, and I saw him in the market yesterday. He mentioned meeting you."

"Really?" Lori raised her eyebrows in surprise.

Eve laughed and shook her head. "Do you mean you just met him and you asked him to work in an orphanage? He must be only a friend. Nobody would ask a lover to do what they do on that farm."

"See," Lori smiled, "what did I tell you? Come on, we're going to be late."

As Lori and Eve made their way to Blackjack, Blue was also negotiating the crowds as he threaded his way down the main street to the orphanage. Despite the heat, he was wearing a pair of jeans and some stout boots with his T-shirt. He was very curious about what was in store for him. He had lain awake a good portion of the night, thinking about Lori. He finally made himself stop worrying about his motives and about what lay in the future. After all, they were both adults and whatever happened, happened. He saw the street to the orphanage that Magic had shown him, and when he turned the corner he bumped head-on into a young girl.

"I'm sorry," said Blue as he caught her, but she dropped her purse, spilling wads of peso notes onto the sidewalk. The wind in the alley was swirling, and the money began to dance away. The girl cried out in frustration, so Blue began to collect the notes as quickly as he could. It was only after he was on his knees, helping her retrieve the money, that he glanced at her.

"Viela?"

Viela looked up at the sound of her name and widened her eyes as she recognized Blue. She looked at all the bills and then back at him. He looked at her and then at the money. He blushed with embarrassment and glanced at his feet as Viela finished scraping the money into her purse. When she straightened, he stood and helped her to her feet.

"Looks like you've been busy" was all he could think to say.

She looked at him for a long time with her sad eyes, searching for some understanding. When she got none, she pulled her arm from his.

"I am going to the post office," she whispered, "to mail this to my family."

Blue's face flushed again with embarrassment, but this time it was for himself.

"Viela, I—"

She pulled her arm away before he could finish and continued up the street.

Blue stood for a while in the alley, leaning against a building. He felt like the true ugly American. He didn't even have to try to make Viela feel bad. He had just done it naturally with his body language, his eyes, and a few stupid words. He had looked at her like some whore scurrying after her ill-gotten gains, and he had transmitted that feeling as surely as if he had said it to her. He sighed and turned down the alley toward the orphanage.

The building sat about two hundred feet from the road, and by the time Blue arrived, a stream of people were marching along the curved gravel path leading to the huge front doors. As Blue joined them, he noticed that the building was constructed of brick, and it contained three floors. There was a main or center building with wings on each end, topped with open patios. A high fence hid the surrounding grounds.

Blue followed the crowd as it entered into a cavernous yet very plain foyer that led to an equally huge main hall. Just off the hall were doors leading to a side courtyard. When Blue stepped into the sunlight, he saw scores of townspeople mingling with the children.

"Blue! Blue! Over here!"

Blue turned and smiled when he saw Lori and Eve. He quickly began weaving his way through the crowd, keeping his eyes on Lori. She was wearing a short cotton dress that was gathered above the waist, as was the fashion back in the States. It was light blue and greatly accentuated Lori's bosom as well as her slim dark legs and delicate ankles. Her long hair shone like ebony as the sunlight danced on her head.

"Hi." Blue smiled at Lori and considered hugging her for an instant and then extended his hand. As he shook hands with her, he smiled at Eve.

"Hello again."

Eve smiled back and accepted his hand.

"So I hear you two already know each other."

"Yes," said Blue. "I had the pleasure of hearing Eve the first night we were in town. She was absolutely fantastic."

"Why, thank you." Eve smiled. "Blue came to the Black Rose with an old acquaintance of mine. Another pilot named Magic Sharentino. Have you met him?"

"No," said Lori. "I'm surprised I don't know him if he's an old friend of yours."

"He's in the US Navy," said Eve. "The times he was in town were when you were back in Manila."

"Oh," said Lori. "I see."

"Well, no matter," said Eve. "I'm sure sooner or later he'll show up."

"Yeah," said Blue. "You'll like him. He's a great guy."

Eve gave him an odd look but then smiled. "Let's go," she said, and they started walking toward the center of the courtyard.

"Hey, Lori. What's up?"

Blue, Lori, and Eve stopped as a young Filipino walked up to them. He smiled and looked at them with sparkling, coal-black eyes.

"Oh, hi, Tony."

"Tony Esparza." The young man extended his hand to Eve. "I know who you are." He smiled. "Everybody in Olongapo knows you." His manner was quick and confident.

"Thank you." Eve laughed.

"Jack Morrison," said Blue. As he shook hands, he noticed Tony was about the same age. Maybe a little shorter and thinner.

"I hoped to see you here, Lori," said Tony. He glanced at Blue, frowned, and then looked back at Lori. "Your grandma said to be sure and find you. You know," he winked, "I think she likes me."

All of a sudden, Blue didn't much care for this Tony character.

"Everybody likes you, Tony." Lori laughed.

"Are you sure?" He looked steadily at Lori, ignoring Eve and Blue.

Blue felt his face redden. He knew it was jealousy, plain and simple. He tried to push it aside.

"Sure." Lori smiled.

"Well," Tony grinned, "if you get lonely, give me a call." He looked at Blue and smiled and then disappeared into the crowd.

"Who was that?"

"Oh, just someone I know. Come on, let's go." She squeezed Blue's arm, and they once again started toward the center of the courtyard.

"What, exactly, are we doing here?" Blue walked beside Lori, enjoying her clean soap smell. Tony was beginning to fade. "What did we volunteer for?"

"We are here for lunch." Lori smiled.

"Uh-huh," grunted Blue, smiling at her upturned face.

"Attention! Can I have your attention! Attention, please!"

Blue and the two women looked in the direction of the voice and walked toward a gathering crowd.

"Who is that?" Blue nodded toward the speaker.

"That is Father Joseph," replied Lori. "He is actually one of your countrymen. He has been working with the orphanage since Evelyn started managing it."

Blue looked at the man and nodded. He stood on an upturned barrel with a bullhorn in his hands. He appeared to be in his sixties, and his smile was kind and genuine. He wore an open-collared work shirt and khaki trousers above a pair of well-worn boots.

"Thank you. Thank you." Father Joseph smiled and nodded to the quieting crowd. "Thanks for coming. As you might have guessed, the rains last week slowed us down somewhat, and we have a lot to do today. My prayers have been answered by so many of you showing up." He smiled again, and a scattered applause rippled through the crowd.

"Today, we need some strong hands to weed the vegetables, some stout hearts to butcher the chickens, and some stout backs to ring the pigs. Some of them are nearly a year old." Father Joseph nodded toward the barn as a groan arose from the crowd. Blue watched him as he jumped off the barrel and started walking in his direction. He waved as he came.

"Father Joseph!" Eve and Lori excitedly introduced Blue to Father Joseph, and he liked him immediately. Blue learned that Father Joseph was Joseph Barnum and he had been born in Manila in 1911 to missionary parents from Ohio. He had studied mathematics and theology in America but had been drawn back to the Philippines in the mid-fifties and eventually took the position of director of Blackjack at Evelyn's request. Blue did not ask how he knew Evelyn.

"Well, I assume you are prepared to help us with some of our work?" Father Joseph fixed Blue with his clear, gray eyes. However, a smile played at the corners of his mouth, and he winked at Lori.

"Yes, sir. I would like to help if I can. I haven't spent much time on a farm though." He was still unsure of what he was getting into.

"Good, why don't we start with the pigs. While we are still strong." Father Joseph put his arm around Blue's shoulders and directed him toward a distant corral. As he walked away, he turned toward Lori and shrugged. She blew him a kiss.

"Have you ever ringed pigs, Blue?" As they walked toward the corral, Blue noticed it was made of wooden posts, and about twenty or thirty men and boys were standing around or sitting on the topmost rails. Blue could hear the squealing and grunting of pigs.

"No, can't say I have."

"Pigs have a tendency to root around and under things, Blue." Father Joseph pointed toward the reddish-brown animals in the corral. "They destroy fences, and they'll even root up trees. We put metal rings in their nose to discourage them."

"Does it hurt?" Blue counted twenty pigs.

"I imagine so. But they don't seem to hold a grudge." Father Joseph reached into a metal toolbox and held up a pair of curved pliers. "This is what we use. The idea is to place the pliers so the bottom tong enters the pig's nostril with the upper one just over the ridged rim of the snout. Closing the pliers crimps the staple firmly through the flesh. Of course, holding the pigs steady during the process is quite an adventure."

Blue looked at the pliers and the rings and then at the crowd of volunteers. Many were sailors. "I didn't expect so many of us," he said, looking toward the corral.

"Oh, yes." Father Joseph smiled. "I always get a great turnout from your navy."

"I guess I expected they would be in the bars or somewhere." Blue glanced at Father Joseph and then back to the corral.

"Sometimes we don't know ourselves, Blue." Father Joseph put his hand on Blue's shoulder. "Many people think all there is to Olongapo is the bars and the hookers. And God knows there certainly is a lot of that. And I imagine your leaders warn the sailors to watch out for disease, scam artists, con men, and thieves. Am I right?"

"Yes, that's right." Blue nodded.

"And such warning is prudent and does good, and I know you must take care of your young people. But most of your sailors tire of the street scene and look for other, more diverse, entertainment. I hope someone on your ship is telling them about all of the other things to do. Blue, do you know you can ride horses, play golf, snorkel, sail, fish, take trips into the jungle, visit our highlands, even ride go-carts right here on this island?"

"Plus, you can ring pigs." Blue laughed.

"Yes, even pig ringing." Father Joseph grinned as he surveyed the crowd once again. "There is much about each other we do not know. Maybe you will learn something about these people before you go."

Blue nodded and continued to look at the corral. For some reason he thought of Viela.

"Maybe you will learn something more about yourself."

Blue glanced at Father Joseph. It was as if the older man was reading his mind. Father Joseph looked at Blue and smiled.

"Come, my friend. Let's go find our cloven-footed friends." As they walked toward the corral, Blue looked more closely at the crowd and laughed as he spotted a familiar face. There, sitting with his back to a fence post and playing with a set of ringing pliers, was Henry.

"Henry, what are you doing here?"

The boy put up his hand to shade his eyes and squinted at Blue. He smiled but didn't answer.

"I'm Blue. Remember me? You met me with Magic the other night by the river."

Henry quickly scowled. "Don't say anything about the river," he whispered. "If Father Joseph found out, he would tell Eve. They would both be very angry."

"What would make us angry?" Father Joseph smiled as he approached the pair.

"Uh, Henry was telling me you and Eve would get angry if he tried to ring one of those pigs by himself." Blue looked down at Henry and winked.

"So, you met Henry?" The father reached down and patted Henry's shoulder. "He's right. I would be angry, and so would his sister. You see, Blue, Henry has something of a wild streak in him. He always insists upon doing what the biggest boys do. But that doesn't mean he can always do them by himself. Does it, Henry?"

"No, Father."

"Okay, enough talk." Father Joseph clapped his hands. "Everybody, get a partner and let's get going. It's already nine and we want to all be done by half past noon." He turned to Blue and grinned. "Why don't you be partners with Henry and me? We will teach you to be the best pig ringer in the fleet!"

"Yeah!" yelled Henry.

Blue smiled at the two of them and nodded. "Let's go."

The corral soon erupted in a melee of squeals and grunts, punctuated by hoots of laughter as the men and boys chased after the pigs. Dust and bits of straw filled the air, and Blue was soon covered. The animals were young and only weighed thirty or forty pounds each, but they were quick and hard to catch. Blue soon found that Henry was the best member of their team to catch the pigs, but he needed help to hold onto the struggling creatures. So they developed a process whereby Henry caught a pig and Blue held its head still. The pigs protested violently to this treatment, but when Father Joseph squeezed the nose ring home, the real pandemonium began.

The teams of men and boys worked quickly, and in a little more than an hour, the corral was empty. Blue was beginning to wonder what they would do to occupy their time until the noon break when Father Joseph walked to the center of the corral and once again clapped his hands for attention.

"I want to commend you on a great job!" Father Joseph smiled and raised his hands to the workers. "But now that you are warmed up, the real work must be done." He looked at his assistants and nodded his head. "Let them in."

The assistants opened a gate, separating the corral from an adjacent holding pen and began shouting and waving their arms. Soon a herd of about twenty grunting, squealing pigs scrambled wildly into the corral. However, these pigs were different. They were much, much larger.

"A farmer up the road donated these fine animals to us," said Father Joseph. "Unfortunately, he neglected to have them ringed when they were small. As you can see, they weigh around 150 pounds each, so we've got a job ahead of us."

Blue heard the crowd of men around him groan as they surveyed the task. The pigs did look formidable, and when they heaved for air or squealed, Blue could see ugly, yellow teeth.

"Do they bite?" he asked Father Joseph.

"Sometimes," he said. "Be careful around their mouths."

Father Joseph turned to the men. "I think it will be best if we divide into four-man teams. You children get up on the fence and watch. You've done enough for today."

"Go on, buddy." Blue gave Henry a pat on the back and grinned. Henry looked at him and frowned and then slowly turned toward the fence.

The pigs gathered in one end of the corral and were eyeing the men suspiciously and grunting softly to themselves as Father Joseph talked. However, it didn't take long for all hell to break loose.

As Blue and his two teammates, Jorge and Hermano, waded into the herd, the pigs bolted away. It took teamwork and focused effort to corner a pig and then dive on it before it could escape. The big animals struggled mightily under Blue as he put all his weight on them to hold them still. They bucked, heaved, and screamed. Spit and slobber flew from their gasping jaws, and as Blue held on their course hair scratched his face and their sweaty stench filled his nose. He also found that there was more than mud on the corral floor. But he and his team worked well together, and Father Joseph's pliers were deft and quick.

Little by little, progress was made, and after almost two hours of backbreaking, hard, and dirty work, all the pigs were ringed—all but one, that is.

Every team had carefully avoided this particular animal, and with good reason. He was a big boar, surely tipping the scales at over 250 pounds. He also had a nasty temper and had snapped at anyone who got near.

Blue and some of the other men formed a half circle around the beast and attempted to hem him against the side of the corral. However, whenever they got close, he would bolt away. After three frustrating attempts, Father Joseph called all the men away from the animal and announced he would give him to whoever wanted him. But as the men began to walk out of the corral, they were drawn back by a sudden scream.

When Blue heard the scream, he ran back to the corral. He stepped on a rail and hoisted himself up to see. There, in the arena, he saw that the big boar had one of the men on the ground.

The man was on his back, shrieking for help as he kicked up at the boar. He desperately tried to push himself backward out of reach. The boar backed up for a moment and stood stiff-legged, his lungs heaving for breath. His hooves splayed against the dirt. His little eyes were red with rage, and long strings of saliva dripped from his open jaws. Suddenly he roared and launched himself at the man, catching a loose pant leg in his long, yellow teeth. He screamed and violently twisted his head. The man kicked with his free leg and caught the boar in the face, but the animal changed his grip and dragged the man closer toward him. The man screamed again as the boar again changed his grip and grabbed the man's shirt. The animal hunched its massive shoulders and ripped his head sideways as he pulled the man toward his dagger teeth.

Blue saw a blur coming from the top rail and caught his breath. *Henry!*

"Henry!" he screamed. Henry leaped from the rail and was on the pig's back!

The boar squealed in rage at this new threat and immediately dropped the man's shirt from his teeth.

"Henry." Blue ran toward the huge boar.

He saw the pig twist his neck as he tried to grab Henry with his teeth. It roared and lurched against the fence.

"Henry." Blue tried to grab the boar, but it pushed by him, knocking him to the ground. He saw Henry's little chest thump up and down against the ridge of the pig's spine and his toes dig into the pig's side. The crowd roared, realizing the danger the boy was in. The boar ran to the far side of the corral and tried to rub Henry off. He shook his shoulders and whipped his head back and forth in an attempt to grab the boy with his teeth. As Blue ran forward, he saw Henry start to slip off the pig's back. He watched him teeter for a moment and then fall to the ground. His heart jumped into his throat as he watched the animal instantly turn toward the boy and charge. Blue dove at the pig, and out of the corner of his eye he saw Father Joseph swing a shovel. Blue rolled against the pig and grabbed Henry. He staggered to his feet and dragged the boy to the fence.

The pig staggered back, stunned for a second, and then squealed with rage and lunged at Father Joseph, who smacked the pig in the snout so hard the shovel handle broke. The big animal squealed in pain and sat down on its haunches, shaking his head. It glared at Father Joseph for a second and then turned and ran for the barn.

Blue loosened his grip on Henry and looked down at him. The little boy was crying. He knelt down, but as he did Henry jerked free and ran to Father Joseph.

"You men are all invited here for next Easter," said Father Joseph as he gathered Henry in his arms and watched the boar lumber out of the corral. "We will be serving ham."

Blue joined a small group gathered around the man who had been attacked. He was anxious to see if the boar had gotten through the clothing, but the man was unscathed. He then turned back to Father Joseph and Henry. The father was holding Henry in his arms, and Blue watched as he hugged him close, rocking back and forth on his feet.

"Henry, Henry, Henry," he whispered. Father Joseph had his eyes closed, and Blue could see a tear trickle down his face.

For some reason, Blue thought of his dad.

After a moment, Father Joseph put Henry down and held his shoulders as he looked sternly into the boy's eyes.

"Why on earth did you do that? He could have hurt you, son. He's bigger than any man here. Hell, he is twice as big."

Henry bowed his head and looked at his feet. Father Joseph knelt on one knee and put his hand under Henry's trembling chin. He lifted his head. "Answer me, Henry," he said. His voice was soft and gentle. "Why did you take a chance like that?"

"I wanted everyone to cheer me," whispered Henry.

"Oh, Henry." Father Joseph hugged the boy against his chest, smiled, and closed his eyes.

Blue spotted Henry's sailor cap laying in the dust and walked across the corral to retrieve it. *Christ,* he thought, *how sad for a boy so young to take such a risk just to get attention! How lonely he must be!* But as he picked up the cap and looked back across the corral, he smiled. Father Joseph was still on his knees, hugging the little boy against him. Henry had his head on the father's shoulder, and his eyes were closed.

While the men were busy chasing after the pigs, the female volunteers were busy butchering chickens. Some of the women cut off the heads, others plunged the still-quivering carcasses into boiling water, and a third group plucked feathers. Lori and Eve shared the final chore of cleaning the birds and preparing them for the refrigerator.

"I bet you don't get to do much of this in Manila." Eve smiled at Lori as she deftly sliced open the abdomen of a bird and emptied its contents.

"No," said Lori, "and to be honest, I haven't missed it that much." She looked at her friend and laughed. A pang of regret swept her as she realized that their old friendship would probably never be the same and wished that she had done more to keep it.

"So tell me," said Eve, "how much do you like this Blue?" She gave Lori a grin that was part mischievous, part something else.

"Oh, I don't know." Lori blushed slightly. "We just met a few days ago."

"Yes, so you said. But in the short time I watched you two together, just now, I think something is happening."

"What do you mean?" Lori frowned and concentrated on her chores.

"I mean the way both of you looked at each other."

Lori shrugged and continued to work.

"Lori, I don't want to get into your business." Eve paused to push her hair out of her face and blew a wisp of it away from her eye. "But please be careful."

"We are just friends."

"Maybe, but I think I see something more."

"What do you see?"

"I see an exciting young man who is very handsome and very appealing. So please be careful."

"What do you mean, 'be careful'?" Lori frowned and looked at her old friend.

"Such men don't know what they want," replied Eve. "Maybe neither do you?"

"What are you saying, Eve?"

"All I suggest is that you project this out to its end. What do you want? A couple of laughs? Heck, then it's okay to have a good time. But if your fantasy is anything more, then be careful."

"Really, Eve, we are only barely friends. We just met." Lori was perturbed that Eve was making such a big issue out of nothing. Besides, it wasn't really any of her business.

"I'm sorry." Eve put her hand on Lori's arm and squeezed affectionately. "But that's the way it always begins. I see our girls with these sailors every day, and I know how it ends for a lot of them."

"Well, don't worry. I'm not going to let anything happen. We are just friends." Lori felt an uneasy tension fall between them. She and Eve worked in silence for several minutes. Finally, Lori looked at her friend.

"Blue reminds you of someone, doesn't he?"

Eve glanced at Lori and kept working with the chicken.

"Since I mentioned his name, you've been acting strange—no, worried, even afraid. Why?"

Eve split open a chicken and flicked the entrails into a waste pail on the floor. "Blue with you reminds me of someone."

"What do you mean?" Lori straightened from her chores and frowned. "Who does he remind you of?"

"Magic," said Eve. "Blue looks at you the same way Magic looked at Solang."

"Magic? You mean Blue's friend? Your old friend?"

"Yes," sighed Eve. "Magic. He's the man Solang loved."

"I don't understand," said Lori.

"Just be careful!"

"Eve? I don't understand. What do you mean 'be careful'?"

"Solang loved a man who wasn't really here, Lori. I watched her. She kept waiting for him and waiting for him. You see, Lori, he was young, and he was handsome, and he was exciting, just like your Blue. And I suspect, like Blue, he didn't know what he wanted and neither did Solang."

"Did he just leave her? Was he coming back?"

"I don't know," said Eve. She took a deep breath and wiped her eyes with her apron. "I guess we will never know. Solang drowned while he was gone."

"Have you talked to Magic about it?"

"No."

"Why?" Lori was intrigued with the story. "Did you write to him about it?"

"I wrote to Magic many times after Solang died. He wrote back, and we wrote about many things. But we never wrote about that. Maybe I didn't want to know the answer." Eve smiled at Lori and laid down her knife. "Magic is special in his own way. He is a wandering spirit and everyone loves him. He may not have realized how much Solang loved him or the kind of love it was."

"I really appreciate your concern, Eve. I really do. But I don't think there is any reason to worry about me."

"Perhaps not. But you have to admit, all of this happened pretty quick."

"All of what?" Lori frowned at her friend.

Eve stood and smiled at Lori. "Let's walk for a moment."

The two women walked away from the work area and down by the high concrete wall of the west side of the mansion. There, they found a bench and sat down.

"What do you think of when you think about Blue?" Eve looked at Lori and took her hand.

Lori returned her gaze and then let her eyes drop. "I … I don't know." She looked at Eve and, finding understanding in her friend's face, continued. "I really don't know what to think."

"It is hard to believe in love at first sight—maybe impossible to believe in it—until it happens to you." Eve squeezed Lori's hand. "I believe in it because it happened to me, with my husband. I think it might be happening with you."

"I … maybe it is," whispered Lori. "It … it is strange indeed."

"But just because it is love at first sight for you doesn't mean it is love at first sight for him. He might not even know the meaning of it. Do you know what he feels?"

Lori shook her head slowly. "No, I mean … I see something in his eyes. I see something in the way he acts, but we have not actually talked about it." She looked at Eve and sighed. "I guess I don't know."

"If you find yourself falling in love—I mean falling hard—at least be smart. Find out how he thinks about you. Find out what's in his heart. Blind love is worse than no love at all, Lori."

"You said Magic looked at Solang like Blue looks at me. If he's as confused as you say he is, how am I supposed to know what's really in his heart?" Lori frowned and the two friends stood. They started to walk slowly back to the work area.

"See how he treats you in front of his friends," said Eve. "See how he treats you when he's with his squadron."

"I don't understand."

"I have worked around men like your Blue and Magic for fifteen years. I have dated them and even loved some of them. I might even still love some of them. They are engaging and even sincere. But I sometimes think they are two men. One man is who he really is, the man of his heart. But the other is quite different. The other person is the man the squadron wants him to be.

Lori stopped and took Eve's hand. "What do you mean?"

Eve slowly shook her head and then continued. "I have often wondered which they are when they are alone. Sometimes I think these young men allow themselves to be taken away from their core, away from their heart. Maybe it is to gain the respect of their friends, or their admiration. Who knows? Magic was two people, Lori. Although his relationship with my sister lasted only a few weeks, I know he loved Solang. The true Magic, the man of his heart, loved her." Eve paused and sighed again. She looked past Lori's eyes, into the surrounding jungle.

"But something happened when he left her to go back to the ship. Something out there took him away from her, or he let it take him away."

Eve continued to stare into the jungle for a few moments and then looked at Lori with sad eyes. "Just be careful."

"How long have you been helping Eve with Henry?" Blue and Father Joseph were walking to the house. Henry was skipping along in front of them, the episode with the boar evidently forgotten. "He has been here since she brought him to Olongapo six years ago. He was just a baby."

"Where are his parents, Eve's mom and dad?"

"Both died shortly after Henry was born. They were from the North, I believe. I did not know them; they never visited here."

"Isn't that strange?"

"A little, I suppose," said Father Joseph. "This society is not as mobile as in America. Besides, I got the impression Eve's parents did not approve of her living here."

"Why is that?"

Father Joseph slowed his pace and motioned to a pair of large tree stumps. "Let's talk for a moment."

"How much do you know about the Philippines?" Blue and Father Joseph were comfortably situated on the stumps, cooled by a canopy of trees.

"Not much," said Blue.

"I see." The father nodded. He leaned over, picked up a twig, and began scratching off the bark. "Filipino history is dominated by a past as a Spanish colony. They have only been independent for seventy-five years, and much of that time they were under the direction of the United States. So, in some sense, they may be struggling for an identity."

"Didn't we pretty much give them everything?"

Father Joseph looked at Blue and frowned. "Before you leave today I want to give you some literature. That is, if you want to know something about these people."

"I do," said Blue.

"Good," the father smiled, "because if you ever tell a Filipino that Americans pretty much gave them everything, your conversation will be finished."

"I see."

"You see, Blue, Americans and Filipinos have a special relationship. We invaded this place after they gained their freedom from Spain."

"We did?"

"Yes. We killed thousands of them, basically took their independence, and cashed it in for ourselves. However, we also brought in our wealth, our education system, and our health and agriculture expertise. We made the Philippines better, but it was forced upon them, and it was at their expense."

Blue nodded and continued to listen.

"We also did nothing to contain the corruption. When we took over we relied on the Filipino power brokers to support us. So the Philippines is run by a handful of families today, just as it was back under Spanish rule. It's just that the overseers are now Filipino and not Spanish."

"Yes, but it's their country."

"True." Father Joseph nodded. "But we are associated with the elite, not the masses. That is important to remember."

Once again, Blue nodded but remained silent.

"So Olongapo is somewhat of a symbol of the Filipino history of being exploited."

"I don't understand."

"Filipinos are embarrassed by some of the things that go on in Olongapo. Prostitution is not an acceptable position in this society. It is regarded much like it is back in the States. Regardless of what your friends on the carrier say, it is not the natural state of this society. Women are revered here. They are wooed with a Latin intensity we Americans may not even understand. Take your friend Lori, for instance. I will tell you I have known Lori most of her life, and she has a constant stream of young men at her grandmother's doorstep, and I imagine the same is true when she is in Manila."

"I can surely believe it," said Blue. "Today, some guy named Tony practically asked her out while she was with me."

"Get used to it." Father Joseph laughed. "Until she is engaged, that is the practice. So, as you can see, women are held in very high esteem. Having them step down to prostituting themselves for foreigners is very embarrassing. It makes them think they are just being exploited by us in a different way."

"Then why do they do it?" asked Blue. "No one is forcing them to be hookers."

"Believe me," Father Joseph chuckled, "I ask that question every day."

"Yes, I guess you do." Blue nodded.

"It's just that when you have nothing here, you literally have nothing. There is no government support system like you're used to. Many of these girls are here without their family having any idea of what they are doing. They make their money and send it home because it's the only money to buy food and medicine and the essentials of life."

Blue thought of Viela and shook his head.

"So when I talk to them, I concentrate on the goodness of their heart and not on the weakness of their condition."

"How do you resolve being an American priest living in a place where Americans are exploiting the people?"

"I firmly believe that it is the condition of corruption and greed that is exploiting the people. The sailors, the hookers, and the rest are just players in that exploitation. At some level it gets to how we behave as humans. Buying a hooker might be a sin, but buying a hooker and treating her with respect is less so."

"So Eve's parents were too ashamed of Olongapo to visit here?"

"I think so." Father Joseph nodded. "For many Filipinos, Olongapo represents the very worst of Filipino culture: corruption, prostitution, drunkenness, robbery, filth, indulgence of the most obscene manner. However, there are people here who defy all of it, and they rise above it. And, Blue, the real beauty is that they pull others up with them. In that regard, Olongapo represents the very best of the Filipino culture."

Blue looked at Father Joseph and smiled as he nodded. "Thanks, Father," he whispered. "I'll be sure to get the material you offered."

"Great." Father Joseph smiled. "Now let's go find the womenfolk."

The women were almost finished when Blue and Father Joseph approached. The feathers and waste were all disposed of, and the fresh poultry was in the refrigerators. Blue spotted Lori washing her hands at an outdoor faucet and walked over to her.

"Hi!" He grinned.

"Did you have a good time with your little piggies?" Lori laughed and threw her towel. It hit Blue in the chest.

"Yes, we had a good time. It turned out to be very exciting. Some of those little piggies turned out to be very big piggies." They both laughed as Lori touched his arm.

"Are you hungry?"

"I am famished!"

"Great, then let's go." They held each other in their eyes for a moment and then walked toward the courtyard holding hands.

# CHAPTER 17

Lieutenant Sanchez sat in his spacious office in Olongapo Police Station 1, reading the morning crime reports and sipping his coffee, when the door suddenly flew open. A surge of irritation brought him to his feet and opened his mouth to scream at the insolence. But he did not get a single syllable to form. In fact, hot stomach acid mixed with coffee in a swallow of horror when he saw the intruder. It was Major Botag!

Sanchez immediately leaped to attention, knocking over his cup. He glanced down to see the brown liquid spread across his leather desk pad and then quickly looked up into the pinched, sallow face of the major. His orderly stood at his side, looking at him like he was a bug.

"Good morning, sir." The stomach acid burned Sanchez's throat.

Major Botag slowly strode across the room to a chair located in front of Sanchez's desk and sat down. He raised his right hand, and his orderly immediately filled it with a large cigar. He kept his emotionless black eyes on the trembling lieutenant's face. Sanchez swallowed bile as he watched the major take a silver lighter from his tunic pocket. He snapped open the cap and rolled the wheel, all the while staring at him with those black eyes. The flame leaped onto the wick, and as soon as the first fragrant coils of gray smoke drifted from the major's mouth, the orderly stood and took his place behind his master's chair. The major snapped the lighter closed and gave Sanchez a slight nod, indicating permission to sit.

"Good morning, sir," repeated Sanchez. He sat and perched forward on the edge of his chair. When the major did not reply, he swallowed and did his best to maintain a level gaze and not let his anxiety show. Although he had only seen the major once before, he had heard terrible things about him. Major Botag was not a man to trifle with, and as the regional inspector general, he could easily make a police chief's life hell.

Major Emilio Vargas Botag glared across the desk at the lieutenant and took a puff from his cigar.

"You know who I am?" He snapped the lighter top.

"Of course, sir." Sanchez quivered and nodded.

"Can you guess why I am here?" Major Botag crossed his legs and stared.

"No, no sir. But you are very welcome." Sanchez smiled weakly and tried to lean back in his chair.

"You have strung up a very large volume of reports, Lieutenant. Reports that indicate you have no control over this city. Reports that indicate you are incompetent." Major Botag slowly put his cigar to his mouth and took a long drag. His eyes never left Sanchez as he inhaled and blew out a stream of blue smoke. He snapped the lighter again.

Sanchez coughed slightly as the smoke went into his nose. He hoped he would not throw up.

"Do you know Ambassador Rodriguez?"

"Yes, sir."

"Oh, that is interesting. He gave me this lighter, did you know?"

"No, sir." Sanchez looked at the lighter in the major's hand.

"See, it has the crest, and it has my initials. It is my most prized possession." The major smiled coldly for a second and then slit his eyes. "How would you know the ambassador?"

"I don't know him, sir. I just know who he is. He visits the admirals when the carriers come in."

"Yes, I see, of course." The major nodded his head gently and rolled the cigar in his fingers for a moment. "Why do you think he does that?"

"For … for friendship?" A drop of sweat fell from Sanchez's nose and fell onto his leather pad, mixing with the spilled coffee.

The major smiled and took another drag. He looked at Sanchez and exhaled. "You are quite an idiot, aren't you?"

Sanchez swallowed and looked at the major. He felt sick.

"Aren't you?"

"Y … yes, sir." Sanchez dropped his head and stared at his desk. He heard the lighter top snap, and snap again. He took a deep breath and slowly looked up.

"He visits because President Marcos puts a very, very high premium on our relationship with the US Navy."

"Yes, sir, I—"

"Shut up." Major Botag's words were icy whispers that caused Sanchez's hair to stand up on the back of his neck. "What happened during the last carrier visit to Olongapo?"

"Sir?"

"What happened, Lieutenant?" Major Botag uncrossed his legs and leaned forward toward Sanchez.

"Well, sir, we had some trouble."

"Yes, you certainly did, and what happened?"

"The navy kept their sailors from the city." Sanchez took a ragged breath as he tried to maintain his gaze on the major.

"And then what happened?"

"You sent some men."

"That is exactly correct, Lieutenant. You could not assure that the Americans would not be ripped off every time they came to town, so I sent some men."

"Yes, sir." Sanchez didn't know what else to say.

"And one of my men shot someone, didn't he?"

"Yes, sir, for stealing."

"Did you think that was too harsh?" Major Botag stood up and walked over to Sanchez. Sanchez stood and swallowed.

Major Botag took a deep breath, and his lips curled around his cigar. He took it out of his mouth and blew more smoke at Sanchez. "Did you think that was too harsh?"

"No, sir. Not at all." Sanchez mustered the courage to look into the major's eyes. "Not at all."

Major Botag looked at him a moment and then walked over to the window facing the bay. He walked with his left hand behind his back, clicking his lighter. He held the cigar in his right. Major Botag looked out at the bay, his profile to the lieutenant. "Last week, I terminated the career of the Mount Zabong city commander, and his reports were not as bad as yours."

Lieutenant Sanchez swallowed as he felt the blood flow from his face. The lighter snapped.

"The American commander of the naval base here called the ambassador. He called him and told him he would have to make Olongapo and the surrounding area off limits to US naval personnel if something wasn't done about the crime." Major Botag studied the ash at the end of his cigar for a moment and then flicked it to the floor.

"It seems the sailors can't walk down the street here, in your city, without having their pockets picked. Material is stolen from the bases, houses are broken into." The major paused and took another leisurely draw from his cigar as the acid in Sanchez's stomach boiled.

"Hardly the type of record that inspires confidence." He turned and gazed at Sanchez and then slowly walked toward him. As he approached, the lieutenant automatically stiffened.

"Don't misunderstand." The major leaned forward until his lips were almost touching Lieutenant Sanchez's ear. The smell of the cigar, mingled with the major's sour breath, almost caused him to heave. Sanchez shivered as the icy voice hissed over him like a cold wind. "I don't give a damn about the Americans. They use us like they have always used us. They deflower our women, plunder our waters, embroil us into God-knows-what with the rest of the world.

But I do care about the ambassador's wishes. All of the ambassador's wishes." He snapped the lighter and put it back in his tunic. "Clean this place up, Lieutenant, or I will clean you out."

Lieutenant Sanchez was still standing behind his desk, shivering, as the major's sedan rolled down the street toward Manila.

# CHAPTER 18

"What do you think the problem is, Chief?" Head looked sideways at his chief and then back at the flight deck.

"I hate to say it, Lieutenant, but I think it's Petty Officer Franks."

Head and Chief Petty Officer Larry Evans were strolling across the Connie's flight deck. It was early morning, and the ship was quiet. They had decided to take the opportunity to get some sunshine while they discussed the performance of their men. Besides being a pilot, Head was the branch officer for the power plants work center. The power plants crew was responsible for the maintenance of the Phantom's J-79 jet engines as well as the fuel systems that fed them. Chief Evans was the senior enlisted man in the branch and Head's most trusted adviser. The chiefs not only oversaw the training of the young enlisted men and managed the flow of work center labor, but they also trained the young officers as well. Of course, this part of their job was not a structured syllabus but more of an observation and advice process. Although the officer was senior, it was a foolish man indeed who did not listen closely when his chief spoke and observe how his chief handled the often-delicate tasks of personnel and discipline.

Head and Chief Evans had been teamed since the cruise had begun and had developed a relationship of mutual respect. Today, as they walked across the gritty nonskid surface of the steel deck, they were discussing a work center problem. The branch had been responsible for the squadron losing several recent sorties. That was bad because the quickest way to bring the wrath of a squadron skipper was to miss scheduled sorties. It made the squadron look bad, but more importantly, it was a failure to meet an air wing commitment. Lives could be jeopardized if sorties were missed.

"What makes you say it's Franks?"

"Well, Lieutenant, Franks is a pretty good technician. If I tell him what's wrong, he can fix just about anything pretty good. However, as you know, sir, the real problem is figuring out what is wrong in the first place. Franks is slow, he's unsure of himself, and he can't troubleshoot worth a diddly shit."

"What do you propose, more training?"

"Sir, Franks has had all the training we give. His problem is that he just won't make a decision."

"So, what do you suggest?"

Chief Evans slowly blew out a breath and looked at Head. "I think we should replace him with Benny—err, Petty Officer Benetiz."

"Benetiz? He's just an E-5. He's years junior to Franks."

"I know he's young, sir, but he's good. He knows the plane better than Franks, and the men really put out for him. He's a damn good leader too."

"Yeah, Chief, but an E-5?"

"Look, sir, let me give you some facts. First of all, Benny is already the night-shift supervisor and has been for three months. We had to do that because the bureau never filled Petty Officer Johnson's billet when he got sick."

"Yeah, I know."

"And, sir, he has done an unbelievable job. No matter how bad we beat the planes up during the day, he has them fixed by the morning's first launch."

"Yeah, we always start the day strong," agreed Head.

"The problem is I can't be everywhere at once. Yesterday, I got all boogered up fixing 203's fuel migration problem and thought Franks could handle 204. As you know, 204 never made the first night go."

"Believe me," Head nodded, "I got hit in the face with that one already."

"Skipper in your shit?"

"Big time."

"Well, anyway, sir. Benny is one hell of a troubleshooter. He figured out 204's problem in about five minutes, and that's why it made the last launch."

"No shit?"

"No shit, sir."

Head slowly nodded. Despite the radical move of putting such a junior petty officer into such a responsible position, he was beginning to see the chief's point. Head looked at the flight deck and rubbed the toe of his flight boot against the rough surface. Such a move would be a slap in the face of Petty Officer Franks and could halt his career. He would never make chief if he didn't get a solid performance appraisal as a work center supervisor. However, Head didn't feel that he had too many choices. If Benetiz was the best man for the job then he should have it, regardless of how many chevrons were on his sleeve.

"Lieutenant." Chief Evans grabbed Head's elbow and looked at him. "I'll keep an eye on Benny. It'll be okay, sir."

"Okay, Chief, if you say so." Head nodded and sighed. "Well, let's go tell Franks."

They walked across the deck, down the metal steps to the hatch cover leading toward the power plants shop, and stepped inside the dark ship. Head led the way as they navigated through the ship to their workshop.

Petty Officer Franks was sitting in the power plants work center, smoking a cigarette, when Chief Evans and Lieutenant McGinnis walked in. He felt a pang of anxiety when he saw the two of them together, because he knew the skipper was putting on the heat. He figured it had to do with the sorties they had dropped in the past few days and immediately began to think of an excuse. Franks stood as the two men entered the space and showed his yellow, tobacco-stained teeth with a smile.

"Where is everybody?" Chief Evans looked around the dark, little room. It was empty except for the three of them.

"They've gone to chow," replied Franks.

"I see," said the chief as he and Head took seats in two gray folding chairs.

"What can I do for you?" Franks sat back down and faced them.

"Listen, Franks, the lieutenant and I want to talk to you about the way things have been going lately."

"What do you mean?" Franks's eyes flicked from Head to the chief. He had guessed right—they were concerned about the missed sorties. This wasn't any social call. *But, hell,* he thought, *it ain't my fault. I don't break those planes; the pilots do.*

"I want to get it out straight with you, Petty Officer Franks," said Head. "We dropped two sorties yesterday, two the day before, and one the day before that. In fact, we've been dropping engine- and fuel system-related sorties for a long time."

"Yes, sir," interrupted Franks. "But, sir," he leaned forward as he shook out another cigarette, "we fixed all the problems. My board's clean." He gestured to a large wall board, containing metal clips. The clips held and visibly displayed the stubs from maintenance action forms. These forms represented outstanding discrepancies, needing work. Franks was right; the board was clean.

"Yes, I know," said Head. "The problem is not the eventual maintenance. You do a good job with that, a real good job."

"Damn right, I do, sir." Franks lit his cigarette and squinted as the smoke curled into his eyes.

"The problem is with your troubleshooting and your decision making." Franks knew he was not good at analyzing problems and discovering solutions. When the aircrew explained a problem, or when he read about it on a maintenance action form, he liked to be able to think about it for a while. In fact, he preferred to have the chief look at the problem and tell him how to fix it. That seemed to work the best. He was very quick, once the chief made up his mind! Franks looked at the lieutenant but didn't respond. He figured he could sit there and listen to the two of them for a while. It wouldn't do any good to argue.

"For instance, yesterday when 204 came back, the aircrew downed it because the fuel gauge rolled back to zero a couple of times during the flight. The plane sat on deck all day and we missed two sorties because of it. Benetiz and his guys fixed it."

"That's bullshit, sir, with all respect." Franks's voice quivered slightly. He didn't want to get into an argument with the lieutenant, but he was absolutely sick and tired of hearing about how great Benetiz was. Super flip son of a bitch anyway! He knew the reason Benny got praise was because nobody could believe a Filipino could actually do anything but mess cook and paperwork. Hell, everybody knew that was all they were good for. *Fucking Benny wasn't shit! If he were a white guy, nobody would give him the time of day.*

"Watch the language, Franks."

"Sorry, Chief. But, hey, Benny had all night to fix that jet. Plus, he didn't have to run the flight schedule at the same time, like I did."

"He fixed 204 in five minutes, Franks." Head leaned forward in his folding chair. "He read the discrepancy on the board, looked back into the history of the plane, and concluded that it was a loose thermistor probe. He changed it, and the jet made the last launch of the night."

Franks stared at the two men and took a final drag off his cigarette. He stubbed it out and immediately fished another out of the pack of Camels on the table. He lit it, took a drag, and exhaled. He didn't know how to respond. He should have known to tighten the thermistor, dammit! Now that he thought about it, it made perfect sense. But he hadn't had the time. Shit, everyone knew the guys on night shift had all kinds of time to think things through. It might have taken super flip five minutes to fix it, but he probably went down to maintenance control before his shift started and read up on the problem. Hell, he probably took hours to figure up a solution and then went waltzing in when the shift started and looked like a hero.

*I hate that fucking gook,* thought Franks. *I hate all those fucking flips.*

"I am going to switch you and Petty Officer Benetiz." Head waited for Franks to look at him before he continued. "You go on nights and he comes on days."

Franks was shocked. His jaw dropped open, and he stared at the lieutenant. He couldn't believe it! *A fucking E-5 taking over the day shift?* It was unheard of.

"That's impossible," he blurted. "He's an E-5. I'm an E-6, and I'm the leading petty officer in the branch."

"You will remain the leading petty officer."

"But no work center has the leading petty officer on night shift."

"You can still manage the administrative functions at night," said Chief Evans.

Franks felt himself beginning to panic. They were serious. He was up for chief this year. *How in the hell would he ever make chief if he was fired? And make no mistake about it, he was being fired and replaced by a fucking E-5. A fucking E-5 flip, to be exact.*

"Do you really think that kid can run days? There's a hell of a lot more to running a work center than making lucky guesses about airplanes."

"I think he can," said Head.

"We'll give him help," added Chief Evans. "I'm sure he would appreciate any help from you as well."

Franks glared at the two men for a moment, and then he slowly began to smile. *Yep,* he thought, *I think I have all this figured out.* He stubbed his cigarette in the ashtray and smiled.

"I get it," he said. "I get it now. You know, ever since those race riots on the Kitty Hawk a few years back, we've been turning the navy over to the minorities. Bending over backward so we won't offend anyone. I always wondered what it would feel like to have some poor, oppressed son of a bitch get my job."

"Franks," warned the chief

"Funny, I always figured it would be to a black."

"Bullshit, Franks," spit Head. "This has nothing to do with minorities. This has to do with getting the job done."

"Whatever you say, Lieutenant." Franks smiled slyly and shook his head.

"Franks, you can believe what you want. The bottom line is to turn the shift over today. I suggest you get some sleep."

Franks remained in his chair for a long time after the two men left. He was oblivious to his crew when they returned from chow and didn't notice when they left again to work on the squadron jets. He smoked cigarette after cigarette as he seethed. In fact, he was more pissed off than he had ever been. He was more ashamed too. *Jesus,* he thought, *fired and replaced by a fucking E-5 gook. God, it's fucking embarrassing.* He could imagine the kind of talk that would be flying through the ranks of the E-6s on board. Everybody would act as if nothing happened, but they'd know all about it before nightfall. And they would talk about it when he wasn't around.

Franks walked out of the work center and quietly slipped into his berthing area. He was thankful no one was in the space and quickly undressed and got into his rack. He lay awake for a long time, hating Benny, hating all of those fucking gook flips.

# CHAPTER 19

The sound of monkeys awakened Blue from a deep, restful sleep. He had left his window open, and at first light the chatter began. At first, Blue could not distinguish the monkeys from the shadows, but as the sun lightened the sky, he began to see the individual black shapes of what appeared to be a single family.

The big male was aloof and sat apart from the others. He maintained an air of nonchalance and quietly watched the antics of his family. The two smaller monkeys were a different story. They raced back and forth through the canopy of trees, chasing each other and jabbering away. Periodically, they would disappear and Blue could barely hear them. Then they would roar back to the large limb their mother used for her morning perch.

Blue smiled at their play. They were so humanlike in the way they related to each other. Every once in a while the two little creatures would stop chasing each other and hug and appear to carry on a secret conversation, just as human children do. Then, as if they had hatched a plot, they would sneak behind their mother and pull the hair on her back. It was the mother's actions that most impressed Blue. She would pretend to be surprised when the little ones touched her, and she would reach for them with a gnarled hand. Her motion would be just fast enough to excite the little monkeys but not fast enough to catch them. Blue watched the monkeys for a full forty minutes, and the mother never lost her patience or tired of the game. Every time a timid little hand reached out and pulled her hair, she would jerk around and make great pretense of trying to catch the perpetrator of the heinous crime. Each time she would just miss capturing the little villains and they would shriek and fall all over each other, trying to escape.

Blue was a romantic. No matter how much he wanted to be an iceman or a hard guy, he was really a romantic. He remembered when he was very young his dad had taken him and his older brother, Wade, to the movies. Blue didn't remember what the movie had been about, but he did remember the cartoon at the end. It was about a mouse shipwrecked on an island that spent the entire cartoon running away from a lion. Eventually, the mouse and lion became good friends, and when a passing ship rescued the mouse, he turned and waved good-bye to his friend. The mouse, the lion, and Blue were all sobbing when the cartoon ended and the lights came on. Blue remembered he had attempted to hide his red eyes, but old Wade had quickly spotted them. As is the duty of all older brothers, Wade sounded out so everyone in the theater would know his brother was a wuss.

Blue had felt embarrassed until his dad reached down and swatted Wade and told him to be quiet. While Wade howled, Blue's dad had reached down and patted him on the head. It was the first memory of his father Blue had, and it meant more to him than any other. He never discussed it with his father, but he often thought of the tender hand and the total understanding and sensitivity it had conveyed.

Of course, such tenderness was absolutely out of place in a fighter squadron. He, like the other guys, built an image of being tough, and the fact that he had won the last two boxing smokers helped. However, he also knew his squadron mates were an emotional lot, despite the fact that any display of it was taboo. He had seen some real tough guys get misty-eyed when they talked about their wife and kids back home, and on the cloudy, rain-swept day they had pushed away from the pier at Norfolk, a lot of guys had been wearing sunglasses.

Blue got out of bed and walked into the bathroom to take his shower. He was soon whistling under the stream of water and thinking about his date with Lori. He was taking her to Grande Island. Chief Mac had told him about the island, and apparently it was a bit of land that jutted into Subic Bay. It was a short distance offshore, and its purpose was to provide recreational opportunities for sailors and their guests. The chief said there were cottages to rent and a hotel, restaurant, and marina. A sailor could rent a sailboat, snorkeling or scuba gear, paddle boats, fishing gear, or just about anything else he would need on a tropical island. It was also very cheap.

Visitors approached the island by sailboat or ferry, but a good swimmer could make it if he wanted to enough. However, such a hardy soul would probably find himself surrounded by the security guards that patrolled the island. The Philippines was unsettled in the southern islands as a fledgling communist party made some inroads into the population. Centuries of feudalism and corruption by Spanish overlords followed by Filipino land barons fueled the movement. Occasionally, disenfranchised members of the People's Liberation Army would push north. They had conducted random acts of terror the prior year. They killed a sailor and his wife on the island, and since then authorities used guards without fail.

Lori sang to herself as she prepared for her date with Blue and remembered the previous evening. Blue had walked her home after the luncheon at Blackjack and had spent the evening talking and socializing. Grandmother had been quite impressed with him, but he had really caught the attention of Uncle Raul. Lori especially liked Blue's care for her uncle after Grandmother scolded him for fiddling with the telephone. Fortunately, it was just as Blue was leaving for the base, so the evening had not been ruined. However, her uncle had been hurt and later, when the telephone rang, he did not make his usual dash to answer. Lori had picked it up on the third ring.

"Hello, is Raul Martinez there?"

"Blue?"

"Yep, it's me."

"What are you doing?" She laughed.

"I am calling for Mr. Raul Martinez. I would most appreciate it if you put him on the line." Lori laughed as she heard him chuckling over the line.

"Okay, Lieutenant Morrison. I'll get Mr. Martinez."

Uncle Raul had never gotten a telephone call in his life. He had made the one fateful call to Australia, but he had never received a call. When Lori told him the telephone was for him, his face lit up like a star. He ran to the telephone, but as he picked it up, his entire manner changed to one of seriousness. He looked at Lori and Grandmother and held up a finger.

"Shhh, I have a telephone call."

He put the telephone to his ear and cleared his throat. "Who may I say I am?" He proudly asked.

Lori put her hands over her mouth to keep from laughing, but tears formed in her eyes. Grandmother stood next to her and squeezed her shoulders.

Blue later recited the conversation word for word to Lori. After Uncle Raul had asked who he could say he was, Blue had responded, "Why, you can say you are Uncle Raul!"

"Thank you," said Uncle Raul as he nodded in agreement. "That is correct." He frowned, trying to remember what he had heard others say.

"You may ask, 'To whom am I speaking?'" said Blue.

"Yes," remembered Uncle Raul. "To whom may I say I am speaking?"

"This is Blue." Blue laughed. "Your friend."

"It's Blue," shouted Uncle Raul. His eyes got big and he smiled. "Lori, it's Blue. Mama, it's Blue!"

"Do you want to speak to Lori?"

"No," said Blue, "I just called to see how you were doing."

"Lori, he does not want to speak to you." Uncle Raul's matter-of-fact tone caused Lori and her grandmother to laugh and hug each other.

Blue and Uncle Raul had talked for several more minutes, and when he said good-bye and handed her the receiver, his smile made a lump form in her throat.

"Thank you," she whispered.

"Sure."

"That really meant a lot to him."

"It meant a lot to me."

"See you tomorrow at the gate?"

"You bet." He laughed. "I'll be waiting."

The following morning, Blue met Lori at the main gate.

"Wow, you look great."

"Why thank you, sir." Lori smiled and held out her hand. Blue took it, and they walked the short distance to the ferry.

Lori had arisen even earlier than usual and had mulled over what to wear for an hour before picking a simple, yellow sundress. She hoped it would be that perfect mixture of cute and classy and that her long black hair would accentuate it. She could tell by the way he looked at her that she must have come close.

As they walked, Eve's words of warning kept popping into her mind, and although she smiled and held his hand, there was a flicker of concern.

*Are you in love with him? How could you fall so fast for a stranger? What made him different from Jose, Tony, or the others?*

But Blue was different! Blue seemed to genuinely care about what other people thought and what was inside them. The way he had treated Uncle Raul had captivated her, and she would always be grateful to him for giving her the precious moment when she and Grandma had held each other and watched her uncle. He had been so proud to receive a telephone call—just for him.

She hadn't realized until they were together at Blackjack how well Blue listened. Lori thought many people pretended to listen but, in actuality, it was only a polite gap between their own expressions of thoughts. Blue wasn't like that. He didn't always immediately respond to her with some standard phrase or thought. He listened, he digested, and sometimes he didn't say anything at all. He would just smile or give her a squeeze from his strong hand to assure her he had heard. Lori had mentioned this to her grandma, who told her most men do not like to trust themselves to silence. There is not enough control of silence, and it makes men nervous. Men need to know what people are thinking so they can address their thoughts and fix any misunderstanding. Grandma said this was especially true when men are talking with people they barely know. She said a man had to be very secure to be comfortable with silence.

Blue paid the fee for the ferry trip, and they had to wait only a few minutes before it was time to board.

It was hot, even beneath the wooden canopy of the ferry's roof, so Blue went forward to the concession stand to buy a couple of sodas. As he waited in line, he looked around the crowd and saw that most were couples. All appeared to be sailors and their girls from the bars out to enjoy a beautiful day.

Magic had told him there were over ten thousand prostitutes in Olongapo, so Blue assumed the sailors' guests were hookers. He knew the assumption might not be fair, but the girls certainly acted the part if they weren't. They continually ran their hands over their sailors' crotches, and their shorts were so short they were literally hanging out of them. Blue finally worked his way to the head of the line and got his order. Grabbing a frosty bottle of Coke in each hand, he turned to leave when one of the sailors touched his arm and smiled broadly.

"Congratulations, man! Looks like you picked a good one. Where did you find her, the Mellow Yellow?" The sailor glanced at Lori and then grinned at Blue. It was a collegial smile of comradeship.

Blue's face flushed with a mixture of anger and embarrassment. The anger was for the sailor, but he wasn't sure about the embarrassment. Was he embarrassed for Lori? Or was he embarrassed for himself? He hated the feeling.

"First of all, my name isn't 'man.'" Blue spit out the words between clenched teeth. "And second, I didn't pick her up anywhere."

The sailor's smile quickly vanished as he realized Blue was not another comrade in debauchery and was probably a damn officer. He took a couple of steps backward and held up his hands.

"Sorry, sir. Didn't mean to piss you off." He turned and walked away.

Blue felt foolish. The sailor hadn't meant any harm. Hell, he probably thought he was paying Blue a compliment of some kind. However, it cut him to the quick to think anybody could mistake Lori for a hooker. Then, for some reason, Blue thought of Viela.

*"Looks like you've been busy,"* he had said.

*The way she had looked at him. The hurt in her eyes.*

As he walked back to Lori, she flashed him a beautiful smile and he immediately smiled back. Fortunately, it was such a gorgeous day Blue was able to cast away the incident with the sailor, and he and Lori enjoyed the rest of the trip, watching the clear water run past their boat. When the ferry docked, they made their way down the gangplank and over to the marina to rent some snorkeling gear.

Blue had been wondering what kind of body Lori had and was curious to see what she would look like in a swimsuit. When she emerged from the changing room, he felt his mouth drop. She was georgeous! Lori's turquoise bikini was a perfect complement to her olive skin, and she filled it exquisitely. Her breasts were ample and proud, her stomach flat and hard. Her buttocks were firm against the fabric of her suit, and her long, slim legs tapered to perfect ankles.

Fortunately for Blue, Lori was looking at a towel she had dropped and didn't see his ogling. He managed to get his mouth shut by the time she looked at him.

"Wow!" For the second time that day, Blue was glad for his sunglasses. He knew he was staring.

"I take it 'wow' is good?"

"'Wow' is very good."

"Well, wow yourself, then." Lori smiled at Blue and threw him a towel. "Let's go."

They picked up their gear and headed toward the far side of the island. The people at the marina told them that was where they could find the best coral formations. As they walked along, Blue kept stealing glances at Lori. *Holy shit,* he kept thinking. *Holy shit.*

They waded out to waist-deep water and put on their masks and fins. The water was clear, and the temperature was perfect.

There are more than two thousand types of fish living in the waters of the Philippines, and Blue and Lori were soon swimming among fascinating, multicolored schools of them. There was the bright yellow-and-black clown fish, the equally spectacular red-and-orange flame angel, and the blue jack fish, and they all displayed their brilliance in the clear, crystal water. Once a shadow floated by and Lori grabbed Blue's arm as she spotted the gray flash of a barracuda. But even its ominous shape and sharp, dagger teeth could not put a damper on their play. They frolicked like that for nearly two hours before deciding to break for lunch.

As she munched on a piece of potato, Lori detected a slight tension in Blue. It was the way he looked away from her and the tightness of his laugh. But the longer they sat she realized that she too was tense. She was tense because she realized she was at the point of needing to understand what was going on between them. And she was afraid the answer might not be what she hoped.

Lori had had not been looking for anyone when Blue just popped up in her life. She was not looking for someone to love. And now something was happening that was too fast to understand. It was wonderful, but it was also frightening. And whatever it was, could it be trusted? Complicating the situation was the knowledge that Blue would not be in the Philippines much longer. She stole a glance at him as he picked at his sandwich, and then she knew why she was so uneasy.

She was falling in love with him! Maybe she was already in love with him!

She shook her head at the improbability of such a thing. After all, she had known him for only four days. She caught another quick glance. His eyes were roaming out the window, and he did not see her looking at him. She knew she was in a rapidly growing love that was blossoming faster than she could ever imagine, and she needed time to try to understand it. But there was no time. She had reached a plateau where she finally admitted to herself that this feeling, this *thing*, was different. Something strange, something possibly wonderful was going on. But did Blue feel the same? Or was she here on this plateau alone? Did he have the same deep ache that accompanied her to bed each night and lay upon her heart until she finally drifted to sleep? Did he have the ache that opened her eyes in the morning and made her happy when she thought of seeing him again, the ache that caused her to shiver each time he touched her? Was it possible he could feel the same?

"Want to walk?" Lori smiled at Blue, who motioned toward the beach.

"Sure," she replied.

He took her by the hand and led her down to the beach, and as they walked along the sand, Lori knew she could not let that day end without finding an answer to her heart's questions.

"I am glad you came with me today."

Blue grinned at her. "So am I."

"I think we're the best-looking couple on the island."

"Pretty conceited, aren't you?"

"No, I mean it."

"Well, I guess I have to agree."

"Do you see many mixed couples in the Philippines?" Blue looked sideways at her.

"Not outside of Olongapo."

"I see," said Blue. "Are Filipinos biased?"

"Oh, I don't know," said Lori. "Some are, some aren't, like anywhere else."

"What do you think about mixed relationships?"

Lori stopped and looked at him. *Why is he asking that?*

"I, ah, I mean in general," he continued.

Lori continued to look at Blue, and then she looked down at the sand. "I think it's important for people to be sure they understand who it is they are in the relationship with," she said. "I think it is important for them to understand all that's involved with the decision. If another race is involved, it's just one more thing to be considered."

*Is she talking about us?*

"For instance," said Lori, "in the Philippines we feel it is families who marry, not individuals. So anyone who married a Filipino would need to know that."

"I see."

"In that way we provide for our extended family—the needy, the very young or old. We believe in the spirit of solidarity of all the family. We believe it is more important than seeking individual desires. In the Philippines we call this *bayanihan*."

"You said you believe people must know each other," said Blue. He stopped walking and turned toward Lori, taking off his sunglasses. "How long does it take?"

The wind whipped through Lori's long hair, sprinkling her with beads of spray. A few strands of hair fell across her face, and she brushed them away.

"Sometimes ..." She paused and looked into Blue's eyes. "Sometimes not long."

"Something is happening to me," whispered Blue. He looked deeply into Lori's eyes. "Something very strange. I can't explain it."

"I know," she replied, "very strange."

"Is it wrong?"

"I hope not."

"Do we know what we are doing?"

"I hope so."

Blue reached into the pockets of his shorts and took out a small stone. He handed it to Lori.

"What is that?" Lori looked at the stone and then back into Blue's eyes.

"It is a *gayuma*."

"A *gayuma*." She laughed softly. "What do you know about Filipino love charms?"

"Father Joseph gave me some books to read."

"I see. Where did you get your *gayuma*?"

Blue paused and looked into Lori's eyes. "After I left your house I tossed and turned and couldn't sleep. Finally, I went outside to watch the night. God shot this star across the sky, and I caught it."

"I see," whispered Lori. "Does it work?"

"I don't know," said Blue. He slowly leaned toward her and gently licked a drop of saltwater from her eyelash. "I read that in Zambales, they believe if a man drinks water that has cleaned a woman, he will be hers forever."

"I see," she whispered again. She looked at him and her lips trembled. "Does it work?"

"Yes." He leaned toward her and gently brushed his lips against hers, and then he kissed her. His lips were sweet against hers, and as he gathered her in his arms, she felt herself melt into him. She felt her breasts heave against his chest, and she felt her head grow light with passion. It was a long kiss, a long and wonderful kiss. But it was also a what-am-I-doing kiss, a kiss that left her with questions after his lips pulled from hers. She knew that she was not on the plateau alone, but that didn't mean she knew where she was.

"Where does it go from here?" whispered Lori.

"I don't know." Blue held her tighter, his voice in her ear.

"Are we doing the right thing?"

"It feels right to me."

She could feel his lips brushing her hair. "But you must leave soon."

"But I will come back." He relaxed his embrace and looked at her. She smiled up at him, and he kissed her again.

"Hello, *Tio*. How are you today?" Lori smiled at Uncle Raul as she walked up the front steps. She had taken a cab from the gate and was hurrying to start dinner. Blue was on his way to Cubi to change clothes. Her step was light, and her eyes sparkled because he was returning for the evening meal.

"Your father is here." Uncle Raul's eyes smiled. He loved being the first to deliver news. "Your father is here from Manila."

"What?"

"Your father is here from—"

"Lori!" Pablo Santiago smiled broadly as he walked out of the doorway, into the sun.

"Papa, what brings you to Olongapo? Is Mama all right?" Lori always worried that something would happen to her mother.

"Sure, she is fine," he said as he held out his arms. "I just thought I would come and see you since you never seem to find time to come home."

"But you should have called." Lori frowned as she embraced her father. What was she going to do about Blue?

"Why? I wanted to surprise you." Mr. Santiago released his daughter from the hug and stood back to get a better look. "You look even more beautiful than I remembered."

"Papa, I have only been gone two weeks. But thank you anyway." Lori glanced at her watch and frowned. "You should call."

"What's wrong? Am I interrupting something?" Mr. Santiago narrowed his eyes.

"Well, I do have a friend coming over."

"Is it a man friend?"

"Yes."

"I see," said Mr. Santiago. "Jose mentioned you seemed preoccupied. He said you would not go out with him when he was here. Who is your friend?"

"It's just someone I met." Lori smiled nervously and walked past her father, into the house.

"Who is he? Why be so mysterious?" Lori heard the screen door creak as he followed her inside.

"Good evening, *Lola*," said Lori as she smiled at her grandmother.

"Good evening, my child."

"Lori, your father's here … from Manila."

"Thank you, *Tio*. I see him."

"He came in a big car." Uncle Raul grinned excitedly and motioned toward the limousine parked by the side of the house.

"Yes," said Lori.

"Come, Raul." Grandmother took Raul by the arm and led him to the door. "Let's go into the backyard and look at the monkeys."

Mr. Santiago paused until he and Lori were alone. "Surely you have not known this young man long. You have not brought him to Manila." Lori's father was reminding her of Filipino tradition. Young men are expected to present themselves to the parents of a girl they are wooing.

"I just met him a few days ago."

"A local boy?"

"No."

"Oh?" Mr. Santiago narrowed his eyes and looked at his daughter. "Oh?"

"He is a young man I met in the store. He came to buy a gun case. For his admiral."

"Admiral! He is in the navy. The American navy?"

"Papa, please don't get excited."

"You know what I think about American sailors! I cannot believe you are doing this. Dammit, I knew it. I told Mama this would happen. I warned her just last week."

"But, Papa!"

"Lori, I don't demand much of you." Mr. Santiago softened his voice and took his daughter in his arms. He sighed and kissed the top of her head. "You know I don't ask much. I try to do what you and Mama want."

"I know," said Lori. "You have given me everything."

"Then why can't you do this one thing?"

"Hello. Hello, in the house."

Lori stiffened against her father's embrace when she heard the sound of Blue's voice. She ran to the door and down the steps.

"Hey," said Blue as he grinned. "What's the rush? Why haven't you changed clothes?"

"Blue, I want you to go back to the base. I will call you later."

"What's wrong?" Blue frowned and looked at the front door.

"My father is here. He is not happy."

"You told him about me?"

"Yes."

"Well, come on then. Let's go see him together. I'm sure we can work something out."

"No!" insisted Lori. "It is not our way. My father will not discuss family business in front of strangers."

"Is that what I am, a stranger?"

"To my father you are."

"What am I supposed to do? Just leave?"

"I will talk to my father. Maybe, tomorrow morning he will feel better. I am sure he has had a long day."

"Well, okay." Blue sighed. "Tomorrow," he said and then turned and walked away.

Lori watched him go and then walked up the stairs and into the house. Her father was sitting on the rattan couch, sipping a glass of tea.

"Sit down, please." Mr. Santiago motioned toward the couch. "Here, beside me." Lori sat beside her father and looked into his face.

"To a Filipino, a child is the most precious gift from God."

"Papa, I know—"

"Please, Lori. Let me speak. And it is even more special when it is a first child—an only, angel child. And it happened to me! Did you know I was fifty when you were born?"

"Yes, Papa, I know."

"I had given up on ever being a father—a father with a baby of my own." Mr. Santiago paused and took another sip of tea. He wiped his lips with a napkin and put the glass on the table. "I went to Obando with your mama. Do you know where it is?"

"Yes, Papa. It is where San Pasqual and Santa Clara are enshrined."

"That's right." He paused again and reached for his glass. After draining it, he returned the glass to the table and took his daughter's hand into his own.

"We could not have children. We had tried and we had prayed, but Mama could not get pregnant."

"Oh, Papa …" Lori placed her father's hand against her cheek.

"I thought it must be something wrong with me, but the doctors said no. So we went to the shrine, we knelt before it, and we chanted the chant of all lonely men and women who have not been blessed with God's most holy of gifts. *Santa clarang pinong pino. Tsang anak, 'sang apo.*"

"Santa Clara, please give us a child and grandchild," whispered Lori.

"That is right," said Mr. Santiago. "We chanted it over and over. We held hands, we wept, and we chanted over and over and over again. And then we left and went home, and we prayed. And then, there was a little, tiny baby inside your mama, and it was you."

"Oh, Papa." Lori felt the warm trickle of a tear roll down her cheek.

"You see, that is the Filipino way, child. We wished for you and for something of you. We wished for our own lonely hearts and for your heart as well. And one day, God willing, we will have our wish completed. One day you two will have a little baby, maybe a girl like you, to complete the circle of our prayer."

Lori placed her father's hand back on the couch and wiped the tears from her face. "Papa, someday I will have that baby and you will have a grandchild. And that baby will be the product of my love."

"And that love is so important, Lori." Mr. Santiago reached his hand to her face and cradled her chin. He looked into her eyes. "The love you find is so important because there is so much false love out there. This business with the American frightens me, and it will frighten Mama. I fear for your heart, dear child. And, I confess, I fear for the heart of your mother and me too."

"But, Papa. I feel something for this young man. He is different."

"Do you love him?"

Lori felt her father's warm hand quiver beneath her chin. She took his hand and placed it back on the couch.

"Do you love him, Lori?"

She looked into her father's eyes and into the love he had for her. Her desire to never hurt him squeezed her heart. Mama loved her. Mama loved her dearly. But he loved her even more. Maybe it was his lateness in life to have a baby, maybe it was his passion to protect his little girl, and maybe it was because she knew he needed her. The reasons didn't really matter because he had always been the one she had run to.

"I do not know," said Lori. She looked away from him and winced at the lie. She didn't want to hurt him. "I have never been in love. I don't know how it is supposed to feel."

"Oh, come, girl! You have never been in love, with all the boys that came to visit?"

Lori heard her father's voice brighten, and she knew why.

"I liked them, Papa. I liked them all. But I did not love any of them."

"What does your American feel? Is he in love with you?"

"I do not know." Lori shook her head in confusion. "We have had so little time, and he leaves in a few days."

"He leaves soon, eh?" Lori heard the relief in his voice. It made her feel empty. It made her feel untrue.

"Good, this will have some time to sort out then."

"Yes, there is time to sort it out ..." Lori's voice drifted to silence.

"Well, come, let's get *Lola*, and Raul. I'm hungry." Mr. Santiago got up from the couch, stretched, and then walked outside.

Lori sighed and shook her head. The sound of her father's whistling blew in softly from the yard, and its melody seemed to only deepen her feelings of emptiness and deceit. But was she deceitful or just wisely guarding her heart? How could it be possible that she was in love with a man she only met a few days ago? How could that be? She stood and slowly walked into the kitchen and began to prepare the fish. It was a special fish she bought in the market, a fish fit to prepare *Sinigang Na Bangus* for Blue. She would have to fix it for Papa, *Lola* and *Tio* now. But as she leaned against the sink she felt something in the pocket of her dress.

*It is a gayuma ... God shot this star across the sky and I caught it.*

Lori put her hand to her mouth and closed her eyes. She could almost feel his lips. She could almost feel the warmth of breath and the strength of his arms. "This must be love," she whispered. "But if it is, why didn't I just tell Papa? Why didn't I stand by it?"

Her hand trembled as she put the knife against the fish, and as she worked she could hear the soft tinkling of her father's whistling.

# CHAPTER 20

The next morning Lori arose early and went to the shop. She didn't feel like talking to her father or to anyone else. But as she worked through the chores of paperwork and inventory, she thought of Blue and began to smile. She even caught herself whistling the tune her father had whistled the night before, and it made her laugh. Her thoughts were good and happy. They were thoughts of things to come and thoughts of joy and love. As she worked through the morning, she kept expecting him to pop through the front door—behind his big smile and blue eyes. And she felt nervous, happy, and confused by the thought of such a thing. When she examined the finished gun case Mr. DeCastro had so carefully created, she felt tremendous pride. Mr. DeCastro had worked in her grandmother's shop for years and was their best artisan. The case was absolutely beautiful. The wood had a rich, soft warmth, and it felt good in her hands. She bent to smell the forest in it, and she found herself smiling. She popped open the brass clasps and ran her fingers over the deep-blue velvet interior. It was an exquisite piece of insert work and a perfect background for the rifle. She smiled again and took a deep breath.

"I love my father," she whispered. She put the case down and re-snapped the clasps. "But I do so want Blue to walk in that door."

She glanced at the entrance to the shop as if to affirm her thoughts. She smiled again. "I am disappointed because he did not come," she said to the empty room. "And that is because I love him. And that is what I must say to Papa."

She left the shop under the watchful gaze of Mr. DeCastro and walked the short distance home. She would have lunch there, visit with Papa, and then return. As she walked up the sidewalk to her grandmother's house, she could not believe her eyes. There was Blue, chopping wood in the side yard.

"What's going on?" Lori walked toward Blue and then spotted her father, sitting under the big mango tree.

"What's going on?" she repeated.

"Lori, Blue is here."

"Yes, *Tio,* I see. What is he doing?"

"Blue is helping your father."

Blue looked at her and grinned but didn't speak. Sweat gleamed on his body, and his arms glistened as he swung the ax.

"Papa, what is going on?" Lori walked to where her father sat and joined him on the grass. "What is Blue doing?"

He looked at her and shrugged. "I don't know. This morning I decided to help with some of the chores that are too difficult for Raul."

"Since when do you do manual labor? You have an army of servants."

"I will have you know I am in pretty good shape for a man who is seventy-five. Besides, I was just going to fill the cooking box."

"And Blue came to see me and you made him work?"

"No, he didn't," said Blue. He held the ax in his hand and grinned. "I asked him if I could do it."

"He is right," said Mr. Santiago. "I was chopping with the ax, and he walked into the yard and asked if he could chop the wood for me. He said it was a Filipino tradition."

"He did?" She turned and looked at Blue. "You did?"

"Yep," said Blue. He picked up the ax and went back to splitting the logs.

"I am surprised an American knows of such things," said Mr. Santiago. "When I was your age, young men were expected to visit the house of the girl they were wooing and help with whatever the family was doing. In this way, the family could observe the boy and decide whether to accept his suit."

"But, Papa, this is the twentieth century. He is an American." Lori looked across the yard at Blue. He seemed not to care about their conversation as he swung his ax without hesitation.

"Maybe so, but I am not an American, and neither are you."

"I know of the tradition, Papa." She glanced again at Blue and looked at her father. "Have you decided to at least talk with Blue?"

Her father stood and brushed the grass from his pants. "It often takes a long time for such things to be decided." He walked past her to where Blue stood, leaning on his ax and catching his breath. Blue had reduced the entire cord of wood to the correct size for the cooking box. Mr. Santiago picked up a piece of wood, examined it, and then grunted and threw it down. He slowly walked to the side of the house, turned on a garden hose, and then picked up a bristle brush and started scrubbing.

"Oh, Papa, not the house."

"It's okay." Blue grinned at Lori and dropped the ax. He walked to Mr. Santiago and held his hand out for the brush. Lori set her jaw in frustration as she watched Blue begin to scrub the side of the house.

"Papa!" She looked at her father but he had his back turned and was intently watching Blue. "Papa," she said again. Mr. Santiago did not turn or answer. He continued to watch Blue. Lori stood for a few more minutes then threw her hands up, turned, and walked back to the shop. She fumed for awhile as she imagined how her father would continue finding tasks for Blue. However, Blue had stumbled into a trap when he had brought up the Filipino tradition angle and she hoped Papa would not take too much advantage. She decided it best to stay away and spent the afternoon working on the accounts. When she finally went home, she half expected to see Blue gone.

"Papa, it's five o'clock in the afternoon. Blue was scrubbing mold from the house when I left to go back to work, and you now have him painting the fence. Have you at least given him something to eat?" Lori stood over her father and frowned. He leaned back in his chair, smiled up at her, and then shaded his eyes to look at Blue.

"Said he wasn't hungry."

"Oh, you ..." She turned to look at Blue. He was covered in sweat, sawdust, and paint.

"Do you intend on working him all night?"

Her father looked at Blue a moment and then stood up. "No, tell him I have nothing else for him."

"But, Papa! Is that all you can say?"

"I have nothing else for him."

Lori gritted her teeth in frustration and hurried across the yard to Blue. He was cleaning the brushes in a jar of turpentine. He smiled as she walked up.

"Boy, you folks know how to fill up a day."

"Blue, I am so sorry."

"Don't be. I think he's beginning to like me." Blue laughed and sat the jar on a workbench.

"Oh, Blue. He said he has nothing else for you."

"Okay." Blue shrugged and started working on the paint on his fingers. "What does that mean?"

"It means he has not accepted you."

"Oh?"

"Blue, you have to understand. This is hard for my father. I am an only child. He is very protective."

"It's more than that," said Blue. He looked at her and sighed. "It's because I'm an American, isn't it?"

"My father does have bitterness for Americans. It goes back a long way."

"Why?"

"He was a baby in the war with the United States, and his family was all killed. His mother and sisters—all of them were killed. The Americans tried to trick his father, and that is the reason they cut off Papa's thumb."

"I wondered how he lost it."

"It will take time, Blue." Lori took Blue's hand and squeezed it. "We will have to be patient."

"Okay." Blue smiled. "I'll say good night and leave. But I'll be back tomorrow to talk with your father." They walked into the house, and Blue nodded to Lori's father.

"Good night, sir." Mr. Santiago looked at him and nodded slightly.

"Good night, *Tio* Raul."

"Good night, Blue."

Blue walked to the chair where Grandmother sat and leaned toward her. *"Mano po,"* he said and held out his hand.

Grandma looked startled for an instant, and then a smile slowly crept across her weathered face. He held her hand, and as Blue kissed it, she made the sign of the cross over his head.

*"Dios to beniga,"* she whispered. "May God bless you."

Blue arose and walked out of the house. Lori watched him go, set her jaw, and marched back inside. She found her father in the living room alone, sitting and sipping a glass of tea. Her grandmother had evidently taken Raul to the back of the house.

"Why are you doing this?" She looked at him, surprised at her anger. She had never been angry with him before. She had been mad at him, but never angry.

"It will take much more than a few words in Tagalog and gestures to our culture to convince me he is genuine. Besides, he is not one of us. He probably doesn't have the slightest idea of the significance of his actions." Her father stared across the room and took a sip of tea.

"But can't you see he is trying? I think he loves me!"

"Love!" Her father sat down his glass and stood. He looked at her and folded his arms. "How can he love you? He doesn't even know you."

"Why do you treat him with such contempt? I have never seen you like this. Today, you would not speak to Blue. Not once did I hear you say a word. When he left tonight, you observed how he honored *Lola*. Yet, you barely acknowledge his existence." Lori felt her face redden as she looked at him. She was very uncomfortable. She had never talked to him like this.

"Acknowledge what, exactly?" Her father returned Lori's stare. His always-kind eyes were hard and set. "Tell me, Lori, what is your relationship? Are you lovers?"

"We have not made love, if that is what you mean." She took a step back, and tears sprung from her eyes. "Is that what you are afraid of, that I have slept with him?" She put her face in her hands and turned to leave. But her father's hands touched her shoulders, and he turned her around. He lifted her face to meet him. "Come, let's sit down. Let's drink some tea." He took her hand and led her outside to the front porch swing. He waited as she sat and then went inside to fetch the drinks. By the time he returned and sat down beside her, she had stopped sniffling and was staring at the sky.

"What are you afraid of, Papa?"

"I am afraid of the dark."

Lori turned to see his face, and his answer surprised her.

"I am afraid of the dark because I cannot see."

Lori sat quiet for a moment and then pushed the swing forward.

"I am afraid of your Blue because I cannot see him. I do not understand him. His acts of respect today, they confuse me. He is not acting as I expected." He looked at her and sighed.

"So you think he is being deceitful?"

"Like I said, I am afraid of the dark. I am afraid of what I cannot see, of what I cannot understand."

"But, Papa, he is my friend."

"I do not think so. You have many friends, and that is not what I see here. I see both of you in a situation neither of you understand. If he were a local boy, this would be fine. Time would be our ally. We could get to know him and his family. But your Blue is not a local boy; he is a foreigner, and he will leave soon. That implies quick decisions because there is no time to know him or his family. I do not think these decisions will be wise."

They sat there in silence a few moments, rocking back and forth together. Lori felt the anger in her fall away with the motion of the swing. Her father's use of the word "afraid" had brought her a surge of love for him. He had never admitted fear of anything.

"Papa, how long did you know Mama before you loved her?"

"I knew your mother a full year before we were married."

"That is not what I asked. How long did you know her before you loved her?" She reached over and took his hand in hers.

"I do not know. Do you think I keep these dates in a little book somewhere?"

"Was it the first time you saw her?"

"I do not remember such things. I was a very busy man." He took his hand from hers and rubbed his forehead.

"Mama told me it was love at first sight, for both of you. Is that not true? Is Mama wrong?"

"Maybe—"

"If you had married Mama on that very first day, would anything be different now? Didn't you love her on first sight?"

"Lori, you are a hopeless romantic." Mr. Santiago turned in the swing to face her. "Besides, we were different. We were both from the same culture. He is an American. It is totally different."

"Why is it different?"

"It just is!" He looked away again, up at the stars.

"Papa, I am aware of your past, of your father's heroism. I remember the stories of the war and how the Americans killed your mother and sisters. How they cut off your thumb."

"What does this have to do with anything?" He jerked his head around sharply.

"You are a racist, Papa." Lori grabbed his shoulder and turned him to look at her. "You are biased against Blue simply because he is an American."

"Nonsense! I have many business associates who are Americans."

"But do you have any American *friends*?"

"I don't know. I don't keep track of such things."

"And that is not all. Blue is a sailor. You are ashamed of Filipino girls that marry sailors. I heard you say so to Grandmother when you told her no American boys were to visit."

"I might have said I was ashamed of a situation whereby Filipino girls are turned into prostitutes to satisfy the lusts of the Americans. Of that, I am very ashamed."

"I think whenever you see a Filipino girl and an American, you automatically assume she is a hooker. Isn't that right, Papa? And you could not think of seeing me that way."

Lori's father did not answer. He just stared at his hands.

"Papa, I have never loved anyone before, except for my family. I have never loved a boy before. I do not know exactly what is going on with me, but, Papa, it is wonderful!" She looked at him and took his hands in hers. A smile spread across her face. "Papa, what I feel, it is wonderful. Don't you understand?"

"But Lori—"

"I also know I love you and I love Mother. But you must let me be free to see where my heart is. I need to know what this feeling is in me. I fear it will tear me apart if I don't." Lori slipped off the swing and knelt at her father's feet. She placed his hand against her cheek.

"Today, when I saw you sitting under the mango tree watching Blue, I was struck by it."

"What do you mean?"

"Do you remember the story you told me about the mango tree and the bamboo tree, about how they argued which was the strongest? And when they could not decide, they asked the wind to decide for them. Do you remember?"

"Yes, I remember."

"You told me how the mango tree was so proud and so brave and he would not bend. But the wind blew and blew, and one day the mango tree's roots could no longer hold. The mighty tree fell. You told me the bamboo tree also felt the wind, but the bamboo tree was not just proud; it was wise. The bamboo tree bent its head, its roots held, and it survived. Do you remember the story?"

"Of course, Lori." Mr. Santiago sighed and stroked his daughter's hair.

"You told me the Filipino people are like the bamboo tree; they bend so that they do not break."

"That is true."

"But it is not true for you, Father. You do not like to bend your head. You are like the mango, not the bamboo." Lori raised her head and looked into her father's eyes. "I am like you, Papa. I am like you and the mango tree. I do not know what's going on with Blue and me. But on the issue of seeing him, of being with him, I will not bend my head."

"And I am the wind?"

"Yes, Papa. You are the wind. I beg of you not to blow too hard."

Mr. Santiago gently touched his daughter's face and then stood and walked to the door. He looked back at her, and she could see his sadness, even in the shadows.

"And if you find you are in love, will he take you away from me? Will you live in America?"

"If I leave, I promise to come back."

Mr. Santiago sighed again and slowly opened the door. He paused at the doorstep and turned his head toward her.

"I will talk to him tomorrow."

# CHAPTER 21

"Good morning." Blue grinned and waved as he walked up the sidewalk.

"Good morning, Blue." Lori smiled back and watched him approach. "Where is everybody?" Blue stepped up on the porch. He glanced over Lori's shoulder and gave her a quick kiss.

"Oh, Blue." She pushed him away and then quickly embraced him and kissed him back. She pushed him away. "Grandma and Uncle Raul have gone to the shop."

"I see, and your father?"

"My father is waiting for you. He is under the mango tree."

"So he will talk with me?" He grinned and hugged her.

"It seems," she said, her voiced muffled against his shoulder.

"How did you make it happen?" Blue dropped his embrace and looked at her.

"We talked for a long time last night."

"Oh?"

"He has many reservations about Americans. Some are based upon the past. Some are based upon his fear of the future."

"He's afraid he is going to lose you?" Blue put his hand to her face.

"Yes."

"And you? Are you afraid too?"

"Yes, I am afraid too." She moved her head and looked down.

"I think I love you, Lori. I don't fall in love every day. In fact, I have never fallen in love. But I think this is love, and I think you love me." He took her hand in his, and she looked up at him.

"Then go and talk with him."

Blue glanced around to see if anyone could see them and then gave Lori another kiss. "I'll see you later, if he doesn't kill me."

Blue walked around the corner of the house and across the lawn to the mango tree. Mr. Santiago was sitting under it on a lawn chair. As Blue approached, he motioned to sit down.

Mr. Santiago looked at Blue for a moment, studying his face. He shrugged slightly and selected a brown *robusto* from a two-fingered leather pouch. After clipping the end and lighting it, he took a long drag.

"Your First Continental Congress met in 1774, in Philadelphia, and the Second Continental Congress met a year later to proclaim your Declaration of Independence." Mr. Santiago looked at Blue and took another puff.

Blue sat and focused on Mr. Santiago, carefully listening to his words.

"I would suspect many Americans do not know this." Mr. Santiago paused and looked at the end of his cigar. Then, finding the ash satisfactory, continued. "At noon on June 30, 1863, Union General John Buford entered Gettysburg from the south. He knew all of Lee's army was close, and when his scouts reported rebels coming down the Cashtown road, he thought they might be on him. But he chose to defend the high ground. Had he not done so and left it for the rebels, the outcome of your Civil War might have been very different."

Blue nodded and continued to look at Lori's father. Mr. Santiago once again studied his cigar and then looked at Blue. "What is the most important thing for a nation to feel?"

"Sir?" Blue frowned in confusion.

"A nation. What is the most important feeling a nation can have?"

"Security? I don't know, sir."

"Relevant," said Mr. Santiago. "The most important word for a nation, or for a man, is relevant."

"I never thought of that, sir."

"No," whispered Mr. Santiago. "Of course you wouldn't. You never thought of it because you take it for granted." The bottom of his cane chair squeaked as he leaned toward Blue. "You see, Americans are always relevant, regardless of the issue. At least, all of the world seems to think you are. You sure think you are. That is why it is so easy to dislike you."

Blue looked at Mr. Santiago. He took a deep breath, held it for a moment before slowly letting it out, and remained silent.

"Do you know why I know things about your country, things that many of your own people do not know?"

"No, sir."

"Because I was forced to learn it!" Mr. Santiago looked hard at Blue and took a puff from his robusto.

Blue saw Mr. Santiago's fingers tremble slightly, where he held the cigar.

"I was forced to learn it because America was relevant, Lieutenant Morrison. Relevant! Did you realize Manila was bombed more heavily by the Japanese than Pearl Harbor?"

"No, sir." Blue could see that Mr. Santiago's breath was coming faster.

"Neither did I," said Mr. Santiago. "Not until a few years ago, and I was told this by a Japanese historian. This was not taught in Filipino schools. This was not taught to my children. Do you know why?"

"No, sir." Blue shook his head and kept his gaze level.

"Because we did not consider ourselves relevant, Lieutenant Morrison!" Mr. Santiago's face grew red, and he stared at Blue. He took several deep breaths and once again returned to his cigar. He checked the ash for evenness and took another puff.

"I wasn't required to learn anything about the Philippines, Mr. Santiago." Blue shifted in his chair so he could look more directly at Lori's father. "My high school history book barely mentions your home, and to be honest, before this cruise I didn't even know where the Philippines was located. But if what I have learned about your people is true, you will not hate me for that."

Mr. Santiago furrowed his brows but remained silent.

"Sir, I have no explanation for the past. I only know I have strong feelings for your daughter and for *Lola* and *Tio* Raul. I also have an appreciation for this town of Olongapo and these people. My history books and teachers did not make the Philippines relevant to me, but please do not fault me for what I did not know. A long time ago, foreign soldiers came to this land and many lands like this and faulted the people they found for not knowing about their ways. Rudyard Kipling called the chore of educating people such as you 'the white man's burden.' Please do not fault me for the past—or present—of others, sir. I promise to give you no reason to fault my future and the future of your daughter."

Mr. Santiago did not answer but, instead, looked toward the jungle. He stared into its green vastness for a long time. Finally, he tossed away the glowing stub of his cigar and looked at the young American.

"My father was a great patriot, Blue."

Blue smiled. It was the first time Lori's father had used his name.

"Yes, sir. Lori told me."

"One day, at the beginning of the war with the Americans, my father came upon a village that had been attacked. In the village was a naked Filipino soldier. He was found dead, sitting in a chair with his hands tied together. A wire was tied around his testicles with the other end tied to a root. Rags were wrapped around his ankles, and they had been set on fire. A large tub of water sat only ten feet away."

"Christ," said Blue.

"Yes, Christ," repeated Mr. Santiago. "The torture selected by the Americans showed a great understanding for us Filipinos. You see, when the Americans set the rags on fire, the young soldier had a choice. He could jump up and run to the tub of water and live.

However, if he did so, he would rip off his own testicles. He could never father a child, Blue. He could never have a family. But he would live. His other choice was to sit while the fire burned away his legs and killed him!"

"And your father found him dead."

"Yes, Blue. He sat there and died. You see, he was a Filipino, and to a Filipino, family is life. Do you understand?"

"Yes, sir."

"Lori is my life. Do you understand me?"

"Yes, sir."

The two men sat back in their chairs and looked into the jungle for a long time. It was Mr. Santiago who broke the silence.

"Toward the end of the war, the Americans came to our village. They killed my father's family. They killed all of them." Mr. Santiago's voice was soft. He kept looking into the forest as he talked.

"They only got my thumb." He smiled slightly and held up his hand for Blue to see.

"So my father captured one of them; he was a captain. He had come to deceive my father and the rest of the patriots. He had been part of the killing party that had destroyed my father's family, my family. And my father gave the captain the same choice. He tied him to the root of a tree."

Mr. Santiago paused and looked again at the jungle.

"What happened?" whispered Blue.

"He lived."

"I see."

"We are different, Blue. But I must do as you say and not fault you for that difference. I fear my daughter is in love with you. She is much like me, stubborn and strong."

"Like the mango tree that we sit under?"

"Yes." Mr. Santiago smiled at Blue. "Like the mango tree. And so I truly believe that if I forbade you to see her, I might lose her. I cannot risk that. And so you have me in somewhat of a predicament."

"I understand, sir."

"Maybe you do understand, Blue. I certainly hope so. But you cannot really understand unless you have a daughter. Unless you have an only daughter and you suddenly risk losing her to a man you know very little about."

Blue looked at Mr. Santiago and nodded, and then he looked up at the mango tree. "I will not violate your trust, Mr. Tree." He looked at Lori's father. "I will not violate your trust either, sir."

# CHAPTER 22

agic met Candi Carlson at the Bamboo Bar in the Manila International Airport. He was trying on the new pair of sunglasses he had purchased in Hong Kong when she walked into the bar and made a beeline for him. He watched her approach through the mirror behind the bar and began smelling the jungle gardenia when she was still thirty feet away. He figured her for twenty-six or so, but it was difficult to be sure with the platinum hair and makeup. Magic was glad he had on his sunglasses, because he was staring at her chest so hard he thought he heard a blood vessel pop. She had absolutely the most magnificent breasts he had ever seen. Magic was constantly waging an internal war, trying to decide whether he was a butt man or a leg man or a face man or a boob man. He decided at that instant that it was boobs forever.

"Excuse me, are you by chance in the US Navy?"

"Why, yes I am." Magic smiled. "Sit down." He figured Georgia or the Carolinas.

"Thank you. I don't mean to intrude. My name is Candi Carlson. That's with an I."

"No problem." Magic grinned as he held out his hand. "My name's Magic Sharentino. That's with a C, and I'm glad to meet you. What are you drinking?"

"Oh, why thank you. Tom Collins, please."

Magic ordered the drink and another beer for himself.

"So why are you looking for a navy man?" Magic prayed she would say for sex, but he didn't think the odds were very high.

"Well, maybe you can help me find someone."

"I don't know," said Magic as he groaned. "The navy's a big place."

"He is an admiral."

"Oh yeah? What's his name?"

"Roy Saratoga. Have you heard of him?"

Magic almost spit his beer in her face. Roy Saratoga. She was talking about his XO, the very prince of darkness himself. The man who thought fun was filing papers.

"Hell, yes, I've heard of Admiral Saratoga. He's a great friend of mine. I just saw him the other day."

"Really?" Candi squealed and clapped her hands. "He's so nice."

"Yes," said Magic, reveling in his lie. "That's what all the guys say. So how did you meet him?"

"I was in Cannes when the *Constellation* visited a few months ago."

"You're kidding. I am in one of the fighter squadrons on the *Constellation*. I was in Cannes too!"

"Really? Are you a fighter pilot?"

"I most certainly am." Magic grinned and took off his sunglasses. "I fly the F-4 Phantom. Ever heard of it?"

"Oh, sure. It's the airplane the admiral flies. He says everyone calls him Golden Eye because he can see the MIGs so far away."

Magic laughed and nodded his head. *They call him Brown Eye because he is so full of shit,* he thought. "Yes, that's right."

"Well, anyway, the admiral told me to meet him in a place called Olongapo on the fourteenth."

"That's a couple of days from now."

"Yes, I know." Candi grinned. "I got bored of Atlanta, so I just took one of Daddy's credit cards, and here I am."

"I see," said Magic.

"I was supposed to meet him at a place called the Marimont Resort."

"Know exactly where it's at," said Magic. "How about another Tom Collins?"

"Sure."

"How did you meet the admiral?"

"Well, I was with some friends and we were in a bar, and the admiral came by and bought us a drink. We just started talking, and pretty soon my friends disappeared and I was left alone with him. Can you believe it? Even his bodyguards had the evening off."

"Yes, that is very rare. He is usually very well protected."

"He even got a call from the president!"

"Carter?"

"He sure did." Candi smiled. "He was going to put me on with him, but the line had too much static."

"Wow," said Magic. "That's too bad."

"Yeah," said Candi. She frowned into her drink.

"I tell you what. I am heading to Olongapo right now. I could drop you off."

"You're kidding. Could I have another Tom Collins?"

"Surely." Magic smiled. "We can get some for the road too."

"Okay!" squealed Candi.

"Go get your bags and meet me here in ten minutes. I'll have my car pulled around."

"Your car! Oh my!" Candi jumped off the bar stool and disappeared.

As soon as she was gone, Magic sprinted for the front entrance. He squinted in the bright sunlight for an instant and then spotted a long, black limousine. Seconds later, he was motioning for the driver to roll down the window.

"Hey, sport, are you for hire?"

"Depend. Where go?"

"Olongapo?"

Julian Cervantes had driven limos for several years. He had never gotten a fare to Olongapo. "Yes, I hire to Olongapo."

"How much?"

"Five hundred."

"Pesos?"

"Dollars."

"Bullshit."

"Okay, three hundred."

"Bullshit," said Magic. "I don't want to put every one of your kids through Harvard."

"Two hundred dollars," said Julian. "But you have to let me see in the mirror."

"What?"

"You know?" Julian winked. "The mirror. You aren't taking a limo because you want to keep your jeans creased."

"Oh, yeah." Magic grinned. "You're right, my friend. It's a deal. Just don't run off the road on the way down."

"Comfortable?"

"Uh-huh," purred Candi as she slipped off her shoes and stretched her long legs. "I just love the way it feels to ride in a limousine."

"Me too." Magic grinned. He was sitting next to Candi with his arm around her shoulders. "But you know the best thing about a limo?"

"What?" Candi batted her eyes and turned toward him.

Magic put his fingers on the zipper on the back of Candi's dress. "You can see out." He smoothly buzzed the zipper down as her eyes opened wide. "But you can't see in."

"Oh." Candi swallowed.

"That's right," whispered Magic as he pulled down her dress. He moaned when he saw Candi's breasts jiggle deliciously free.

"What about the admiral?"

"Let's not tell him," said Magic as he reached for heaven.

Magic entertained Candi all the way to the main gate at Cubi and was able to convince the guards to let them pass through. He dropped Candi off at his BOQ room to freshen up and headed down the hill to check on the jet.

"Hey, Chief, how we looking?"

"Great, Mr. Sharentino. When did you get back?"

"About an hour ago. In fact, I got a hot date over at the BOQ waiting for me."

"All right!"

Magic reached into a bag at his side and took out a cigar box. "Got these in Hong Kong." He grinned as he handed them to the chief. "Be sure to smoke 'em before you get back to the States. They're illegal, you know."

"Oh, great! Thanks, Mr. Sharentino."

"Think nothing of it, Mac. How's the bird?"

"She's in great shape, sir. Ready to go when you are."

"We'll be heading out tomorrow. Seen Lieutenant Morrison around?"

"Shoot, no. Not for four or five days, not since you two kicked them air force boys in the ass."

"Surely he's not spending his time in the BOQ."

"I don't think so, sir. I think he has something going on out in town. The first class told me he seen him going out the gate every night since you left. Plus, some of the boys say they seen him out there in the daytime too."

"Is that so?" Magic frowned and rubbed his chin.

"Yes, sir." Mac chuckled. He took one of the cigars out of the box and carefully trimmed the end. He closed his eyes as he put it to his nose and inhaled deeply. "Yes, sir," repeated Mac as he grinned at Magic.

"Lieutenant Morrison has turned into a regular mayor of Olongapo on us."

Magic looked at the chief and frowned again. He nodded and picked up his bag and headed for the door. "See you tomorrow, Chief."

When Blue returned to his room late that afternoon, he found a note laying on the floor under the door. He picked it up. It was from Magic.

> *Hey, kid!*
> *I'm back from old Hong Kong. Wait until you see the loot I got. Six pairs of sunglasses and some Cuban cigars. I even got a souvenir little red book by that cocksucker Mao See Tongue. Drop by the Black Rose when you get into town. You have to see the chick I found in Manila. She has the biggest fun bags you have ever seen!*
> *Stud of all Asia,*
> *Magic*
>
> *P.S. Be ready to go to the ship tomorrow. We'll zoom out around noon.*

Blue laughed as he read the note before tossing it into the wastebasket. No time to meet Magic's girl tonight. He had a date with his own girl, and she was going to present him with a custom-made gun case.

# CHAPTER 23

**B**lue rolled over, shut off his alarm clock, and sat up in bed. He had been awake for a couple of hours, thinking about Lori. The past days had been marvelous, and he and Lori had been inseparable. He was sure he was in love with her, but he wasn't sure what lay in their future. He planned on flying back to the Philippines after the cruise was over so he and Lori could spend more time with each other.

Blue smiled when he thought of the dinner the night before. Grandma had prepared spicy dishes of pork and chicken adobo, and Lori had concocted a delicious platter of pancit noodles. They had eaten until they were stuffed and then spent the rest of the evening talking about everything from Filipino history to how a steam catapult works. Blue learned that the University of Santo Tomas was older than Harvard, and Lori learned that the catapult was stopped at the end of its stroke by a water brake system.

Of course, the highlight of the evening had come when Lori presented him with the gun case. It was beautiful! The dark mahogany gleamed with a rich, buttery finish, and the carefully fitted insert was testimony to the superb craftsmanship of the Martinez artisans. Lori had even included a vinyl cover to protect the case in transit.

Blue paused at the front door, just before he had left.

"I leave tomorrow to fly back to the ship."

"When will you be back?"

"We'll tie up in Subic Bay the day after tomorrow. It'll probably be on the morning tide."

"I see."

"Maybe you can come down to the pier and meet me?" He kissed her soft lips.

She returned his kiss and grinned at him. "Maybe."

Blue continued to think about Lori as he got dressed, and she was on his mind as he ate breakfast. He was still thinking about how much he was going to miss her when he walked into the hangar.

"So he lives." Magic boomed across the hangar as Blue approached the battered desk where he and Chief Mac were sitting.

"Alive and well," said Blue with a smile. "Sorry I couldn't meet you last night. Had a date to pick up this." He held up the gun case.

Magic took the case, unzipped the vinyl cover, and showed it to the chief. "Wow, this is nice! It sure is a beauty, Mr. Morrison."

"Man, somebody knows what they're doing. This is fucking fantastic!" Magic grinned at Blue. "I mean it."

Blue stood between the two men, feeling proud he had succeeded in his mission. They continued to examine the case for a few more minutes before Chief Mac covered it in plastic Bubble Wrap for the trip back to the ship. The case would travel with their luggage in a metal container attached to one of the Phantom's weapons pylons.

Magic and Blue discussed their flight plan for a few minutes and then walked out to the flight line to inspect their plane.

"What did you do last night?" asked Blue.

"I took this chick I met in Manila to the Black Rose."

"Oh, yeah? Eve there?"

"Yeah, she was great as always. She really looks tired though. Must be working too hard. But, hey, you should have seen the chick I had."

"What was she like?"

"She had the biggest tits you ever saw. Man, they were out to here." Magic held his hands out in front of his body. "I almost lost my head in those things. And get this. The best thing is she is in Olongapo to meet Prince!"

"What?"

"No shit." Magic laughed. "He told her he was the admiral."

Blue laughed and continued to tighten his harness. He climbed up the ladder and inside the cockpit.

"So the boys say you've been out in town pretty regular since I've been gone." Magic zipped the leg of his G-suit and looked up at Blue.

"Yeah, I guess."

"You tapping the girl from the wood place?" Magic grinned and put on his sunglasses.

"It's not like that. I've been seeing her, that's all."

Magic studied Blue for a moment and then slowly nodded his head and grinned. "Sure, kid, that's what they all say." He stepped onto the boarding ladder and climbed up into the cockpit.

Thirty minutes later, Magic and Blue were rolling down the runway in full afterburner. At 140 knots, Blue felt the nose gear break the surface of the runway, followed quickly by the main mounts. He heard Magic slap the landing gear handle up and bunt the nose down, leveling the jet about six feet off the runway. At three hundred knots, Magic smoothly rotated the nose to a forty-five-degree angle, and they zoomed into the sky toward the South China Sea and the *Connie*. Since the ship was only two hundred miles away, it didn't take long for Blue to establish communications with the ship's approach control.

"War Chief, Angel 207."

"Angel 207, War Chief center, go."

"Angel 207 is a single Phantom on your 180 at 45 miles."

"Roger 207, radar contact, cleared to the tower with a visual."

Moments later ...

"Boss, 207 sees you five miles astern."

"Cleared for the break, 207."

The break is used for day flight operations, and it consists of an approach up the right side of the ship followed by a sharp left-hand turn. It is designed to allow aircraft the ability to enter the downwind leg of the ship's visual traffic pattern. It is executed at 800 feet and between 250 and 350 knots, depending on aircraft type. Much faster and the pilot has too much trouble slowing the aircraft down enough to lower the gear and flaps and get trimmed prior to rolling into the groove and calling the ball.

Of course, the faster you come into the break, the more impressive it is. It shows you aren't just some ordinary kind of guy—as long as you hack it, that is. Many pilots try to look like "John Wayne in the break," only to look like "Slim Pickens in the groove." Also, the LSOs don't show any mercy for a bungled attempt at landing, no matter how "shit-hot" the break is. In fact, if it's too much out of safety parameters, they will wave the pilot off and have him try it all again: the ultimate embarrassment. If he is only shitty but not unsafe, they will just give him a bad grade. Since landing grades are publicly posted in every ready room, nobody wants to get bad grades.

Magic and Blue hit the break at five hundred knots. Magic snapped the Phantom into a six G, left-hand turn while he simultaneously slapped the throttles to idle and extended the speed brakes. Observers on deck saw the plane disappear into a vapor ball and then rocket out the other side.

As he approached the abeam position, Blue saw they were still doing 325 knots, much too fast to lower the gear and flaps. He smiled to himself. This was going to be interesting.

They continued the left turn, and as soon as they reached 250 knots, Magic lowered the gear and flaps. They intercepted the final approach path at 200 knots and rolled wings level just to the left of centerline. Blue heard Magic turn on his hot mic, so he could talk to him during final. It was the way Blue and Magic always flew.

"I'm fifteen knots fast, slightly left, slightly high."

"I'm looking good, on centerline, ball coming to the center."

"Slowing down, come on, Magic. Add a little power, baby. Little more to catch the ball right in the middle. Good."

"Slight drift to the right. Little left wing down to catch it, squeak on the power now to keep the ball from sagging."

"On airspeed, on lineup, on centerline."

Magic was still flying the ball and chatting to himself as the Phantom slammed onto the deck with all the grace of a falling safe. The hook engaged the number-three wire and slowed the big jet to a quick stop. It was a perfect landing.

"God, I love this shit!" Magic screamed into his oxygen mask and raised the hook and taxied out of the landing area.

"Well, look who's back." Spot smiled as Blue walked into the ready room. Spot was sitting at the duty desk, surrounded by the usual pack of JOs. They all turned toward the door, and a chorus of welcomes erupted.

"Blue boy, good to see you."

"Look at the sand crab. Nice tan, pal."

"About time you came back to work."

"I smell monkey pussy."

Blue smiled and laid the gun case against the skipper's chair. He expected to take a lot of shit, as anyone returning from a genuine "good deal" should.

"Hey, Blue, what's it like?" Head shouldered through the knot of officers gathered around Blue.

"Yeah, what he means is, what are the women like?" added Face.

"It was fantastic." Blue smiled. "Absolutely fantastic."

"So, what'd you do?"

"Yeah, Blue. Exactly, what did you do?"

"Well, I got some sun and—"

"Bullshit! We don't want the *Reader's Digest* version," said Spider. "We want the *Playboy* version. What's the pussy like out there?"

"Stand back, boys! The king of the jungle's back!"

"Magic! Welcome back!"

Magic walked to the duty desk and was immediately surrounded.

"How fast were you going in the break? You looked supersonic."

"What kind of airspeed were you looking at when you rolled wings level?"

"Super break, man!"

"Thanks, boys. And, before you ask, I will personally lead the first night's beaver hunt when we pull into Olongapo."

The men cheered, and Magic smiled broadly. Blue grinned as he watched the guys crowd around. For some reason he was glad that Magic had them as friends.

"Magic, Blue was just starting to tell us about the town. What was it like?"

"Well, boys," Magic put a booted foot up on the arm of a chair and lit a cigar, "for starters, money ain't a problem. A twenty-dollar bill will take you through the night in the 'Po." The men all cheered again. The excitement was growing.

"Did you tell them about Evelyn's, kid?"

"Not yet." Blue shook his head and grinned. He was glad Magic was taking the lead. He had a way of making everything seem even better than it was.

"I tell you, boys, that's one place designed for the human male species. It is like an adult Disneyland."

"What's so great about it?"

"The rides, son. The rides."

"Look who's back." Heart came through the door, followed by the XO. He shook hands with Blue and Magic.

"Any trouble with the jet?"

"She don't slow down too good." Magic grinned.

Heart and the rest of the officers laughed. "Super break, Magic." He grinned. "The pass looked great too."

"Thanks, Skipper. Blue boy even fixed the radar good enough for us to beat up on a couple of air force pukes."

"Great." Heart smiled. "I hope you gunned their brains out."

"We did." Magic smiled.

"How did the mission go?"

"Mission success, Skipper," said Blue. He pointed to the gun case.

Heart opened the vinyl cover and whistled when he saw the case. "Man, that is beautiful. Who did you find to do this kind of work?"

"One of the shop owners out in town," said Blue.

"Yeah." Magic grinned. "Blue had a real good working relationship with the manager."

"Oh, is that so?" Heart looked at Blue and smiled. "That's the way to do business, son. Well, I'm taking this to my room for safekeeping. Great job, guys!" He walked through the door and was gone.

"I would also like to offer my congratulations for a job well-done." The XO had gone unnoticed until he spoke. He leaned against the duty desk and looked at Blue. "Of course, I expect a written report of all transactions, with receipts." His smile was small and cold.

"Yes, sir. I will have it to you this afternoon."

"Well, I've got to go and unpack my Hong Kong loot," said Magic as he moved toward the door.

"By the way, Blue, two more things before you go."

"Yes, sir."

"You need to see the skipper about your fitness report, and you need to call Captain Joplin. He says he needs you to call him today. What's that all about?"

"Well, sir. I guess it's about his daughter. I used to date her."

The XO slowly nodded his head, his eyes fixed upon Blue with the intensity of a cat watching a bird. He turned and walked out the door.

*Shit,* thought Blue. *That's all I need, a conversation with Cathy's father.*

Blue took his flight gear to the parachute locker and quickly hurried to the skipper's room. He knocked and entered. "Skipper, the XO said you wanted to debrief me on my fitness report."

"Come on in and sit down," said Heart. "We'll take a look at it together."

Heart handed Blue the form he used to report on an officer's fitness. It was the critical record that led to promotion and success or stagnation and failure. Heart gestured to the paper. "First, on the front side, I want you to notice I have given you all A marks," said Heart. "I have also recommended you for early promotion."

"Thank you, sir. I appreciate your confidence."

"It's not just me, Blue. These marks were compiled by all the department heads and the XO. I make the final choice on who goes where, but you have strong support throughout the command. Fact is, you are impressing a lot of people."

"Thank you, sir."

"Now look on the back at the narrative."

Blue flipped the paper over and read the first sentence. *LTJG Morrison is the number one of five lieutenant junior-grade officers in this command.*

Blue swallowed and looked at the skipper. He had no idea he was thought of so highly. He didn't spend much time worrying about things like fitness reports or how he was ranked. He just tried to do the best job he could, regardless of the tasking. He blushed and looked at the floor.

"Your strongest capability is your trustworthiness." Heart moved his chair back and rocked it against the wall. "For instance, I know when you say you're going to do something, you will do it. You don't just talk; you execute. It's a great trait, Blue."

Blue sat quietly and nodded his head.

"Now you can read the rest of the back later. Let me take a few minutes to give you some advice." Heart brought his chair forward and looked intently into Blue's eyes.

"Right now, you are doing a superb job. I couldn't ask for more. But tomorrow, or the next day, it may not be enough."

Blue frowned. He didn't quite understand.

"In this business you can never stand still, Blue. I imagine it's the same in the corporate world. Being number one or achieving a certain level of performance must be a process of evolution, not an end state. What you are today is only good today. Tomorrow, the race starts all over again, and I'm not saying that because the goal is to get a number. I'm saying if you try as hard as you can to improve on your own personal performance, you will elevate everyone else around you. Understand?"

"I think so, sir."

"Eventually, your peers will figure out you're the number-one guy, and some of them will resent you. But most guys will just try to race with you, and that kind of performance-based leadership makes the whole squadron healthy."

"Yes, sir."

"One final thing, Blue. Don't confuse leadership with popularity. You're not ranked number one because everyone likes you the best; it's because of your performance and potential. Some people can't make the distinction. Remember, Blue, there's a big difference between being in front of something and leading it. A lot of real popular officers aren't the ones who actually make things better."

"Yes, sir."

"Good, then go ahead and get to the ready room. I think the XO is having an all-officers meeting to talk about tomorrow's arrival in the Philippines."

"Aren't you going to be there?"

"No, I've got to go down and meet with CAG. He is giving me *my* fitness report." Heart winked at Blue. "I just hope I do as good as you."

"Good luck, sir." Blue stood and shook hands with Heart before walking to the door. He opened it and looked over his shoulder. "We're going to miss you, sir." He turned and hurried to the ready room.

"Anybody else have any comments?" Doc surveyed the ready room for upraised hands. As the operations officer, he was responsible for conducting officer training meetings and insisted upon keeping them on schedule.

"No? Okay, XO, I guess you're on, sir."

Blue watched Doc take his seat and Prince stand and walk to the podium. He felt a new tension in the atmosphere. It was the first time the XO had addressed the ready room without the skipper present, and Blue felt nervous. He did not trust the XO.

"I just want to make a few comments about our next port visit."

The crowd emitted a muffled groan, and Prince's eyes flickered across their faces. He smiled an iceberg at them and continued. "I am going to take leave for the first day in port, and I don't want a bunch of trouble to force me back to the ship."

Blue saw Magic turn and look at him. A huge grin was plastered on his face.

"Between now and the time we pull in, I want you to meet with your troops and stress the following three points. First, the Philippines is an underdeveloped country. They don't have the modern sanitation and sewage systems we are used to. God knows how they prepare their food. Tell your men not to eat anything out in town and not to drink anything that doesn't come out of a bottle or a can."

Blue felt himself getting angry. He squirmed in his seat and looked toward Magic's seat. Magic was looking straight ahead, his face contorted by a frown.

"Second." Prince held up two fingers and paused until all eyes were on him. "Tell your sailors to really watch themselves. There are con men on every corner, just waiting to cheat them out of their money. There isn't one thing in Olongapo worth buying. Tell them to beware of the girls—no matter how sweet they look or innocent they act. Most, if not all, are carrying syphilis, gonorrhea, or both. Third, every one of them is a hooker. In fact, there are ten thousand hookers in Olongapo, and all they want to do is find a sailor to marry. Then they can move their entire family to the States and become his dependents. Tell the men there is absolutely no way they can make any commitment to a girl without command approval."

"You mean a legal commitment?" Doc raised his hand.

"Yes, if any of our sailors wants to make any kind of commitment like engagement or, heaven forbid, marriage, he has to have a chit signed by me."

"Got it, sir." Doc lowered his hand.

"And you officers." The XO unfolded his arms and put his hands on the podium. "I do not want to see any of you so much as look at one of those girls. If I see or hear about you having anything at all to do with them, I will consider it conduct unbecoming. Do I make myself clear?"

The room was absolutely silent.

"You mean … no pussy?" Spot frowned.

"We can't go to the bars?" Head raised his hand.

Blue couldn't believe what he had just heard.

"What are you talking about, XO?" Blue looked at the XO and frowned. "I mean, I have only been there for a few days, but they seem okay."

"Okay, then what does one of your sailors think when he pops into a bar and sees a hooker grinding down on your lap?" The XO glared at Blue and then at Spot and Head. "I'll tell you what he thinks. He thinks if it's okay for Mr. Morrison, it's okay for him. But you see, Mr. Morrison, that young sailor doesn't have your … sophistication. This might be the first girl he has been with. Poof! He falls in love. Get where I am coming from?"

"But, sir, these are grown men—"

"Enough, Blue, enough." The XO gripped the podium until his arms shook. "I will not have my officers mucking around with these sluts, and believe me, every girl in Olongapo is a slut."

"Well, sir, that isn't true."

Blue couldn't believe he had said the words so forcefully. He had all but shouted at the XO. He swallowed and felt himself blush.

The XO glared at him, his normally cold eyes narrowed to slits and his face reddened with anger.

"What did you say?" He spat each word as if it were poison.

"Uh, I said what you said wasn't true," stammered Blue. "Sir," he added.

"Oh, and in what way is it not true?" The XO gritted his teeth and looked at Blue like he wanted to strangle him. "I suppose now that you have spent ten days in the Philippines you are an expert on their society. Would you please come forward and share your wealth of experience with us?"

"Uh, sir?"

"Please, I insist." The XO pointed at a spot beside him. "Come up here and tell us how I am wrong."

Blue stole a quick glance at Magic, hoping to see him rise in his defense. After all, Magic was the expert on the Philippines. If he said something, the whole problem would defuse. However, Magic was avoiding him and staring at the floor. Blue was on his own.

"I meant no offense, sir." Blue slowly walked forward.

"You correct me in front of the entire ready room and then say you meant no offense? It's a little late for sensitivity, don't you think?"

"I guess so, sir."

"Just get on with enlightening us. Tell us of your vast experiences."

Blue swept the room with his eyes, looking for some sign of support. However, the faces turned toward him were set in frowns of confusion. They were wondering what Blue was up to and what could have possessed him to challenge the XO.

"Sir, it's just that you can trust the Filipinos. They are regular people, for the most part. True, some are bad, but most aren't. All the girls aren't hookers either. Many work in the local shops and … and …" Blue trailed off. He felt like an absolute idiot.

"Well, well." The XO looked at Blue like he was a tick. He curled his lips and shook his head in disgust. "Looks like we have a regular Albert Schweitzer among us. Eh, boys?"

It irritated and hurt Blue to hear the other officers laugh. Clearly, the XO was trying to embarrass him.

The XO's eyes lit as he heard the laughter. "How do you know about their philosophy, Blue? Did you study about the Philippines in school?"

"No, sir."

The laughter grew a little louder, and Blue felt the eyes of everyone on him.

"Learn it from … from … a whore, perhaps?" Prince grinned broadly.

"No, sir."

"Well, what then? Who told you these things?"

Blue looked at the floor and swallowed. His face flushed hot.

"I asked you a question, mister! You embarrass me in front of what will soon be my command with some crap about philosophy. Tell us how you know so much about the Philippines."

"A girl—I mean a lady—told me."

"A lady! A lady!" The XO opened his eyes wide in mock amazement. His smile gradually widened.

"Was she a hooker, Blue? Did you get your information from a streetwalker?"

"No, sir!"

"No? Well, perhaps some nice girl you just happened to … bump into?" The XO chuckled and was joined by many in the crowd.

"Yes," said Blue.

"So you meet a girl and immediately you start talking all the fine points of culture. Sounds like you're a bigger risk than the troops. I tell you what, LTJG Morrison, don't counsel any of my troops."

Once again, Blue looked at the floor. He felt humiliated and alone. All he had done was defend Lori. He looked at Magic and frowned … and he had defended Solang and Eve … and he had defended Viela and Evelyn. He felt angry and confused.

"Christ, Magic." The XO shrugged his shoulders and grinned. "What happened? You were supposed to keep him from going native."

Magic looked at Blue and then at the XO. He smiled slightly and shook his head. "I don't know, sir. I wasn't watching him all the time."

# CHAPTER 24

"Well, look who's here? Blue of the jungle." Spot grinned as Blue walked into the bunk room. He looked at Spot, Head, Face, and Spider and groaned inwardly. He didn't want to put up with any of their shit.

"Where have you been?" asked Head.

"Walking on the flight deck." Blue went to his bunk and flopped down.

"So, what was that all about in the ready room?" Head swiveled in his chair to see Blue's face.

"What are you talking about?"

"You know. The bit how you challenged the fucking XO in front of the entire ready room four days before he takes over as the skipper." Head and the others laughed.

"Yeah," chirped Spider. "He means the bit about how you took your dick out and let the XO tap-dance on it." They all laughed again—all except Blue.

"Shit, I don't know." Blue sighed and kicked off his boots. "It's just that the XO is so full of shit. The stuff he was putting out was bull. And, hey, he put the girls off-limits to all the officers. I was watching out for you too."

"We appreciate that, Blue, but you picked a fight for no reason. You know the deal with handling him. Just listen, nod your head, then do what you have to do. We are all going out in town, despite what he says. He'll never go there and will never know what we do."

"I don't know," repeated Blue. He looked at his hands and then stared across the floor. "I just felt like I had to say something." He shrugged and looked around the room.

"I'm glad you did it, Blue." Spider grinned and threw his pillow into the air. "Now the XO hates you so much more than me."

Even Blue had to chuckle with everyone else.

"Back to the subject," interrupted Head. He grinned suspiciously at Blue. "What happened to you while you were in the PI? You were really weird in there tonight. Not the old Blue boy I know. What's going on?"

"Yeah," said Spider. "You stick your dick somewhere it doesn't belong?"

"Blue, did you fuck a monkey?" Face asked with mock seriousness, and everyone but Blue laughed.

"No." Blue sighed. He leaned his head back and looked at the ceiling. For a few minutes he just stared.

"It's kind of strange," he finally said. "It's just that, well, I did meet this girl." He sat up and leaned his arms on his knees. "And she was real nice. I guess I was thinking of her and her family when the XO said every woman in Olongapo was a hooker."

"Nice, huh," said Spider. "How was she in the sack?"

"Beats me," said Blue. "We never had sex."

"Okay, let me get this right." Head hopped from his perch on the top bunk and landed next to Blue. "We have been on this deployment for months. We have spent up to six straight weeks on this ship between port visits. You get a chance-of-a-lifetime good deal to fly into a place with ten thousand hookers and you fall in love with Olongapo's version of Sally Field?" Head looked at Blue and held up his hands. "Then you race back here and defend her honor by committing hara-kiri. Is that about the size of it?"

"I didn't say I was in love with her."

"No." Head narrowed his eyes and looked closely at his friend. "You didn't say as much. But you sure sound like you are."

"I tell you what," cackled Spider. "I'm going to jump on the first whore I see, and the XO can say anything about her he wants."

"Seriously, Blue, what is going on?" Face frowned and shook his head. "You're acting goofy. I used to run around with you before you hooked up with Cathy. You were a real player. Remember Fridays on the back deck at Oceana? Fort Story on Sunday? You used to have radar for finding just the right girls. You know, the ones who were just breaking up with the boy back home in Kansas?"

"Yeah." Spider laughed. "Big tits and no brains."

"Shut up, Spider," growled Face. "Blue, I just can't believe the same guy is sitting here mooning over some chick he met in the middle of nowhere. Who knows if you ever see her again, and if you do, what then?"

"Who says I'm mooning? I just said I met this girl, that's all."

"Well, buddy, you aren't acting right. You looked real bad tonight at the AOM."

"He's right, Blue," said Spot. "I don't want to get into your shit. You're a big boy. But take it from your pals and think about what's going on. How can this girl really mean anything to you? She isn't one of us. Think about it."

"All this love talk makes me sick," said Head. "Christ, we sound like a knitting bee in here."

"Yeah." Spider laughed. "We are the Yarn Angels of Knitting Squadron 57."

"Well, what say we pull on our panties and go to chow." Head stretched and scratched his stomach.

"Good idea. Grease and fat goes well with love talk. You coming?" Face stood and looked down at Blue.

"No, thanks. I'm not hungry."

"I have a *National Geographic* if you want to beat off while we are gone." Spot smiled and reached for the door.

Seconds after they filed out, Blue heard a knock. "Come in," he said.

The door opened and Magic walked in, carrying a bottle of Jack Daniels and two glasses of ice.

"Figured you were in here." Magic grinned and sat down.

"I could have used some help in there tonight."

Magic grinned again and shrugged. He poured a generous helping of liquor in each glass and handed one to Blue.

"Cheers." Magic tipped his glass, took a big gulp of whiskey, and leaned back on his perch on a bottom bunk. He looked at Blue, raised an eyebrow, and then took another sip.

"I could've used some help in there," Blue repeated.

"Look, kid, I'm sorry if I left you in a lurch, but it was for your own good."

"My own good. What do you mean?"

"You needed to feel what it's going to be like."

"What are you talking about?"

"Look, Blue. I don't know what you are calling this feeling you have for the girl you met. But it looks like you got the hots for her. You need to know what it's going to feel like being on the outside." Magic swirled his glass; the ice tinkled in the bourbon.

"Outside?" Blue leaned forward and frowned.

"Yes, outside. You get mixed up seriously with this girl and you are going to be all alone with her. Tonight was your first lesson."

Blue held up his hands in exasperation, sloshing a little bourbon in the process. "I give. I still don't know what you mean."

"Kid, I wanted to give this to you easy, but you refuse to understand. Olongapo is a fantasy; it doesn't really exist anywhere but in Olongapo."

"What do you mean 'doesn't exist'? There are people there, real people."

"The idea is not to take it seriously. The idea is to blow into town for a couple of days, have some brews, have some good times with the girls, then you leave. Period! That's the way the game is played. You fuck 'em and then you leave 'em."

"You sure don't sound like a guy that fell in love with a Filipino girl. What about Solang?"

Magic looked at the floor, and Blue heard him sigh. He slowly nodded his head and looked up. "I admit it. I had it bad for that kid. But don't you understand? That's why I'm here. I know what you're going through. I saw it developing all along when you first started talking about her back in Olongapo." Magic shook his head and drained his glass. He reached for the bottle. "I hoped reality would set in, once you were back here on the carrier. I should have known you were going to say something stupid when I saw you fidgeting at the meeting." Magic refilled his glass.

"But you looked pissed too! You heard what the XO was saying. Don't you feel any loyalty to those people back there? To Solang?" For the first time since he had known Magic, Blue felt his hero might not be all he thought he was.

"Sure I do, but not enough to make an ass out of myself."

"So when you stand up for someone you're an ass? Bullshit!"

"You pick your battles, kid. It wasn't worth the fight. You looked like some lovesick idiot in there." Magic's eyes hardened, and he leaned forward.

"Christ, Magic! Are you that hung up on what people think?"

"Grow up, kid. Standing up for someone isn't the issue. Controlling your emotions is the issue. Do you think falling in love gives you the right to be stupid?"

"Fuck you!" Blue leaned forward, his face growing red.

"No, fuck you." Magic stood up and glared down at Blue. "And get used to the sound of that, because it will be what everybody tells you. I know, kid! I was stupid! I fell for Solang so hard my heart ached whenever I wasn't with her. But I had no right to fall in love with her. Don't you understand? When you begin to take it seriously, you break the rules. You ruin the fantasy. You make all the pixie dust turn into dirt. The point the XO tried to make is we can't afford to let our young men take any of this place to heart."

Blue stood and glowered at Magic. "The XO is a prick. Who cares what he says?"

"He may be a prick, but he will soon be the skipper prick and that means you have to deal with him." They stood like that for a few moments, both breathing hard and glaring. Then Magic sighed and sat back down on the bunk.

"Sit down, kid." He gestured to a chair. Blue stood looking at him a moment and then sat down.

"I have been on cruises when ten or fifteen guys think they have found true love and want to get married by the second day in port. And I am talking about young, enlisted kids. Jesus, kid, what do you think it looks like for an officer to get strung out on a local? What chance does the command have to protect their young people if the officers go native? The last thing Heart needs is an officer running for the job of the mayor of Olongapo."

"I still can't believe you can say all of that and still say you ever cared for Solang."

"Kid, when I first left her, I did love her." Magic looked at the floor and coughed softly. "I ... I. Shit, kid," he whispered. "Things changed."

"What kind of things?"

"When I went back to the ship, I started thinking about all the things that went into loving her. I started thinking about how it would really be back home. Think about it for a second. Do you really want to be the thirty-third guy in the rice line at the commissary?"

"Bullshit!" Blue leaned forward and glared. "Magic, can't you ever get over worrying what people think of you? Do you embarrass that easily?"

"Look, Blue." Magic took a deep breath and gritted his teeth. "I'm not proud of this. Do you think I'm that shallow? If all I cared about was myself, I would be back in my stateroom, listening to music. I wouldn't be sitting here with you, exposing a bunch of fucking crap about myself. I don't share who I am with anybody!

I'm here because I have walked in your shoes. I fell in love with an island girl when I had no right to. It wasn't right for me, and it wasn't right for her, and it isn't right for you."

"How can you be so sure it wasn't right?"

"Because when it came down to crunch time, I realized I didn't love her enough to overcome how much I loved myself." Magic sighed and took another sip from his glass. He looked at Blue and gave him a weak smile. "After I bagged my MIG, I had a reputation. After I bagged my second one, I was somebody. I was the only guy in the wing that had a kill, and I liked the way it made me feel. I liked being a hero. I liked it a lot. You see, Blue, everybody wants to be a hero, and every time you hear otherwise the guy is bullshitting. I will say it again—the truth is everybody wants to be a hero. They just don't want to admit it. And when you get to be one, you don't want to let it go. So I did some thinking about what I was prepared to give up, and my ego wasn't on the list. You can fault me if you wish, but it would have been worse if I had pursued her when I wasn't totally committed."

"How would loving Solang interfere with your ego?"

"Oh, come on, kid. Everybody who ever made a Westpac cruise would look at her like she was a hooker. They wouldn't say anything, at least not to my face. They would just give me that look like, 'Hey, buddy, don't you know Olongapo is like bluegill fishing? You catch 'em and throw 'em back. You don't keep 'em.'"

Blue thought of the sailor on the ferry to Grande Island. He had automatically assumed Lori was a hooker. But would the same thing happen away from Olongapo? Surely not. Besides, if he loved her it didn't make any difference. Did it?

Magic stood and picked up his bourbon bottle. He hid it in his shirt and walked to the door. He turned around and faced Blue. "Once you get her out of the jungle, what then? Can you love her then, with all the stares? Can you put up with the prejudice? It's worse than if she was black, because then people would think you have something for diversity or something. But she is Filipino, so if they have ever heard of Olongapo they will think she used to be a hooker and you are some weak piece of shit that bought her out of a bar. Think about it, kid. Today, maybe it doesn't seem like it would matter to you. How about when you take her home for Thanksgiving? Do you want your kids to look like her grandparents or yours? I know all this sounds small and selfish and racist, but I bet you are already thinking about some of what I'm saying. Maybe you don't want to admit it. Maybe you don't want to admit you would walk away from a girl because you don't have the balls to put up with her baggage. After all, isn't it ironic to walk away from a girl who never asks you to explain your friends just so you can get acceptance from your friends who demand you explain her? How much sense does that make?" Magic shook his head and chuckled.

"I don't know, kid. Maybe you do have the guts to do all these things. You do what's right for you." He turned and stepped into the hall.

"At what point did you know you weren't coming back for Solang?" Blue stood in the doorway, looking at him.

Magic turned and started to speak and then let out a breath of air and shook his head. "I guess I don't know. It's something I never let myself think about." He looked at the floor and then back at Blue. "Then she died. She died and I never had to face it."

# CHAPTER 25

**B**lue lay awake and listened to the sleeping aircraft carrier. The *Connie* slept because no planes flew, but her sleeping carried the never-ending sounds of the life inside her. Blue heard a generator start up somewhere above him, and on the other side of the ship he heard the whoosh and thud of a catapult piston test firing into its water brakes. He heard the *Connie* creak and moan and the faint sound of a needle gun ripping off old paint. And as he listened he struggled to understand his feelings. Did he love Lori, or was it just some infatuation? Was it love, or was all this just the result of something new? Was Olongapo real or just a place to dip your toe into for a moment and then hurry away? Finally, just before dawn, he crept out of the dark room to the showers. The hot water helped refresh him, but it did not ease his mind. He kept replaying the previous evening's conversations. A lot of people he kept in high esteem seemed sure he was making a mistake with Lori. He was glad he was on the early-morning flight schedule. He needed something to take his mind off Lori. He was crewed that morning with Spot, and they were flying on the skipper's wing on an area familiarization flight over the Philippines.

The flight was relaxing, and Heart took the section of Phantoms on a leisurely cruise around the islands. They flew south from the carrier's position down the western side of Mindoro until they reached the Semirara Islands. Then they headed north through the Tablas Strait and back up the eastern side of Luzon.

Although Blue was busy with navigation chores and keeping a lookout for other aircraft and logging cables, he took the opportunity to examine the landscape below. But as he looked out his cockpit he didn't just see the magnificence of deep valleys and plunging rivers or the deep green of the lush jungle. He saw mango trees and bamboo trees, and he thought of Mr. Santiago. He saw banana trees, and a smile gathered under his oxygen mask as he thought of uncle Raul and *Lola*. When he saw the occasional pillar of gray smoke from a cooking fire and when they flew over cultivated fields where startled laborers looked up from knee-deep rice paddies or from behind the traces of water buffalo, he thought of the people on the streets of Olongapo. And when the jungle opened to show a village and when he looked down and saw the hovels of tin-covered shacks clustered like barnacles against a piling, he thought of Evelyn and of Viela and all the girls like her. He saw these things, and he thought these things, but most of all, he thought about Lori and what Magic had said.

*"Can you take her home for Thanksgiving? Do you want your kids to look like your grandparents or hers? Do you want to be the thirty-third guy in the rice line at the commissary? Anybody who ever made a Westpac cruise will think she's a hooker."*

He knew that Magic had been right about one thing. Blue *had* been thinking about those things. He had shoved them deep into the back of his mind, but he had been thinking about them. He had thought about them ever since encountering the sailor on the ferry to Grande Island.

All too soon the flight was over and they were back on the ship.

"Blue, telephone." Screech Moran, the duty officer, handed the phone to Blue. "I think it's some captain."

"LTJG Morrison."

"Blue, it's Captain Joplin."

Blue immediately felt tired and depressed. *Jesus Christ,* he thought. *The last thing I need is a conversation with Cathy's dad.*

"Yes, sir."

"I was wondering if you could come down and see me, when you get the chance." Captain Joplin's voice was pleasant and friendly.

Blue assumed he wanted to know if he had called Cathy while he was off the ship.

"Yes, sir. I'll be right down." He hung up the receiver and sighed.

Five minutes later, Blue knocked on Captain Joplin's stateroom door.

"Come in, Blue. Come in." Captain Joplin smiled widely as he held his door open. "Sit down and make yourself at home." Blue sat in the offered chair and noticed that a Joplin family photo was facing him from its place on the captain's desk. Cathy was smiling at him.

"How was your trip?"

"Fine, sir. Just fine."

"I've seen the gun case and it is superb, Blue, just superb. You did a remarkable job on such short notice. I'm surprised you could find any of those people who could do that kind of work."

For the second time since he had returned from Olongapo, Blue found himself noticing a slur. He wondered if he was oversensitive.

"How long did you have to search for the right company to do the job?"

"Actually, it was the first place I looked." Blue noticed a smugness in his voice. Was it payback for the slur? Captain Joplin appeared not to notice.

"Is that right? I would never have guessed such quality workmanship was commonplace. Unless, you just got incredibly lucky."

"No, sir. I got the feeling a lot of places in Olongapo could have done almost as good a job." Captain Joplin frowned for a second, as if some private thought had been disproved, and then brightened and continued. "Well, you are to be congratulated." He turned to his family's photo and touched the frame.

"My wife sent me a telegram. I just got it yesterday." He paused and looked at Blue. "Maureen says you and Cathy are having a little trouble." He smiled and rocked back in his chair. "Now, as you know, not much can be said in a telegram. But Maureen was able to convey that Cathy was very, very upset. Did you two have a spat?" Captain Joplin's smile was replaced by a frown.

"Well, sir. We didn't exactly have a spat." Blue shifted uncomfortably in his chair. "It's just I told her I wasn't sure we should continue in our relationship."

"I see." Captain Joplin nodded. He picked up the framed photo and looked down at it, holding it in his hands.

"What happened? I thought you two were really getting serious. Have you met someone on cruise?" He frowned, as if he couldn't believe such a thing was possible.

Blue looked at the captain, trying to decide where their little chat was going. He found himself getting impatient and frustrated. It sure seemed like a lot of people were interested in his love life.

"Sir, I don't think Cathy and I have as much in common as we thought we did. I think, maybe, we stayed together because other people wanted us to. I think it is best for us to go our separate ways. It's as simple as that, sir."

"No, Blue, it is not that simple!" The captain bolted upright in his chair. A drop of spittle hung on his lips, and his eyes were bright with anger. Blue realized he had been a loaded gun all along, waiting for him to say the right thing to pull the trigger.

"I love my daughter very much. I do not appreciate you taking advantage of her!"

"Sir, what are you talking about?"

"I am talking about a young officer who winds his way into a girl's heart and then casts her away when he gets to sea. It's an old story, Blue, and it's always an ugly one."

"Sir, we entered into our relationship with our eyes open. We never even discussed engagement, at least not seriously."

"Maybe you weren't serious! She was. She was damn serious, and you used her!"

"Sir, I did not make any promises to your daughter. I never told her I loved her. I never lured her—"

"Shut your mouth!" Captain Joplin rose from his chair and towered over Blue. His lips quivered, and his face was contorted with rage. "I talked to your XO, Blue. He told me about your little scene in the ready room. I find it quite interesting you decide to dump my daughter at the same time you meet some girl in Olongapo."

"Sir, it's not like that at all." Blue was desperately trying to keep calm and not make Captain Joplin any angrier than he already was. "Cathy and I weren't hitting it off long before I met Lori."

"Lori! Lori! Christ, I'll tell you what, boy. If you think you are going to humiliate my little girl by dropping her for some Filipino hooker, you had better think again! That is, if you value your career at all!"

"Captain Joplin, Lori Santiago is not a hooker. She is a girl I met. She has absolutely nothing to do with your daughter."

"You break my girl's heart and I'll break your back! Now, get out of here and get your goddamned head out of your ass and act like an officer in the United States Navy instead of some modern version of Fletcher Christian. This is not the fucking mutiny on the *Bounty*. This is real life!"

# CHAPTER 26

At six o'clock Lori finally gave up on getting any more sleep and threw back her covers. She smiled at her excitement. It was so different, so unreal from anything she had ever experienced, and she couldn't believe how much she had missed Blue. He had been gone two whole days!

She must have made some noise in the kitchen because, while she was filling the coffeepot, her grandmother appeared behind her and gave her a big hug. Her thin brown arms felt comforting and good. Lori turned and hugged her and found the old woman's body still warm from her bed. She loved her grandmother very much.

"You cannot sleep?"

"No." Lori blushed.

"When does his ship come in?"

"At ten o'clock."

Grandmother smiled, squeezed Lori's arm, and then shuffled back toward the bedroom.

"Don't you want coffee?"

"No," she said over her shoulder. "I do not have the thoughts of a young man to drink it with."

Lori smiled as the coffee filtered and the aroma of it filled the room. She poured a cup and walked outside. She drank her coffee there on the porch, slowly, with the coming of the sun. And when the shadows lifted enough to see, she walked over to the mango tree and put her hand against its trunk. "*Puno ng mangga ...* mango tree, I do love him. I love this American and, like you, I will not bow my head to that." She lifted her head to look at the glossy green leaves and smiled. "I will not bow my head to that love." She turned and ran into the house to get ready.

First came the chore of deciding what to wear. She had spent much of the previous night's sleepless moments contemplating her wardrobe, because she would doubtless be meeting some of Blue's friends. She wanted to look just right.

*Hmmm, the blue dress with lace top? Or perhaps the green?*

He had seen her in yellow and had liked it very much. *What to wear? What to wear?*

In the end, she selected a simple white dress she had gotten in Manila. Although it was not bold and striking, Lori chose it because it exhibited an understated class and charm she thought most appropriate for the occasion.

After selecting her dress and accessories, Lori drew herself a bath and took a long soak. The hot water felt good, and she was surprised at how tense she had become over the simple matter of choosing a dress. It was crazy!

Lori finally arose from her bath and put on the dress she had selected. She gave herself a final check in the mirror and then walked out to the kitchen.

"Good morning, *Lola*." She kissed her grandmother on the cheek.

"Good morning, child. My, you look pretty."

"You look really, really pretty," said Raul. He looked at her and smiled. He wore his only suit and held a banana in one hand.

"Thank you, *Tio*, and why are you dressed up in your best clothes?"

"He is waiting for you," said Grandmother. "He thinks he is going with you to see Blue."

"What do you mean?"

"I am taking this banana for his lunch," said Raul. His eyes were bright with excitement. "Blue said he loves bananas."

"But you have eaten part of it." Lori walked over to her uncle and put her hand on his arm.

Raul looked down at the nibbled end and quickly folded the skin over to cover it. He smiled up at Lori.

"Only a small bite. Blue will not mind."

Lori bent forward and kissed his forehead. "It is better I go alone this time." She smiled at his disappointed face. "I will tell him that you have a banana for him. He will eat it when he comes home with me."

"I wanted to see the ship and the airplanes."

"Next time. I promise." Lori gave him another kiss and squeezed his arm. Then she walked out the door. She turned when she heard the screen door open and close behind her.

"Will you take this banana to Blue?" Raul stood on the steps, holding the fruit.

"You go ahead and eat it, *Tio* Raul. He can have another one."

"Okay," said Raul as he bit into the fruit. "But you are bringing him here for a visit?"

"Of course, *Tio*." Lori walked to him, kissed him on the stubble of his chin, and smiled. "We will be back before you finish your Cheerios."

Other than waiting in line, Lori had no trouble getting a visitor's pass. She joined a crowd that consisted of young women, and Lori assumed by their conversations and dress that they were representatives from the local bars. Many carried signs, advertising the establishments where they worked.

As Lori walked onto the long pier, she could see the huge, gray warship slipping quietly beside Grande Island. Its sheer size was startling. She had wondered what the carrier would look like but did not realize it was so gigantic. It was more massive than any building in Manila, and its representation of power and technology and wealth was a stark contrast to the little city of Olongapo. As the ship drew nearer, she could see the sailors, standing around the edge of the flight deck in their crisp white uniforms. Blue had told her the crew would be "manning the rails" as a customary display of honor.

Although the ship was still too far away to distinguish individual faces, she nevertheless began to scan the men for Blue.

Like Lori, Blue had also spent another restless night, and after a breakfast of toast and orange juice, he returned to his stateroom. He sat at his foldout desk and attempted to work on enlisted evaluations. The room was dark except for his desk light, and his roommates snored away. But he couldn't concentrate because his mind kept drifting back to Lori. He thought about talking to the skipper about the situation. But he was too embarrassed to take his time. After all, the other guys had told him he had made a fool of himself, and he was thankful Heart had not been there to see it.

But could he be so wrong? Was his feeling for Lori love, or was it just a bout of immaturity and overreaction to the romance of the jungle setting? Was he experiencing something that could only exist here, in Olongapo? Had he fallen for the siren song of this strange place? But was he rejecting his true feeling for her because his friends were biased? Did he love her but just didn't have the courage of his convictions?

By nine Blue gave up and got dressed. He climbed the ladder to the flight deck and walked into the bright, tropical day.

Just like the night before, a part of him was excited about seeing Lori again. He had missed her greatly. However, he also felt very unsure and anxious. He hoped once he was with her again, things would all settle.

Blue saw the crowd on the pier, so he walked to the side of the ship to get a better view. As he mingled with the sailors, a young airman smiled at him and winked.

"Sir, you better pick one out now. Save time when you get into town."

Blue nodded and smiled, but he felt like a conspirator. Would it always be like this?

"Hey, baby!" a sailor called to the crowd below. "Hey, you. Up here, honey. You, with the cute ass."

Blue frowned as he looked at the young petty officer at his side.

"Hey, man, they all looking up here now!"

Blue swallowed and set his mouth in a scowl.

"Jonesy, I thought you said they were all flat-chested. Look at the one in green!"

"Man, look at those girls! I forgot how good a body can look. I got to get off this ship. Hey, Ernie, take my duty?"

Blue began to feel more and more uneasy as he heard the remarks. Some were just exclamations of excitement, but others were rude and crude. As the ship drew closer, he could also hear the calls from the girls on the pier.

"Hey, baby, I love you."

"Throw me your hat, baby. We be married."

"Hey, Joe. Come with me to the Wild West Club. I treat you good all night."

"You like French love? I good at French love."

Blue felt himself getting more and more embarrassed. He knew he was blushing, and his face felt like it was on fire. He flicked his eyes around to see who might be watching him.

"This is ridiculous," he muttered. "Christ, nobody is looking at me." He began a nervous search for Lori. He was surprised to realize he hoped she would not be there. He shook his head in disbelief and disgust. What was wrong with him? Why was he hoping she would not show up?

"Why are you embarrassed?" he whispered to himself. "Am I afraid someone will say something to offend her? Say something about how she looks? Or am I embarrassed for myself? Am I afraid someone will think I'm with a hooker?"

"Hey, Blue!" Blue cringed at the sound of his name, even though it came from behind him. He turned and saw some of the JOs from the other squadrons had also come on deck to check out the scenery.

"Hey, Blue, you probably already have one of these picked out, don't you?"

"Blue, I think that kid over there kind of looks like you."

"Very funny, guys. Glad you could get out of the rack to join me." Blue attempted a smile and then turned back toward the crowd on the pier.

There she stood.

She was as pretty as a flower, standing next to a girl with burnt-orange short shorts and a see-through blouse.

"Christ," he muttered. "She showed up."

Blue began to edge to the back of the crowd, and he ducked behind a tall marine when he saw Lori scan the crowd. He watched her head as she looked at each face before moving to the next, searching for him. Her expression was one of excitement, anticipation, and concern. She looked like she wanted to find him more than anything, and Blue realized then that she needed him to validate her. She was standing in a sea of hookers and bar girls who were all dressed for the kill and spewing sexual promises like confetti. Lori needed him to signify she was not just another one of them. Blue saw frustration begin to build across her face.

The hooker in the orange shorts moved away to yell at a sailor, leaving Lori in a small hole in the crowd. She looked so alone, and Blue could not take his eyes off her. Her beautiful hair moved gently with the faint breeze, and her forehead knotted in concentration as she scanned the row of faces, looking for him.

Blue saw her eyes moving along the crowd where he stood. Soon she would see him, and her face would light with recognition, and her eyes would grow large, and she would stand on her tiptoes and wave at him. She would call his name and smile.

Her eyes were coming closer, scanning to Blue's right. All he had to do was wave and call her name.

But then everyone would look at him, and all they would see is one Filipina out of a sea of hookers waving at him. She would wave to him from a horde of cleavage-bearing, short shorts–wearing, cheap-looking whores all screaming at the sailors on the rails.

His mind flashed back to his mother. *"Jack, tell your dad not to wear that old blue suit to church this morning. He won't listen to me. I swear, if he wears it I am sitting by myself."*

Suddenly, he ducked and ran for the other side of the ship. The hot rush of shame pounded in his head, and tears filled his eyes. He felt an incredible guilt as he stumbled out of the crowd and crossed the flight deck. His mind flickered images like snapshots, each washing a fresh wave of shame over him: the excitement she must have felt to meet him, the anticipation of their reunion, the excitement that she would have shared with Grandmother and Uncle Raul, the care with which she fixed herself for him to please him, standing on her tiptoes, needing to find him, needing to see him, needing him.

He knew all along she would come.

Blue stumbled out of the brightness of the deck into the gloom of the ship's interior. He walked rapidly toward his stateroom and then realized he couldn't go there. The other guys would be getting ready to hit the town. He couldn't face them in his condition. He turned and headed toward the darker reaches of the ship, places where his friends wouldn't be likely to go.

Blue wandered about the ship for over an hour, carefully avoiding the spots where his fellow JOs would be congregating. They would insist he go ashore with them. He knew he couldn't do that. Besides, Lori would be watching the departing men for who knew how long? He couldn't face her either. Finally, he found himself outside the skipper's stateroom.

"Come in. It's open."

"Skipper, you got a minute?" Blue cracked the door and saw the skipper shaving in the little sink against the wall.

"Absolutely! Come on in. Hey, did you get the note I left in your mailbox last night?"

"No, sir."

"Actually, the note is from the admiral. He really loved the case."

"Oh, thanks, sir."

Heart frowned as he watched the young man reflected in his mirror. He turned around and flung his towel at Blue.

"Hey, you don't look so good."

Blue caught the towel but just sighed and looked at the floor.

"Well, Skipper," Blue's voice was thick, and he fought to control it, "I feel like the biggest asshole in the world."

"Son, you're in a fighter squadron. You're supposed to feel like that!" Heart laughed and poured them both a cup of coffee and motioned to a chair.

"Have a seat."

Blue smiled faintly and then cleared his throat as he sat. "Skipper, I'm in trouble." He leaned his head against the back of the chair and closed his eyes.

Heart continued to sip his coffee and remained silent. Finally, Blue rocked his head forward, opened his eyes, and told the skipper the whole story. He told him how he and Lori first met, the way their relationship had developed and blossomed. He told of the initial confusion and about his doubts. He told him about the conversations with Father Joseph and Lori's father.

Blue also told about the advice he had been given since he returned to the ship, the shame of that morning, and how he had let Lori down so badly. That part was the most difficult, because he knew he telling a man he respected so much just how much of a weakling he really was.

Heart listened through the story, occasionally nodding and grunting encouragement.

"So, that's it, Skipper." Blue leaned forward and put his head in his hands. He rubbed his eyes and then sat back up, looking at Heart. "That's it."

"When I was in high school," said Heart, "I dated this girl that was the best-looking thing in town. I was a pretty good football player in those days, and she was the head cheerleader. On homecoming night, she was crowned queen and I scored five touchdowns. We were not only in love, we were the town's perfect couple. A photo of us was in the picture window of the dime store!" Heart chuckled and took a drink of coffee. "I tell you, Blue, homecoming night was the most perfect night of my life! But, you know, on the day after football season she walked up to me and handed me my letterman jacket and started dating the captain of the basketball team. You want to know why?"

"Yes, sir."

"Because she was the hottest thing in school. She was a Junior Miss America, and she won every beauty pageant in the county for about four years in a row. Her girlfriends told her she was supposed to go out with the guy that was her counterpart. They put her on this pedestal and expected her to be what they wanted her to be."

"Did she care for you at all?"

"I think she did." Heart looked at the wall and nodded his head. "The funny thing is I think she really had a feeling for me. I think she wanted to be able to love me, but it wasn't in the cards. Her girlfriends insisted on something else."

"Well, that sucks."

"Indeed," said Heart. "Look, son, you are a popular guy. All the JOs think the world of you. They decided it was not in your interests to have a relationship with Lori and convinced you of the same. The problem is it was not their choice to make. It was yours and yours alone."

"Yes, sir, but I don't really know what I feel for Lori."

"Of course you don't. How could you? You spent a few days with her, thought you had something special going on, and then had to separate. You're not children. It takes time to understand your feelings, especially in complicated situations that cross cultures. You would be pretty shallow if you didn't have doubts and concerns."

"I guess I need to find her and apologize."

"Yes, but not quite yet."

"What do you mean?"

"Do you really know how you feel about her, Blue? I mean, really feel? Do you love her? Do you want her to be the mother of your children? Do you want to introduce her to your parents? Do you want to grow old with her? How does her family enter into this? Think about all these things, Blue, and then go and find her. Beg her to listen to you, and tell her what she means to you. Don't go to her to just tell her you're sorry. She's perceptive enough to know that."

"Yes, sir."

"You did a terrible thing to her, Blue. You hurt her to the very inside of her soul, and you weakened yourself tremendously in her eyes. You basically let her know you didn't have the courage to love her after her heart told her you did."

"Yes, sir, I know."

"Can you do this, Blue? Can you make this right?"

"Yes, sir. I think. I know I have a lot of sorting out to do." Blue stood and extended his hand. "Thanks a lot, Skipper."

"Blue, I want you to do one more thing."

"What's that, Skipper?"

"I want you to go talk to Master Chief Davis."

"The master chief? Why, sir?"

"Doc told me about the AOM. He told me about you and the XO."

"He did?"

"Yes, and I took the liberty of talking to Master Chief Davis about it. He and I have known each other for a long, long time, Blue. I think you need to talk with him."

"Okay, Skipper, if you say so."

"Good. I'll see you later, Blue."

Lori waited for a long time after the carrier tied up. She waited and scanned the crowd, anxious to see her young man again. She watched the deck crew throw over the large, hemp mooring lines and tie them to the steel bollards. She watched tractors place the steel-latticed boarding platforms and she heard the ship's boatswain's mate announce the shifting of colors as the carrier was moored.

"Where can you be?" she asked as she scanned the crowd. "Where are you, Blue?"

Then the sailors began to stream off. Some wore crisp white uniforms, and others wore what looked like working clothes. Still others had on all manner of civilian clothes, and these sailors were the most exuberant: whistling, crying, and waving to the women on the pier in front of them.

"Where can you be?" Lori patiently watched the crowd of young men come down the ramps. Occasionally, she would turn and look behind her, in case she had somehow missed him. She stood there for two hours, shifting her weight from one foot to another as she watched the constant stream of men gradually trickle to groups of two or three. She felt a tear gather at the edge of her eye.

*He isn't coming.*

The thought crept into her mind, but she frowned and looked at her watch. He was just late. He would come popping down the ramp any minute.

*He isn't coming.*

Once again, the thought hit her, and this time she couldn't dismiss it so easily. Why was it taking him so long? She looked at her watch again. Men had been leaving the ship for over two hours. Where was he?

And, then, she allowed herself to say the words—the words she had swallowed and held all morning. "He isn't coming." As she said the words, she looked around her. Most of the sailors had already left the pier, surely headed for town. Only a few remained, and they were hand in hand with the girls from the bars. She felt her face glow, and she swallowed a tear. She looked around to see if anyone was staring, pointing. She looked to see whose joke she was. But nobody was looking at her. She was alone. Slowly she turned and headed for the gate and the bridge across the river. What had Eve told her about Solang and Magic?

*Something happened when he left her to go back to the ship. Something out there took him away from her, or he let it take him away.*

Had something happened to Blue? Did being with his friends somehow turn him against her? Or had she been wrong all along? Was she just some foolish little island girl who was a diversion?

Once, her heart soared when she thought she heard him call her name. But when she turned toward the sound and smiled, she realized her mind had played a cruel trick. It was just two sailors hailing a cab.

She walked through the gate, across the river, and down the street toward her grandmother's house. Grandmother's house was quiet and mercifully empty, a blessing for which she was tremendously thankful. She didn't want to talk to anyone, and she surely didn't want to have to explain anything to Raul. Her *tio* would never understand.

She didn't cry until she looked into the mirror. That morning, it was a tool used to ensure that her dress was perfect for him. Now, it scoffed at her because he didn't care. She cried quietly as she stepped out of the dress and carefully hung it in its place, and her thin shoulders shook as she placed her new shoes in their box. She held a tissue to her wet eyes and curled into a ball on her bed.

Blue left Heart's stateroom and started walking toward the squadron's maintenance spaces. Although he was sure the master chief would be ashore on liberty, he found him on the flight deck.

"How are you doing, Mr. Morrison?"

"Fine, Master Chief. Good day for the beach."

"That it is, sir. That it is." The master chief was standing beside one of the squadron Phantoms when Blue found him, looking across the bay at the city.

"The skipper told me you might have some words for me."

The master chief glanced at Blue, smiled, and then returned his gaze toward the beach. He took a couple of chews on his toothpick and then threw it into the water.

"First time I saw this town I was a seventeen-year-old airman apprentice, fresh off the farm." The master chief grinned at Blue and shook his head. "It was my first cruise, and when I saw this tropical paradise with all these little women, I thought I was in heaven."

"Yeah." Blue nodded. "It's something, all right."

"First night in town, I got a gut full of mojo and San Miguel and don't remember much after sunset, but the next morning I woke up with a chicken staring at me and a headache you wouldn't believe." The master chief laughed, and so did Blue.

"I was in this little shack, like one of those." He pointed to the row of hovels lining the river's edge. "The bar girl I was with had evidently taken me home and put me to sleep on her bed. Anyway, I was sicker than a dog and couldn't get out of the rack all day. I thought I was gonna die. But she took care of me, wiped my head with cool rags, and gave me water and juice to drink. A little after noon, she fixed me some chicken broth, and it was about then I knew I was going to live after all." The master chief chuckled and looked at the shacks along the river. He turned to Blue and grinned. "Her name was Pilar."

"Where was her family?"

"She ran them off to her aunt's shack."

"But the night before. How did she explain you?"

"Nothing to explain, sir. She was a hooker. Her pa was a one-legged drunk, and her ma was a two-legged drunk. Pilar earned the family living for all of them, including her two sisters and little brother."

"Christ," whispered Blue.

"Fortunately my chief looked out for me and didn't tell the division officer I was gone all day, but he did give me the duty for two days in a row. So the minute I got free, I went back to that bar and there she was, sitting on a yeoman's lap. Hell, a damn sit-in-air-conditioning-all-day yeoman! Can you believe that?" The master chief laughed and winked at Blue again.

"I looked at her and asked her how much to buy her out of the bar for all day and all night, and she said it'd be one hundred pesos. I gave her the money and we went to the ferry and spent the day at Grande Island. Then I asked her how much it would cost to buy her out of the bar for the rest of her life."

"You did what?"

"I asked her to marry me."

"After only knowing her for two days?"

"Yes, sir. I knew she was the one when I saw how she looked at me and when she had the cool rags on my face. I thought about her for the two days I had the duty, and then I asked her."

"What did the command say?"

"Oh, they told me I was out of my mind. I must have talked with half the officers on the ship, including the chaplain, before it was over. They wouldn't sign my request, so I put in an application to swap with another guy on the carrier coming over to relieve us. It was approved, and I jumped onto it and came right back here to the PI."

"No kidding? What did your friends say? What did your family say?"

"Well, my family didn't much care, as long as I wasn't asking for money and my friends all told me about the same things your friends told you the other night."

"Yeah," murmured Blue.

"But they were my friends. She was my lover, so I didn't much listen to them."

"But, Master Chief. Wasn't it hard? I mean, the fact she was … you know?"

"A hooker?"

"Yes, a hooker."

"Well, look, sir. I believe that a person's past can be just that, their past. Hell, I bought me a big ugly girl at the fair in Sedalia before I got into the navy. So I wasn't a virgin. I figured if I didn't tell Pilar about that girl, then Pilar didn't have to tell me about anybody she had known."

Blue shook his head and swallowed. "What ever happened to her?"

"I married her." The master chief laughed. "We got four kids, and the oldest is in college."

"Married her?"

"Yep, she's a damn good woman. Best thing I ever did was get drunk that first night in town."

"But doesn't it make you feel funny when you're around navy guys with her? I mean, they probably all think she's a hooker."

"She was a hooker! So what? She's a good woman, Mr. Morrison. She was a hooker, but now she's my wife and she's the mama to my kids. I love her and she loves me. Fuck anybody who doesn't like it. Sorry, sir."

"No need to apologize to me, Master Chief. I'm the one who needs to apologize."

"Well, sir, if you don't mind, 205 was pissing hydraulic fluid all over the deck this morning and I need to go forward and check her out."

"No, go ahead, Master Chief. And thanks a lot."

"No problem, sir. No problem at all. And good luck with your situation."

# CHAPTER 27

enry sat squatting in the dirt with his friend Paulo. They were in a small alley, located next to the bridge. Henry was very busy, dividing the proceeds from the morning's take as canoe rowers for the girls in white, and Paulo was very busy watching him. Henry knew Paulo couldn't count, but he wasn't going to cheat him anyway.

Henry grinned as he put the pesos into two piles. It was a good time to make money on the river. The *Connie* sailors were rich!

The two boys were very preoccupied with their business and the noise of the street crowd and rumbling jeepneys masked the approach of booted feet.

"Don't move!" Henry heard the guttural voice and slowly turned his head. He saw three Olongapo policemen.

Despite the order not to move, Henry and Paulo slowly stood. Henry glanced down the alley for a possible escape route. Unfortunately, there was only one way out, and the three policemen blocked it.

"I said do not move."

Henry recognized the speaker as the new Lieutenant Sanchez. Although he had been posted to Olongapo for only three weeks, the word to stay away from him was already out on the streets. Several times during the past few weeks, the lieutenant and his henchmen had been seen beating people for minor offenses. The rumor was he was friends with President Marcos.

Henry watched the lieutenant walk up to him and looked up into his glare. The lieutenant's peaked hat sat squarely over his cruel face, and as Henry bowed his head he saw his highly polished boots gleamed through the darkness of the narrow alley. The lieutenant held a braided leather riding crop in his right hand, which he kept slapping into his left palm. He also wore a pistol at his side. When Henry looked up into his face again, the lieutenant's thin, cold smile caused Henry to shiver.

"What are you boys doing?"

"Nothing," said Pablo. He looked down and began to pick at a scab on his elbow.

"We were just playing," added Henry.

"Is that so?" The lieutenant's eyes brightened slightly above the cruel lips. "And were you playing money games?" He pointed to the pile of coins in the dust at the boys' feet.

"We earned those pesos," whined Paulo.

Henry didn't say anything. He wasn't worrying about money any longer. He was looking for a way to escape.

"You earned it, how?"

"By helping the girls down by the river," said Paulo.

"Were you rowing the canoes?" The lieutenant's voice softened.

"Yes, sir."

"Where did you hide the radio you stole?"

"What radio?" Paulo whimpered and looked at Henry. Tears began to fall down his face.

"The radio you stole from the sailor. It was about fifteen minutes ago in front of the Top Rail Club."

"We didn't take it, sir," said Henry.

"The sailor said two boys stole his radio."

"It wasn't us," cried Paulo.

"Liar!" Lieutenant Sanchez screamed, and his riding crop whirred through the air, biting into Paulo's cheek. It cut him just below the bone, laying open the flesh like carved beef.

Paulo screamed and sank to his knees, clutching his cheek. Blood streamed through his fingers and down his arm. Henry grabbed his friend and steadied him. He quickly tore off his shirt and wadded it into a bandage, pushing it to Paulo's face. Paulo kept screaming and crying.

"I don't like liars," said Lieutenant Sanchez. "They offend me."

"He did not lie, sir," said Henry. "We did not take any radio."

The crop blurred through the air like the head of a snake, but Henry was too quick. He had anticipated such a move and had readied himself to spring clear. The crop missed his head and smacked against the side of the building with an ugly thump. Paulo jumped and screamed, his eyes wide with fear.

Henry had noticed there was about a small space between the wall and a row of trash cans, so he grabbed Paulo's hand and pushed him into the opening. He dived in behind him but felt strong hands on his foot. He clawed against the dirt and rocks, but he felt himself being dragged back into the alley.

"Gotcha, you little bastard." Sanchez pulled Henry into the alley. Henry took one look at the hand holding his foot and then bent over and bit it as hard as he could. As the man screamed and jerked his hand away, Henry scrambled back through the opening. He tasted blood on his lip as he and Paulo raced to the monastery.

# CHAPTER 28

A fter leaving the master chief on the flight deck, Blue spent the day in his stateroom and wandering about the ship. It was strangely quiet, as most of the crew had bailed into town. He could hear only the occasional sound of a radio or the ship's television. The sounds of the music and the going-to-shore smells of Right Guard and Old Spice made him even more depressed.

"You're looking glum," a buddy from the tanker squadron grunted as he moved to the side of the passageway.

"I'm doin' pretty glum," said Blue as he sighed and moved past him.

Blue spent most of his time thinking about Lori, and fortunately his roommates were all out shopping for "good deals" in the huge exchange complex at Subic Bay. All kinds of electronic gear, china, jewelry, furniture, and other assorted treasures could be had for substantial savings. Sailors could browse the latest Pioneer and Thorens turntables, Marantz receivers, Frazier and Bose speakers, and the newest Akai reel-to-reel tape decks. There was even the Nakamichi 700 cassette player on sale! It was a must-stop for Westpac sailors. But none of this interested Blue. He was engaged in a soul-searching exercise that was depressing.

He had really surprised himself when he failed to meet Lori at the pier. He figured it was the weakest, most disgusting thing he had ever done to anyone. He was not able to rationalize his actions, regardless of how he dissected the event. There was just no excuse for his spineless behavior.

But by around three o'clock in the afternoon, Blue could take his confinement no longer and dressed in civilian clothes. He had no destination or plan but knew he had to get out of his stateroom and clear his head. Before long he was passing over the Magsaysay Bridge into Olongapo.

He wandered around the main street for over an hour, looking into the various shops and stalls. He wasn't really interested in shopping, but the activity was at least a diversion from his depressing thoughts. He also noticed the streets were much more crowded since the *Connie* battle group had pumped more than eight thousand more sailors into town. Although it was still early evening, there was already a tremendous energy of excitement and anticipation running in the air. Even Blue in his depressed mood could feel its charge.

Blue was unaware of any conscious decision to see Lori. After all, the skipper had made a lot of sense suggesting he give the situation some time. But he needed to talk about it. He needed to set things straight as soon as he could—to stop the hurt. So he found himself walking toward Grandma's house, trying to think of what he could possibly say. He considered using an excuse, but he knew Lori would see through it. He would never be able to lie to her. He knew he would have to tell her the truth.

Grandma opened the door and blinked at Blue from behind her spectacles. Her friendly smile slowly changed to a grim stare when she recognized the caller.

"Hi, Grandma, is Lori here?"

She looked at Blue for a long, agonizing moment. His gaze was so fierce, for an instant Blue thought she would slam the door in his face. Finally, she spoke.

"Yes, she is here." The chill in her voice matched her eyes.

"May I see her?"

"Did you come to see her cry?" Grandma looked up at him, defiance in her dark eyes.

Blue felt his face redden, and he looked at his shoes for a second to avoid Grandma's merciless stare.

"No."

"Then you had better go."

"I've got to see her, Grandma. I have to apologize." He looked up and swallowed.

Grandma stared for a few moments and then pushed open the door. It creaked as she leaned against it and slammed shut when she walked down the steps toward the mango tree.

"Come," she said.

Blue followed her to the spot where the chairs were circled and took a seat when the old woman pointed.

"What have you done to her?"

Blue swallowed hard and coughed to clear his throat. There was no easy way to tell her.

"I did not meet her when she came to the ship."

"I do not understand. Lori went early. I watched her go out the door. How was it you missed seeing her?" Grandma sat across the circle from him.

"I did see her, Grandma."

"But, then, how did you not meet her? Could you not get off your ship? Did you have some duties?" She leaned forward and glared more.

"No. I had nothing to prevent me from leaving the ship."

"So you saw her, but you could not bring yourself to meet with her. Why? Did you not like the dress? It was her favorite. Was something wrong with her hair? Did she act in some manner to offend you?"

"No." Blue choked. "She didn't do anything to offend me. I … I—"

"So why didn't you meet with her?"

"Well, I …" Blue fought to keep the whine out of his voice. It made him feel even more like a weasel. "It's just—"

Grandma abruptly stood and began to walk to the porch. Blue watched her, surprised at the abruptness of her movement. When she reached the steps, she turned and gave him a look of utter disgust.

"Just what did you plan to say to my granddaughter?"

"Well, I was going to say I was sorry." Blue stood and walked toward her.

"Sorry? Sorry? Young man, she has been in her room all day. She is sick." Grandmother took a few steps toward Blue. "And all you have to say is you're sorry?"

Blue swallowed and looked at his hands. He clenched his fists and looked back at the old woman.

"I do not know how you captured her heart, how you captured all of our hearts. Mine, Raul's, even Lori's father became reluctantly impressed with you. You certainly must be a powerful demon."

"I'm not—"

"How could you? How dare you? You are sorry? Telling her you are sorry will not do what's left of *her* heart any good. All it will do is make you feel better."

Blue stood as Grandma stepped toward him again. He could think of nothing to say. He deserved every word, every hard look.

Grandma raised a bony finger at him and pointed. "Do not come back here until you can explain what you have done." Her voice quivered in anger. Little flecks of spittle gathered at the corners of her mouth. "That is, if you can explain it. Which, I cannot." She turned and stomped up the steps and slammed the screen door in his face. Blue watched her disappear in the darkness of the house. He took a few steps toward the door and then stopped and sighed. He turned and started walking back to the ship. As he walked, he felt like such an idiot. The skipper had warned him of such an event, and he had disregarded his advice. He couldn't believe he had just walked up to the house with no plan or understanding of why things had happened the way they had. What was he going to say to Lori anyway? What did he feel?

Blue walked back through the crowd to the main gate, and as he walked down the street, he passed the blaring loudspeakers of the Sunshine Club. Magic was sitting inside and watched him walk by, but he did not hail his friend. Magic had left the ship alone. Despite the offers to join all manner of groups, he begged off and slipped across the brow by himself. He considered heading to the Marimont Resort to find Candi but quickly rejected the idea. The XO would surely be there.

He eventually entered the Sunshine Club because it had three things he needed: cold beer, bar girls who didn't leap into a sailor's lap, and D-7 on the jukebox. Magic needed the cold beer to think better, and he didn't want to fight off a bunch of "eager beavers," as he called them. And D-7 was his favorite song: "Duke of Earl." He had already played it four times and had finished off five beers by the time Blue passed by.

Magic suffered from a growing feeling of frustration and depression, and when such a mood hit him, he liked to be alone to work it out. It wouldn't do his image of happy-go-lucky confidence any good to have others see him moping around. What bothered him was the fear of wasting time, and Olongapo reminded him of many things he had wasted. He failed to promote to commander twice, and he knew he was finished in terms of a career. He knew the only reason he had a spot in the Death Angels was because Heart still appreciated a man who could fly an airplane and train others to fly one, despite a complete lack of administration and management skills. But Magic wasn't kidding himself. There was no war, and there was no prospect of war, and his kind of officer was not much good in times of peace. He knew the navy expected much of their warriors, and that included the ability to be good ground officers, stewards of the taxpayers' interests, and supporters of the navy's policies. Magic had never proven good at any of those things and, in fact, he reveled in rejecting them. He was also beginning to doubt just what kind of man he really was. After all, just how much of Magic Sharentino was genuine, and how much was bullshit? He thought that when he shot down the MIGs he would be a hero forever. He thought he would always be one of those guys everybody looked up to. But lately he had begun to experience a horrifying feeling of irrelevance. What would Magic Sharentino be doing ten years down the road? Would he be some beer-gutted loser, standing in some officers' club, desperately trying to find somebody to talk to about his MIG kills?

Blue had shown some real balls and some real leadership when he risked his reputation and his "place" in the squadron to set the XO straight. He had proclaimed that the emperor had no clothes while Magic had sat silently. Blue had been right all along about everything. Olongapo was not just a fantasy. There were real people there, and the sailors who visited them were real people too. Magic finished his beer and signaled the waiter for another. When it arrived, he took a big gulp, stumbled to the jukebox, and put all of his change into the slot. He heard the record for D-7 begin to spin, and he thought of Solang. She had really liked that song. She said it reminded her of him.

He sat there for a while longer, but as the beer coursed through him, he pulled himself out of his depressed, maudlin state of mind. He stood up and threw some pesos on the bar. "This is bullshit," he hissed to himself. "I am fucking Magic Sharentino, and it is time to party." He walked out of the bar and right into the path of Spot, Head, and Face.

"Magic, we have been looking for you!" Spot grinned and pounded him on the shoulder.

"Well, you found me. What are you guys up to?"

"Don't know," burped Head. "We have been drinking since noon. What do you suggest?"

"We think it might be close to time to fuck something." Spot smiled as he staggered against Face.

"Come with me, boys." Magic grinned. "I know exactly what you need."

He turned and started up the sidewalk as his troupe followed in tow. They walked a few blocks, and then Magic led them inside a noisy bar called Victor's Place.

Victor's was packed. Sailors with girls sitting on their laps occupied all of the chairs and tables. Nevertheless, Magic led the group to an open spot along the mahogany bar. Soon they were drinking ice-cold beer and watching the band, which was amazingly good. Their music was a mix of oldies and country and western, and the man crooning "You Were Always on My Mind" actually sounded a little like Elvis with an Asian accent. The band played a couple more tunes, but when they took a break, they announced a special floor show.

"Hey, guys, pay attention." Magic leaned toward Spot, Head, and Face, who were busy arguing over whether Elvis was born in Nashville or Memphis.

"I know for a fact it was Nashville," slurred Spot. "I'll bet you."

"It was Memphis, man," corrected Head. "Down on King Street. For a fact."

"Hey, shut up, you guys," interrupted Magic. "He was born in Tupelo. Now watch this show; it is a classic."

"Where the fuck is Tupelo?" Face swallowed and tried to focus on Magic.

"Mississippi. And by the way, it is Beale Street in Memphis, not King Street. Geez, you guys are stupid. Now watch."

The men turned to the small stage and watched as the band exited to a nearby table. A moment later, a woman walked on the stage and placed a beer bottle on the floor. She smiled into the microphone and yelled, "*Connie* sailors, welcome to Victor's!"

Everybody cheered, and a few pesos plinked upon the stage.

"What is number of *Connie*?" the woman asked. "What is number on side of ship?"

"Sixty-four," roared the crowd.

"Sixty-four," repeated the woman. She reached into her bag and began counting the metal pesos as she placed them on the top of the beer bottle. She shaped the stack as it grew to keep it straight. With a final clink of metal, she stood and faced the microphone.

"Sixty-four." She looked at the crowd of sailors and smiled. "I put all sixty-four in my pussy. What you bet me?"

"What are you talking about?" asked a sailor from a table next to the stage.

"I squat and pick all sixty-four pesos with my pussy." She grinned. "No drop one."

"Bullshit." The sailor laughed. "I'll bet you ten pesos you can't."

"I'll bet you twenty pesos you can't," shouted another.

"I'll bet you fifty pesos that she can," shouted Magic.

The two sailors looked at the tall stack of pesos on the bottle and then at each other. They grinned and turned toward Magic.

"You're on."

"If she does it, you owe her and you owe me." Magic laughed.

"You're on, man," replied the two.

The woman smiled at the crowd and then walked over to the bottle. She walked around it, as if inspecting the right angle of approach. Finally, she stood over the bottle and gathered her dress up to her waist. She was not wearing any panties. She looked down at the stack of pesos for a second, adjusted her aim, and then squatted down. As the entire stack disappeared into her vagina, the crowd started yelling. When she stood up with no pesos left on the bottle, the crowd roared.

"You owe her some money," yelled Magic.

The two sailors looked at each other in disbelief, and then they laughed and shook their heads and walked up to the stage. They paid the woman what they had bet, but when they turned and started toward Magic, he held up his hand.

"Give the money to her, boys." He laughed. "She is the one that earned it."

The sailors shrugged and returned to the woman on the stage. The woman took the money and looked at Magic. She waved and smiled, and then she squatted and a stream of pesos gushed onto the floor. The crowd groaned as they watched.

"Man, that is disgusting." Face scowled.

"Wow, did you see that?" Spot stood looking at the empty stage. "I can't believe it."

"Now you know why your mama told you to never put money in your mouth." Magic laughed. "Barkeep, how about another round of beers."

They sipped the new beers and watched as another young woman walked upon the stage. She too approached the microphone and smiled at the crowd.

"I take peso off your nose."

"What?" The crowd of sailors mumbled in confusion.

"Spot, get up there." Magic grabbed Spot's arm and pushed him toward the stage. "Get up there, man. She will sit on your face."

"Wheee," yelled Spot. He stumbled up on the stage and lay down on his back. The crowd started clapping and cheering.

The young woman placed a peso on Spot's nose, and as she raised her dress and squatted down, he closed his eyes.

"Yeah," yelled the crowd as she stood up, lifting the peso from Spot's nose.

"Again," Spot slurred at the top of his voice and plopped a peso onto his nose.

But Head moved quickly from his perch alongside the bar. He ran to the stage, and as Spot closed his eyes in anticipation of the young woman's squat, Head pushed her aside, dropped his pants and underwear, and sat down on Spot's face. He attempted to pick up the peso with his butt cheeks, but as he stood the peso fell back onto Spot. Spot opened his eyes and, instead of seeing a young woman's vagina, found himself staring at Head's huge hairy ass.

"Ahggg," he coughed as the crowd jumped to their feet, yelling and clapping.

"Jesus Christ," he spewed.

Head could barely keep his balance as he pulled his clothes back up and stumbled back toward the bar. He was crying with laughter, and the whole bar was in pandemonium.

Magic shook his head as he watched. "Now, that is one I haven't seen before."

"Hey, barkeep, another round of beers. And do you have any napkins in here?"

# CHAPTER 29

The morning after a ship pulls into port can often be painful, and this was surely the case for many in *Connie's* crew. Although the day dawned bright and clear, many of the previous night's revelers never saw it as they clung to their racks, suffering the curse of Bacchus.

It is something of an occupational hazard in the navy to go ashore after weeks, sometimes months, of the often boring and mundane life on a ship at sea. It is easy for a fellow to overdo it on his first night of freedom. This is especially true in a city like Olongapo, with its cheap prices and many vices.

Blue was not suffering from such problems after his meeting with Grandma. He had had no desire to whoop it up out in town after her tongue-lashing, and despite the urging of Head and Spot, he stayed in the stateroom. Of course, when Head and Spot returned they were so drunk they passed out with their clothes on.

Blue arose early and spent the morning catching up on the paperwork he had neglected while in Olongapo. He went to breakfast, roamed around the flight deck, and then went to his stateroom to get dressed for the skipper's change-of-command ceremony. He had to awaken Spot and Head, and with a lot of urging he got them to figure out how to put on their uniforms and get into formation.

At one o'clock that afternoon, the Death Angels of Fighter Squadron 57 mustered in ranks in *Connie's* cavernous hangar bay for Heart's change of command with Prince. They formed by divisions with rank and file dressed down to perfection. They wore the crisp white uniforms appropriate for the tropics, each man further adorned with multicolored ribbons he had earned. Officers wore black shoulder boards with gold stripes, and chief petty officers wore the fouled anchors and stars of their rank. The sailors wore the crow and chevron, topped with the navy's most familiar fashion statement: the Dixie cup. Blue found the event very impressive, and he was proud of his squadron as they stood in ranks, resplendent in their uniforms. It was a perfect affair until Spot heaved and ran for the toilets. Blue later found him asleep on his rack, still in uniform but with vomit all over his shirt.

The ship's crew had rigged the cavernous hangar bay with colorful signal flags and had placed a huge American flag behind the speaker's podium. CAG was the guest speaker, and he talked about the future of naval aviation and how important aircraft carriers were. Blue thought the speech was pretty boring, but the skipper was great because he talked about what it meant to him to associate with such a great group of men and how much they meant to their country and how he had often prayed that no harm would come to them. Blue enjoyed the speech because it was just like the way the skipper had run the squadron. It was personal and funny and emotional but controlled. Blue felt tightness in his throat when Heart said, "Monika waits for me now, just as she always has done, just as she always will as long as I wear this uniform." Blue swallowed hard when he heard Heart's voice catch. "I doubt that I will ever come this way again, but if I am privileged to do so, I can only pray it's with men like you." Blue laughed when the skipper said, "The difference between a Phantom and a cactus is that in a Phantom, the pricks are on the inside."

After the ceremony, the entire squadron gathered in the DJ Club for one final bash with the skipper. Blue stood with Magic, Face, and Head. They were still mighty hung over, but the beer was beginning to make them feel better. They were sparing no details as they recounted the previous night's adventure, and when Blue told them about Spot's condition, they laughed even louder.

Blue laughed along with the crowd. He laughed despite the fact that nothing was funny. He clapped backs and shook hands when all he wanted was to be alone. He was in the middle of long and animated conversations, but despite the fact that his lips moved and words flowed, all he thought about was Lori. The beer didn't even taste good.

"Hey, kid, how we lookin'?"

Blue turned and looked into Magic's familiar grin. He had not seen him or talked to him since the night in his stateroom.

"Doin' okay." Blue took a drink of beer.

"Eve called me."

Blue hesitated and turned his head.

"She called the quarter deck this morning around six." Magic shook his head and let out a sigh. "Anyway, said she needed to talk. She's down at the Black Rose. Want to come along?"

"No, I don't think so."

"Are you sure?"

"You probably have a lot to talk to her about."

"Kid, I don't want to spoil your party. I know you got some things to sort out. So do I, to be honest. I guess what I'm saying is I could use your company if you got the time. Besides, maybe Eve can give you some help with Lori. The guys told me you've not been yourself, and I figured it was because of her. Hell, it couldn't hurt."

Blue looked at him but didn't respond. He wasn't sure he wanted to talk to anybody about Lori.

Magic shrugged, finished his beer, and turned to leave.

"Wait a minute," said Blue. "I'll go with you. I mean, you're right, it can't hurt."

Down the street, the crew from the Death Angels' power plants work center was in the Sunshine Club, having a good time with the local talent. All seemed to be enjoying themselves except for Petty Officer Franks. He was furious. He was furious because across the table from him sat the king of all fucking gooks, Benny.

"Can we sit with you, Petty Officer Franks?" Benny had led a dozen or so of the guys over to his table. He had extended his hand and smiled.

"Sure, shipmate," Franks had said, shaking the bastard's hand. And now they all sat nice and cozy. Franks had hoped to use the port visit in Olongapo to unite the power plants crew behind him. He felt that if he could get the guys to really support him, he could use that unity to get the lieutenant and the chief to change their minds and put him back as the day-shift supervisor. After all, he had witnessed what kind of power Benny had gained from the devotion of the men. He thought his plan was sound, and the guys were really excited about the visit and had begun to rally around him in several question-and-answer periods.

But today was all screwed up. Today that bastard gook, Benny, sat in the middle of the room with everyone hanging onto his every word.

"Damn it," muttered Franks. "The whole fucking navy is turning into a bunch of pussies and gook ass-kissers!"

Franks hid his hate behind his chain-smoking and drinks of mojo. The only good thing about the party was the fact that the Sunshine Club made good mojo. He also had two girls who had wormed inside the circle of men. They made him feel good, and he bought them drinks to make them happy. He hoped they would make Benny feel bad, but he didn't seem to notice them. Franks slurped at his mojo as they rubbed his arms and kissed the side of his face. Normally he would have taken one of them up to a room and fucked them good. But he was too pissed off for that now. He took another slurp of his drink; they used a lot of rum in the punch, and Franks knew he needed a lot to put up with all the shit.

Franks lit another cigarette off the one he was smoking and took another drink. He absolutely did not understand what the others saw in Benny.

"Hey, Benny, you want a beer?" Henry's cheerful voice penetrated Frank's black thoughts. "No, thanks, little man." Benny smiled. "The last one is still cold."

"I could use a mojo." Franks looked at Henry and smiled with yellow teeth. "Your two whore sisters will have something too." He laughed and looked around the tables at the others, and it pissed him off when they stopped talking and looked at him.

"Sir, my sister is not a whore. My sister is a singer." Henry turned and walked away, and the whole table erupted. Franks faked a laugh. Inside, his hate for gooks continued to grow.

At the same time Henry was walking away from Franks, Blue and Magic entered the Black Rose. It was dark and empty, and Eve stood by the bar alone.

"Hey, Eve." Magic hailed her as they walked in.

Eve turned and squinted against the bright sun as the door swung shut. "I did not realize you would bring Blue."

"Well," Magic smiled, "I didn't think you would mind. Besides, maybe you can help Blue and Lori. They are having a problem."

Eve looked at Blue and frowned. "I talked with Lori's grandmother last night," she said. Her voice and eyes were cold. "Lori doesn't have a problem, other than she fell in love with a coward and a fool."

Blue turned and started to leave. This wasn't going to do him any good.

"I think you should stay, Blue." Eve's black eyes flashed, and her pretty mouth turned to a scowl. "Since you are here, what I have to say to Magic may do you some good as well." Eve motioned to two chairs beside her table. "The bar is closed so we won't be bothered."

"Good," said Magic, his eyebrows knitting in surprise.

Blue took a seat in the chair next to Magic and looked across the table at Eve.

Eve returned his look and then shifted her gaze to Magic. She started to speak, swallowed, and then stood and walked to the piano. She sat down and gently brushed her fingers against the keys.

"I am dying," she whispered as she looked at the table.

"What?" Magic swallowed and took a step toward her. "Evie, what do you mean, dying?"

"I have cancer." Eve looked up at him and then back to the piano. She gently stroked the keys.

"What do you mean, cancer?"

"I have cancer of the pancreas."

"But surely it can be treated. What do the doctors say?" Magic walked to the piano and touched her arm.

"I just returned from Manila. It has spread through me. They thought I was quite a curiosity, as a matter of fact." Eve chuckled softly and shook her head. "They called in all their colleagues to discuss what could be done."

"How much time?" Magic knelt down beside the piano stool. He took Eve's hand and held it. "A week, a month. Not much more, I'm afraid."

"Christ, Eve," said Magic. "What can I do?"

"That is why I called you. Please, sit." She turned and pointed back to the table, and Magic and Blue returned to their seats. Eve once again placed her hands on the keys and began to play. "Do you know this song?"

"Of course," said Magic. "It's the 'Orchid Forest.'"

"Solang wrote it. Did you know that?"

"Solang? I thought you wrote the song. Everyone thinks you wrote it."

"Solang had an understanding I do not have. I have a gift for singing she did not have." Eve continued to play, and she hummed softly to herself as she did. "Solang wrote another song. I want you to hear it."

"Okay." Magic swallowed.

"Yes, please sing," said Blue.

"It's called 'Gift of the White Raven.'" Eve softly began to sing:

*He spoke with an open face, his heart, so I could see.*
*I fell in love on that very first day*
*with the stranger from 'cross the sea.*
*He was strong as a bull and king of his land*
*and stood taller than all the rest,*
*but strong hands are often the most gentle*
*when they touch the face of loneliness.*

*A darkness grows on the glass of my life.*
*The sun can't warm this body and bone,*
*but my strange heart welcomes its ending.*
*It's so much better than being alone.*
*A darkness grows on the glass of my life.*
*The sun can't warm this body and bone,*
*but my strange heart welcomes its ending.*
*It's so much better than being alone.*

*Love's heat can cook the marrow of our souls*
*and allow truth to run wild and free,*
*but my father's fear couldn't love my stranger*
*and soon it couldn't love me.*
*But sweet sap is an alluring nectar.*
*The wildest flower brings the sweetest song.*
*I turned my back on father's garden.*
*True love can never be wrong.*

*A darkness grows on the glass of my life.*
*The sun can't warm this body and bone,*
*but my strange heart welcomes its ending.*
*It's so much better than being alone.*

*A darkness grows on the glass of my life.*
*The sun can't warm this body and bone,*
*but my strange heart welcomes its ending.*
*It's so much better than being alone.*

*Then one day he went away with the wind,*
*the morning the sun stayed 'neath the sea,*
*and the heart can be the loneliest place,*
*searching a horizon forever empty.*
*Waiting becomes a word of anguish.*
*Love's time can hurt more than heal.*
*Too many days without sunrise*
*brings the strongest passion to kneel.*

*A darkness grows on the glass of my life.*
*The sun can't warm this body and bone,*
*but my strange heart welcomes its ending.*
*It's so much better than being alone.*
*A darkness grows on the glass of my life.*
*The sun can't warm this body and bone,*
*but my strange heart welcomes its ending.*
*It's so much better than being alone.*

*I fear it's two men who sought me,*
*one a hawk and the other a dove.*
*He was a mix of clouds and sunshine.*
*It's a white raven I will always love.*
*He's gone but he grows inside me.*
*The white raven's gift is my soul,*
*but it's my island god I pray to.*
*Please watch my gift as it grows old.*

*A darkness grows on the glass of my life.*
*The sun can't warm this body and bone,*

*but my strange heart welcomes its ending.*
*It's so much better than being alone.*
*A darkness grows on the glass of my life.*
*The sun can't warm this body and bone,*
*but my strange heart welcomes its ending.*
*It's so much better than being alone.*

The bar was eerily quiet as Eve's final notes died. Magic sat looking at his hands. The song was so beautiful, yet so haunting.

"What do you think that song is about?"

Neither man answered. They both just stared at Eve. She rose from the piano and joined them at the table.

"We have known each other for a long time, eh, Magic?"

"Yes," he whispered. "Yes, we have."

"I have known you since you were young, like Blue here."

"Yes." Magic smiled.

"And now you are older, but you have not changed a bit."

"What do you mean?" Magic frowned and shifted in his chair.

"Nothing about you has changed but the insignia on your collar. And now, that isn't even changing. I don't know much about your navy rank, but shouldn't you be promoted by now? Your old pal Jimmy Smith was in here two months ago when the *Enterprise* pulled into port. You and he were both lieutenants when we first met. He is now a squadron commanding officer. What happened to you?"

Magic looked at a cigarette burn on the wooden table. He slowly traced it with his finger. "What are you getting at, Eve?"

"You are still a JO, Magic. You are the oldest JO in the navy."

"Is that why you called me here? To give me some career counseling and humiliate me in front of my friend?"

"Maybe I better go." Blue pushed back from the table.

"No!" said Eve. "Now you are here and you will stay. You came to find out something about Lori. Well, maybe you will find out something about her ... and maybe you will even find out something about yourself. Maybe in the process you might find out something about being a man." Eve's eyes glistened with tears as she looked first at Blue and then at her old friend.

"The song is about you," she said as she looked at Magic. "'The Gift of the White Raven' is a song Solang wrote about you."

"Me?"

"Yes."

"I don't understand."

"Solang did not drown." Eve whispered the words, and as Magic heard them, he felt sick. He felt sick because for some reason he felt guilty.

He swallowed and looked into Eve's wet eyes. "What do you mean, she didn't drown?"

"She died in childbirth. She wrote the song when she found out she was pregnant. Pregnant with your baby."

"What are you talking about?" Magic stood and frowned down at Eve. "What do you mean, childbirth? What child?"

"Your child, Magic." Eve stood and pointed at his chest. "Your child."

"Why did you lie about it? Why didn't you tell me the truth?"

"And what would you have done if I had told you, Mr. MIG killer?" Eve thrust her chin in Magic's face. "Would you have come back for the funeral? Would you have given a shit about the child?"

"Hell, yes!" roared Magic. He was so confused and angry he couldn't breathe. He grabbed the back of a chair to steady his shaking arms and took a deep breath. "Hell, yes, I would have come back!"

"Bullshit! Bullshit! The only reason I am telling you now is because I am dying! I'm the only one who knows the secret. If you cared, you would have come back for her in the first place!"

"I couldn't come back. I was fighting a fucking war, remember?"

"Your war with the Vietnamese was almost over, Magic. It was your war with your ego you were fighting, and you didn't want it to ever end. You could have come back, but you chose to go home and show off your medals."

"The navy made me do that."

"Did they? Did they, Magic? The child was conceived in June, the same month you shot down your MIG. When you didn't come back with the ship, she waited for your letters so she could know how to tell you. So she could know if you wanted her to tell you. But the few letters you wrote were about you. Your letters were about the crowds and the parades and about meeting the vice president. You didn't mention anything about her."

"And she didn't say a thing about being pregnant."

"No," said Eve. "That was not her way. She was too proud. If you did not come back for her, she did not want you to come back for the child."

"Christ, Eve ..." Magic dropped his head and looked at the floor. Then he slumped into his chair.

Eve looked at him, and her features gradually softened.

"Do you remember how you first dated Solang?" She reached across the table and put her hand on Magic's arm. "You dated her here, in the bar. She would make the pretense of helping me set up the band. That's the only reason Papa let her come and stay with me. I told him I needed her to help my career."

"I remember."

"Papa and Mama had no idea she was dating anyone, let alone an American. When she got pregnant, she didn't know what to do. I told her to stay here, but she was too afraid word would get back to Papa. He would die if he knew she was not a virgin, let alone pregnant."

"Where did she go?"

"She went to Manila. She stayed with a friend of the band. She died in her house, having the baby."

"And your parents never knew?"

"There was a typhoon that swept through the Philippines at that time. Many people died, and there was much damage. I lied to

Mama and Papa. I told them she had been trying to cross a bridge and had slipped."

"And the baby, was it buried with her? Was it a boy or a girl?"

"Magic, it *is* a boy."

"*Is!* You mean the baby lived?"

"Yes, Magic. Your son is alive."

"My son!" Magic stood up and reached for Eve. He held her shoulders, and a shocked smile crept across his face. "Eve, he is alive? What happened to him? Where is he?"

"He is here, Magic. He is here in Olongapo."

"Where? Was he adopted? Who is he with?"

"He was not adopted, Magic. He is at the orphanage."

"At the orphanage?"

"Yes, Magic." Eve closed the piano keyboard and let her fingers caress its wood. "Your son is Henry."

"Henry! You mean little Henry, your little brother, Henry?"

"Yes, I mean him. I passed him off as my little brother because I did not want him to go through life thinking he was the bastard son of an American sailor. In a way, I was fortunate my parents died so soon after Henry was born. No one was alive to spoil the secret."

"Christ, Blue, did you hear? I have a son! Henry is my boy!"

Blue grinned at Magic and shook his hand.

"But, Eve, after all of these years? Why didn't you tell me? We wrote regularly. I don't understand."

"Think about it, Magic. Think about it. Over the years when we exchanged letters, I wrote you about Olongapo and me ... and Henry. I told you about our lives. I told you about the people at the Black Rose. But your letters were all about what fun you were having. Your letters were written by an energetic and happy young man who was living his life to the fullest. Your letters were so wonderful in their passion ... yet so very selfish in their content. Magic, all you wrote about and seemed to care about was having the life of a bachelor with no concerns and no worries. There was nothing in them that indicated any interest in anything but you."

"But—"

"Magic, this is why I said the things I said to you—about growing up and about your career. So listen carefully and think. Think and do what is right. If you do not want the boy, Father Joseph will take him. Father Joseph loves him like a son. And I think it would be best for him to stay with Father Joseph."

"What do you mean, stay with Father Joseph? He is my son. Henry is my son, and I sure as hell want him!" Magic grabbed Eve and hugged her close. "I want him! I want to be his dad!"

And as he hugged her thin frame, Magic thought of the last time he had hugged Solang. He thought of her tiny, warm, loving body and how she had cried because he was leaving. He still remembered the smell of her hair, the faint scent of gardenia and soap. But now, holding Eve, he didn't shove the thoughts of Solang from his mind. He didn't hide them, as he had done a thousand times before. This time, he drank them in. He welcomed his memories of her, and the exquisite sadness of it seemed somehow to cleanse him. He hugged Eve tighter, tears began to form at the edges of his eyes, and he blinked hard to hold them back. But they came, a tiny trickle of remembrance and then a stream of realization of the colossal waste of it all. The waste of a lonely woman, a woman who might be alive today if she had given birth in a modern hospital. A young girl who had been so ashamed that she had hidden herself from the very people she needed. The waste of a selfish man who didn't have the spine and the decency to be honest with her. The waste of a little boy growing up within the lie that his father had created.

And so Magic stood there and hugged Eve and buried his face against her neck and long dark hair. And when he found the faint trace of gardenia there, he thought of Solang's sweet face, and he cried. He cried the dry-throated, halting cry of frustrated grief and shame, a cry he had never known before. But after a while, after standing there holding Eve for a while, he cleared his mind. He thought of what Eve had told him, slowed his breathing, and swallowed his tears.

He looked at Eve, turned her face up to him, and kissed her on the cheek. Then he turned to Blue and wiped the tears from his eyes with the back of his hands. "You want to come with me? Do you want to come with me to find Henry?"

Blue looked at Magic and nodded his head.

"How will you tell him?" Eve touched Magic's hand.

"I will bring him back here, if it's okay." Magic looked down at Eve and smiled. "Please help me. We will tell him together."

Eve blinked back her tears and reached to embrace him again.

Blue quietly waited as Magic and Eve stood together in their embrace. As he watched them and as he listened to Eve's soft cries, he knew he had to find Lori. He knew he had to tell her he loved her and somehow convince her he needed a second chance. The master chief was right. The important thing was that she loved him. He would work through all the other crap that didn't make any difference anyway.

# CHAPTER 30

Lieutenant Sanchez pushed open the door of the Sunshine Club and waited for his eyes to focus in the darkness. The cool breeze from the air-conditioner felt good against the sweat under his shirt. He surveyed the large, open room for a moment and then walked into the bar. His two deputies followed him.

Sanchez liked these military parties. He felt he was welcome. After all, he was not only a man in uniform, he was also responsible for protecting the Americans who also wore uniforms. He felt that the Americans respected him.

A momentary lull in the buzz of conversation was the unofficial announcement of his presence but, after a cursory glance, the sailors returned to their drinks and their girls.

Sanchez stood for a moment and watched an older sailor hurry over with his hand extended. "Can I help you, sir? My name is Chief Petty Officer Evans. We are having a party here." Chief Evans smiled and waved his arm around the room. Lieutenant Sanchez took his hand. "I am Lieutenant Sanchez, Chief of Police in Olongapo City. We are here to make sure everything is as it should be."

"Everything here is just fantastic. Won't you please join us?"

"Yes, but only for a moment. My men and I are still on duty. Thank you for the kindness." The table where Benny, his buddies, and Petty Officer Franks sat was the closest, so Chief Evans led Sanchez there. A cold San Miguel appeared in front of him.

"Of course, we all thank you for your fine work. Although we are only going to be a short time, we feel very safe in your fine city." Chief Evans smiled at Lieutenant Sanchez.

Lieutenant Sanchez smiled, nodded, and took a sip of beer. He loved the praise.

"Please, let me extend the offer for you to be my personal guest and visit the *Constellation* tomorrow."

"Why, you are most gracious," said Lieutenant Sanchez. "How much longer will you be in port?"

"We leave in a few days. Why don't you visit tomorrow?"

"In that case, I will try to find some free time tomorrow."

"Good. Just hand this card to one of the sailors, and they will find me so I can escort you on board."

A loud whistle caused the room to hush. Lieutenant Sanchez and Chief Evans turned toward the sound.

Sanchez's heart almost stopped when he saw who was there. Framed against the sunlit doorway was Major Botag. His orderly stood by his side, a silver whistle clinched in his teeth. Sanchez leaped to his feet and hurried to the major's side. "Sir, what—what are you doing here?"

Major Botag pushed him aside and strode up to Chief Evans. He extended his hand and smiled. "I am Major Botag, Regional Chief of Police." He nodded toward Sanchez. "The lieutenant here works for me."

"Glad to meet you, Major." Chief Evans shook the offered hand and motioned to the room. "Care to sit with us?"

"For only a moment, thank you."

Lieutenant Sanchez returned to his chair while Major Botag took a seat next to Franks. He took his lighter from his tunic, snapped it open, and lit a cigar.

"Drink?" Chief Evans gestured toward the bar.

Major Botag took a puff from his cigar and shook his head. "I cannot drink, as I am on duty." He eyed Sanchez and then looked at the San Miguel in front of him. "Perhaps the lieutenant will have another though?"

"Sanchez stared into the black eyes and vigorously shook his head. "Oh, no, I, too am on duty." He smiled lamely and shoved the beer aside.

"I am glad," said the major. "I feel safer already." He snapped the lighter open and then snapped it closed.

While the chief was talking to Lieutenant Sanchez and Major Botag, Magic and Blue were working their way up the street. Magic took one side and Blue the other, and they stuck their heads into each bar, looking for Henry.

"I notice from the decorations on your tunic that you have had duty in the South." Benny smiled at Major Botag and pointed to his chest.

"Why, yes, I have." Major Botag turned toward Benny, a surprised smile on his face.

"I am from the South," said Benny.

"And now you are an American sailor?"

"I am a Filipino American sailor." Benny smiled and held out his hand. Botag smiled too and put his lighter down. As he reached to shake hands with Benny, it fell to the floor.

Sanchez saw it fall and started to say something. Then he remembered how much he hated the sound of it, the snap, snap, snap. He smiled and remained silent.

Franks saw the lighter fall too. Then he saw Henry walking toward the table, a tray of San Miguels balanced in his hands.

Henry bent over the table and placed the tray down. At that instant, he saw Lieutenant Sanchez and drew back.

Franks bent over, picked up the lighter, and slipped it into Henry's baggy shorts pocket.

Sanchez saw Henry and rubbed his sore hand. He opened his mouth to speak.

"My lighter." Major Botag looked at the table and then anxiously checked his tunic pocket. "My lighter. Where is my lighter?"

"Something wrong?" Chief Evans moved his chair back and looked at the table.

"My lighter. It was here a moment ago, on the table." Major Botag stood and pushed his chair back. He looked down at the floor and then knelt and looked under the table. "Don't just stand there," he screamed at his orderly.

"The kid's got it," said Franks, nodding toward Henry.

"What?" Major Botag frowned and looked at Henry.

"In his back pocket. I saw him take it."

Lieutenant Sanchez stood and started toward the boy. The boy that bit him.

Henry stepped back. He reached in his back pocket and took out a lighter. He looked into the hard, black eyes of the major and then at the advancing figure of the lieutenant. He ran for the door.

"Stop!" Sanchez yelled and ran after the thief. The kid bolted through the door, and Sanchez burst out into the sunlight behind him. He reached for his Beretta.

*I'll shoot a couple into the air. That'll stop him.*

Magic rounded the corner just in time to see Henry burst out the door. He never had such a feeling of joy. There was his son!

"Son of a bitch!" he cried as he saw Henry sprinting in his direction. "Someone must have already told him. Somebody told him he's my kid. Here he comes!" The improbability of such a thing never crossed his mind as he sped toward the little boy.

As Henry jumped off the sidewalk, Magic suddenly noticed the man behind him. He focused his eyes, and then they widened in alarm when he saw the man raising a gun. It was pointed right at Henry!

"Stop!" he screamed. "Stop!" He began running toward Henry as fast as he could.

Lieutenant Sanchez started to raise his gun into the air, but as he stepped off the sidewalk, he tripped. His gun kicked into his hand as it went off.

Magic saw Henry stumble and then sprawl onto the street. He quickly ran to his side and turned him over. A wound on his son's left side spit blood at him over the ragged edge of a rib bone. The sight of his son's blood made him sick, but it enraged him even more. He gently laid the boy back on the street and stood.

"My boy!" he screamed. "You shot my son!" Magic began walking toward the man with the gun. His temples pounded as blood gushed to his head.

*He killed my boy,* he thought, and tears sprang to his eyes. *Finally, I have something in my life besides that fucking MIG, and that son of a bitch took it from me! That fucking bastard killed my little boy!*

Blue ran to where Henry lay in the street. He tore his shirt off and put his hand on the wound. Henry moved beneath him and moaned. He was still alive!

Magic was shaking so hard he could barely breathe. He felt a red-hot rush flood his brain, and his hands balled with the desire to kill. He increased his stride. "I am going to rip out your fucking heart!"

"Magic, stop!" screamed Blue. "He's alive. Henry is alive."

Magic did not hear Blue. He did not hear anything but the pounding of his blood and the scream of frustrated rage in his heart. He looked up the street where the man with the gun stood. He was only twenty feet away, only a couple of big steps if he was really quick. He started sprinting.

Lieutenant Sanchez looked at the man running toward him, raised his gun, and squeezed off a shot. Magic never felt the round as it pierced his left hand.

The lieutenant took a step back and frowned. He fired again. His aim was good, and the bullet penetrated Magic's left shoulder just above the heart. Magic thought he had been hit by a hammer and looked to his left. Blood spurted but it didn't matter. Nothing mattered except getting his hands on that son of a bitch with the gun. He was going to kill him.

Lieutenant Sanchez took another step back.

He aimed and fired a third shot.

The bullet hit Magic in the solar plexus, passing just to the left of the heart. The tumbling bullet nicked the edge of the aorta and then veered into his lungs.

Magic staggered and fell to his knees. He felt like he had been hit in the chest with a mallet.

"Christ," he coughed and stared at the blood in his hand. "Christ," he coughed again.

Suddenly, he was so tired. He couldn't keep his hands from trembling, and he shook his head and tried to shake off the numbness and ringing. "Got to get there," he gasped. He tried to stand but couldn't move his legs. "Got to get moving."

His ears began to ring, and he shook his head again. He felt so weak and tired. Then he vomited. He looked down in surprise at how bright and red the blood was. It splashed out of his mouth and down the front of his shirt. He mustered the last of his energy and staggered to his feet, turning toward Henry. He bent over, coughed up some more blood, and fell onto the street. He stretched out his hand toward his son.

"Magic!" Blue ran to his friend and tried to turn him over, but Magic groaned.

"Nooo."

Blood gurgled and foamed from his mouth. He looked into Blue's eyes and then glanced toward Henry. "Please, Blue," he panted. "Please help me get to him."

Blue took Magic's good hand and dragged him toward Henry. Tears trickled down his face.

Once, twice, Blue pulled at Magic's body. He heard him groan with each yank, but he did not stop. One more hard pull and Magic lay next to the boy. Blue gently lowered his friend's palm on top of Henry's hand.

Blue sank to his knees as tears coursed down his cheeks. He watched Magic slowly close his bloody fist over his small son's hand and squeeze. It was a reassuring squeeze that fathers give to sons who are sick—gently, so they know everything will be all right.

Magic moaned softly, and then he died.

# CHAPTER 31

Blue lay on his back in the darkness of his room. He felt the wetness of his tears on the pillow and the occasional trickle as a new one slipped down his cheek onto his neck. His efforts to breathe through swollen sinuses caused him to cough, rekindling the ache in his head.

He was surprised at the extent of his grief. Magic was a good friend, but do men lie in the dark, crying over lost friends? As Blue lay there, he realized his sorrow involved more than just the loss of Magic. His sorrow involved the futility of it all. If Magic had been more honest with himself, if Solang had been more forthcoming, if Eve could have been a little more trusting, these events would not have transpired. Henry could have been raised in a happy family of people who loved one another instead of growing up on the edge of a sewer, making money from men who didn't care a thing about him.

But, despite his tears, Blue was happy about one thing. At least the little boy was only wounded. The lieutenant's bullet had not done any irreparable damage. If only Magic had stopped to inspect Henry instead of flying into a rage. But Blue knew Magic's rage had as much to do with his personal frustration as it did with the actions of the lieutenant. That was just the last straw.

Blue sighed and turned on his light, blinking against the sudden brightness. He also knew he was sorry for himself. Sorry for the fact that he had set down the very road Magic had traveled before him, a road strewn with personal weakness, denial of self-understanding, and betrayal. A road leading away from the person he now knew he must find.

Blue was splashing cold water on his face when the telephone rang. It was the duty officer, informing him the skipper wanted to see him. He groaned as he hung up the phone. He didn't want a conversation with Prince. He quickly threw on a uniform and headed for the new skipper's stateroom.

"Blue, I want to tell you how terribly sorry I am. Here, have a seat by the desk." Prince pointed to a chair and smiled. "We all lost a good friend in Magic. I know it was a terrible thing to have to watch it happen."

"The boy?"

"I'm sorry." Prince cocked his head. "What did you say?"

"The boy, Henry. How is he?" Blue sat heavily in the chair.

"Oh, the boy. He will be just fine."

Blue nodded and looked at the floor. Prince frowned as he looked at him.

"The police are still piecing the story together. I understand the boy was Magic's son? Something about the mother dying in childbirth?"

Blue nodded, sighed, and then looked up. "Yes, sir."

"Do you know Magic listed you as his next of kin in his service record?"

"What?" Blue was stunned.

"Yes, he did. You knew he had no living relatives?"

"Yes, I knew that," said Blue. He couldn't believe it.

"Magic's son's aunt, a singer named Eve Mariposa, is looking after the boy. She also wishes to have Magic buried in some local cemetery next to her sister. You will have to talk to the guys down at legal about all this."

"Yes, sir."

"Blue, I know what I am about to say will sound harsh, and I hope you do not misconstrue it as any sort of punishment." Prince paused as Blue lifted his head and looked at him.

"I think you need to learn a lesson from the tragedy that has just unfolded. A lesson that warns against getting romantically involved in times of stress and, Blue, a deployment is a time of stress. You leave your home, your culture, and your people for six or seven long months. It places great stress on the strongest among us. That is why we must temper the things we do, guard our emotions and actions, when in this situation."

"But, sir."

"Blue." Prince held up his hand. "Magic would still be alive if he would have followed a few simple rules."

"But he loved the girl, Skipper."

"Blue, please! He didn't know what he felt, and I think you are in danger of repeating his mistakes."

"I am in danger of repeating his mistakes, sir, but not in the way you think."

"Well, no matter," said Prince. "I think it best if you avoid the town for the rest of the time the ship is in port."

"What? Are you restricting me?"

"Of course not, Blue. I am just suggesting that you not depart the ship until we leave for home."

"But, sir! I've got to talk to Lori."

"Blue, I am telling you this for your own good and to protect you. In a few days or weeks you will thank me for this."

"I can't stay on the ship, sir. I can't do it."

"What do you mean, you can't do it?" Prince narrowed his eyes and stiffened in his chair.

"Sir, a couple of days ago, I promised a girl something and I let her down. I have to explain it to her."

"Look, Blue." Prince stood and walked around to the front of his desk. He leaned against its edge and smiled. "I've heard all about Lori."

Blue frowned in surprise.

"I talked with Miss Mariposa down at the police station. She told me about you and the girl."

"So you surely see why I have to talk to her."

"That's just it, Blue. I surely see why you should not talk to her. Son, you are too emotional and too distraught to know what is good for you. You have no business going into town. Now, if you give me your word you will forget about her and not try to contact her, I think all of this can be forgotten. If not, I am afraid you need to find a different line of work."

"What do you mean?"

"Do you expect me to allow an officer in the United States Navy to make the kind of decisions you have made? Look at the situation you are in. You make a fool of yourself in front of the entire ready room. All the troops know about your little love affair. Everybody is calling you the mayor of Olongapo, for Christ's sake. Blue, you have embarrassed the entire squadron. Quite frankly, I would give you an unsatisfactory fitness report and end your career right now if it were not for the chief of staff."

"Cathy's father?"

"Yes," said Prince. "For some reason he thinks you have merit and this will all blow over. He convinced me to give you a second chance. But only if you do exactly as I say."

"And if I don't?"

"Look, mister. Let me spell it out for you. You stay on the ship until eight o'clock tomorrow morning. Then I am having you escorted to Cubi Point for a DC-9 flight back to the States. You will check in with the advanced detachment and work on getting our spaces in order when we arrive. I don't want the squadron to have to put up with you for a month-long boat ride back home. I don't want them to have to be reminded how foolish and amateurish one of their officers was. I want you out of our sight, Mr. Morrison. Now, get down to legal and straighten up the stuff about Magic. Then get to your room."

"Yes, sir."

"Good. Because if you can regain your sense and integrity, we can all forget about this. Despite your immaturity, you have a future in the navy if you can just grow up. However, if you insist upon chasing after this island girl, I will personally prevent you from ever making lieutenant. Do you understand?"

"Yes, sir."

"Good. Now, get out."

Blue went to the legal office, and after filling out forms, he slowly walked back to his room. He was deep in thought and didn't see Master Chief Davis until he bumped into him in the gloomy passageway outside his room.

"I'm sorry about Mr. Sharentino, sir. I'm sorry about everything."

"Thanks, Master Chief. Thanks a lot." Blue opened his door and started to walk inside.

"Did you ever see the girl, sir?"

Blue turned and looked into the master chief's eyes. He sighed and shook his head. "I haven't seen her," he said. "I haven't, and now I can't."

"What do you mean, sir?"

"The skipper gave me an ultimatum. If I forget Lori, I keep my career. If I try to see her, it's all over."

"What are you going to do, sir?"

Blue looked at him for a moment and then took a deep breath. He crumpled up the forms in his hand.

"I'm going to get dressed and go see her."

The master chief looked at Blue and smiled. He stuck out his hand. "Good luck, sir."

"Thanks, Master Chief."

Blue quickly changed clothes, walked down to the quarterdeck, and handed the lieutenant duty officer his ID.

The lieutenant looked at the card and then at Blue. "Just a minute."

"Is there a problem?" Blue was puzzled. He had never had anyone stop him before, ever.

"Just a minute," repeated the lieutenant. "I need to make a call."

"Does legal need me back topside?" Blue frowned in confusion.

The duty officer put his hand up, palm out. "Just a minute." He walked over to the duty podium and picked up the phone.

Blue waited for several minutes as the duty officer made one call and then another. He turned around when he heard the hatch behind him open and two burly petty officers with military police gear strode in. They walked over to Blue, one on each side of him.

"We can't let you leave, sir."

"What are you talking about?"

"Sir, we got a call that said you were not authorized to leave the ship."

"What's going on?" Blue looked at the petty officers and then back at the duty officer.

"I took the precaution of calling," said Prince. He slowly walked across the quarterdeck, where Blue and the petty officers were standing. "I told him who you were and asked them to keep you on board."

"But, sir."

"You just tossed your career away for some girl you don't even know," said Prince as he slowly shook his head. "You're a fool."

# CHAPTER 32

"Yes?"

"Excuse me, ma'am. Are you Miss Lori Santiago?"

"Yes. What can I do for you?"

"Ma'am, my name is Wayne Davis, Master Chief Wayne Davis, from Mr. Morrison's squadron."

Lori looked at the man for a moment and then opened the screen door. "Would you like to come in?"

"No, ma'am. I can only stay a moment."

"Did Blue send you?"

"No, ma'am. He has no idea I am here. I thought I would come because I think you should know what's going on."

"Yes."

"LTJG Morrison is in hack on the ship."

"Hack?"

"Yes, ma'am, hack. It means he is restricted to his room."

"Is it because of Magic's death?" Lori had heard all about the morning's tragedy in the street. She also knew Blue had been involved and, despite the way he had treated her, felt deeply sorry for him.

"No, ma'am," said the master chief. "It's because of you."

"Me." Lori frowned. "How could I have caused that?"

"Our commanding officer gave him an ultimatum. He could continue with his career or he could continue with you. He chose to come and see you and was caught. Now he is forbidden to leave the ship. I thought it was good for you to know."

"He risked his career for me?"

"I was there when he made the decision, miss. He knew what the stakes were. He tried to get to you."

"Then I shall go to him."

"No, ma'am," said the master chief. "They won't let you see him. You'll just make trouble for the both of you. In the morning they are putting him on a plane for the States."

Lori closed her eyes and sighed. *So this is how it finally ends,* she thought. *I won't ever see him again.* Although she had been badly hurt, she continued to believe, somehow, things would still work out. She refused to believe Blue would just walk out of her life.

"Well, thank you for coming." She held back her tears and turned to go to her room. "Ma'am?"

"Yes." She looked at the master chief.

"Ma'am, I talked with Mr. Morrison about you. You see, I married a girl from Olongapo years ago and, well, I told him about what I went through. Mr. Morrison has been in a lot of pain. He truly feels terrible about what happened, and I'm betting he is very much in love with you. I'm just sorry he can't come and tell you himself."

"Thank you, Master Chief. Thank you for coming."

The following morning, Staff Sergeant Windle L. Royce, United States Marine Corps, stood under the awning and squinted at the gray DC-9 as it taxied into takeoff position. He was on the runway side of the Cubi Point operations building, sipping black coffee and smoking a Marlboro.

"Christ," he muttered. "What a fucking bunch of pantywaists. Now I'm a babysitter! I go and roust some officer out of his rack, take him to the airport, put his sorry ass on the plane. Christ!"

*Be sure he gets on the plane, Sarge. Don't leave until it takes off, Sarge.*

"Christ, I hate being called 'Sarge,'" muttered Royce. He took a drag from his smoke and allowed himself a smile. "But, by God and the Marine Corps, I put Mr. Morrison on that plane." He took another drag. "I sure as hell did that."

He looked at his watch and shook his head. It was only thirty minutes until the *Connie* pulled up her brows and began to head down the channel. He would have to drive like hell to make it on time. That is, if the damn airplane with the mysterious Mr. Morrison would ever take off! He shook his head again in disgust, took a final drag off his smoke, and dropped it into the half-full cup of coffee. As the cigarette hissed into the cup, he heard the engines begin to howl and watched the big jet begin its roll. Staff Sergeant Royce smiled for the first time that day and ran for his car. The gray airplane was climbing eastward as he sped out of the parking lot.

# CHAPTER 33

Despite her lack of sleep and terrible feelings of depression, Lori made herself arise early and go to the office. She knew she had to keep busy, and moping around the house all day would be the worst thing she could do. So she pretended it was just another day, a day like all the others before she had met Blue. She pitched into her work with a fury and tried not to think about him. She filed papers, updated inventory accounts, and wrote checks. She plunged so totally into her work that for a while she forgot her problems. Then the long wail of the *Constellation's* navigation whistle announced the carrier's departure and shattered her momentary calm.

Lori stood and walked to the window and stared into the green jungle. She had hoped against hope that somehow he would come. She prayed he would come. Now, as the tears coursed down her cheeks, she knew he would not. By the time he got to the United States, he would not even remember her, and even if he did, they would be thousands of miles apart. Besides, if he forgot her, perhaps he could regain his career.

"Does anybody here know how to make a gun case?"

Lori's shoulders tensed, and she heard herself gasp at the sound of the voice. She turned and there he stood. She looked at him for a long moment, unsure what to do.

"Something happened to me out there."

A tear fell from her cheek.

"I lost my way."

And then another fell.

"I lost my way, Lori." He was walking toward her.

"I am so sorry, Lori. God help me, I have wished over and over I could relive the other morning, that I could spare you the pain I caused."

"Why, Blue? Why didn't you come?" Lori said. Her voice was thick.

"Because I was weak." Blue stopped and looked at her. He opened his hands out in front of him and then let them drop. "I saw you in the crowd, with all the other … girls, the girls from the bars. I heard all the catcalls, the guys whistling down at them. I … I just gave up, I guess. I gave up on us, on me. I did not think I could love someone enough to overcome all the baggage. I had no idea what you meant to me."

"You hurt me, Blue." She stood still.

"I know," said Blue. He closed his eyes, exhaled, and then looked at her again. "I know. And it will be a long time before you can trust me again, if you ever can. But, please, just give me a chance."

"Are you sure that is what you really want, Blue? Are you confusing your shame with love? Do you really love me, or are you just ashamed of yourself and just trying to make yourself feel better?"

"I have tossed that question through my mind over and over," said Blue as he walked to her. His hands shook as he gently placed them on her shoulders. He shut his eyes and drank the sweet smell of her hair.

"And?"

"And I am here. I am here because I know you mean more to me than anything. You mean more than the approval of my friends, more than my career."

Lori put her arms around his waist, and they hugged each other close.

"I love you, Lori," he said as he kissed the top of her head.

"Are you sure?" She turned up her face and looked at him.

"Yes," he whispered as he first kissed her eyes and then softly kissed her lips. They embraced like that for a long time, holding each other tight.

"Master Chief Davis came by."

"Master Chief Davis? What for?"

"He told me about your commanding officer. About the choice you were given. Is it true? Have you destroyed your career?"

"I imagine so," said Blue as he hugged her even tighter. "But it's worth it."

Lori smiled into his shoulder and hugged him back. Then she frowned and pushed away. "How did you get off the ship? I thought you were going to be put on a plane for the States."

"I am." Blue laughed. "Or, at least, somebody with my name tag is."

"I don't understand."

"Well," Blue grinned, "my roommate, Spot Smith, was going on leave anyway. He bought a commercial plane ticket for the States that leaves in a few days. The navy was sending me on the C-9 shuttle this morning. So we switched places. He put on my name tag, and the marine that escorted LTJG Morrison to the C-9 was really escorting Spot Smith."

"And it worked?" Lori grinned into Blue's eyes.

"Yep, all you need is a name tag and a set of travel orders, and you are good to go."

"So everybody thinks you are on the plane?"

"Well, everybody but Spot and you."

"You are going to get into a lot of trouble."

"Maybe. I figure if I can show up at the advanced detachment in San Diego in a couple of days it will be okay. I am a JG. I am supposed to screw up." Blue laughed, leaned over, and kissed her again. "Besides, girl, I have been in a lot of trouble since I met you. And most of it was trouble with my heart."

They held hands, walked to the window, and looked out into the jungle. It was a beautiful day, and through the open window came the smell of the jungle. Blue lifted his head to hear the cheerful titter of the birds, and his face opened into a smile when he spotted off at the edge of the clearing, a mango tree.

"Eve told me about Magic," said Lori. She looked at Blue and squeezed his hand. "Why didn't he come back for Solang?"

"He let himself drift with the crowd, Lori. He let himself drift with a crowd of brave and intelligent but sometimes selfish young men, men who can consume each other if they are weak. Unfortunately, he didn't allow himself time to really understand what was in his heart. I think Magic blamed himself for not going back to her, for not sharing himself with her for a long time. In the end, it was that guilt that got to him."

They stood like that for a few more minutes. Then Blue took Lori in his arms and held her again.

"I want to take a trip to Manila."

"Why?"

"I want to meet with your mother and talk some more with your father. I want to talk with them about my parents visiting Manila."

"Your parents? I don't understand."

"I called them last night. I told them about you. They want to come and visit. They want to talk about our engagement."

"Engagement?"

"Yes." Blue smiled.

"What makes you think my father will accept such an idea?"

"I think he will." Blue grinned. "After all, I am an important man."

"Oh." Lori grinned. "Just who do you think you are?"

"Me? Heck, lady, I am the mayor of Olongapo."

# EPILOGUE

In 1977, almost a year to the day after he shot Henry and killed Magic, Lieutenant Sanchez was rushed to the burn unit in Manila. The team of doctors operated for hours in the hope he would keep at least one of his legs. They failed. They also operated to stabilize his groin, since his scrotum, testicles, and penis had been ripped away. He was in the unit for six weeks, and rumors swirled about a strange revenge ritual in the jungle, connections to a beautiful singer in Olongapo, and that a rich man in Manila was responsible for what happened to him. Upon release he shot himself to death with his service revolver.

Eve Mariposa died shortly after the incident in Olongapo.

Heart Valentine retired from the navy with the rank of rear admiral. He lives in Burke, Virginia, and is a defense consultant.

Prince retired from the navy as a commander. He was relieved of command shortly after taking the helm of the Death Angels due to conduct unbecoming an officer, specifically a relationship of a sexual nature with a woman who was not his wife.

Head, Spot, Just Ed, Face, Spider, and the rest of the gang of junior officers all left the navy after their tour with the Death Angels. Most fly for the airlines today.

Petty Officer Franks retired as an E-6 petty officer, having failed to make chief. He lives in Georgia.

Benny Benitez retired as a master chief petty officer, an E-9. He lives in San Diego, California.

Blue resigned from the navy eighteen months after the incident in Olongapo, and he and Lori married that summer. He is an author, and he and Lori share their time between their homes in Los Angeles and Manila. When they visit the Philippines, they always make a trip to Olongapo. Eve, Grandma, and Uncle Raul are all now dead, but Blue and Lori like to visit Blackjack and Father Joseph. Often, during these trips, they journey to a small village northeast of Olongapo, where they stop by a local cemetery. It is there they pay respects to two graves placed side by side. The graves are marked with the names Solang Sharentino and Paul Sharentino.

Blue and Lori are usually joined there by Father Joseph and by their adopted son. He often wears a sage-green flight suit, and the patch on his shoulder and the gold wings on his chest mark him as an F-14 Tomcat pilot. The young man is somewhat of a legend in navy fighter circles. He is considered by many to be the best fighter pilot in the navy, and besides that, he knows a lot of important things. He knows what computer systems are the best buys and how to tune a fuel-injected engine. He knows what waters hold the tastiest prawns. He knows how to install a hot tub and where you can buy the best bowl of *tinola*. He knows how to plan an air strike on a heavily defended target. Nobody knew how or when or why Henry got the call sign Magic. But it didn't make any difference. Magic just seemed to fit.

# CUTTING-EDGE NAVAL THRILLERS
## BY
# JEFF EDWARDS

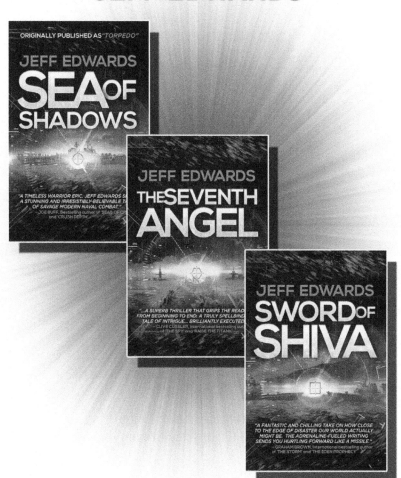

**THEY STOLE HIS FUTURE.**
**HE STOLE THEIR SUBMARINE.**

# JOHN R. MONTEITH

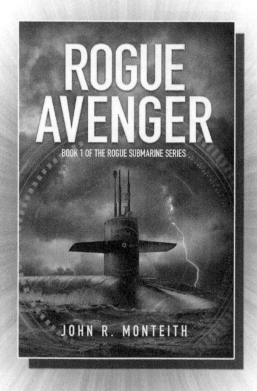

Jake Slate only knows one thing...
He *will* have his revenge.

www.braveshipbooks.com

**HIGH COMBAT IN HIGH SPACE**

# THOMAS A. MAYS

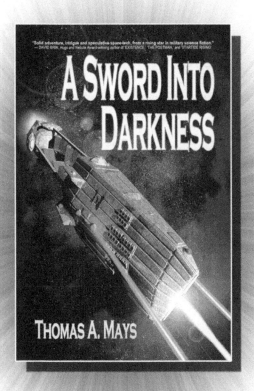

"Solid adventure, intrigue and speculative space-tech, from a rising star in military science fiction."
— DAVID BRIN, Hugo and Nebula Award-winning author of 'EXISTENCE', 'THE POSTMAN', and 'STARTIDE RISING'

# A SWORD INTO DARKNESS

THOMAS A. MAYS

**The Human Race is about
to make its stand...**

www.braveshipbooks.com

**HIGH OCTANE AERIAL COMBAT**

# KEVIN MILLER

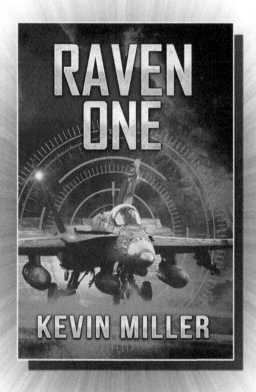

Unarmed over hostile territory...

www.braveshipbooks.com

**THE THOUSAND YEAR REICH MAY BE ONLY BEGINNING...**

## ALLAN LEVERONE

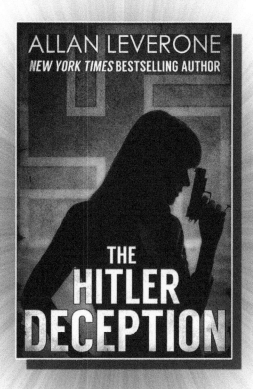

A Tracie Tanner Thriller

www.braveshipbooks.com

Made in the USA
Las Vegas, NV
05 February 2021

17289303R10208